The Pittenweemers

V.E.H. Masters

NYDIE
BOOKS

Books by VEH Masters

The Seton Chronicles:

The Castilians
The Conversos
The Apostates
The Familists
The Pittenweemers

First Published in Scotland in 2024 by Nydie Books

Copyright © 2024 V.E.H. Masters
The right of V.E.H. Masters to be identified as the Author of the
Work has been asserted by her in accordance with the
Copyright, Designs and Patents Act 1988
All rights reserved.

No part of this publication may be reproduced, used, stored or
transmitted in any form by any means, electronic, mechanical,
photocopying or otherwise without the prior written
permission of the author.

This is a work of fiction. All characters in this publication – other than
the obvious historical characters – are fictitious and any resemblance
to real persons, either living or dead, is purely coincidental.

A CIP catalogue record for this book is available from the
British Library

Paperback ISBN 978-1-9174920-1-0

Also available as an ebook, ISBN 978-1-8382515-9-8

Cover Artwork and Design: Mike Masters

Maps and images reproduced with kind permission of the
National Library of Scotland, Deutsche National Bibliothek

For some free short stories which tell more of The Seton Family
please go to www.vehmasters.com

For Mike

And for our children's fantastic partners, Mayuko, Pete and Sarah

Anster

Pittenweem

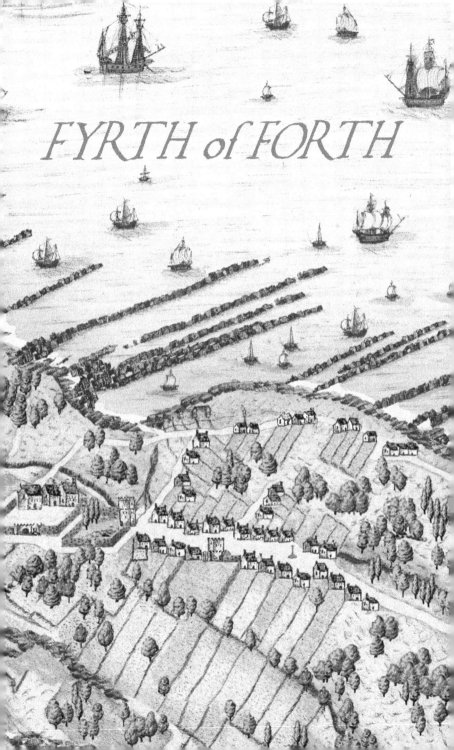

FYRTH of FORTH

The Players

Bethia, now a widow and a Catholic, who has returned to Scotland after forty years – much of which time was spent in Constantinople.

Will Seton, Bethia's younger brother, minister to the parish of Pittenweem, a widower and a leading defender of a Protestant Church without any clerical hierarchy.

John Seton, Bethia's youngest brother, a wealthy Protestant merchant living in Pittenweem with his wife Violet and ten children, the eldest of whom is Symon.

Ephraim, one of Bethia's grandchildren who has travelled with her to Scotland and who was brought up as a Jew.

Grissel, who has been Bethia's servant since they were both children and now learns she is related to the family she serves.

Cecy, Will's beloved only child who is married to Andersoun, with whom she has six children, the eldest of whom is Edane.

Nannis, Andersoun's mother, who is very busy about all her neighbours' affairs and constantly at Will's door.

King James VI (1567-1625) of Scotland and later James I of England. Son of Mary, Queen of Scots, who was beheaded under instruction of Elizabeth of England in 1587. He is a Protestant who is tolerant of the Catholic nobles who surround him, and a poet.

James Melville (1556-1614), minister to four parishes within the East Neuk, including Anstruther; diarist and poet.

Andrew Melville (1545-1622), a religious reformer, theologian, poet and James Melville's uncle. He is principal of St Mary's College at the University of St Andrews.

Juan Gómez de Medina (dates unknown), commander of the wrecked Armada ship El Gran Grifon and known to his men as El Buen (The Good).

Traditionally in Scotland, *good sister* was a common way of referring to your sister-in-law, *good mother* your mother-in-law, and so on. I have used those terms throughout the book – as both a mother-in-law and sister-in-law, I much prefer the epithet *good* (and hope I am so deserving).

The village of Anstruther is locally known as Anster and I have used both names

There is a Glossary of Scots words to be found at the back of the book.

Part One

Pittenweem

March to June 1587

Chapter One

Pittenweem

All was peaceful in Pittenweem – well, as peaceful as it could be in a country riven with fury that their queen, however wrong thinking, had had her head removed by order of the queen of England. It was not safe to be English in Scotland, and Will had to intervene one day to save a man taking a beating from a group of lads.

'What are you about?' he shouted as he hauled them off the fellow who was curled up on the ground, covering his head with his arms. 'This is a Christian country, and I will tolerate no barbarians.'

'He's the barbarian,' muttered one of the youths, who'd been about to swing for Will until he realised it was the minister holding him back.

'Christ's bones,' said Will, recognising the lined face of the pedlar who'd been coming to the village every spring for the past ten years, 'do you not know him? It's McGarroty.'

'Aye we ken him weel, and we dinna want ony English here, what'er they're selling,' said the vocal lad amid the group. The others nodded their agreement while keeping their distance from their minister.

'He is *Irish*,' said Will wearily.

He helped McGarroty to his feet and offered the man his handkerchief to stem his bleeding nose.

'Where do ye think you're going?' he called to the lads, who were intent on slinking away. He gestured to the packman's bundle of wares scattered across the muddy path.

Will led McGarroty to his home and left him outside the kitchen door, while the lads following behind with McGarroty's wares dropped them and fled.

'Whit dae ye want me to dae wi' him?' Nannis said, arms akimbo.

'Patch him up, feed him, and he can bed down for the night in the stable.' Will held up his hand as Nannis opened her mouth to complain, no doubt about the likelihood of McGarroty stealing something.

He bent to look the pedlar in the eye and as quickly straightened up, recoiling at the blast of foul breath emanating from a mouth of rotting teeth. 'I am placing my trust in you,' he said, with the same stern tone he used when trying to place the fear of God in his congregation.

McGarroty nodded his head so vigorously Will feared it would fall off, and proffered the bloody handkerchief.

Will waved the handkerchief away. 'You may keep it,' he said, hoping the poor fellow would not have reason to use it again while he journeyed across Scotland.

'Your dinner is ready, Meenister,' said Nannis tapping his arm.

Will sighed. Fond though he was of his son-in-law Andersoun, there were days when he secretly wished his daughter had made a different choice of husband. If he had understood quite how interfering Andersoun's mother Nannis was, he might have forbidden the match. A smile crept across his face and he shook his head. He was as soft as new-made bread in his daughter's hands and could never refuse her anything.

He rose the next day and went to the stable, where he

4

discovered the small round figure of Nannis standing over the pedlar, steaming bowl of porridge in one hand and ceramic jar of honey in the other. She turned quickly when she heard Will saying, 'I wis telling McGarroty here we maun put some honey on they cuts on his face but—'

She stared indignantly at the packman. '—He doesna like the idea.'

'Our good Nannis is correct,' said Will. 'And you may as well submit now, if you want your porridge.'

'Here, hold this,' said Nannis, thrusting the bowl at a surprised Will and liberally applying the spurtle dripping with honey to McGarroty's forehead and cheek.

Ministrations over, Will passed the bowl to the packman. As soon as Nannis's back was turned, McGarroty ran his finger down his face and licked the honey from it. Will shrugged and went to saddle his horse.

'You'll be off to see Ma Beattie at Grangemuir, Meenister,' said Nannis. 'I hear she's terrible sick.'

'Amongst other visits,' said Will stiffly, thinking he'd had more than enough of Nannis already and the morning bell had not yet rung. Then he espied the nest of straw and blankets McGarroty had slept warmly amid, and the eagerness with which the man was now spooning porridge into his mouth. Nannis was a good Christian woman, and if, at times, she was as irritating as a tick burrowing into the flesh, then that was Will's cross to bear.

Sick parishioner soothed, Will rode his horse along the path to Anstruther to meet with his fellow minister there. It was a cold yet clear March day, and Will shivered, wishing to return quickly to the warmth. The horse kept slowing and Will kept nudging it faster. The animal was a recent purchase, and although Will had always considered himself a good judge of horse flesh, he now understood why the seller had rubbed his hands together once they'd agreed the deal.

'He's a spirited one,' the seller had said. He was clearly an astute fellow, for Will was persuaded it was the animal for him from that moment.

But the horse did not want to do more than plod today, as though, despite his dainty feet, his ancestors were plough horses. He spurred the animal, encouraging it to lope, holding the head straight despite the beast's desire to lower it. Just when he thought he'd successfully imposed his will, the horse cast his head down mid stride, and stopped. The saddle girth broke and Will went flying. He found himself lying on a bank with the saddle between his legs and the foolish beast somersaulting so it landed next to him with all four hooves in the air, before rolling and, with considerable effort, rising to its feet.

Will disentangled himself from the saddle and staggered to his feet to find two men working the nearby field staring open-mouthed. He grabbed the reins and, leaning in close to the beast's ear, whispered, 'You will not best me.' But actually the horse had, since with the girth broken Will could no longer ride.

James Melville, the minister for Anstruther, Abercrombie and Kilrenny, chuckled when told of the tumble Will had taken. Melville was a clever fellow, and more importantly a good and kind man. However, it was said he wrote poetry, which Will did not consider a proper pursuit for a man of God, although of greater concern was the diary Melville kept. What did Melville write in it and was there anything about Will therein? He hoped his mishap with the horse would not be written up – no, for surely Melville would be focused on matters more spiritual.

They discussed parish affairs, and in particular the need to appoint another schoolmaster since the teaching of reading was a matter of some urgency. He borrowed a saddle and left the broken one with Melville's servant to take to the saddlers for repair. Then he most determinedly rode his ill-natured nag along the seaweed-strewn shore where the tide was creeping slowly in, clattering over the wooden bridge that crossed the Dreel burn and up the hill, where he saw a sight that had him spurring the horse into a gallop.

He rode along the cliff and back down the hill to the harbour at Pittenweem. And people seeing their minister urging his horse ever faster followed behind. Before he even dismounted and rang the bell calling all to gather, there were many running after him.

'Spaniards,' shouted a man, and a great wailing arose from the crowd. Stories of the immense Armada that Spain was building to invade England and avenge the death of Mary, Queen of Scots, now seen as a Catholic martyr, had been spreading fast as the plague. And all good Protestants were fearful that Philip would seize Scotland too. Will had more faith than that. He knew God would protect his true worshippers and foil those papist sinners.

'No, these are pirates,' he said breathlessly. 'One small ship does not an Armada make.' He could see his parishioners turning to one another – *whit was the meenister blethering aboot?*

He stood shielding his eyes from the light as he peered out to sea. It was surprising to find them here this early in the spring.

'It is likely those bastards who attacked *The Fair Maid* out in the Forth off Anster last year. Their audacity knows no bounds to come this close. We must take the fight to them.'

Will could see the men looking to one another, and one of the wives tugging on her husband's arm urging him not to go. And others with mouths hanging open, no doubt shocked to hear the word *bastard* drop from their minister's lips. There was a murmuring among them, and at the edges of the crowd people began to creep away.

'The meenister is richt,' shouted Will's son-in-law, Andersoun, who had appeared in their midst. 'If we dinna stop them, then next they'll come ashore and attack us in our very homes. Do ye want that? Your houses destroyed, wives, daughters and mothers ravaged, and your bairns enslaved? DAE YE?' he roared.

It was enough. Men left their wives and came to stand beside their leader. And those that did not were dragged there by the wives and mothers.

Will told Andersoun to pick his captains, and the captains chose their men. They ran across the rocky skerries where the boats were moored and cast off. Will went to climb down into Andersoun's boat, *Merry Japes*.

'You maun stay ashore,' called his son-in-law.

'I think not,' said Will, who leapt down and took an oar. He could see his fellow oarsmen looking at him uncertainly. 'I have much experience in rowing,' he said as he settled himself on the plank.

'Aye, we ken. We're only afeard we canna keep up wi' you,' said one.

Will laughed, and the men, who'd looked askance at their fellow for speaking to the minister in such a familiar fashion, smiled their relief.

But the smiles faded as they bent to their task and drew near the much larger ship, where the cannon being prepared for firing was clearly visible. Will's back and shoulders were screaming – it was near forty years since his body had last suffered such punishment. He shouted to the other two boats, directing them to surround the ship. There was a burst of flame and the deafening sound of a cannon fired. The men instinctively ducked, some dropping their oars to cover their ears. The cannonball fell into the sea close enough to their boat for the spray to soak them.

The crew had stopped rowing and Andersoun roared at them to put their backs into it. They began rowing again but in a listless fashion and with much muttering about *whit can we dae agin sich a big ship, and well armed at that?*

The sloop was raising its sails in any case, amid shouted commands, and as the breeze freshened they soon passed between the three fisher boats and out into the Forth.

'They *are* English,' Will said quietly.

'Aye, so it seems,' muttered Andersoun. 'No content wi' beheading oor queen, they are now sending these sinners to tak whit is oors. But we saw them off, lads.'

'There was a ragged shout in support.

'Nay, we can do better than that,' Andersoun shouted back, as the other two boats drew near and they all made for the harbour. 'A hearty cheer, lads. For oor meenister who is both a man of God and a man who is no shy to fight for what is right and true, in protection of our village.'

The men cheered and shouted. 'Weel done, Meenister.'

Will felt himself flushing like a schoolboy. But when he stood once again on the skerries and gazed out to sea watching the sails of the receding ship grow smaller and noting the cloud banks building on the horizon, presaging a storm, he knew they had to be better prepared – for these wicked creatures would come again.

He left Andersoun ordering the mooring of the boats, released his horse from the pole to which he had hurriedly tied the reins, and walked up the steep close where he was stopped every now and then by a member of his flock who came to humbly thank him. And all the time he puzzled what wee boats could do against an armed ship and men who made their living by taking from those who were fishermen, not fighters.

Reaching home, he found the tale of his afternoon's work had preceded him. His daughter Cecy came, and taking his arm, leant her cheek against his shoulder, saying, '*Je suis heureux que vous soyez en sécurité, Papa. S'il vous plaît, ne vous battez plus. Nous avons besoin de notre ministre et vous sont trop vieux.'*

Will snorted then could not help but laugh. 'Very prettily, and formally, said, my girl, but I must help protect us – even if you do think I'm too old to fight. A minister must stand up for what is right – and what of your husband? I could not let him go alone.'

He patted her arm and detached himself, going into his workroom for a moment of quiet restoration and prayed for all those who must fight for survival. He thought of Bethia then. They'd had word near ten months ago that she was returning to Scotland. The perils of her journey, where even a peaceful village like Pittenweem was beset by men intent on stealing from them, or worse, did not bear thinking of. But his sister was always a most determined woman – although perhaps she had changed. The last time they were together was just after his marriage to his beloved Cecile, and Cecile died in childbirth thirty-two years ago. He pressed his hand to his heart and sighed. Soon after, Bethia and her family had fled Italy, escaping a vengeful Pope, and she'd lived in Constantinople ever since.

Will bowed his head and prayed for his sister, and for her servant Grissel, that both would soon be safely restored to their family in Scotland.

Chapter Two

Nannis

It was more than twenty years and shortly after the great and sudden reform of religion in Scotland that Will had been called by the presbytery of Pittenweem to minister to its parish. Around the same time, his father and brother John, along with John's large family, had removed from St Andrews to the village. John had determined that it was better situated for the salt pan business he'd recently acquired to add to his other trading interests. Will had wondered why John hadn't chosen Anstruther with its deeper harbours. John had shrugged, saying property in Pittenweem was to be had for a good price. Yet Will had a strong suspicion it was more that John preferred to be a giant amongst the lesser merchants of Pittenweem. Although this was immaterial now – John, as he took on more and more of the running of Father's many business interests, was soon the wealthiest burgher to be found not only in Pittenweem but all of the East Neuk of Fife.

Will's house, in comparison to his wealthy brother's, was not large. There had been talk of his congregation building a more substantial manse befitting the minister of the parish but nothing had come of it. There were three bedchambers and he had insisted on moving into the smallest when his daughter married. Cecy now shared his old chamber with Andersoun and the two girls, who slept on truckle beds, while her four boys lay like pegs in a row in the bed which filled the third chamber. The ground floor was taken up by the large kitchen and the small room which Will used to work on his sermons, meet his elders and parishioners, and of course study and pray.

He had always suspected that Cecy had made it a condition of her marriage that she and Andersoun live with him. But Andersoun had been the soul of discretion and never let slip by any hint, word or glance that he would've preferred their own abode – especially in the beginning when he was too in awe of his minister father-in-law to mumble more than a few words when encouraged by Cecy to speak.

'You barely know this lad,' Will had said to his daughter, when the red-faced youth had crept out of the room after stammering out his request for Cecy's hand.

'I know him as good, honest and hard-working.'

'But he's a fisherman.'

Cecy had come behind where Will sat and, wrapping her arms around his shoulders, had laid her head on the top of his. Will could feel the soft warmth of her hair cascading over his bald spot. '*Les disciples étaient des pêcheurs, Papa,*' she had whispered, and of course she was correct. Peter, Andrew, James and John, the Lord Jesus Christ's disciples, were indeed fishermen.

And that was that. His resistance was broken, for he could refuse this child, all he had left of his long-dead and much-loved French wife Cecile, nothing. For all her gentleness Cecy had a core of iron much like her mother, and he would not, and could not, place himself in a situation where they were estranged. As the minister's daughter, he had expected she would marry the son of a minister, or even better another minister, but she'd shown little interest in the young, and sometimes not so young, men who were beginning to sniff around. And truth be told, he'd not been sorry, for her companionship was all he had. Of course, he could have remarried himself, but he had taken a vow to God that no other would, or indeed could, replace his Cecile.

And so Cecy had married, and Andersoun had soon surprised Will. He was a smallish man amid the great height of the Seton men, yet there was a strength in him and a clarity of purpose that had taken him from being the scrawny fatherless youth aboard another man's boat to a broad-chested fellow who planted his feet on the ground, or deck, as though nothing could sway or overturn him. Fishing vessels, of course, were owned by merchants and not the fishermen who worked them but marriage to the minister's daughter elevated Andersoun and John, ever quick to spot an opportunity, helped fund the purchase of Andersoun's first boat.

Andersoun now owned two vessels and was saving towards the building of another three.

'I have four sons,' Andersoun said. 'One boat each, and one left for me.'

Privately, Will was aware that Andersoun did not have four sons who wanted to go to sea but, for all he was a sound fellow who had made his own choices, it didn't seem to have occurred to him that his sons should be accorded the same. Donald, for instance, was a scholarly lad, who Will was eager to send to the university in St Andrews as soon as he was old enough.

Sitting in his tall oak chair at the head of the board, he gazed at his family seated around it. Notwithstanding his daily communion with God, his services which people came to listen to from as far away as Perth, Falkirk and even Glasgow, his moments when he spoke at the General Assembly of the Protestant Estates in Edinburgh and was listened to with great respect, this was what gave him his greatest joy. Of course, he knew it was wrong to be prideful about his family, but it was also directed by God that he should care for them. And each

13

time he raised his head, after they all prayed together, his heart near overflowed.

He gazed at Cecy as she bent to speak with her younger daughter, smoothing the child's hair, while she explained why Jesus would always watch over her, even when she had got lost in the woods as had happened today.

'Of course, if you had not gone in amid the tall trees when I have expressly forbid it, then you would not have found yourself lost,' she added.

'I will not do it ever again,' the child said softly. 'Even if the boys do throw dolly in there.'

Cecy frowned. 'Which boys?'

Edane, Will's eldest grandchild sniffed. 'You have a big imagination, Syffy,' she said.

Syffy, thinking herself unwatched, stuck her tongue out, but Edane just rolled her eyes. Will hoped Syffy would be the last child because six seemed more than sufficient, and his fear each time Cecy gave birth that it would end as it had done for his Cecile had never gone away. That first time with Edane, the midwife claimed Will had suffered more than the mother.

'Niver hae I seen a man in sich a state,' she'd said. 'And you not even the father. Away ye go to the kirk and get on yer knees and I will send a message when it's all o'er.'

And so beside himself had he been that he hadn't even chided her for suggesting he should kneel to pray – a papist practice which was an anathema to the Church of Scotland.

Edane looked like Bethia had at that age, with the long thick dark hair and bright eyes and he very much worried she had his sister's determined nature too. Already a local laird had come saying his son wanted to marry her. Will had looked doubtful but said he would discuss it with his son-in-law. Fortunately, Andersoun had agreed that, although it was not unknown for girls to

14

marry as young as fourteen, she was too young. He appeared untroubled that it was Will's permission that had been sought.

'Ye are the meenister, after a' and would need to agree to carry oot the marriage, for I'll have nae hand fasting but a proper ceremony which binds.'

And it seemed, when the laird's son's proposal was mentioned to Edane, that she had neither intention nor interest in him.

'We'll wait a few years,' Will advised.

'But no too long,' said Andersoun, 'for 'tis a good match.'

The meal was drawing to a close and Will thought what words he might say in prayer at the end. There was a common prayer, but he liked to vary it else it became rote and no one listened. God's word should never be treated lightly, but soberly, wisely and righteously.

'Let us place our hands together and close our eyes,' Will said. He looked pointedly at Syffy, who grinned gap-toothed back at him. 'Bow our heads and pray to our great Father who watches over us and,' he added, eyes now on his youngest grandson, who was quite the naughtiest child he'd ever encountered – and that was saying something after the exploits of his own brother John – 'sees all that we do,' his gaze fell on Edane once more, 'knows what is in our hearts and sees our sinful pride.'

The prayer over, Will rose and retreated to his workroom. He had barely sat down when there was that familiar, and insistent, tap on the door which heralded the arrival of Nannis.

'Come,' he called, suppressing a sigh. He had tried silence in the hope she would think him out and leave, for – as she was quick to tell anyone who would listen – she never presumed to enter the *meenister's* chamber without his permission, even though they were related and really she need not wait for an invitation.

'She leans against the door listening,' Cecy had told him, trying to suppress her giggles, for she did attempt to be respectful towards her mother-in-law, however trying Nannis might be.

'I know,' Will had said ruefully. 'I can hear her breathing.'

At which Cecy let out a peal of laughter and Will could not but help smile in return, however inappropriate, for Nannis was a good, God-fearing woman despite her stentorious breath.

In bustled Nannis, grown stout and toothless from an excess of sugary foods since her son had become comfortably-off. Her neck was so short as to be almost invisible and her head appeared to rise direct from her voluminous chest.

'There's grim work afoot, Meenister,' was her opening salvo.

'Aye, so you're aywis telling me, Mistress Nannis.'

'The blacksmith is in the jougs in the mercat, and so he should be, but he has knocked aff the crown which he is required to wear. And ye ken it has all they important words on it which tell o' his crime.'

Will rose immediately. The smith was a wicked man before God and his fellow parishioners, and Will would not have him flout the law or his punishment. He grabbed his cloak and bonnet from the peg and bent his head to go out through the front door. It was market day and busy outside, the man's punishment being enacted now for that very reason. All his neighbours would both see his humiliation and take heed in how they behaved towards their own family members.

The smith was as broad as he was high, with the jutting shoulders of a plough horse and a face contorted with rage, eyes daring anyone to come near. The watching crowd stood well back. Will knew he must approach with caution for the man was angry enough to do something very unwise – like swing for the minister –

which would have him locked up for some considerable time. And, although punishment for assault was always merited, Will did not think longer incarceration was needful. The fellow's temper was erratic and easily activated, but he was their only blacksmith and skilled at his work. The village could not do without him.

He bent to pick up the paper crown, but one of the circle of watching visitors darted in before he could, handed it to him and backed away bowing. The crown was still wearable, having fallen too far from the smith for him to stamp on it, manacled as he was to the mercat cross. Will made sure to stay out of reach himself; the man might be barefoot and dressed in sackcloth as part of his punishment, but it didn't mean he couldn't deliver a powerful kick.

Behold the unnatural son thus punished for putting a hand on his father and dishonouring God in him while holding hammer and stone.

The writing was cramped and barely legible, but then there was little space on the crown for such a long sentence. The deacon might have done better to be less wordy.

The blacksmith tugged on his manacles growling like a rabid dog but they were fastened firm.

'Calm down, man,' said Will. 'Do you want to be back here tomorrow, for the elders will call for your sentence to be extended if you continue to behave thus.'

The fellow glared at Will but at least he was no longer baring his teeth. Will realised he should not have left this up to the presbytery. He should have met with the smith himself, and talked him down. He took a step forward and lowered his voice. 'Show true humility before God and take your punishment like a man and all will think better of you for it.'

The smith stared at the ground and so did Will. He

was rolling a stone back and forth beneath one filthy bare foot and curling his toes around as though to get a grip on it.

'You will be freed from the jougs and I will send for your father. We will go to the kirk where you will make an apology for striking the man who gave you life under God. Then you will be released.' Will spoke loudly so that all could hear. 'But only under faithful promise made before the Lord that you will never again lay hand upon your father, whatever the provocation. Can you undertake to keep such a promise?'

The fellow glared once more and Will held up his hand. 'This is your final opportunity. Otherwise I will have no alternative but to refer you to our good bailie and a hanging may be the outcome.'

He could see the bulbous Adam's apple in the man's neck wobble as he swallowed.

'Well, what is your answer?'

There was a long pause and Will wondered what it would do to discipline within the village should the man refuse.

'Aye, I'll no lay a hand on the auld bugger again. But,' he thrust his face at Will, 'ye'd better hae him telt too.'

Will had to bite down on his lip to contain the smile. 'Our fathers can be thrawn, believe me, I know,' he said in quiet voice.

The smith stared at him then gave a shout of laughter, while the crowd leaned forward with curious faces, desperate to know what the minister had said to the sinner to provoke such mirth.

Will handed him the crown, and the smith, with a wink, placed it back on his head and suffered himself to be paraded along the street to the kirk. The father was waiting, and Will thought it was going too far when the smith sank to his knees and begged forgiveness – especially when he touched his forehead to the ground before his father's dirty feet, giving a distinctly papist feel to the act – although it left the auld man open-mouthed and the congregation sighing with satisfaction. Ah well, at least it was over and done with.

'Weel done, Meenister,' said Nannis, catching up with him as he left the kirk. 'Now I hae something else of a maist serious nature …'

Will sighed and could not help but roll his eyes heavenwards.

But before Nannis could hurry him away to the next thing of import, Will's nephew, Symon, was before him face alight with excitement. 'They are here,' he said. 'Aunt Bethia and Ephraim are come.'

Chapter Three

Father

Father had never been a man to display much emotion beyond making it plain to all if anything displeased him, but Bethia was left in no doubt of his heartfelt delight in being reunited with her. He sat by the fire in his high-backed oak chair with Bethia on a low stool by his side holding her hand tight between both of his.

'My lass,' he said, 'my lass has come back to me.'

Even John was seen to surreptitiously brush his eyes, while her grandson, Ephraim, watched quietly from the settle and Bethia wept freely.

For a man nearing his ninth decade, Father was remarkably sharp-witted still, but then why wouldn't he be with his daughter-in-law attending to his every need and John's many children flowing freely in and out of his domain. Bethia soon observed how he was like a king among his people, for the townsfolk of Pittenweem were mighty proud to have an octogenarian in their midst. It gave hope to all that they too might live long, and remarkably healthy, lives. Perhaps there was some power hid in the cave for which their village was named, or some quality of the air, or a special benefice from God which might be cast over them all too. And look at the auld man's children, all of them a good age, and the daughter and younger son rich forby, not to mention the other son a minister of the Kirk. Aye, Master Seton was indeed a man of great bounty in wealth, health, faith and family.

Father did not sit long holding Bethia's hand between his before he grew restless, turning his head to look around. 'Grissel? Where is she? I must see my Grissel.'

And there she was smiling shyly in the doorway.

'Come, lass,' he called, and Grissel came and stood by him. He freed one hand and reached up. Grissel took it, kneeling down at his other side.

'My girls,' he said. 'Baith ma girls.'

Bethia glanced over at her brother, John, who shrugged. Was Father getting wandered?

They sat thus for a while until John's youngest appeared. 'Our wee surprise,' John had called him, for Violet had birthed the bairn when she was forty and thus well past child-bearing age. He tottered around the chamber, treading on the spreading skirts of Bethia's dress, and she, fearful of damage to the silks, released Father's hand and rose to her feet. Grissel stayed where she was, seemingly reluctant to let go. It was sad for Grissel that her mother had died only two years since. If they had left Constantinople when the plan of returning to Scotland was first mooted, then Grissel would have seen Agnes again. Father, Bethia noticed, was now using his other hand to stroke the back of Grissel's hand curled in his.

And so it continued. They had been in John's home for five days now and Bethia had been reunited with her other brother Will and met her niece Cecy and extended family. It was good to be among them and especially to see Father. He did not like her to venture far from him, unless Grissel was there. It seemed Grissel, despite being Bethia's servant, was a satisfactory substitute, and Bethia was made uncomfortable by this. She sat in the hot and airless chamber feeling the sweat trickling down her back watching while Grissel crouched by Father's chair telling him stories of Constantinople and the sultan's harem in her inimitable way. She looked over to her grandson Ephraim, but he was in deep discussion with John's eldest, Symon, who was a younger version of his father complete with the mischievous expression. John was complaining about a special tax raised by the king to pay for some visit or other and Father interrupted, shouting that one good thing about the recently beheaded Mary of Scots was she only raised taxes in this way once while she was queen – to celebrate the christening of her son. Having made his point, he bent his head to Grissel once more.

Bethia motioned to John and they left the room, descended the stairs and went out into the bright spring sunshine. It was preternaturally still, no wind blowing for once, and the waves rippled gently onto the narrow stretch of sand between the jagged shoals of black rock with which this coastline abounded.

Bethia ran her finger lightly across one eyelid and then the other. The brightness of the day, the light reflecting off the water and the dazzle of a sun unobscured by cloud was both delightful and piercing – and showed up just how wrinkled John's face was. It was hard to believe this grizzled, slightly stooped man was once her naughty wee brother.

'Is Father often confused?' she said.

'Why would you say that?'

'You know, the way he is with Grissel. She is our *servant* after all.'

'You think that's all she is to us?' said John wryly.

'I know she's more than a servant and no one could have been more loyal – and I to her in return,' said Bethia sharply.

'That is *not* what I meant,' said John.

Bethia shook her head slowly. 'No, that cannot be.'

'Why can it no be? Father would not be the first master to dip his wick where it shouldna go. And we hae talked of this afore. What's mair, Grissel may no bear much likeness to you, who take after Mother, but in height and colouring she favours me and Will, certainly before we all went grey heided.'

Bethia chewed on her lip. 'I can remember when Grissel was born,' she said slowly. 'Do you think Mother guessed?'

John shrugged. 'Perhaps, for she rejoined Father in the marital bed for long enough tae mak me.'

Bethia smiled sadly. Mother and she had shared a bed for much of her childhood. It was one way to avoid the endless pregnancies to which John's wife had been subjected.

'And what o' Grissel?' John said.

'What of her?'

'Should we acknowledge she is oor sister since it seems Father is sae doing?'

Bethia stiffened. 'I see no reason to change the way things are.'

John frowned and then shrugged. 'As you think best. But we will aywis look after her.'

'Yes, as I have done my whole life, I will continue to take care no harm comes to Grissel – despite her sometimes errant ways.'

John grinned and squeezed Bethia's arm.

The door of the house opened and Grissel came down the narrow path of this long narrow garden that stretched up the hill behind the house and commanded a view of the sea. They drew apart then as she observed them, hands on hips.

'Your faither wants ye,' she said in her usual abrupt way. 'He's feart ye've disappeared back tae Turkland already.'

'Tell him I will be with him in a moment,' said Bethia.

Grissel's eyes widened but she said nothing further, simply turning around and rubbing her hip as she hirpled down the path.

'Are you going tae speak tae him about it?'

'Speak to who about what?' said Bethia.

John widened his eyes much as Grissel had done.

'I assume you mean am I going to ask our father if he fathered a bastard which he has hidden in plain sight these past fifty years.'

'At least he took care of her, and Agnes.'

Bethia thought that if Grissel's mother Agnes had still been alive she would've asked her who Grissel's father was. She smiled then, for Agnes could be fierce and most likely would have sent Bethia about her business with a flea in her ear at the impertinence of such a question. She was sad indeed not see Agnes and unfortunately the same could not be said of her own querulous, demanding and long-dead mother.

'Why don't you ask him yourself?' she said.

John stared out to sea. 'Whether Grissel is my bastard sister or your servant makes little difference to me for she will aywis be a beloved member of this family.' He gazed shrewdly at Bethia. 'But whatever her position is, you seem discomposed, and perhaps you dinna want to share Father. As his only daughter you hae occupied a special place, but this pettiness isn't worthy o' you, my sister.'

One of John's sons came seeking him then, which was as well, for Bethia was close to boxing his ears, indeed might have done were he not so tall. She sat down on the trunk of a severed tree, her skirts spreading around her, uncaring that the damp ground might mark the cloth. Grissel was adept at removing spills and stains. Resting her elbows on her knees and her chin in her hands she gazed out at the unusually tranquil scene. The boats were on their way out for a night's fishing as the half-light of evening spread, the men at the oars rowing mightily while some women were at work still mending nets and baiting lines on the shore. The near perfect full moon rose behind long streaks of cloud, one moment obscured and the next shining an uncanny light upon the scene below. She hunched against the creeping chill, pulling her shawl close up around her chin. She heard the backdoor open but felt reluctant to turn away from the eerie sea and sky. Then John's middle daughter stood before her, a wee sprite of a child.

'Aunt Bethia, Pa asks if you will come.'

Bethia nodded but didn't move.

The child, already halfway down the path towards the steps to the shore and clearly bent on escape, called back, 'There is a man come to see you.'

Bethia sighed. She stood up and walked slowly towards the half-open door where the golden light of candle spilled onto the rough stone path while behind her John's fey child made good her escape.

One of the first things that Father had spoken of to Bethia was how her old friend and one-time suitor Gilbert Logie had come seeking her.

'He came riding doon frae his big tower hoose awa up in the hills,' Father waved his hand vaguely, 'jist tae find oot if the rumours were true and if the grand lady frae Turkland arrived in Edinburgh wis you.'

And so Bethia was not at all surprised to find Gilbert seated by Father when she came in from the garden. She was, however, decidedly put out to be discovered with stains on her skirt from where she had been sitting on a damp tree stump. She put her hand up to smooth her hair, which was no doubt dishevelled, wishing she'd had forewarning of his visit.

Gilbert rose and bowed low and Bethia curtsied in return. He was grey-headed with deep furrows across his forehead, which surprised her, for she remembered him as a man who smiled more than he frowned. He'd always been of stocky build but fortunately had not developed the fat belly common among men of wealth. Gilbert had never been handsome like her husband Mainard, but he was not unattractive, even now, she thought.

They made their obeisance to one another and he inquired how her journey had been, remaining standing until Bethia sat down.

'It was long, uncomfortable, frequently stormy, occasionally perilous but, as you see, we endured.' She was aware of the entire family watching and listening, and Father most especially leaning forward, his hand cupped around his ear, while Grissel sat on the stool by his knee.

She would've preferred to have had private conversation with Gilbert for their first encounter and not this public display. Gilbert did not look any more at ease than she, and she was grateful to her grandson Ephraim, who began to tell tales of some adventures from their journey which soon had everyone laughing. And Father was near to bursting with pride at having a grandson with such proficiency, and confidence, in conversing with his elders.

Gilbert did not stay long, saying he was on his way to Dreel Castle and must arrive there before curfew, to which they all laughed, since curfew did not apply to men as wealthy as he.

Bethia was glad the awkwardness of the first meeting was now over. He made no arrangements to come again but no doubt they would encounter one another on occasion.

'He was niver bonny like Master Mainard,' said Grissel, echoing Bethia's thoughts of earlier, while she was brushing out Bethia's hair, once a deep rich brown and now a lead grey shot through with silver, although still satisfyingly thick.

Bethia wondered if she would've recognised Gilbert if she'd encountered him in the street. She would have known him though by the purple scar puckering one side of his face. And no doubt he too had been surprised by how much she had aged.

'He was ay a guid yin,' said Grissel softly.

'Yes,' said Bethia slowly. 'He was the kindest man I have ever known.'

Chapter Four

Ephraim

Father was remarkable, Bethia, John and Will all agreed. He was frail, as one would expect of a man entering his eighty-ninth year, but he was alert as ever. He sat in his great chair in a chamber which was not small but so overfull was it constantly with family and frequent visitors that the room felt cramped as a seaboard cabin and humid as a wet summer's day in Constantinople. Nevertheless, Bethia spent much of her time sitting with him. He was reluctant as a small child to let her out of his sight, and she was only released when Grissel would take a turn for a while.

'My girls, my girls,' he would say frequently, a note of great satisfaction in his voice.

He was also exercised about keeping Ephraim occupied, which was a relief in a way. Bethia had been concerned when first she introduced her grandson, made uncomfortable by Father's remarks.

'Aye, yer a dark yin, like yer grandfaither,' was Father's opening salvo. 'Bonny wi' it, but I'm guessing ye ken that.' He glanced at his eldest granddaughter watching intently from her corner, with three other sisters clustered around her equally open-mouthed.

Ephraim looked to Bethia, and she realised that for all

his Scots had come on since he arrived in the country, Father's speech was beyond him. She moved to stand behind the lad where he was seated and smooth his curly hair. Closing her eyes she could almost imagine her dead husband was back with her once more, for the tight curls felt the same.

'Father says he's right glad to have you here,' she said to Ephraim.

He glanced up at her and laughed. 'I may not have fully understood the words, Nonna, but I surmise it was more a comment on my appearance than salutations on my arrival.'

Bethia smiled fondly down on him.

'But I *am* richt glad to see ye,' said Father. 'Come close by me, laddie, and tell me all aboot yerself.' He reached out and took the lad's hand. Bethia could see there were again tears in Father's eyes. Old age seemed to have made him surprisingly lachrymose, she thought, wiping her own eyes.

Being Ephraim, he found his feet in no time. It would've been natural for him to look to the sons of the local laird with which to pass his days, but Ephraim, with his easy manner, made friends with the sons of the fishermen and was soon to be found out on the boats learning their trade.

John, perhaps unsurprisingly, approved of his enterprise, saying Ephraim was in a fair way to become a skilled buyer and seller of goods if he learned well about the product from the sharp end.

'He'll ken his fish,' he said. 'And naebody will be able to sell him anything that's been oot the water for a few days for he'll see by the glaze of the dead eye and its stiffness if it's auld and long caught.'

Ephraim, who had been reluctant to leave the friends he'd quickly made in Edinburgh during their brief sojourn there, appeared to forget about his desire to return to that city. His Scots came on apace and, immersed as he was in the fishing and new friends, he seemed content. The folk of Pittenweem grew used to him, and he would stop for a blether with anyone, often returning home with some sweetmeat that one of the fond auld women had given him, much to John's wife's indignation.

'I can bake ane far better than that. Ma MacNiven hasna put ony spice in it, it's tasteless,' said Violet, after a wee nibble at the corner.

Nannis too, who had fallen out with Violet a long time since, suddenly found reason to refriend her. 'I ken 'tis only cause she wants to let a' her neighbours know she's spent time wi' oor Ephraim,' Violet said to Bethia.

But for all she seemed a difficult woman, Nannis could exert some charm herself, if she wanted something. When she brought Violet a length of lace she had crocheted and some gossip about a neighbour, all was made good between them.

'Aye,' muttered John to Bethia as Nannis appeared for the fourth day in a row and she and Violet bent their heads together. 'We'll see how long it lasts this time.'

'It is Passover, Nonna,' said Ephraim sadly, after they had been in Pittenweem for over a month.

Bethia went to her grandson and wrapped her arms around his long, lean frame. 'It is also Lent,' she said, 'and soon it will be Easter. And these dour Protestants do not believe in celebrating any festival.'

'I do not think I want to go to a Scottish heaven,' said Ephraim. 'For it will be very dull.'

Bethia gazed up into his face. 'You are not wrong, my bonny lad.'

He sighed as she released him.

'Do you miss Constantinople very much?'

'Sometimes – but I like it here well enough and I'm learning more Scots every day. Papa says the more languages you speak, the better you can connect with folk and the better your business will grow.'

Bethia nodded. Her son Samuel was a wise man, she thought.

Ephraim's skin, which had faded to a pale olive after the time spent in smoky, dreich Edinburgh, grew darker with all the outdoor activity which made the blue of his eyes even more noticeable. His shoulders acquired a breadth and strength which had been lacking and the lassies of Pittenweem followed him giggling and peeping from behind their hands when he turned his gaze upon them. Bethia kept a close eye on her charge. She loved her grandson's winsome ways but she was also accountable to his father for Ephraim's safety. And so she watched, ready to intervene with a word, or several, of warning should he appear to be fixing his attentions on any of the young women. It would seem to him that they were easy and available because of the freedom with which they gathered together and roamed in the long twilight of the Scottish spring evenings when it did not grow dark till late – something that would never have been permitted to the young women of Constantinople, be they Jews or Moslems. The bewitching hours, Bethia thought, but Ephraim did not fall under any lass's spell, indeed was careful to keep his distance.

'He's a canny one,' said John when Bethia voiced her concerns, more as a way of ascertaining whether John was aware of anything that she was not. She was relieved to hear John's assessment. Although when he added thoughtfully, 'Edane likes him,' she stiffened.

'Will's granddaughter? But they are cousins,' said Bethia.

'Aye. Neither the Bible nor Will would like it. But I havena seen the laddie show her ony special attention in return.'

Then why mention it, Bethia wanted to say, but instead went with all possible haste up the steep close and along the street past the mercat cross – where the traders were packing up for the day and a particularly ugly small dog tried to attach itself to her – to her brother Will's house to ascertain if there was indeed anything more than cousinly friendship between his granddaughter and her grandson.

She arrived breathless to learn Ephraim was in the workroom with Will. There was no sign of Edane nor any other child, for once, and Bethia sat down at the long table in the kitchen to have a blether with Cecy. They had barely begun when Will came into the room saying the minister from the neighbouring parish of Kilrenny and Anstruther was here. It seemed James Melville had heard from Will about his nephew and expressed an interest in meeting him. Would Bethia care to join them, Will asked?

Bethia would much rather have continued with Cecy but suspected she was to be paraded before Melville and rose slowly to yet again play her part as the foreign lady from the land of the Turks.

'He does know I hale from these parts?' she muttered as she followed Will out of the room.

'Of course.'

'My son is called Ephraim too,' said Melville, after they had exchanged greetings. 'From Genesis, as you will know.'

'He was Joseph's second son, his firstborn was named Manasseh. I'm glad I was not named for him,' said Ephraim. He dipped his head as he spoke and Bethia was pleased to see the deference shown to James Melville.

Melville's eyes brightened and he nodded his approval at Ephraim's biblical knowledge. He was a small, darting man, quick of movement who took an eager interest in all around him. It was strange to think he lived in Kilrenny, a village once owned by Cardinal Beaton. Bethia shuddered as she remembered the cardinal watching the burning of George Wishart from the tall window of St Andrews Castle. And it was this most terrible event which had precipitated everything which had happened to both her and Will since.

'And when Joseph saw that his father laid his right hand upon the head of Ephraim, it displeased him: and he held up his father's hand, to remove it from Ephraim's head unto Manasseh's head, saying unto his father, Not so, my father: for this is the firstborn; put thy right hand upon his head.

'And his father refused, and said, I know it, my son, I know it: he also shall become a people, and he also shall be great: but truly his younger brother shall be greater than he, and his seed shall become a multitude of nations,' said Melville.

'That is perhaps too much greatness to aspire to,' said Ephraim. 'I am happy to be a latter-day Ephraim who lives a good and righteous life before God.'

'And Jesus Christ,' said Will quickly, and Bethia shifted on the settle next to Ephraim.

'You must come and meet the other Ephraim. Although he is only a child, he is quick and keen to learn – but there speaks a father as fond as Joseph,' said Melville, smiling.

They all laughed, and Bethia could see why his parishioners loved their minister.

'But I had another reason for wishing to meet with you. Your uncle,' he nodded towards Will, 'tells me you are fluent in Hebrew and have knowledge of some other Oriental languages. Hebrew is the language of the Old Testament and the foundation on which our Lord Jesus Christ stood in creating the New Testament. I have some Hebrew but want to learn more.' He looked to Will. 'We hoped to form a small study group while you are among us and can teach us fluency in this most sacred of languages.'

Bethia could see Ephraim swallow and knew it was not how he wished to pass his time in Pittenweem. But he deferred to his elders, bowing and saying, 'I would be honoured.' And she was relieved to know he would pass at least some of his time in study, and it would do him no harm to do some teaching.

Melville then said he would have welcomed a daily lesson, 'But the demands of my ministry and flock are too great to permit it.' And so they agreed to meet four times a week while Ephraim was among them.

Bethia could see Ephraim's brow furrow as Will and Melville blethered about parish matters.

'I do not know how to teach, and especially to such learned men,' he said after Melville eventually rose and Will went to see him out.

'Melville says you are not to worry,' said Will coming back into the chamber. 'He has a copy of the good book in Hebrew and we will simply work from that.' He rubbed his hands together. ''Tis a grand idea. I'm looking forward to our wee group.'

Bethia stroked Ephraim's back and, after a moment, felt him relax.

'I must away to the kirk,' said Will, 'before the synod come seeking my whereabouts.'

''Tis more likely to be Nannis who will,' muttered Ephraim, and Bethia stifled a laugh.

Will stared at him, then let out a guffaw himself. 'You're no wrong there, lad, well observed.'

And off he went stomping out the room in great good humour. Bethia too felt lighter. It was in moments such as these that she remembered she liked her brother, which was a welcome relief from feeling burdened by the excess of self-righteousness he frequently displayed. She sent up a small prayer to the Virgin thanking her that Will's sense of humour saved him from being a most dour fellow. Then gave a wry smile thinking how angry Will would be if he knew she had importuned Mary, Mother of God, on his behalf – for these Protestants did not venerate the Virgin as they should.

Chapter Five

The Kirk

Will inevitably was not long in leading Bethia into his workroom and interrogating her about attendance at the kirk.

'You were several weeks in Edinburgh,' he said stiffly, 'and I assume you worshipped within St Giles or one of the other many churches with which that city abounds.'

There was something so solemn and yet pompous about him she could not resist saying, 'John told me that many of the nobles who surround the king are Catholics, as is the woman who was as near to a mother as our poor King Jamie ever knew.'

'The Countess of Mar is an honourable woman,' said Will sternly, 'and it was the king's tutor George Buchanan, a most right-thinking man, who took charge of his education, both academic and spiritual, and a stern and able taskmaster he was too. Fortunately, the queen was gone before she could bring any influence to bear and impose her papist ways.'

Bethia shivered. She had not long reached Scotland when word came of the death of Mary, Queen of Scots. Inevitably there had been delays in their journey and it was winter when they finally made landfall. She had sent up a prayer of thanks to the Virgin for again watching over her, because John had been easily located, lingering in Leith awaiting her arrival. And then one storm followed close on the heels of another and John said it was not safe to make the final push across the water to where Father impatiently waited, for why would she wish to risk drowning in the Firth of Forth when she had survived the long sea journey from Constantinople?

Instead, he had taken their party up the hill to his crowded land of tall tenements in Edinburgh's High Street where he kept a few rooms and let out the rest to respectable townsfolk.

Eventually, one day the weather was suddenly calm; no wind whipping around the corners and howling down the long narrow closes which dropped to the stinking Nor' Loch below.

'I think we may finally depart for Fife,' John had said, '… although the lack o' wind may only be the presaging of another storm tae come.' Nevertheless, he had gone to arrange passage.

Grissel was standing with an armful of clean linen while Ephraim knelt tying up his trunk when the commotion began.

'That doesna sound good,' Grissel had muttered.

The noise spread and soon all the church bells were ringing. Bethia clutched hand to breast while Grissel covered her ears and Ephraim hung out of the window. The door was flung wide and John had rushed in bringing a great draft of cold air with him.

'The queen is dead.'

'What did you say?'

'I said Queen Mary is dead,' John bellowed.

'So Elizabeth did it.'

'Aye, she chopped her cousin's head off. Glad I'm no a member o' that family.'

Bethia had gone to her kist in the corner and dropped down onto her haunches, which was not at all comfortable for her creaking bones. She glanced over her shoulder but John and Grissel were leaning out the

35

window while Ephraim was already gone thundering down the spiral stairs and out into the throng. She slid her hand into the secret compartment and removed her gold crucifix and small image of the Virgin. Lowering her knees to the ground, she had clasped the crucifix and Virgin between her hands, closed her eyes and began a prayer for the dead ...

'De profondis clamavi ad te
Domine exaudi vocem meam
Fiant aures tuae intendentes in vocem deprecations meae
Si iniquitates observaveris Domine, Domine, quis sustinebit?
Quia apud te propitiatio est; et propter legum tuam susttinui te, Domine
Sustinuit anima mea in verbo euis ...'

'Out of the depths I have cried to thee O Lord.
Lord hear my voice
Thine ears be attentive to my supplication
If thou, Lord, shouldest mark iniquities, O Lord, who shall stand?
But there is forgiveness with thee, that thou mayest be feared.
I wait for the Lord, my soul doth wait ...'

Bethia thought on this as she gazed at the shelves of books lining Will's workroom and the Genevan Bible lying on the board and knew that Will would send her immediately back to Constantinople should he ever catch her, as John did that day, on her knees with crucifix in hand.

'We do not pray for the dead within the Protestant Kirk,' John had said, roughly hauling her to her feet. 'They are in God's hand and have no need of our paltry supplications.'

'You seem distracted,' said Will. 'What are you

thinking of, sister?'

Bethia shook her head.

'I want you to come regularly and take lessons with me. I will have no false witness within my kirk. There is an English Bible at John's house and you will spend some time each day studying it and I will hear your lessons.'

Bethia swallowed.

'Does everyone attend the kirk, even the Catholics?' she had asked John while they were still in Edinburgh.

'Oh, aye,' he'd said. 'What they do in private is their own business provided they are discreet – and wealthy. But you must display expected behaviour in public.'

'So I should not make the sign of the cross nor eat fish on Friday.'

She'd expected John would understand she was being light-hearted but saw his face growing red and knew an explosion was imminent unless she averted it. 'It is of no matter,' she'd quickly said. 'As you well know I attended church in Geneva so have already been exposed to, and survived, the Calvinist form of Christianity. Since John Knox was a disciple of Calvin's, I should imagine it's not much different here.'

The flush had faded from John's cheeks and a smile crept over his face. 'Will says the Kirk in Scotland is more austere than that of Geneva.'

Bethia had groaned, but they all went the next day, John with Bethia on his arm and Ephraim by her other side and Grissel following close behind. She had tried to give Ephraim some instruction on how he must act in church but he'd told her he would just watch and follow.

'I am curious to see how you Christians go about your worship,' he'd said.

She'd placed her hand on his arm and looked earnestly up into his face, saying, 'Ephraim, please do not ever refer to the congregation as *you Christians* again. You must behave as a though you too are a Christian for the time we are here.'

He'd looked at her in that careless way of his, but after a moment, he inclined his head in acknowledgement. 'I know, Nonna, you told me frequently enough on the journey. But I am curious, why do they assume you are one of them? You've been away for so long, and you married a Jew?'

'He was not a Jew when I married him. You must know that.' She'd stopped then, for Ephraim had been told little of the family history. Samuel, his father, behaved as though his family had always been staunch Jews. And yet the antecedents of many of the Sephardim living in Galata across the Golden Horn from the sultan's palace were the same – expelled from Spain, they had been forcibly converted in Portugal and fled across Europe until they found sanctuary in Constantinople. There had been a story told among the grandchildren of how Nonna had been saved from the sea by their grandfather and they were never parted from that day. A tale which had elements of the truth but owed much to daughter-in-law Mirella's fondness for weaving a chivalrous story, for Bethia had met Mainard when he saved her from attack by a group of the men who took St Andrews Castle – and it was Gilbert who rescued her from drowning.

The service that day in Edinburgh was as dour as she remembered and St Giles devoid of colour and ornamentation. The many altars – Bethia was sure there had once been at least thirty – were gone. The rood screen, behind which Mass was once celebrated, ripped down, leaving only a broken rod to indicate where it once was, and the soaring arch of the chancel now had galleries built in, packed with worshippers. And it was loud with chatter – like a synagogue, she had thought wryly. Some people had even brought their dogs, as though they had come to a theatre, not a place of worship.

Bethia became aware that Will was standing arms

folded awaiting a response from her.

'I will take instruction from you,' she said, trying to keep the hint of weariness from her voice.

'And Ephraim will attend too?'

'Of course,' said Bethia.

Will sat down, opened his Bible to begin the lesson, but before he could speak there came a tapping at the door.

'Enter,' said Will wearily.

Nannis's head appeared. 'Oh, Meenister! The lad that pipes the hours around the village …'

'… has been playing the pipes on the Sabbath,' said Will.

Bethia stifled a laugh. Nannis looked so cast down that Will already knew.

'He will do his penance this Sunday,' said Will.

'Aye, aye,' said Nannis gazing curiously at Bethia.

'My sister and I are undertaking a course of study,' said Will.

'I'll away then, mustna interrupt ye.'

The door closed very slowly behind her, as though to catch them in conversation.

Bethia and Will looked at one another and burst out laughing.

Chapter Six

Visitors

Bethia had observed that the only books John seemed interested in reading these days were those which detailed his accounts: buying and selling, profit and loss, notes about the merchants he had done business with, who was to be trusted and who, in future, avoided. So she was touched he was now inquiring of Ephraim what he was reading.

John and she looked to one another awaiting a response, but Ephraim seemed unaware he'd been addressed.

'Ephraim!' said Bethia sharply.

John shook his head at her. 'Leave the laddie be. 'Tis good to see his pleasure in books.'

But Bethia called his name again and eventually Ephraim lifted his head, eyes unfocused. 'Your uncle wants to know about the book which is so absorbing you.'

'*Codice sul volo degli uccelli,*' said Ephraim, and bent his head once more, but before Bethia could remonstrate, he added, ''Tis that Italian fellow inquiring into how birds fly.'

'Leonardo da Vinci or the other one?' said Bethia.

'Aye, da Vinci,' said Ephraim.

John gave a bark of laughter. 'I see your Scots is

coming along. You'll hae it tae add to all the all the other languages, for I take it ye are well versed in Italian?'

Ephraim nodded to his grandmother. 'At one time it was thought I might study in Padua. Nonna sometimes speaks to me in that language of when she lived in Venice, and it's not so difficult when you know Latin.'

John grunted. 'Never found a great use for Latin, but French is spoken everywhere. Would be most inconvenient for business if I didna ken it weel.'

'My brother the pragmatist,' said Bethia fondly.

'French is also useful in Constantinople,' said Ephraim.

'Aye, the language of trade,' said John.

'And diplomacy,' said Bethia.

There was silence in the chamber, apart from the crackle of the fire in the grate, a soft snore from Father and the inevitable noises from outside where the fishwives worked on mending nets and the gulls circled high above calling harshly to one another.

'So what does yer Italian hae to say aboot birds?' said John, scratching his head.

'Well, 'tis not him exactly but someone who claims to have had sight of da Vinci's notes.' He raised his head again. 'Such a great trove of knowledge for whoever has been tasked with preserving them.'

'Who is the copyist?' said Bethia.

Ephraim sifted through the pages. 'There is no name.'

'How can we know it is genuine then?'

'Look at this drawing,' said Ephraim.

Bethia and John rose to peer over his shoulder at the sketch of a winged contrivance which would carry a man.

'Hah!' said John. 'This is not unique. We had ain such in Scotland, an abbot obsessed with flying.'

'An abbot?' said Bethia. 'That seems most unlikely.'

'It was a benefice he was gifted by our king's great grandfather, James IV,' John added for Ephraim's benefit. 'But I dinna believe the abbot was at all holy, for the king

41

employed him as an alchemist, a costly business by all accounts.' He shook his head, a parsimonious man shocked by profligacy. 'By the time furnaces were built and ingredients purchased, yet no transmutation of matter converting base metals into gold ensued, the king was baith oot o' pocket and oot o' humour. As a distraction the abbot claimed he would fly to France, or perhaps it was Turkland.'

'Why is Turkey always brought into play where anything outlandish is to occur?' said Bethia.

'I think it was that fellow Dunbar who introduced the Turks. He wrote a poem about it called the *False Friar of Tongland's failed flight to Turkey*, or some such nonsense.'

'But what of his flight?' said Ephraim.

John got up and went over to the large kist at the side of the chamber. Kneeling on the floor, he rummaged, digging deep until he emerged holding a rather tattered manuscript aloft. 'The poem is in here somewhere,' he said laying it on the board. 'That's it – *Ane Ballat of the Fenyeit Frier, How He Fell in the Myre Fleand to Turkiland.* I wisna far wrong wi' the title.'

'He fell in a midden flying to Turkey?' said Bethia.

'It's as well he did else he'd have been flat as a badger run o'er by a cartwheel when he crashed to the ground. He took to the air from the battlements of Stirling Castle but dropped like a stone, falling in the midden up to his eyes in muck, wi' the king and all the court watching.'

'What did he use for wings?' said Ephraim rising to read over John's shoulder. 'I cannot make out what the poet is saying.'

'I would not rely on the veracity of what you're reading here,' said Bethia. 'It's verse writ to entertain, not inform.'

'Aye, dinna think ye are the Archangel Gabriel. Hens cannot fly so why would wings made oot of hens' feathers take flight? There's a moral somewhere in this sorry tale.'

Ephraim shrugged and went back to his papers while Bethia determined to go out rather than sit watching him reading. She donned her cloak and bonnet and set off, skirts carefully gathered in one hand so they did not catch on the creels and fish boxes lying outside the houses set back from the shore. She stepped over a pile of thick rope and skirted around the drying poles from which nets and clothes hung, nodding to a group of fishwives and their daughters baiting lines. They stopped work to stare and she felt a great weariness. John said the villagers would grow used to her, but when?

The wind blowing off the sea today had a chilliness which belied they were about to move into the month of May and she was glad to reach Will's house.

Will's eldest granddaughter, Edane, opened the door, curtsied and asked after Bethia's health. As she followed Edane into the house, Bethia thought what pretty manners the girl had to match her bonny face.

'You look like your dear grandmother,' Bethia said as she sat down on the proffered chair. 'She had the most remarkable green eyes too.'

'Like a cat,' said Edane, and smiled.

There was a sweetness of nature about the lass, which, in Bethia's experience, had been entirely lacking in her grandmother. A most determined and rather humourless woman entirely focused on her spiritual life and the push for Church reform. Yet Will had loved her with such a fierce intensity he'd never taken another – and there would have been many willing. Not only was he the minister, he was a good-looking man still. Would she remain as steadfastly true to Mainard, if she were ever given another chance at love and companionship? Her mind drifted to Gilbert. He had been a widower for a long time, or so Father had impressed upon her. Was he a man such as Will, who would have no other?

'Where is Ephraim today?' said Edane.

'Preoccupied with how to take to the skies like a bird,'

said Bethia abruptly. She too had observed that Edane liked to linger around the lad and would give no encouragement.

Will came to join them at the long table, saying Cecy should soon return from tending to a sick neighbour.

'Grandpa,' said Edane rising and coming over to lean her cheek against Will's. 'Tomorrow is May Day.'

'Yes,' said Will slowly, although Bethia could see he was trying to contain a smile.

'The girls are all rising at dawn to go to the shore and wash their faces in the morning dew. Mama says 'tis a pagan ritual and not suitable for the granddaughter of the minister to engage in, for we must lead by example.'

Bethia thought she might have been better to stop at *pagan ritual* without raising Will's obligation to his flock, for Will's smile had faded.

Edane straightened up, hands pressed together in supplication. 'But I thought as long as we lassies say a prayer together first it would show true rightness of spirit.'

'I think that might be appropriate,' said Will slowly.

'Oh thank you, my favourite grandpapa,' Edane said, kissing his cheek. 'I will go and tell the girls it has your blessing.'

Bethia could see how startled Will looked, but the lass, clearly as quick of foot as she was of mind, had gone before he could remonstrate.

'Wound around her little finger,' said Bethia, smiling. 'But then she is the sweetest natured lass.'

'Aye, and so like my dear departed wife,' Will said, and she could hear the emotion in his voice. 'And,' he said, straightening his back and speaking with his more usual gruffness, 'I will speak at my Tuesday service about how Christ lived a joyous life and of how these Mayday rituals do not belong to either Catholics or pagans but are a celebration of innocence and virtue, which our Lord would not have objected to.' He leant back in his chair.

'And I will instruct Edane on the prayer she and her friends should say and we will practise it together.'

Privately Bethia thought Will had twisted things a little conveniently to suit his ease, but frankly anything to enliven this dreich faith should be welcomed. She only wished she could join the girls.

When she returned to John's house, she found Ephraim with pen and paper, calculating the dimensions for wings.

'I think it might work with eagle feathers instead of hen feathers,' he said.

She was about to wish him good fortune finding enough of the former in Scotland for his purposes, but held her tongue. It was only an exercise of the mind that he could come to no harm engaging in. And at least he was safely occupied and showing no particular interest in Edane or any other lassie, so far as she could ascertain.

There was a knock on the door and all Bethia's maunderings about Ephraim vanished when Gilbert was ushered in. Bethia felt her spirits lift until she caught sight of a woman aged about five and twenty following behind him.

She rose to make her curtsey as Gilbert bowed.

'This is my daughter Isobel,' he said. 'Although we ay call her Izzy.'

'And which do you prefer,' said Bethia gaily. 'Are you an Izzy or an Isobel?'

'Oh, she is an Izzy,' her father said.

Bethia smiled at the young woman but there was no answering response. Definitely an Isobel, she thought.

Gilbert went to make his obeisance to Father, who told Gilbert how glad he was to see him and he shouldn't be a stranger.

Bethia could feel a trickle of sweat run down the back of her neck and wished Father was not being quite so hearty.

The guests, invited to sit, began a desultory conversation about how fearsome the weather had been.

Isobel sat in silence gazing at the painting which hung behind Father's chair, while the conversation flowed around her. Ephraim, who was holding his own amongst the men, added his piece, telling of how one of the fishermen had got his foot caught in the net and was near drowned when he fell overboard trying to free himself.

'It was painted by an Italian' said Bethia quietly to Isobel. 'Of my mother and myself.'

'I can see that,' said Isobel.

Bethia blinked.

'I have been meaning to come for some time, for we had barely an opportunity to speak on my first visit.' Gilbert said quietly. Bethia saw Isobel stiffen.

'Yes, it is unusual to find this chamber so empty.'

'John has many children.'

'Ten, at the last count.'

'He is a fortunate man.'

'I think he would consider himself so.' Bethia was aware Isobel was listening intently as they spoke.

Ephraim, good lad that he was, asked Isobel how they had travelled to Pittenweem. 'For I understand you live some distance from the village,' he said courteously, 'and should imagine it was not comfortable given how muddy the paths are after all this rain.'

'We came on horseback,' said Isobel. 'I would not subject myself to the cart.'

'Izzy is a fine rider,' said Gilbert. 'And a knowledgeable plantswoman.'

Bethia, understanding that Gilbert was attempting to build some connection between her and Isobel, felt a surge of affection for him.

'We had many beautiful plants growing on the hillsides around Constantinople, and Suleiman himself took a great interest in his gardens,' Bethia said to Isobel, and Ephraim looked grateful to be relieved of any further attempt to engage her in conversation. But the lure was again not taken as Isobel only inclined her head.

Gilbert looked to his daughter, evidently expecting her to speak, but when she did not, he continued, 'You might be interested to see the work we are carrying out to create a garden in the English style.'

Bethia was aware of Father leaning forward in his chair eagerly watching and listening.

'I would like that,' she said softly.

'There is little to see at present,' said Isobel.

Gilbert pressed his palms together. He looked as uncomfortable as Bethia felt.

'Perhaps when the weather has improved. I had forgot how much it rains here,' she said, and then regretted her words as she saw a flicker of disappointment in Gilbert's eye. But, really, what was she to do in the face of Isobel's hostility?

After a moment Gilbert rose to his feet, saying, 'Come, Izzy, we must away.'

Even Izzy looked surprised, if relieved, by the speed with which she was being hastened from the chamber.

Ephraim followed them out, saying he was off to find his cousin Symon.

Bethia was left with only Father gazing at her out of hooded eyes.

'Hah!' he said. 'Ye are going tae have tae dae better than that. Gilbert is nay some laddie to be played.'

'I don't know what you're talking about,' said Bethia, leaving the room in search of Violet and the company of a sensible woman.

But that evening found her penning a note in the quiet of her bedchamber. The light of the setting sun fell on the writing case balanced upon her knee, while through the open window she could see the swallows, released from their long winter slumber, darting and swirling, swooping and diving.

Dear Gilbert,
It was delightful to meet Isobel today. Thank you for

your kind invitation. I would very much like to see the
garden she has created. If it is convenient I will come
next Thursday accompanied by my grandson,
Ephraim, who is eager to make your further
acquaintance.
Your friend
Bethia de Lange

She read the letter over several times, folded it ready to be sealed, unfolded it and read it once more. She did not like the sentence about Ephraim being *eager* to make Gilbert's acquaintance. It inferred a desire for greater intimacy between the families and might be misconstrued. She rewrote the letter leaving out any mention of Ephraim's eagerness or otherwise to accompany her or any suggestion of when, better to let Gilbert propose a date. She sealed the letter and passed it to John's servant, giving him a coin to deliver it with all possible haste and without John's knowledge. Then she chided herself for a fool – there was no reason to keep it secret. She was making a mystery of something that was not at all mysterious.

Gilbert's reply took eight days to come, and Bethia was annoyed with herself for noting that, and for the eagerness with which she looked for it daily. It was brief and abrupt – almost rude.

Dear Bethia
I thank you for your note. Come next Tuesday. There is
someone I would like you to meet.
Your most humble and obedient servant
Gilbert of Logie

She wondered who he wanted her to meet – his other daughter, or perhaps he had a lady love. It was not her affair if he did, and she was by no means certain she would trouble herself to make the journey.

Chapter Seven

Balcarrow

It was Tuesday and the day of the visit to Balcarrow, the home of Gilbert Logie. He had written again, particularly mentioning that his other daughter was also eager to meet the *grand Turkish lady* of whom she had heard so much. Bethia was very tired of this epithet and not at all sure this daughter would view her any more kindly than Isobel had – but she *was* curious to see Gilbert's home.

She arrived in great state, which had not at all been her intention, but when John heard she was going he insisted on accompanying her.

''Tis unsafe times,' he said. 'By all that is being said, we may soon have Spaniards roaming our land.'

'When do we ever have times which are safe? And I doubt very much the Spanish will come here. Their quarrel is with Elizabeth, not us. Ephraim will accompany me, and I know you are busy elsewhere. I did manage to cross Europe without falling into Spanish hands, so a wee trip into the Fifeshire hinterland does not trouble me in the least.'

'But it troubles me,' said John stiffly.

Bethia gazed at him. 'You are made curious I think, wee brother.'

John drummed his fingers on the board while Violet watched the interplay between brother and sister, her forehead wrinkling more at each exchange until it was as rutted as the tracks which led from the village.

After a moment John leant back and grinned at Bethia and the wrinkles on Violet's forehead smoothed out. 'I *am* curious. Balcarrow is said be a bonny estate. I think I shall bring Symon. He'll learn something about managing a place like yon.'

Bethia wondered if John was considering building a tower house. There was already one in the village but that would not matter. Nothing would surprise her about her wee brother. There he was with all the people crammed into the land on the High Street in Edinburgh, the comfortable but overfull house here in Pittenweem, and Father's old house in St Andrews to manage alongside all his other business interests. Surely that was sufficient! And John had spent the previous hour much exercised about Edinburgh merchants buying up all the boats in Pittenweem they could lay their hands upon and how he and Andersoun were like to be the last of the local owners. 'The amount o' customs tax being charged to the East Neuk is monstrous,' he'd groaned. 'We are only a few wee villages and yet we are paying mair than Dundee, a toun of at least seven thousand souls. How can that be fair? The merchants' guild must dae something tae stop a' they outsiders frae stealing our business, not to mention English merchants trying to take over our salt trade in France.'

Bethia, who had perused John's daybooks, investigated the many pieces of paper in the array of pigeonholes in his work room and studied his accounts, could not but help point out how John took advantage of the benefice of other ports and especially in exporting salmon out of Dingwall, Wick and Inverness, which he sold on at a large profit.

John narrowed his eyes. 'And what would you ken aboot it?'

'My dear brother,' she said, 'as you well know, I ran a

profitable business supplying goods to the women of the sultan's harem.' She narrowed her eyes in return. 'And I understand as well as you what is needful for success.'

John sniffed but said no more. Bethia was hopeful he would decide not to accompany her, but John's sulks were of short duration, especially when there was information to garner.

She went to sit with Father before they left. He was cooried up by the fire with a shawl around his shoulders and a further one upon his knees, which Violet was busy tucking in. As soon as Violet left the chamber he tossed the one over his knees on the floor and tried to tug the other from his shoulders.

'She takes very good care of you,' said Bethia as she lifted the shawl from where it was trapped at the back of the chair and folded it.

'Bah!'

'Now, Father, you are fortunate indeed to have such a dutiful good daughter.'

He glared at her from beneath bushy eyebrows, then as suddenly subsided. 'Ah ken I am, but still I'd prefer no tae be treated as though I'm in my dotage.'

She sat down on the other side of the grate and told him they were off to visit Gilbert.

He listened but said nothing, although she could see the way his eyes brightened he approved of the outing.

'Tell John to tak Symon wi' ye,' he called as she was leaving the room. 'It's good for the lad to get an airing and see how a grand estate is run.'

'John is already beforehand – Symon is to accompany us.'

She smiled to herself as she went to fetch an extra shawl – as was the father so was the son.

It would be cold on the cart. It might be summer but there was little sun to show for it, she thought, as she slid on her gloves while Grissel beside her wrapped up warmly too.

51

They wound their way through the Fife countryside, the wind less strong as they moved inland, the pap of Largo Law rising in the distance. They passed several tower houses on the bone-rattling journey and each time Bethia would draw herself up in the hope she was soon to be led into a warm and comfortable chamber where she would make sure to beg a cushion for her relief on the return journey.

'It's further than I understood,' John called.

He sat astride his horse with seeming ease and she could not think what he had to complain of. Symon and Ephraim rode behind the cart blethering away and Bethia caught snatches of their conversation which was all about how man might take flight. Ephraim was still determined on eagle feathers replacing the hen feathers and Symon was equally curious about the choice of wood to build a light enough frame. 'Perhaps it was because he used dense wood that the abbot plummeted to the ground,' he said.

Bethia was pleased the lads had a shared interest to occupy them on the journey and even more pleased that Ephraim and Symon were becoming fast friends. Her grandson never complained but it could not be easy in this strange land, which followed a different faith to that he had been raised amid, and where he must always be on his guard.

The track led them along the side of a burn whose banks regularly overflowed judging by the state of the road, the cart lurching from side to side and the wheels whipping the mud around and splattering it widely. The puddles grew broader and deeper and Bethia wiped the spray from her face.

'We'll be in a fine old state by the time we arrive,' she muttered to Grissel perched next to her.

Grissel remained silent, which was most unlike her. Her face was white under the bonnet-wrapped shawl. She was gripping the blanket tight and mumbling to herself.

'Stop!' Bethia shouted, and the carter leading the horses turned to stare at her.

'Stop at once.'

John, who had moved ahead as the track narrowed, reined in his horse. 'Ye cannie stop there, you'll get stuck in the mud.'

'Well it's either that or have Grissel ill. She's not the best of travellers as I well know.'

She could see John's mouth open to say *then why bring her*, but clearly he thought better of it.

'Move to where the ground is drier and let her doon sae she can walk the rest of the way,' he ordered the carter. 'It canna be much further.'

The cart drew to a halt and John directed his servant to get off his horse and help Grissel. The fellow looked surprised by the instruction to give aid to another servant but obeyed. And, as Grissel recovered, she was clearly regaling him with some tale that he found amusing, for Bethia could hear the bursts of laughter.

The road went between banks of gorse then curved around a hummock. Grissel's colour improved now she was safely walking, and Bethia wanted to get down and walk beside her but John absolutely forbad it.

'Dinna be daft,' he said. 'You'll arrive with yer skirts ankle deep in muck.'

The cart bumped through a particularly deep hole and, just when Bethia felt she could not take one more moment of being jarred and shaken, a tower house of most pleasing proportions rose in the near distance. On the large side, it was of square dimensions topped by a small pitched roof surrounded by a broad parapet. The windows dotting its five stories were glazed and there was a gatehouse attached, which looked to be of recent construction since the stone was fresh and unweathered. The colour of the stone was soothing to the eye: a soft grey with pinkish stones picked out on the sides and corners. A high wall enclosed the house with further walled gardens to one side, above which reached a plethora of trees in blossom. All in all it was most attractive, and Bethia, from feeling decidedly grumpy that she had undertaken this uncomfortable and dirty journey, was enchanted by the prospect.

The cart climbed the steep slope to the gatehouse, which had a coat of arms engraved above it, and there was Gilbert hastening to meet them, a large dog by his side, the willowy figure of Isobel trailing behind and running to catch up a small yapping terrier.

Gilbert stepped forward as the cart drew to a halt. He helped her down, saying quietly, 'Welcome to Balcarrow.'

'I am happy to be here.'

He held her hand a moment longer than necessary then let it gently go and turned to greet John.

Bethia and Isobel curtsied stiffly to one another while the fluffy dog circled them and the deerhound curved itself protectively around Gilbert's legs without actually touching him.

'Come away in,' Gilbert said. He walked ahead with John, who was full of questions about the tower house – how long since it was built, what improvements Gilbert had made, did he get a good yield from the fruit trees and kitchen garden, how much land came with it?

Bethia suspected the questions John most wanted answered were how costly was it to maintain and how much the new gatehouse extension had set Gilbert back, but she hoped he would restrain himself.

She was glad to get in out of the freshening wind and grateful there was a rope at the side of the spiral of stairs with which to haul herself up. She arrived in the solar breathless and sank thankfully down on the chair Isobel directed her to. The small dog settled across Gilbert's feet and the deerhound sat by his side, both watching Bethia. A light repast was served by an elderly retainer, who had no qualms about chiding Gilbert for not eating more – 'Ye'll fade away and the devil'll seize ye,' she said.

John stared and then guffawed. 'I see you have a Grissel to contend with too.'

Gilbert smiled weakly and Bethia hoped he would have a word with the auld woman later. Even Grissel would know better than to speak thus in front of visitors. Grissel had not joined them, of course, but had gone around the back of the house with the other servants when they arrived – which Bethia did not feel was entirely appropriate now. She wished Father had not brought them to a realisation, however indirectly, that Grissel was his child. For now Grissel was neither fish nor fowl – not family but also no longer a servant to them. It was common enough among royalty and nobles to have a wheen of bastards who were, if acknowledged, given houses and pensions and titles. But they were a merchant family, not nobility, where bastards were kept well hidden and often unacknowledged. It was all very awkward, and since it was Father's doing, it should be up to him to resolve what Grissel's position should be. Bethia chewed thoughtfully on the stew of jugged hare and decided it was best if Will approach Father, in his guise as both the elder son and exemplar of the village morals. She would speak to her brother.

Bethia then attempted a few conversational forays with Isobel but received only monosyllabic responses. She gave up and sat in silence while the men blethered, feeling decidedly put out that Gilbert was not engaging more with her. She may as well have let John come alone.

Chapter Eight

A Surprise

Eventually Gilbert turned to Bethia, suggesting they make a tour of the gardens, 'if the wind is not too strong for you.'

She was reminded of the sweetness of nature hidden beneath the gnarled exterior, especially when he insisted his daughter lend Bethia a second shawl to tie over her headdress, in spite of Isobel's obvious reluctance.

The dogs rose ready to follow, but Gilbert, glancing at Bethia, ordered them to stay. The deerhound obeyed his command but the small dog kept coming and was shut in the chamber barking.

Bethia was glad of the extra shawl for otherwise the wind whipping round the corner of the tower house would've sent her carefully arranged hair flying. Once in behind the shelter of the walled gardens though, she was impressed by the care with which they were laid out and tended.

'I am glad you have left a little wilderness here,' she said as they walked beneath fruit trees through the drifts of fallen blossom. 'Rose gardens are all well and good but they have an unnatural stiffness about them.'

'We have a rose garden but there is not much to see as yet since it is so new planted. I was fortunate the fruit trees were already here. But I hope you will come back when everything is better established.'

'I should like that,' she said, and noticed Isobel, who had drawn close, frowning at her words while Ephraim, John and Symon followed behind deep in discussion.

'And where is this surprise you have so vaunted in enticing me to visit,' Bethia said gaily.

'Ah, I think ye'll be both surprised and delighted.'

He guided her past a small but well-stocked herb garden and through the gate in the wall. Down a broad path they went to where several stone-built cottages were huddled together. Drawing closer, Bethia could see a thatcher working on the roof of one and that the stonework looked well maintained – a sign that Gilbert took care of his wider family of servants and tenants.

He knocked on the sturdy wooden door of the nearest cottage and it opened quickly.

'I have brought her to you,' he said to the woman who stood in the doorway looking past him to Bethia. A little old woman, she was, but with bright eyes peering out from a careworn face. Bethia stared at her; there was something familiar but she couldn't grasp it. She was uncomfortably aware everyone, including John hovering in the background, seemed to be awaiting a reaction from her.

'I fear you do not recognise me,' the woman said.

Bethia gasped. 'Elspeth,' she cried. 'Oh, my dearest friend, is it you?'

They fell upon one another, hugging and crying with delight.

'We will leave you to get reacquainted,' said Gilbert, leading the others away. And Bethia was reminded yet again of how thoughtful he was.

She dipped her head as she followed Elspeth through the low doorway. The single-roomed cottage was sparsely furnished yet seemed to have everything anyone would require. There was a fireplace in which a cooking pot hung over well-spread embers, a board on which to prepare food, and a bed recess. Elspeth insisted Bethia sit on the only stool while she sat low to the ground on the pallet which made up her bed, hugging her knees close to her chest like a young girl.

'I have thought of you often,' said Elspeth, 'and wondered how your life turned out married to the Converso.'

Bethia swallowed. 'Mainard died five years ago.'

'Yes, Master Logie told me you were a widow now.' She leant forward. 'He is a good man, you know.'

Bethia shifted, made uncomfortable by the intensity of Elspeth's gaze. 'I am well aware of Gilbert's kind nature. But how did you come to be living here?'

'Master Logie found me. He came searching soon after everything changed and Scotland turned to the new faith.'

'You were in the nunnery then?'

'No, there was no nunnery any more. Those were perilous times and you were fortunate to be far away.'

Elspeth spoke almost accusingly and Bethia thought to tell her of the life she had led fleeing across a Europe where religious allegiances shifted constantly and never knowing how long it would be before they came under scrutiny and would have to flee onwards once more. Of Mainard with a permanently damaged foot after an accusation of proselytising led to his incarceration and torture in Antwerp, and of how they had only reached a place of relative safety once they'd arrived in Constantinople. She studied her friend. Elspeth's skin was as wrinkled as last season's apple, her eyes darted as though constantly on watch, and the way she hugged her knees to her chest – as though to protect herself – spoke of vulnerability. At least Bethia had had Mainard and, on occasion, Will to watch over her. Only when she first arrived in Constantinople had she been without male protection, and then Dona Gracia had stepped into the breach. But Elspeth had no siblings and her parents had sent her to a convent after she'd disgraced the family by running away with the Italian artist who had painted the portrait that hung by Father's chair.

'I assume your parents were unable to assist you – or were they gone?'

'They are long dead. I think my father would've done what he could at the time of the reform of the Kirk, if he'd been alive.' Elspeth winced and straightened up, rubbing her lower back.

'But you will be happy to be reunited with *your* father,' she said almost accusingly.

'Indeed. He has barely let me out of his sight since I reached Pittenweem.'

'Fortune has always favoured you.'

Bethia reached out and tapped Elspeth lightly on the arm. 'We were troublesome lassies at times. Do you remember the day I first met Mainard in St Andrews and you stabbed that fellow who was threatening us. Quick as a snake you struck and laid his arm open from elbow to wrist.'

Elspeth leaned back and let out a peal of laughter, and they were restored to being friends. It had aye been thus, thought Bethia. They knew one another too well and could poke away at the tender spots.

'And how were the thirteen-odd years you spent in the convent?'

'Better than marriage to an old man.'

'You would've been a wealthy widow by now.'

'Like you, you mean?'

The laughter left Bethia as quickly as it had come. 'I wish every day Mainard was with me still.'

'Of course you do. But we are not all so fortunate as to have a union of love.'

'Yes, I was fortunate.' Bethia fell silent. 'But from what you say, you also have had your moments of good fortune. Did Gilbert actually come seeking you?'

Elspeth waggled her head. 'He came to help the nuns,

for we were all without a home when the convent was ransacked and torched.'

'Did he offer them all sanctuary?'

Elspeth shook her head. 'They either returned to their families or he found places for them. It was only me he took in.' Elspeth spoke almost defiantly then her shoulders sagged. 'It was not difficult for those among us who chose to embrace Protestantism,' she said softly.

'And have you?'

Elspeth gazed at her speculatively. 'It is rumoured you are a lingering Catholic yourself.'

Before Bethia could decide how to respond, John stuck his head around the door. 'It is good to see you, Elspeth, but Bethia, we must away if we are to reach home before the gloaming and not have Father fretting.'

Bethia and Elspeth rose.

'Promise you will visit again soon, my friend,' said Elspeth.

'I promise.'

It was a thoughtful Bethia who climbed aboard the cart. 'Did you know Gilbert helped Elspeth escape?' she called to John once they were underway.

He shook his head.

'But you knew she was here?'

'No, why should I? Logie is not someone I come in contact with ower much and I had no reason to come to these parts till today. In any case, I dinna think he would want it widely known he's harbouring a former nun.

'He was always a good man,' said Bethia quietly.

She became aware of Grissel sitting next to her on the cart, arms folded and staring straight ahead.

'Did you enjoy your visit,' Bethia said, made strangely uncomfortable by the unusually silent Grissel.

'No' really.'

'Oh! Did they not treat you well.'

'*They* treated me fine,' she said, not looking at Bethia. 'I would hae liked to see Elspeth. She was ay good to me.'

'Next time,' said Bethia.

They sat in silence. Bethia was left perplexed by how to solve the difficulties of their change of relationship. It might have gone unacknowledged so far but likely Grissel had deduced for herself who her father was. All that had been easy – Bethia swallowed – was now made awkward and uncomfortable, and she wished with all her heart they could go back to how things were before this unwelcome revelation.

Just before they reached Pittenweem, Grissel spoke suddenly, her voice loud in the heavy silence between them.

'I dinna belong in Pittenweem. I want tae go back tae Edinburgh.'

Bethia swallowed. 'Of course, if that is what you prefer.'

'You will let me go?' said Grissel eagerly.

'I do not think it is up to me to order your comings and goings any more,' said Bethia, finding it difficult to get the words out. It was the closest she had come to an open admission that Grissel could no longer be treated as her servant. She did not care to think of how Father would react to the news that Grissel was to leave him. They had only both been permitted out of his sight today since it was Balcarrow they were to visit.

'Aye, weel, I shall be awa …' Grissel frowned, '… as soon as I can sort oot how tae get there.'

'I am sure John will arrange your travel, if you ask him.'

'Aye, I'll dae that,' said Grissel straightening her back.

'And of course you must seek his permission to stay in his house, for I assume that is what you intend?'

Out of the corner of her eye she could see Grissel hunch her shoulders.

Bethia felt herself slump. But it was for the best – even though it didn't feel that way – for Grissel and she had rarely ever been apart.

They arrived home to find an irritable Father. 'Whit took ye sae long?' he shouted as they came through the door. 'It'll be dark soon. Ye should've been back hours ago.'

'Let me at least divest myself of my cloak,' Bethia called in return. She gave Violet, who was carrying one child while another was clinging around her legs, an inquiring look.

'He's been in a richt state since a note came for John.'

'What now?' muttered John, following Bethia into the overly stuffy room where Father sat by a glowing fire. She could feel her chest constricting both at the heat and the expression on Father's face, and a little at the prospect of a life without Grissel by her side.

He flapped the paper at them. 'There's trouble.'

John took the letter. 'This is directed to me,' he said.

'Aye, weel, if you will go gadding aboot all o'er Fife, what can I do but open it.'

'What does it say?' said Bethia, ready to snatch the letter herself if John didn't get on with reading it.

John scanned the lines and looked to Symon. 'There's been another attack.'

Chapter Nine

Pirates

Will edged down the steep close which led to the sea. It was slick with mud after recent heavy rain and he'd no desire to land on his arse again – it was still paining him after his most recent tumble from that wretched horse.

The wynd opened out onto the shore, where John's large stone house was perched on a rocky promontory with an excellent view out into the Forth and dominating the scattering of fishermen's cottages set back from the shoreline.

He found Father looking remarkably content, despite the tumble, John's wife whispered to Will, that he'd taken down the stairs yesterday.

'Ah can hear ye, Violet,' Father shouted. 'I'd niver hae fallen if they bairns o' yours didna leave their ball lying around. Tripped ower it,' he said, glaring at Will as though it was Will's fault. 'Coulda happened to ony one.'

Will could not help but feel some sympathy given his own recent undignified landings.

Violet retreated to the kitchen herding her younger children before her and mumbling to Will that she would leave him to it.

'Ah heard that too,' the auld man bellowed.

'You have the most selective hearing of anyone I know, Father' said Will sitting down on the settle.

'Ah weel, there's nay benefit in being deaf if ye canna pick and choose whit ye hear.'

Will burst out laughing and Father hid a smile that his sally had gone down so well.

'Where is Bethia? I had thought to find her with you?' said Will.

'John has taken her to Balcarrow,' Father said, making no attempt to hide his satisfaction.

'Father ...' said Will slowly.

'I ken, I ken. Just because Logie offered for her once ... but he has hankered after her all these years. I niver met the man, but he would ask if there was any news of *the family in Galata.*'

'Father, do not start planning a wedding. Bethia has her family in Constantinople and, from my observation, likes the freedom that being a widow brings, however much she may have loved her husband.'

'Pah! No woman can manage without a man to oversee her. And Bethia is a perfect example. Look at the way she jaunters aboot like a queen.'

'I rest my case,' said Will, folding his arms and grinning at Father.

Father scowled but said nothing and Will thought the matter finished. He should've known better. As he was about to inquire when Father expected them back, Father spoke again.

'Anywis, wi' the Armada aboot to invade England, nae doot Scotland as weel, she cannie travel. It's nae safe.' He spoke as though there was no further argument to be had. And giving a firm nod of the head, added, 'So she may as weel just git on wi' it and marry Logie.'

'That,' said Will, 'assumes Logie wants a wife and all the upset it will cause in his extremely well-ordered household with his daughter, who I have heard, is determined to remain unmarried.'

But Father was made so downhearted by his words he wished them unsaid.

'I wanted to speak to John … and you … of what action we should take about these pirates.'

Father stared at him from beneath bushy eyebrows, no doubt suspecting it was a distraction. Will was silent for a moment, gathering his thoughts.

'Weel?' said Father impatiently.

'I do not think we can wait for them to catch us unawares again – but then maybe we did enough to scare them and they'll no come back. I worry we have been complacent yet I'm uncertain how to act.'

Father stuck his chin out belligerently. 'They'll be back. Ye hae tae tak the fight to them.'

'That's not so easy.'

'Naething easier. Ye sail doon the coast o' England till ye find them.'

Will burst out laughing. 'Well, when you put it like that, there seems no impediment.'

'Ye need mair help than jist Andersoun and his boats though.'

Will nodded.

'Weel, whit are ye waiting for? Away ye go and speak to yon fellow Melville.'

'I thank you, Father,' he said, rising and briefly resting his hand on Father's shoulder.

'Aye, aye. Get awa wi' ye,' said Father, brusque to mask his pleasure.

Will left and rode his reluctant horse to Anstruther. He was directed to a field which commanded a view of the village scattered directly below. Beyond it was the broad expanse of the Firth of Forth, where the Isle of May sat low and sleek like a lurking sea monster, and, in the far distance, the coast of East Lothian.

He found James Melville standing mid field, the long grass brushing his kneecaps and a thoughtful expression upon his face. So absorbed was he that he didn't hear Will approach and started when he came into view.

'Ah, good day to you, Reverend,' Melville said. 'You

65

find me in a brown study considering the layout of my new manse.'

Will stood next to him and looked around. 'It is a good-sized plot.'

'Aye, I am happy with it. My parishioners have been most generous in the sums raised, and Laird Anstruther has gifted the land.'

Will swallowed, aware it was a most ungodly envy that he was forcing back down his gullet.

'You are fortunate to be so valued,' he paused, 'but it is well deserved for you are a good minister to your flock.' He turned to look at Melville as he spoke and was surprised by how emotional the younger man appeared.

'I thank you. That means a great deal coming from you, who have suffered for your faith.'

'Ach,' said Will, thinking of his time of trial as a galley slave, 'it was a long time ago.'

'There was your part in the siege of Rouen and the aid you offered poor Renée of France in Ferrara.'

'Sad to say that made little difference, and all I can do now is provide succour to those Huguenots who were fortunate enough to escape France. And that gey few, for we have no more than half a dozen families we are supporting in Edinburgh. Anyway, I am happy to see the site has been agreed for your manse, but what I came to speak to you about are these raids come from England. I fear we have been dilatory and should not just wait to see if they will return. We must show our strength else they'll continue to treat us as easy targets. If we do not curb them now then I fear there will be deaths on our hands.'

Melville nodded and the two men turned and walked companionably together down the hill to the ale house in the village. Melville said he liked to show his face there on occasion so his flock knew that he was, if not as all-seeing as God, aware of most of what transpired in his parish.

'Can representations not be made to the queen of

England to deal with the pirates? Our king is her heir after all, and surely she will not tolerate English buccaneers attacking us?' said Melville once they were comfortably seated with a wooden tankard of ale apiece.

'Perhaps. I think she is preoccupied by the threat of the great Armada Spain is building, and in any case, I understand relations are not as cordial since Elizabeth had our queen executed. 'Tis said that King James wrote to her in terms that were verging on scathing saying that her father, Henry VIII, *was not impeded in anything but the beheading of his bedfellow but yet that tragedy was far inferior to this.'*

'Strong words indeed to mention the killing of Elizabeth's mother, especially from a king who hopes to inherit her throne. So what *are* you proposing then?'

'I think our parishes need to work together to mitigate this peril. We should arm one of our drifters at least,' Will said firmly.

Melville hesitated, and Will thought for a moment he was going to refuse to get involved, but, as was often the case, young Melville surprised him.

'We will need a fast-moving vessel to be swift enough to apprehend them. We must get the good burghers of Anstruther and Pittenweem together along with a fighting crew.'

Will clapped him on the shoulder. 'Good man!'

'It never fails to surprise what a minister must take the lead on,' said Melville.

'Aye,' said Will, 'very true.'

But the pirates did not wait for any action the East Neuk villages might take and this time a man died.

Chapter Ten

Andersoun

Will's good son, Andersoun, was fishing off the Norfolk coast when his boat was attacked.

'They came at us frae the landward side so the sun was in our eyes. It was a good haul and we were heid down and busy. We thocht it was just a merchant ship bound for the Low Countries, and afore we knew what they were about, they were upon us. They took the catch and everything else they could lay their hands on. I swear the only reason they didna throw us intae the sea and commandeer our boat was because they were sae few.' Andersoun shook his head. 'We were bested by fewer men than we had.'

'But they would be armed,' said Will.

'Aye, they were, and the cannon pointed at us too.'

'Then we must give thanks to God you escaped with your lives.'

Andersoun shook his head, and Will could see the tears in his eyes.

'You lost a man?'

'Collysoun is dead. I have just come frae telling his wife.'

'The poor woman. I will go to her immediately.'

'She has five bairns,' said Andersoun, and Will could hear the anguish in his voice.

'I know,' said Will, feeling a terrible ache within for these poor fatherless children and the hard lives they would have as a consequence. 'The parish will not see her or her children starve.'

'Collysoun acted maist unwisely. They had taken all and were going tae leave us without a shot fired when ane o' they bastards noticed the amulet Collysoun wore around his neck.' Andersoun breathed out through gritted teeth. 'It wis of no value apart from tae him. His son who drowned had found it on the beach, only a smooth pebble wi' a hole in it through which he had strung a lace. But Collysoun wouldna gie it up, and when the fellow tried to tak it there was a fight.' Andersoun rubbed his forehead so hard that Will feared the skin would break.

'There was nothing you could've done except what would have likely seen you all dead.'

'I ken, I ken. But still I canna help but wonder. At least if we'd had a watch we might hae got away.' He paused. 'They stabbed him and tossed his body overboard. The blood is there on the deck still, I didna have the heart tae wash it off.'

'Go to Cecy and your children, man. They will give you what comfort they can and I will visit Collysoun's wife. When I come back we'll make a plan to put an end to this piracy.'

The folks of Anstruther and Pittenweem were slow to rile, but once their blood was up then it was remarkable how quickly action was finally taken and all the dragging of their heels about what to do was over. Will and James Melville, as their ministers, worked to maintain an ordered calm as far as was possible. The decision taken, a vessel was quickly purchased and equipped, with the assistance of Lord Anstruther, who was made purple with rage when informed of the further depredations by the pirates. None could attack his folk, steal, abuse and kill without retribution. A vessel which was both swift and well equipped was commissioned and the challenge was then to choose the crew, for every honest able-bodied man, and several angry women, from both villages wanted to be among them. But more was to come, for Andersoun had met with a counterpart in St Andrews, and the boat owners there were similarly alarmed by what they learned had taken place. *Your fight is our fight,* was their opinion, *for if they are left to run unchecked, we will be next.*

And so it was not one but two ships which Will watched set sail. Each fast, for they appeared to be racing one another in the rising wind, and soon the white tips of sail vanished behind the Isle of May.

Andersoun was home within three weeks, unharmed (which in both his wife and father-in-law's opinion was the most important thing), and triumphant. Will hurried from church to house as soon as an excited parishioner burst in to let him know all was well, and to hear the tale from the fountainhead.

'We bested them, oh how we bested them,' Andersoun said, while his children listened with shining faces. 'And ye know they English are nay say bad – they gie'd us a helping hand once they realised we weren't the Spanish Armada.'

'How did you come to be in contact with the local people – for I'm assuming that is what they were?' asked Will.

'Weel, it was like this,' said Andersoun, slowly lowering himself into his oak chair, while his family, perched on the settle and stools, leaned forward to listen.

'We werena althegither certain whenever we saw anither ship if it wis oor pirates or no, so each time we rolled the cannon out and demanded they pay homage to King James VI of Scotland.'

The bairns clapped and Will burst out laughing.

'And did they?'

'For the most part they did, although one pompous old arse – Will noted that Cecy was so caught up in the tale she allowed the blasphemy without correction – of an Englishmen refused to give obeisance.'

'What did ye do then, Pa?' said Donald.

'We fired off a shot which took half his mainsail away. Then he roared at us that he was a fine, upstanding merchant who would never again trade with the heathen Scots, so we decided he couldna be a pirate and let him go.'

The lads cheered and clapped one another on the shoulder. 'Then what happened, Pa?' said an eager Donald, once the tumult had died down enough for him to speak.

'We sailed on down the English coast, further than I have ever been – for usually we are wary of drawing too close and stand well out. Past the flat lands of Norfolk we went ...'

Will, watching Andersoun as he dwelt on each detail, saw how much his good son was enjoying recounting his adventure. The laddies shifted restlessly as Andersoun described the landscape, how fertile, well drained or otherwise it looked and then made a diversion into the fishing grounds close to the coast and that perhaps he'd been missing an opportunity by being overly cautious and staying well out. 'Because now we hae friends there, it is not so perilous.'

There was a shout from his frustrated audience. 'Pa, tell us whit happened. How do we have friends in England?'

'How can we hae friends there when they killed our queen?' muttered Nannis, who'd come rushing the moment she heard the news her son had safely returned.

Will could see by the twinkle in his eye that Andersoun was enjoying teasing his audience, but now the smile faded from his face, while Nannis folded her arms tight across her chest as though to contain the fear.

'One day, just when we were thinking we could go nae further and those devils had given us the slip, we caught them. And it was ane o' our own they were attacking.'

'No!' cried Cecy as she leant forward, as absorbed in the story as her children. Syffy came to clamber in her mother's lap and hide her face in Cecy's bosom and Will reached out to stroke his granddaughter's hair.

'It was off the coast of an area they call Suffolk, which is, unsurprisingly, south of Norfolk ...'

'Pa!' the lads shouted, and Nannis shook her head at her son.

Andersoun held up his hand. 'The topography is important, for we had recently sailed past a sizeable place where we saw a large boatbuilding yard swarming wi' busy men.' He looked to Will. 'The English are immersed in preparation for the repulse of the Spanish Armada. We saw signs of it mair than once.'

'Hush,' said Cecy, dipping her head towards Syffy.

'Aye, aye,' said Andersoun, apologetically.

'Pa ...' howled Edane this time, as caught up in the tale as her brothers.

'Before us was a crear from St Monans. I recognised it immediately for Tam has a figurine o' the Virgin attached to the prow still.' He looked apologetically towards Will. 'And the pirates were there, caught in the very act. They didna see us at first, so intent were they on attaching their grappling hooks and climbing on board to plunder what they could. We drew close and suddenly a shout went up. They had seen us. They scrambled back on their boat fast, since they saw we were twa good-size ships and not some wee boat they could easily overpower. They hoisted the sail but there was no place for them tae run, for we had hemmed them in, and they were on the lee side of the boat they'd attacked. The wind was blowing on shore and all the sail did was take them towards the beach, and we fired a broadside to show we meant business.'

'You used the cannon!' said Donald. 'Did it fire well, was it a big explosion?'

Andersoun held up his hand up to stop the clamour as Donald's siblings urged him to haud his stupid wheesht and let Pa speak.

'They were bold, I'll gie them that. They ran their vessel onto the broad flat sand where a river meandered through, which is common in that part of the country. We came after them taking our boat onto the sands too while the St Andrews ship kept watch in the bay. We soon had them caught and bound.'

'Did any of the locals inquire what you were about?'

'Oh aye. We had caused a great uproar, and men came running from the nearby cottages carrying pitchforks when they heard the cannon. Then the lord of the nearby manor came on horseback, galloping alongside half a dozen men waving swords. They thought we were the pirates, which our captors loudly proclaimed to be true, saying they'd been attacked by fierce Spaniards.'

Cecy had her hand over her mouth by now.

'But the lord was naebody's fool, and he kent as soon as he saw the flags we were flying and heard us speak that we were no Armada. They locked the pirates up in the cellars of the big hoose and we were all invited into their great hall and fed, and our skill in capturing the brigands was toasted. Then we bedded down for the night before a warm fire with right full bellies and the next day they escorted the corsairs, whom we had bound together with rope, to our ships and we sailed away bringing the pirate sloop with us – for when I told of the damage they had wrought and the death of poor Collysoun at their hands, not to mention leaving a wife and five bairns unsupported – there was no argument but that it was rightly ours. And so we have made some friends in England and they said we maun aywis put ashore whenever we are at the fishing grounds off their

73

coast and we'll be accorded a richt good welcome.' Andersoun sat back and rested his hands upon his belly, a smile of satisfaction on his face, his cheeks rosy from the press of bodies within the chamber listening to his tale.

'But what of the men you captured? They looked to be a most sorry collection that I saw led off the ship,' said Cecy.

Andersoun sat up. 'Ye need waste no pity on them, my love, for they showed not a mite of compassion for Collysoun.'

Will rose and left the room. All praise to God it had turned out well. But he knew the likely fate of the pirates and it was a just fate. He would go to these men confined in the tolbooth prison in Anstruther and offer them the chance to repent.

They were brought before Lord Anstruther the next day and John was among the burghers tasked with determining their punishment. Although there was little to decide ... *a hanging and quickly, for there is no reason why they should linger – and us having to spend parish funds to keep them fed.* They were hung the following morning from the end of Anstruther Easter's pier before a subdued crowd. Will was thankful the villagers watched quietly. He remembered witnessing a similar hanging on the Thames many years ago during his brief stay in London with good John Knox, and the pleasure the crowd had taken in the spectacle.

But it was over and Anstruther and Pittenweem would be free of piracy ... for a time at least. Will went quietly to his church, where he prayed until he was disturbed by a fussing Nannis, who said that Cecy was worried about him and he must come home for the porridge was burned and the spit-roasted heron would soon follow, since they had delayed their meal in anticipation of his return.

Will stood up and quietly followed her out into the splatter of rain blown in off the Forth by a rising wind.

Chapter Eleven

Anstruther and Izzy

Bethia had hoped once she was in Pittenweem folk would grow used to her, and, at least here, that she could walk the few streets and narrow twisting closes, all of which led to and from the sea, alone without fear of attack. And now these pirates had been caught and punished she again felt safe to do so. But it seemed she was ever an object of curiosity. Men bowed and women dipped a curtsey when she so much as glanced their way. Then a message came from Dreel Castle. Lord James Anstruther was requesting, or was it commanding – for its tone was imposing – that she visit with him.

'You maun go,' said John. 'He is the most important man around these pairts.'

Bethia tilted her head. 'I thought that was you.'

She could see Violet, bent over her sewing, quietly smiling while Father leant forward, hand cupping his ear, saying, 'Whit are ye blethering aboot.'

John ignored him and addressed his reply to Bethia, while two of his children squabbled on the floor by Violet's feet over possession of a dolly which Ephraim had whittled from wood for them. 'Johannes taught me,' he had said in response to Bethia's question about where he had learned such a skill. Her eyes had filled with tears when she thought on the faithful family retainer and his deaf wife Ysabeau, both now dead, although their daughters continued to serve the wider de Lange family in Constantinople.

'Anstruther is a friend to the king and I am naught but a merchant, and must keep him onside. He owns much of the land around here and was appointed searcher to the customs,' said John, his voice reverberating around the room. He clapped his hands on his knees. 'And you can charm him with your stories.'

Violet shook her head at her sewing.

Symon came bounding in and passed Bethia a note. 'Gilbert of Logie's servant brought it,' he said in response to Bethia's inquiring look.

John leaned forward expectantly.

She read the note and refolded it.

'Well?'

'He is coming to Pittenweem.'

'Strange Logie so frequently has business here now when we never saw hide nor hair of him before you came,' said John, winking at Violet.

Bethia left the room to go to her own quiet space.

'You must not tease her so,' she heard Violet mutter to John. 'He is a fine man whom any widow, however rich, would be fortunate to have.'

Bethia was getting wearied by these inferences of Gilbert's intentions – and of her limitless wealth. She could've married again in Constantinople, and very easily if she had converted, but she had not forsaken the Virgin for her beloved Mainard so was most certainly not going to do it for some pale imitation of him. There had been a Frenchman sniffing around, as her son Abram so charmingly described it, but why would she want the added complication of a husband who, although a Catholic, would at some point return to his native country? No, she had not wanted to marry again, for who could ever replace Mainard.

'It is not a replacement, Mama,' her daughter-in-law

had said. 'The Frenchman would be a companion, and a charming one too.'

Bethia had gazed thoughtfully at her good daughter. 'It would be pleasant for you to have sole command of this household.'

Mirella had blinked and the tears came to her eyes. 'I was thinking of you and how lonely you are without Papa.'

She had gone to Mirella then and hugged her. 'I know you were only thinking of my welfare.' Bethia had dropped her arms and taken a step back, smiling at Mirella. 'But I also remember the satisfaction I felt when finally I took charge of the household many years after my marriage. For all I loved my mother-in-law dearly and was sad to lose her, there was also a certain joy in ordering everything as I wished.'

And taking note of this discussion, Bethia withdrew from the running of the house more and more – although it was seen as a sign she was growing old, which she considered most unfair.

She sighed, thinking of her beloved family so far away, and turned her attention to dressing as the grand lady of Pittenweem for her visit to Dreel Castle, tugging out the farthingale from where it had been rolled up in her kist, and tying it on. She missed Grissel, but Edane had come to help. She lowered the fine satin overskirt of richest blue over Bethia's head. A pink silk bodice delicately embroidered with tiny rubies went on next, then the sleeves were slid up and Edane tied them, making the lacing on the tight side, which Grissel would not have done.

Bethia had forsworn ruffs, which she found both constricting to the neck and injurious to the chin, for the stiff pleats rubbed the skin raw. Instead, she donned a collar to edge the low neck of the gown, and which rose high at the back of her head. She tied a girdle of blackwork embroidery, beaded with pearls, around her waist, and was done. John's youngest daughter, who had sat on the floor big-eyed as she watched proceedings, let out a small sigh of pleasure.

Violet came into the room then, arms full of linens whipped dry in the wind, the fresh, briny smell of the sea rising from them. 'Gilbert of Logie is here. He is coming with you to Dreel,' she said as she laid the linens on the bed. She gazed at Bethia. 'Ye look verrie bonny,' she said slowly.

Bethia waited, thinking Violet had more to say, but, when nothing was forthcoming, she turned sideways to edge through the narrow doorway. Descending the stairs, her skirt caught, trapping her till Violet came behind to free it.

John looked dubious when Bethia appeared before him. 'You are dressed too finely,' he said abruptly. 'We have sumptuary laws here which mean that you may only dress so richly if you are a noblewoman.'

'I can always cover myself with black robes as I had to whenever I went out in Constantinople, if that is what you desire,' Bethia said tartly. 'In any case, it was you who told me to wear my finest clothes.'

'I didna realise they were quite sae fine,' John muttered.

Bethia looked to Gilbert.

'We are only going to Anster,' he said softly. 'There should be no issue.' But he did not look comfortable either.

'I will change my raiment,' said Bethia stiffly, but her dignified departure was spoilt when her skirts again trapped her in the doorway.

'No, we must awa. Just dinna wear them again, not without removing some o' they jewels first,' said John.

When they arrived it transpired that James Anstruther had been called away urgently to Stirling.

'The king had need of him, and he asked me to give his apologies,' said Alexander of Anstruther, 'and I will endeavour to fill my brother's place.'

He was a youngish man of medium height, so that he could look Gilbert straight in the eye but must lift his gaze to meet John's. Bethia liked his quiet confidence immediately.

'Sit ye down,' said Anstruther once the obeisances were complete, and all became more comfortable. 'It will be gey strange for ye to be back in Scotland after so many years,' he said to Bethia, and she was touched by his perspicacity.

'It is, but I am happy to be here.'

'How is Izzy?' Anstruther said, looking to Gilbert.

Gilbert shifted in his seat. 'She is well.'

'She is busy about the gardens,' said Bethia filling the awkward pause, and interested that Anstruther had used the diminutive to refer to her. 'Perhaps you have seen the work Gilbert has been undertaking at Balcarrow? There is even to be a knot garden in the style that Elizabeth of England favours. Isobel is taking a keen interest in its creation.'

'Ach, that sounds grand. 'Tis a while since I have visited and I should verra much like to see it,' said Anstruther.

'Then you must come with me when I go next week.' She turned to John, who was staring at her. 'Gilbert has invited me.'

John blinked. 'Father will be pleased,' he said dryly and, Bethia considered, most inappropriately.

'The garden is nothing as yet,' said Gilbert, 'hardly worth looking at. Better to wait till the work has been completed.'

Anstruther gazed down at his hands, shifting in his seat.

'Oh, come with me anyway. John is busy and it will be good to have pleasant company on the ride.'

John coughed and Gilbert stared at her. Surely Gilbert didn't mind. This younger Anstruther seemed like a nice fellow.

There was an awkward silence and then John brought up the topic of conversation on everyone's lips – the rumours that Spain was intent on gathering the largest fleet the world had ever seen to invade England.

'And what of Scotland?' said John. 'Philip of Spain will likely attack us too if he takes England.'

'I understood that an agreement existed between our king and Philip,' said Bethia, and the men, including Gilbert, gazed at her, clearly surprised she should venture an opinion.

'That agreement is to do with trade,' said John gruffly.

'I would have thought our king will certainly support his cousin,' said Gilbert.

'Aye,' said John, 'for if Philip takes Elizabeth's throne then all hope o' James becoming king of England and Wales will vanish.'

Bethia squeezed her hands together tightly. Gilbert reached out and placed his hand over hers while John was distracted, responding to a question from Anstruther. Bethia sat very still. The warmth of his hand on hers was comforting – and strange.

After a moment Gilbert withdrew, saying, 'England has recently demonstrated mastery of navigation and exceptional sailing skills with both Drake's and Raleigh's circumnavigations. I do not think the country will be easily taken.'

Bethia was grateful to receive such reassurance, but John snorted, and she shifted on the settle. John's behaviour was verging on rudeness.

'We must keep you no longer,' she said, standing up suddenly. Thankfully, after a moment, John and Gilbert followed her lead.

Chapter Twelve

The Priest

'I understand you are a woman who can read Latin, and Greek too,' said Alexander of Anstruther as they travelled in his comfortable conveyance together to Balcarrow some days later.

'I never learned Greek, but have always seized any opportunity to peruse whatever books have been available to me. Unfortunately, my eyesight is poor now and it's a struggle unless I am surrounded by candles, and even then the dancing shadows mock my attempts.'

'Do you not have eyeglasses?'

'I did not find them helpful.'

'There is a man in Cupar who makes them. I can give you directions to him. They helped my poor departed mother very much.'

'Thank you, I will try there.'

They sat in silence, until Anstruther said suddenly, 'I understand you have met Izzy?'

'Yes,' said Bethia, and could think of nothing further to say on the subject.

'My wife is dead and our son with her,' Anstruther said slowly.

'In childbirth?'

'Aye.'

Silence again fell between them but it did not feel

awkward. She hoped Isobel would treat him kindly.

'I have known Izzy since we were children.'

Bethia, who had been near falling asleep despite the jolting she was being subjected to, came awake.

'She was ay a thrawn one. Even a thrashing did not stop her if she wanted to do something, and she could climb trees like a laddie – which earned her another skelping when her mother caught her.'

'What was her mother like?'

'Not a happy woman. Logie is a gentle soul behind that scarred face, and she was a harridan, shrieking her displeasure for all to see. And especially at her daughters. The older one, Helen, takes after her, I fear, not helped by choosing to marry a fool of a man.'

'She chose her own husband?'

'Aye. Logie was not keen on the match, but he is weak where his daughters are concerned.'

'I do not think it at all weak to allow a girl a say in who her husband is to be.'

Anstruther raised his eyebrows at her tone, but he was young and would permit an older woman a certain leeway. 'Well, she did not make a wise choice it seems. I have heard she's always at Logie's door seeking funds to keep her home in the comfortable style she desires.'

Bethia could think of no response to this and changed the subject. 'It is curious there has yet been no account released of Sir Walter Raleigh's circumnavigation.'

He looked startled but gave a considered reply. 'Perhaps Elizabeth does not want the Spanish to know where Raleigh's been and for her people to realise how much our understanding of navigation, and colonisation, comes from Catholic Spain. Too much was probably told of Drake's travels, especially since his purpose was piracy as well as discovery.'

Bethia was surprised, and pleased, he should speak so openly. It was wearisome to forever be tiptoeing around. 'Yes, there was talk of Drake's voyages even in faraway Constantinople. I understand the English merchants of *The Spanish Company* were not much pleased, saying he caused great damage to trade and a constant danger that English-owned goods and property in Spain would be seized as a consequence of the raids he made and the silver bullion he seized.'

'You think like a man,' said Anstruther, and Bethia laughed.

'I was my father's helpmeet and he taught me well.'

'I hear you also ran a profitable business among the sultan's many women.'

'I did indeed, for many years, and my daughter-in-law, and her daughters in turn, have now taken on the mantle.'

Gilbert, as ever, was a welcoming and attentive host, although she saw him look briefly askance that Anstruther had indeed come. He quickly recovered, making his obeisance and ushering them into the house. The small dog stayed close to his heels but the deerhound came to Bethia and thrust its wet nose against her hand. Unused to dogs, Bethia stiffened.

Holdfast wants you to stroke him,' said Gilbert.

'I am honoured,' said Bethia, and Gilbert gave an awkward smile,

'No, I mean it,' she said, smoothing her hand across the rough hair of Holdfast's back. 'He seems an animal that is selective about who he befriends.'

'That is an astute observation,' said Gilbert, and this time his smile was genuine.

'My daughter Helen sends her apologies. She hoped to join us, however is indisposed.'

Bethia dipped her head. 'Please give her my compliments and I wish she may feel better soon,' she said, although she was relieved not to come under Helen's scrutiny. Isobel was difficult enough.

Isobel flushed when they entered the chamber where refreshments were already set out upon the board. She rose and curtsied but would not meet Anstruther's eyes. Anstruther in turn became overly hearty, rubbing his hands together, saying what a fine day it was and expressing a hope that Izzy would show him the new garden which he had heard she was much occupied by.

Izzy did not respond.

Anstruther awaited a reply, but Isobel – behaving as though she hadn't heard – removed herself to the other side of the table.

'Perhaps we will have some refreshments first and then Izzy will show you the plans for the knot garden, which are most beautifully drawn.' Gilbert looked pointedly at Isobel while he spoke.

'This looks to be a cunning and a clever design,' said Anstruther when they were eventually unrolled before him. 'What plant are you using to create it, Izzy?'

'Izzy!' said Gilbert.

She rose slowly and, beckoning Anstruther to follow her, left the room.

Bethia had found Isobel to be not the most approachable of women but never before so ill-mannered.

'Tell me more about the ideas for the garden,' she said to Gilbert.

Gilbert smiled. 'You are ever the emollient to troubles.'

She wondered what he meant but chose not to ask. Glancing out the open window she was surprised to see Isobel and Anstruther arm in arm, strolling in the garden.

'They bicker and then they make up,' said Gilbert coming to stand by her side. Bethia thought that Isobel was frankly rude, not childish, but she held her peace and simply nodded her understanding.

'He wants to marry,' he said quietly. 'But Izzy, I think, is reluctant to leave me alone here.'

'I am going to Elspeth now,' said Bethia turning away before he could say anything further.

Today Elspeth fluttered around the small cottage like a trapped moth. At first Bethia thought it was because Elspeth was excited to see her, but she seemed distracted. Eventually she sat down and stirred the pot while Bethia spoke of how Alexander of Anstruther was out walking in the gardens with Isobel this very moment.

'He has been patient,' Elspeth said. 'He wanted her before he married the first wife but Izzy kept him dangling and eventually he looked elsewhere.'

'Gilbert says Isobel will not leave him alone in that house – although he would hardly be alone with such devoted servants.'

'It's not the same,' said Elspeth.

Bethia, thinking of Grissel and their long companionship, was about to disagree and then thought better of it. In any case, Grissel, as far as Bethia was aware, was happy in Edinburgh and without a care for what Bethia might be feeling. She became aware that Elspeth was up and flitting restlessly around once more.

'What *is* the matter with you today? You're as fidgety as though you'd sat on an ant's nest.'

Elspeth looked at Bethia, her eyes narrowing. Then sat down again at the other side of the fire.

'You have another stool now!'

'Master Logie had it brought to me.' Elspeth straightened up and stared almost defiantly at Bethia. 'He said I must have a second one since I now have a regular visitor.'

Bethia swallowed. 'Did you not have visitors before?'

Elspeth shook her head. 'Folk are nervous to be around someone who was once a nun.'

'But it's nigh on thirty years since Scotland turned!' Bethia put her hand to her heart, thinking what it must have been like for Elspeth to be alone and mostly shunned for all that time.

'People have long memories,' said Elspeth, sticking her chin out.

'Do you still paint?'

'Aye, I do. Master Logie's wife had me paint their ceilings.'

'Oh my good Elspeth! You became a painter of ceilings after all!'

Elspeth smiled, a smile of such sweet joy that Bethia felt a lump in her throat.

'In my end is my beginning,' she said.

They stared at one another then both burst out laughing.

'Unfortunately, Master Logie does not seem to care for painted ceilings overmuch, and I've not been asked to do more since his wife died. But I did have commissions elsewhere, for it has become quite the thing to build a tower house and have them so decorated.'

'And now?'

'And now I am old – as are we all.'

They sat in silence gazing into the fire until the pot began to sizzle and Elspeth leapt up to deal with it. Watching her quick movements, Bethia reflected that Elspeth could probably still climb a scaffold with ease.

'You will eat with me?' said Elspeth, doubtfully.

Bethia, realising that Elspeth expected rejection, accepted as graciously as though the invitation had come from a queen. She would arrange to send Elspeth a basket of provisions when she reached home. She shifted on her low stool, trying not to spill any of the soup onto her spreading skirts and uncomfortably aware that *sending Elspeth a basket of provisions* would formerly have involved her in no more effort than directing Grissel to do so.

'There has been an unfortunate case among one of the men who work the land here,' said Elspeth. 'He has leprosy and must leave. But Master Gilbert has said the leper must first be allowed to harvest his crops so his family will not starve.'

'Where will he go?' said Bethia.

Elspeth sighed. 'It is not so easy now there are no monastic orders, for it was ay they who took care of the sick, but I know the master will see him right.'

They finished the soup which Bethia pronounced to be delicious, inquiring as to what herbs Elspeth had used to flavour it, which Elspeth responded to in a distracted fashion. She stood up, and taking the empty bowl from Bethia's hand went to place it on the board beneath the window, bending to peer out as she did.

'Are you expecting someone?'

Elspeth swung around so fast Bethia was fearful she might overturn. She slid her hand into her pocket and then extended her arm, fingers curled around something gripped tightly in her palm. Slowly, she uncurled her fingers until Bethia could see a silver crucifix.

Bethia sat very still for a moment then reached deep into her own inner pocket and brought out her gold crucifix inlaid with tiny rubies and emeralds.

'There is a priest coming,' said Elspeth.

'Gilbert is a Catholic still?' Bethia said slowly.

Elspeth nodded.

Bethia felt her throat constrict. She had not realised until this moment how terrible it had been to be alone with her faith. She leant forward and hugged Elspeth and Elspeth hugged her tightly in return.

Arx Epifcopi.

Part Two

St Andrews

July to September 1587

Chapter Thirteen

A Summons

Will was packing his saddlebag ready for a fast ride to St Andrews. Andrew Melville, Principal of St Mary's College and uncle to the minister of the neighbouring parish, James Melville, had requested his attendance. Will had great respect for this man who was younger than him by fifteen years, considering him clever, erudite and clear thinking. Andrew Melville, like Will himself, had spent time in both Geneva and France, before returning to Scotland two years after Knox's death.

It was hard to believe John Knox had been dead for near on fifteen years. There were things Knox had advocated that Will had never agreed with – he still considered kneeling to pray, which Knox declared an anathema, made for a humble and better connection with God. But there was no doubt Knox was a great man who led the way in peacefully turning Scotland from a Catholic nation into a Protestant one.

Yet there were many who were determined to follow England's lead in holding tightly to some aspects of the Catholic Church. The current Archbishop of St Andrews, one Patrick Adamson, a perfect such example. Recently he had given the vicarage at Flisk to a child of eleven years old who was the bastard son of a priest – which was exactly the kind of action the corrupt Catholic Church had once taken. In turn, Adamson faced a charge of heresy for trying to overturn the presbyteries. Will ground his teeth just thinking about it.

Bishops were about land, money and power, not about service to God, and yet the king, and many of his papist-leaning nobles, were determined to retain them. Will, Andrew Melville and many among their fellow preachers were equally determined they would not have this quasi Church which England had adopted. England had bishops and archbishops, they had saints, they had their churches over-adorned with nearly all the accoutrements the papists had – the only thing they did not have was a Pope. Henry VIII had seized the position as head of the Church at the same time he took possession of the wealth of the monasteries. And, of course, Scotland's king wanted to be head of the Church too and have the power which came with it.

Administration at a local level by presbyteries was the foundation upon which the new Kirk was built. Whatever the risk – and it was perilous to oppose any king as Will well knew having had to flee with Melville and others into exile in Berwick a few years ago – the synod must resist any return to the abuse of position which had previously existed. Archbishop Adamson seemed equally determined to cling onto the power that bishops once wielded. He was now hiding out in St Andrews Castle, with rumours rife that the healing woman he had called to cure his belly thraw was naught but a witch.

Will fastened his satchel containing the few items he would need and slung it over his shoulder, conscious that the strap was so worn it was close to breaking. He ran down the stairs to the kitchens to say a farewell to Cecy and was disconcerted to find Bethia there.

'I have made you a package of bread, cheese and the last of the apples. They are wrinkled and a little soft, but still surprisingly sweet,' said Cecy, handing him the cloth-wrapped bundle.

'Where are you off to?' said Bethia.

'To meet with Andrew Melville in St Andrews. I may be away for up to a week,' he said, bending to kiss his daughter's cheek.

Bethia, arms folded, surveyed him through narrowed eyes. 'William Seton, I have been wanting to visit St Andrews since I returned to Scotland.'

Cecy too gazed on him with disappointed eyes. 'Yes, you have,' she agreed.

Which is why he found himself leaving several hours later than planned and, instead of having only one stout companion to provided him with protection, with a considerably expanded group. And somehow Cecy, as well as Bethia, was of the party when she mentioned to Bethia that she had never in all the years she had lived in Scotland – and she had come here so young she remembered nothing of her place of birth in Geneva – visited this once holiest of Scottish cities.

Will wondered at his own weakness. Bethia he might have resisted, but never Cecy. And what was Andersoun going to say when he arrived home from the fishing to find his wife gone and Nannis in charge of the household?

Even the suggestion that Bethia might await Ephraim had not held sway. 'Surely,' he had said hopefully, 'you will want to wait till Ephraim has returned from wherever he and Symon have gone so he can come with you.' But no, as long as Ephraim had Symon's company it transpired the lad would be happy. In desperation, Will suggested that an inquiry into the doings of that pair was needful but was swiftly rebuffed by the assurance that Violet, ever watchful over her own son, would likewise keep a vigilant eye upon Bethia's grandson.

And now here was Will on the way to St Andrews but starting so late they would have to stop in Kingsbarns and beg a bed for the night from Robert Archibald, local landowner and staunch man of the Kirk.

Will had been by no means certain about turning up at Archibald's door. Of course, hospitality to travellers would always be given, but it was one thing to arrive as a solitary traveller, with only a stout fellow to guard him, and two horses. It was quite another to appear at man's doorstep late in the day with two gentlewomen, all the baggage that entailed, servants, and several horses. But if he was surprised, Archibald hid it well.

'Come awa in,' he said, flinging the door wide and shouting over his shoulder for his servants to bring basins and linens so they might refresh themselves, demanding of his cook that she lay food on the board with all possible haste and requiring a chamber to be prepared for the women – 'For I am assuming you will have no objection to bedding doon in the hall wi' the men,' he said to Will, and all was hustle and bustle from the moment of their arrival.

His five sons, who each appeared to be a replica of the other, were called to join the company in breaking fast.

'My lads,' Archibald said proudly when they stood in a line to make their obeisance. 'I'll no tell ye their names for ye'll niver remember which is which.' He laughed loudly and his sons with him. He led Bethia to the board, sat down next to her and proceeded to question her about the wonders of the Orient while his sons leaned in to listen. Will was growing accustomed to the fascination with which every word that dropped from his sister's lips was greeted, as though she was the most exotic creature anyone had ever seen and not just a lass from Scotland who'd gone a-wandering.

They set off early the next day and were in St Andrews by the time the noon bells were ringing. Bethia, who'd been blethering merrily away to Cecy, grew silent as they reached the crest of the hill which looked down on the town. It was a bonny sight, Will had to admit … from a distance. The curve of the bay with the glistening sea and serene sky a rare deep blue today, the long pier stretching out into the sea – the wood so rotten you took your life in your hands walking upon it – the square of St Rules Tower and the sharp spires of the cathedral, the castle's solid grip on the top of the cliff, the yellow-brown hue of the sandstone of the city walls, and the green fields surrounding it where slowly ripening wheat, barley, beans and oats rustled in the breeze.

He heard Bethia's intake of breath even from the back of his horse.

'It looks … different,' she said.

'Aye, well, 'tis forty years since you were last here.'

'There are still ships. I thought John said trade had fallen away?'

Will narrowed his eyes against the light and gazed at the half dozen ships rocking at anchor and another one sailing around the point in the freshening breeze.

'There are no more pilgrims, and they brought money in return for food and services,' he said. 'There are no monks and the current archbishop does not live in the lavish fashion of his predecessors. And yes, the folk o' the toun still need goods but there is not the same wealth with which to purchase them.'

They followed the path which descended the brae, past a pair of oxen plodding steadily, heads sunk with the effort of pulling the plough through compacted soil. Over the hump of the bridge that crossed the burn they went, skirting the mill. The wheel wasn't turning; there was little to grind until the crops ripened. Then they were through the unmanned port and into the streets of the town.

Will, leading on horseback, turned to glance back at his sister. Bethia was leaning forward in her seat on the cart, mouth agape. He turned back to gaze at the street with fresh eyes. It was dirty, the middens piled high outside the houses as though no one cared how the entry to the town appeared, but then visitors were few now.

The numbers of students had fallen too since Will attended university here, although Andrew Melville's appointment as principal of St Mary's had begun to reverse that decline.

Will dismounted and helped Bethia and Cecy down. There was stabling for the horses and a place to store the cart in the farm steadings which butted up against the town wall, and he left his servant to deal with it and paying off their guards. He proffered his arms and Bethia took one and Cecy the other. The servant would follow behind with the baggage.

Cecy squeezed his arm, and he smiled down at this beautiful daughter he so rarely got to spend time with alone.

'You are not responsible,' she whispered.

Gazing upon the filth, the badly maintained buildings and some of the townsfolk they passed, the poverty evident in ripped clothing and thin faces, Will felt himself shrink inside. John had said on more than one occasion that *the good burghers of the toun needed to get their fingers oot o' their arses and do something about the state o' it*. And Will could not but agree. It hurt him to see, through Bethia's eyes, what the town of his birth and once Scotland's centre of faith had descended to now it had lost purpose.

They turned right along the broad way to their old home. This end of Southgait, close by the cathedral, was where the wealthy merchants of St Andrews were domiciled, some of whom had shops jutting out from the front of their homes. Here the houses did look more prosperous. All was not lost – there was still money being made from trade and the fishing.

Will was relieved to find the message he had sent ahead yesterday, once he realised there was no escape from bringing a party, had been received. The chamber was clean, windows wiped, floor washed and fresh bedding laid out. Cecy and Bethia would share, while he slept on a truckle bed on the floor.

'The auld bugger willna let me sell the hoose,' John had frequently complained. 'It's an inconvenience to hae to gang a' the way tae St Andrews tae mak certain the tenants are no abusing the place.'

'Does the factor not do that?' Will had said.

John had sniffed. 'Aye, and I need to keep a watch on what he's aboot else he'll fleece me.'

The house looked like the rest of the town, worn and neglected … he needed to halt this train of thinking. He would settle his sister and try to have some private words with Cecy on keeping Bethia occupied while he went about the true purpose of his visit – which was not to be a guide to his sister and daughter – but to meet with Andrew Melville. He opened the shutters to gaze out the window and Bethia came to stand by his side.

'Queen Mary's house looks to still be in good order,' she said.

He peered through the smoke drifting from nearby chimneys, and choked, coughing till both Bethia and Cecy were thumping his back.

Bethia closed the shutters and fastened them. 'God's blood,' she said. 'It stinks. But it is still the best laid out town I have ever been in.'

Will stared at her and then he was laughing in between coughs, and Cecy too. He realised he should have known that his sister, a woman who had demonstrated over and over that she could adapt to whatever occurred in her life, would find something to celebrate in their decrepit town.

'Off you go,' she said when Will could breathe again without coughing. 'Cecy and I will be fine.' She smiled at her niece. 'It is our opportunity to spend time together without children, fathers, husbands or brothers interrupting.'

He went out with a light heart, crossed the street and passed through the archway into the courtyard of St

Mary's College where Andrew Melville, as principal, had his chambers. The hawthorn tree said to have been planted by their poor beheaded queen was thick with leaves – at least something was thriving in the town. Mary had loved St Andrews and visited often. It was a relief to think that sad queen had had some happy times, but then it was her own choices which made for her end. If only she had joined the true religion instead of determinedly cleaving to the Pope of Rome. Will quailed, thinking of Bethia, who he suspected was following a similar path, however devout she might appear in the kirk.

Chapter Fourteen

The Cathedral

Bethia awoke to the crack of wood on wood. Thud, thud, thud.

'Git oot o' it, ye wicked brats, and on a Sunday too. I ken who ye are and I'll be telling the meenister,' came the cry from an outraged householder.

At least one thing had not changed in St Andrews – laddies playing golf in the street and making use of front doors to whack their small wooden balls off, which had been forbidden even in her day, Sunday or no.

Will had said more than once than anyone caught engaging in any Sunday activity, other than reading their Bible, was to be brought before the presbytery, and Bethia had wondered how Scotland's people, large numbers of whom like Grissel could still not read, would manage.

'We are teaching them as fast as we can. Schools are being set up in every parish and the supply of Bibles in our language is increasing daily. And those who cannot read must memorise. It is remarkable how much a willing child, or adult, can remember and repeat back with great accuracy,' said Will abruptly.

'And what of the teaching of writing?' asked Bethia.

Will had shaken his head. 'Writing is a different matter althegether. We don't need most folk to be able to do more than sign their name, and that rarely. But most important of all is to have sufficient students at the university studying divinity so we have a well-educated ministry of sound doctrine.'

Bethia, curled up in bed, was aware of movement beyond the curtains but reluctant to leave her cosy nest. She wondered what the punishment was for playing golf on a Sunday. No doubt to be placed on the repentance stool and shamed before the whole congregation. They must need a wheen of repentance stools in the kirk in St Andrews, all laid out in rows. She giggled to herself imaging a Sunday where more of the congregation were sat in their shirts and shifts on the stools than were in the pews.

'Surely it is better to own your sin to the priest and do your penance before God than have your neighbours inform on you?' she had said to Will.

But Will inevitably did not agree. 'John Knox called Catholics apostates and traitors,' he had responded.

And then she had been furious. 'How could I be an apostate?' she had shouted, nay screamed at him. 'Even when my beloved husband begged me to join him and become a Jew I have never faltered.'

He blinked at her vehemence but responded calmly enough 'You are being dishonest before God and Christ in sitting in a Protestant church.'

'I am not,' she had said. 'There is much in Protestantism to commend it and I am faithful to God, Jesus Christ and the blessed Virgin.'

'Worshipping Mary is naught but idolatry,' Will had muttered, but he did not pursue it further.

The bed curtains were tugged apart and Cecy stuck her head in. 'Papa has gone to St Mary's College and says he will meet us in church. Shall we go out and have a walk around the town beforehand?'

Bethia bestirred herself as eager, if not more so, than Cecy to revisit her childhood. Cecy helped her dress. Then Bethia dipped wet linen dipped in rock alum and wiped her teeth while Cecy brushed out Bethia's hair, doing her best to style it.

'I have not Grissel's skills,' Cecy said, but Bethia did not want to speak of Grissel. John told of how she was busy and happy in Edinburgh. Bethia had asked no more. She and Grissel had been mistress and servant for the past forty years and it hurt that Grissel could so easily abandon her.

Once in the street she linked her arm in Cecy's, turning away from where the cathedral towered. She was not ready to see the destruction wrought there, and instead led Cecy down Baxter's Close. There was not the usual heat blasting out from the ovens, but then it was Sunday and no bread would be baked on the Sabbath. They turned into Mercatgait and lifted their skirts. The street was dirty from the detritus of the market and, at the far side, dark from the pools of dried blood where the beasts were slaughtered. The market was deserted apart from a few dogs scavenging and a beggar asleep against a wall, his leather badge prominently displayed on his chest to show he was both deserving of charity and licensed for it within the burgh of St Andrews. Cecy dipped into her pocket and laid a coin upon his lap. He didn't open his eyes but his hand curled around it.

Crossing the street, they made their way down the lane to Northgait. Fishertoun was opposite, leading to the castle, but Bethia turned left down the broad street, which like Southgait was made wide for the many religious processions and mystery plays which had once marked the Catholic calendar year but were now forbidden. Would Jesus Christ truly have objected to some joy, amid the seriousness of life – after all he was the light of the world?

Then they were before St Salvator's and Bethia gasped. This was the church of the university, and she had expected it would, as such, have been protected from the ravages wrought elsewhere on ecclesiastical buildings when the Reformation swept through Scotland. But the niches where the statutes of the saints had sat along its frontage were empty. The evidence that they had been toppled and smashed still there scattered on the ground even twenty-seven years later. Worse was the beautiful coloured glass in its tall windows all gone, apart from some jagged pieces visible along the sills. Just as with St Giles in Edinburgh, the windows were patched with leather hides and torn oiled paper sheets. It would be dark inside and only on the sunniest of days would light penetrate the gloom. The beautiful old church looked neglected, almost derelict. She tilted her head back, gazing up at the square tower which rose high above it and remembered standing with Gilbert watching as its wooden pinnacle was torn down by the French soldiers so they could drag cannon up to the top and bombard the castle. It was this which had broken the long siege and precipitated her departure for Antwerp, with Mainard. She sighed. It was all so long ago.

The church bells began to ring, startling Bethia.

'We should go,' said Cecy as the students emerged from the nearby college and flowed past them into St Salvator's.

She took Bethia's arm. 'Is it so very different from what you remember?'

Bethia nodded. She averted her head, brushing the tears from her eyes. They retraced their steps, arriving at Holy Trinity in time to join the flow of people entering. Bethia looked around, wondering where to sit. She assumed their family pew would likely have been given up and they might have to stand. But no, it seemed they were known and the deacon waved them forward while fellow worshippers stood aside to let them pass. Bethia was aware she was the recipient of curious looks, indeed open stares, but she was used to that. She sat down, leaving a trail of whispers in her wake.

Holy Trinity had always been the church of the

merchants, craftsmen, burghers – the church of the townsfolk – who rarely, if ever, entered the hallowed aisles of the once great cathedral. The minister came in led by the deacon, with Will in his train. They bowed their heads and the service began with a prayer spoken by Will.

Holy Trinity was where John Knox had preached his first sermon, while the castle was under siege. Bethia had sat in this very place with an eight-year-old John asleep by her side and Mother nodding off on her other side while Knox's voice thundered off the roof beams so that God himself could not but listen too. And, according to John, it was at Knox's instigation when he was again preaching in this very church in fifteen hundred and fifty-nine that its beautiful coloured glass windows were destroyed.

But worse was the destruction of the magnificent decoration within. She pressed her hand to her heart and wondered why it was engendering a physical pain. She had seen how St Giles in Edinburgh was stripped bare, yet here it hurt. This was the church she had come to for Mass, confession and spiritual comfort, where once as many as thirty priests had ministered to the townsfolk. Cold, bleak and echoing it was now. Where was the beautiful altar piece wherein the Archangel Gabriel rose above a crowd of supplicants spreading his wings protectively? Where were the panels which had once hung from the walls: the Holy Trinity with God on his throne cradling Christ Jesus after the crucifixion and the dove of the Holy Spirit flying above; King James IV and his queen kneeling at prayer and overseen by a cluster of angels; the Virgin gazing upon the infant Christ held tenderly in her lap; and Saint Andrew, a halo of gold around his head, seated on a throne with the good book slipping off his knee; the altar piece of haloed Saint Peter holding a huge key and Saint Andrew with the diagonal cross he had requested, for he did not consider himself worthy to be crucified on the same shaped cross as Christ?

They stood to sing psalm six …

O Lord, rebuke me not in thine anger,
Neither chasten me in thy hot displeasure.
Have mercy upon me, O Lord
For I am weak

These had been beautiful works of art. She wondered if some were to be found still, hidden away in the homes of the good burghers of St Andrews. All the statutes too, of Jesus, the Virgin and the saints, brought from Flanders at great expense, were gone. She remembered Father grumbling when he'd been required to dip into his pocket to help fund them.

The psalm ended and she sat down. There were only two people on the repentance stools today, a man and a woman, and not so young either. Most probably adultery, although she would learn soon enough, for their offence and penance would be proclaimed to all within the kirk. They were positioned in an empty space between the altar and the body of the kirk, and she realised this was where the rood screen once stood. It had been a richly carved piece of finest oak veneer, with painted panels inset along the base.

There was nothing to look at now in this church of bare walls, apart from the pair on the stools and the minister, of course. But then that was the purpose no doubt – all thoughts should be of God. Yet surely it was easier to see the magnificence of the Lord surrounded by evidence of it rather than amid this bleak sternness?

'Should you not be at home with your Bible?' said Bethia when Will indicated his intention of joining Cecy and her as they recommenced their walk around the town that afternoon.

'The healthy exercise of body and mind is another form of godliness,' he said.

Cecy looked as astonished as Bethia felt.

'Come let us to the castle. I think you will be pleasantly surprised when you see it,' said Will

'Then we shall pass by the cathedral first so we can finish on a more joyful note,' said Cecy.

Bethia noticed Cecy glancing anxiously at her as she spoke and felt a surge of affection towards her gentle niece.

St Andrews Cathedral, the largest church in Scotland, was derelict. They passed through the gate, once controlled by the monks, and stood before the arch which led within. The stonework here was untouched, although the great doors were gone.

Will took Bethia's arm and she was glad of the support. They climbed the broad steps, avoiding the lumps of stones which littered them, and peered inside. Broken glass glinted on the flagstones and the walls were as bare as those of Holy Trinity. Bethia, taking a step into the gloom, could make out that part of the roof had fallen in.

'The central tower collapsed a few years ago bringing down much of the roof with it,' said Will.

There was the flapping of wings, and Bethia tucked her head in as pigeons took flight above them. Gazing up, she could see they were nesting everywhere – a ready source of meat for the local citizens. She took another step forward but Will stopped her.

'It's not safe. Come, we can walk the grounds and see the friary. St Rule's is undamaged too.'

'What's St Rules?' said Cecy.

'The church that was here before they built the cathedral next to it,' said Bethia before Will could answer. 'They always said the cathedral did not have God's favour. An ower grand testament to the pride of the good burghers of the town and not to the Lord. The west front blew down soon after it was built, whereas St Rule's has stood as a beacon to any pilgrim since the eleven hundreds.'

'We do not require a beacon for pilgrims,' said Will stiffly.

'Where did all the monks go?' said Cecy in her measured voice.

Will looked at her strangely and Bethia too thought it a naive question.

'They were expelled,' he said.

'No doubt violently. My friend Elspeth, the one who was a nun,' Bethia said to Cecy, 'told me they were attacked and she was fortunate to escape without a beating or worse.' She paused. 'Gilbert helped her,' she said softly, almost to herself. She stopped with a suddenness that had Will near falling over her. 'What happened to the relics?'

'What are relics?' said Cecy.

'An abomination is what they were, naught but papist idolatry which was destroyed, as was right before God,' said Will, and stalked on.

Bethia sighed. 'Some of the bones of Saint Andrew were held in the cathedral in a most exquisite reliquary. It's why this town is so named and was once a centre of pilgrimage. People came from France, Russia and many other countries to worship before them. But let us say no more of it.'

They followed Will while swallows flitted above and a couple of bairns darted past pursued by a bigger lad.

'Hey,' shouted Will, reaching out a long arm to collar the boy. 'What are you about?'

The lad twisted out of Will's grip and fled in the opposite direction.

They rounded the corner into the cloister where monks once walked in silent contemplation. Bethia had only been inside the cathedral a couple of times as a lass and had never freely wandered its, then, sanctified grounds before. She had not realised how spacious and gracious a place of living it must've been for those in holy orders. There was movement beneath one of the archways and she caught sight of the white of a bare arse where a man was crouching to defecate. A woman and a man slid away from behind another of the pillars.

'I am surprised the toun council are not keeping a better watch on what goes on here,' said Will. 'It looks to be a den of vice where any vagabond may hide out, or worse.'

'I think their attention might be more on controlling the quarrying of the stone,' said Cecy pointing.

Bethia and Will turned to where it was evident stone was being systematically removed, block by block, although there were no men at work today since it was Sunday.

'I do not think this is a safe place to wander,' said Will. 'Let us away.'

'I want to go home,' said Bethia. And realised she did not mean the house in Southgait where she had spent her childhood or even John's house in Pittenweem. She had a sudden terrible longing for her home in Constantinople. She stumbled, and Cecy caught her arm, looking anxiously into her face.

'Are you quite well, Aunt Bethia?'

She regained her balance. 'I am fine, my dear. Only a little tired.' Which was true.

'Then you must rest.'

Reaching their lodgings, Bethia lay down upon the bed and Cecy drew the curtain around it. She could hear the rising and falling of voices on the other side, through her dreams. Then she was back in her home in Galata, and Mainard came to her, hands outstretched, but she shook her head. It was not her time to join him, he must wait a little longer.

The next day she awoke refreshed and ready to complete her tour of St Andrews.

'Papa has gone to see Andrew Melville, for there are rumours the king is coming. He says to await his return,' Cecy told her.

'Nonsense,' said Bethia. 'I will eat a handful of those delicious dried prunes which John imports, I suspect through those English merchants in Spain, drink some watery ale and out we shall go.'

Chapter Fifteen

Andrew Melville

Andrew Melville was ebullient when Will climbed the steep stone steps within St Mary's College to his chambers.

'The king is on his way to St Andrews,' he said. ''Tis an opportunity to again put to him how unnecessary bishops are to a well-run Kirk of presbyteries. He is now the perfect age to ratify the laws of our established religion and purge the land of papists and priests. They must be sent from his kingdom, under pain of death should they return. No exception should be made whether they are of noble birth or not, for they pollute the land with idolatry.'

Will removed his bonnet, wiping the sweat from his brow with the back of his hand, made uncomfortable by Melville's unequivocal position. He could feel the sweat gathering beneath the tight black cap he wore too. Cecy had extracted a promise before he left the house in Southgait that Will would not allow himself to again be placed in a position where he was sent into exile. He had only just got his presbytery running the way he wanted after his last enforced absence and had no desire to be kicking his heels in Berwick once more.

'Let us focus on addressing the issue of bishops,' he said firmly. 'One thing at a time.'

Melville paused in his pacing and gave a slight nod. 'The king is travelling with a Frenchman, Guillaume de Salluste du Bartas.'

'The poet?'

'Aye. 'Tis not often a literary man will cross the Tweed, and James is showing his delight with a deluge of gifts, including a knighthood. This is in part because Bartas is translating the king's poem, *The Lepanto*, into French.' Melville paused and scratched his head. 'Have you read anything Bartas has written?'

Will shook his head.

'Bartas is no a bad poet, no bad at all. He combines the divine with world history. *La Semaine, ou Création du monde* is the title of his first epic and inevitably draws heavily on Genesis. I have it here somewhere. You may borrow it if you wish,' he said, going to the shelves on which were stored many large leather-bound volumes.

Will, who didn't much care for poetry, even that which was biblical in origin, was about to refuse the kind offer when he thought of Bethia and graciously accepted. He took the book with its red leather engraved cover and bowed his thanks. It was only when he went to slide it into his satchel he remembered that Bethia's eyesight was failing and he'd most likely be the one who ended up reading it to her. Too late to refuse now though.

'Why is Bartas in Scotland?'

'Word is that he was sent at the behest of Henry of Navarre to negotiate a marriage between our king and Henry's sister.'

'I thought James was set on the Danish princess.'

'Did you not hear? They could not agree a dowry and Frederick of Denmark wanted Orkney and Shetland restored to him – which will never happen. In the end that daughter was married elsewhere, although there is a younger sister, for which reason I suspect nothing will come o' Bartas's visit. Denmark is the better alliance, and Protestant forby.'

Melville dropped down into his chair and waved a hand inviting Will to sit. 'We are blethering like two auld men …' He paused then grinned, staring straight into Will's eyes, inviting him to laugh at himself.

'Aye, but I am the old man. You have a way to go before you reach my august years.'

'With age comes wisdom …' Melville said.

'… for some,' added Will.

'We have the king in thrall to poetry – and a poet. Although I can see nothing to object to in Bartas's doctrine, yet it is a distraction from the king addressing the more important matter of our Archbishop Adamson, who has again incurred the wrath of the synod. They are demanding he be excommunicated.'

'What has he done now?' said Will.

'Oh, more of the same. Adamson's three years as ambassador to the English court has given him a misplaced confidence in both his influence and his abilities, as you well know. He is still determined bishops and all the power associated with them will endure and that the governing and influence of lower level upwards, which our presbyteries represent, must be o'er turned.'

Will rested his hands upon his belly. 'Adamson does not have the influence to carry this through. He's not a bad man, just wrong thinking.'

'Aye,' said Melville leaning back, hands crossed over his own larger belly. 'I will see what can be done with both the king and Adamson.'

Melville went off to teach his class and Will decided to join the student body and listen. They were sharing a small repast afterwards, intent on a most satisfying discussion of some of the finer points Melville had made, when they heard a commotion below. Before they could rise and find out what was about, the door suddenly opened wide and the king came sauntering in, bursting with youth and energy. Will and Melville leapt to their feet, bowing low. The king waved a hand and took the

111

chair Will had vacated, but was soon on his feet again roving around the chamber. He stopped before Melville's bookshelves and tugged out a volume while Will and Melville watched in silence.

'I have read this *Dialogue between a papist and a Protestant*,' said the king excitedly. I do not know that I agree with all George Gifford has to say, but then he is an Englishman, and, as we well know, they have taken a different perspective on the true religion than we have in Scotland.' The king looked directly at Melville and grinned.

Will smothered a smile. The king was teasing Melville about their different stances on bishops. There was a gentleness about it, like the son to a beloved father. Yet Melville, and Will, had had to flee to Berwick for standing strong, insisting that the Bible and the Protestant cause outweighed any secular and kingly authority. The king had still been in his minority then, and the country ruled by men among whom numbered several unrepentant Catholics.

James leaned forward. 'Have you seen Gifford's new book – *A Discourse of the Subtle Practises of Devils by Witches and Sorcerers*?' he said, and Will could not help but lean away. 'A subject which we in Scotland should attend to, for we have a fearful abundance of witches, conjurors and sorcerers which Satan makes ready use of. I am very glad Gifford wrote this discourse since his sound sense refutes much of what Reginald Scott had to say in his *Discoverie of Witchcraft*. Gifford is a sensible man who recognises the peril we are in, while Scott is a fool who does not take it seriously.'

The king dropped back into the chair and swung his legs over the side.

Will, watching, thought he looked like a spindly colt with those skinny shanks, and yet this attention on enchantment left Will fearful.

The king had left his entourage outside, but a man of

middle years appeared in the doorway, hand resting on hip, taking in the scene.

'This is my good friend and fellow poet Salluste du Bartas,' said the king waving his arm languidly.

Bartas extended a leg and bowed and Will and Melville bowed in return. Will was relieved Bartas had come, hoping it would distract the king from any further discussion of witches and their craft. There had been mutterings about Bethia in Pittenweem recently, which Nannis, inevitably, had apprised him of. He was dealing with it, largely through some thunderous sermons on the wickedness of spreading false allegations about your neighbours.

'I translated some of Bartas's poems from the French,' said the king, and Will sighed in relief.

'I gave my copy to Seton to read, Your Grace,' said Melville.

All eyes were now upon Will and he was glad to be able to report that he planned to read some aloud to his sister this eve, 'for she greatly enjoys poetry too.'

Both king and poet looked gratified.

'Your sister is the lady come from the land o' the Turks,' said the king, narrowing his eyes and staring at Will.

Will swallowed, quite unnerved by how well informed the king was. 'Aye, Your Grace, she is.'

'And she lived there for many years.'

'She did, sire,' said Will slowly. He could feel his heart thumping in his chest, and wondered where this conversation was leading.

'She will know of the Battle of Lepanto.'

Will opened and closed his mouth, and could not think what to say.

James swung his legs off the chair and sat up. 'I have come for a lesson,' he said, looking to Melville. 'And Bartas is eager to hear you speak too.'

Will let out the breath he'd not realised he was

holding. The king's attention was leaping about like a frog on a lily pad.

Bartas inclined his head, saying to Melville, 'I understand, sir, that you are a great orator.'

'You are too late, Your Grace. I have already teached my ordinary this forenoon and am done till tomorrow,' said Melville stoutly to the king.

The king's eyebrows shot up. 'That is of nae matter. I maun hae a lesson, and that within the hour.'

'I am sure we can call the students back. It will be the greatest honour to have you amid them, Your Grace,' said Will firmly.

Melville narrowed his eyes but said nothing. Will wondered at him. Did he want to be sent hunting for Jesuits around Scotland again, a condition the king had required before allowing Melville back into the country after his most recent exile? A pointless and futile exercise it had been too, for no Jesuits had been discovered. 'Likely because there are none,' Melville had said wearily when he was finally permitted to return to his post in St Andrews.

'We will be ready within the hour,' said Will.

Servants and bursar were sent out in a great flurry to gather all the students, regents and any sundry others they could find to come and listen. Will thought how eager Bethia would've been to accept such an invitation but no women were permitted within the university.

'Dinna forget to go to the Bow Butts, for likely there may be some there practising their archery,' said Will.

'Mair likely to find them at the golf,' muttered Melville's stout servant.

'Well go there too,' said Will.

Within the hour the student body was collected in the hall with the king in prominent position amid them. Will took his seat by James, as commanded, and watched Melville swinging his arms as he waited for those congregated to settle.

The young king, who could have merged very nicely with the student body – were it not the richness of his dress and his guards – held up his hand for silence. Melville drew himself up from his habitual hunch and spoke quietly to begin with but soon his voice deepened and grew louder till it filled the hall.

'I am here as the messenger of God far above you, and it is by the authority of His Word herein that I speak to you today.' He banged the Bible, which Will could see by the engraving on its cover was in Hebrew and which Melville considered the truest version. They had not taught Hebrew when Will was a student in St Andrews and Will was happy Ephraim was now helping him to repair that woeful gap in his knowledge.

'The right government is that of Christ, and none must set themselves higher, for it cannot be. There are two kings and two kingdoms in Scotland,' he thundered, his thick black beard waggling as he spoke. Will risked a glance at the king and could see the colour rising up his neck, above the neck ruff. 'As well as King James, there is Christ Jesus, the King of the Church, whose subject *our* king is. Before God, King James the Sixth is not a king nor a lord but a *member* of the Kingdom of God and Christ.'

The king's face was puce by now and Will felt sorry for him.

'The mighty right and governance of Christ takes precedence over all, and no acts of Parliament, which are the work of men, may gainsay that. We will yield to you your place, and give you all due obedience, but again I say, you are not the head of the Church. You cannot give us that eternal life that we seek nor can you deprive us of it.'

There was a rumble of agreement around the hall and the audience leaned forward, listening intently. Will could hear the doors at the back of the hall opening and closing as more people flowed in. Word that the king was here would be spreading fast as the plague around the

115

streets of St Andrews.

The king shifted in his seat and all those seated near him were shifting their eyes from Melville to the king and back, watching for a sign that James was about to halt proceedings. But he'd been brought up by George Buchanan, that sound theologian and strict disciplinarian. It was likely the memory of all those thrashings he'd received which kept their monarch fixed to his seat. At some point Will became aware that Archbishop Adamson had crept out of his bishop's palace and taken a seat at the side of the hall. Adamson half rose to refute a point Melville was making but Melville waved him down, speaking louder and faster. The heat in the hall was stultifying, the smell of bodies ever more pungent. There was a thump from behind as a student fainted, and more clattering as he was half carried out in a clumsy fashion by a couple of his fellows.

Adamson again went to rise and Melville frowned at him. A bishop should outweigh a college principal but Adamson was a weak man already under threat of excommunication by the Presbytery. Will could well remember the visceral sense of fear when he, along with his fellow Castilians, had been excommunicated. He smiled now, wondering that he should ever have been so under the dominion of that scion of Satan, the Pope of Rome. A man's connection with God and Christ was a direct one defined by godly behaviour and right living. No intermediary was needed else they became a crutch … and a path to sin.

Melville was winding up now. He had spoken for an hour and the bell for three hours after noon had rung. It was wise he stop anyway, for the expression on the king's face indicated he would likely not tolerate much more.

Melville bowed to the king and thanked his grace for his attention. James stood up and strode from the hall, his entourage stepping smartly behind. He did not look back to see if Melville was following.

116

Meanwhile, Melville had slipped out a side door as soon as the king turned his back to leave. The crowd dispersed slowly, with much animated discussion.

I doubt King James will again insist Melville hold a lesson, Will thought, as he set off for the house in Southgait.

Chapter Sixteen

The Lepanto

'I Sing a wondrous worke of God,
I sing his mercies great,
I sing his justice heere-withall
Powr'd from his holy seat …'

The king was watching her, and Bethia tried to keep her face impassive as she listened, head tilted to one side, hands hidden in the lap of her voluminous skirts twisting together.

'You read the rest, Bartas,' he said. 'You declaim better than I, and I want to listen again and see where it might be improved.'

'… Which fought was in LEPANTOES gulfe
Betwixt the baptiz'd race,
And circumcised Turband Turkes
Recountering in that place …'

'Why does the king want to see me?' she'd cried to Will when the summons came. 'How does he even know of me? What did you say to him?'

'Me, I said nothing,' Will had responded. 'It is the king's business to know what passes within his dominions.'

'But why would I be worthy of his attention?'

Will huffed. 'You are among the most exotic creatures to reach his shores this year. You can tell him of the land of the Turks and Sultan Murad. And you knew Suleiman …'

'I would hardly say I *knew* him. I was not even supposed to look upon him on the single occasion I was summoned to his presence but must keep my eyes fixed upon my feet.'

'… but most important of all,' Will continued, 'the king believes you will have knowledge of the Battle of Lepanto from a Turkish perspective and, as such, can give sensible comment on his epic poem of that very subject.'

Actually, it was a fine poem which the king was rightly proud of. And she didn't think it was false modesty that had him listening intently to his own words but a desire to improve them.

Strangely, this battle did have a great significance for her family. Jacob, her second son, had fought in it, on the Turkish side of course since their home was Constantinople. He had witnessed the death of his beloved commander Ali Pasha, whose decapitated head had adorned one of the Holy League's victorious ships. Jacob had been restored to them but he was irrevocably changed and soon after converted to Islam. Bethia gripped her hands tight. There were days that she missed her sons so much she was in physical pain. Then she thought of Ephraim and sent up a small prayer to the Virgin that this most beloved of grandsons was in Scotland with her.

'No more shall now these Christians be
With Infidels opprest,
So of my holie hallowed name
The force is great and blest,
Desist o tempter. GABRIEL come

119

O thou ARCHANGEL true,
Whom I have oft in message sent
To Realmes and Townes anew.
Go quicklie hence to Venice Town,
And put into their minds
To take revenge of wrongs the Turks
Have done in sundrie kinds.'

It was odd, Bethia thought, that James should so laud
the triumph of a Catholic force, but then with all this talk
of Spain likely to make a direct attack on England, he was
no doubt mindful of the dangers that would pose for
Scotland. And yet why would he attempt to appease the
Spanish king? James had signed an agreement with
Elizabeth of England, although the terms were said to be
vague. And Elizabeth had still not confirmed that James
would be her successor, even though there was no
impediment now the king's mother, who had been next
in line of succession should Elizabeth have died first, had
been beheaded.

There came eight thousand Spaniards brave,
From hotte and barren SPAINE,
Good ordour kepars, cold in fight,
With proud disdainfull braine

It was curious how positive the light in which
Catholic Spain was portrayed in this poem by a
Protestant monarch. But then Philip of Spain was the
richest king in Europe and should be kept onside. John
had frequently said there were Scottish merchants in
Spain anxious that their king did nothing to upset Philip.

Yet James seemed eager to demonstrate that the battle
was fought with honour – and on both sides. What was
the Latin phrase that described that … *jus ad bellum* …
praise be to God her mind was still able to function. Of
course, it was widely known how well schooled the king

was. It was even claimed the first language he learned to speak was Latin.

But there was no honour in battle. What her son Jacob had described had been brutal and bloody – and all for what? The Christian alliance may have won at Lepanto but it was the Turks who retained the prize of Cyprus. The king was a clever young man but naive in the extreme. *Jus ad bellum* was all well and fine as an idea for how a battle should be fought, and all honour to the king, he was careful to credit the Turks while still declaring them wrong thinking. Yet how could any engagement in battle ever be fair?

'This ended was the Angels song,
And also here I end:'

Bethia had been drooping but now sat upright at the prospect that the end was nigh, but there was more.

'Exhorting all you Christians true
Your courage up to bend,
And since by his defeat ye see,
That God doth love his name
So well, that so he did them aid
That serv'd not right the same.
Then though the AntiChristian sect ...'

She could feel her eyes closing and forced them wide, pinching the soft skin between thumb and forefinger as hard as she could in a body ready to pitch forward into sleep.

There was silence and Bethia realised the poem was finally over. Will filled the gap with hearty congratulations on such a fine and clever work. The king said nothing, but Bethia was aware of him watching her shrewdly.

'You did not like my poem?'

121

Bethia dipped her head. 'It is a great work, my king, and written on an epic scale such as the famous poets of ancient Greece and Rome.'

His face lightened. 'I am glad you think so, for it is what I was attempting.' He leaned back in his chair, legs thrust out. Then suddenly sat up. 'But do you think I captured the spirit of the time? You were among the Turks then, were you not?'

Bethia hesitated, choosing her words carefully. 'I think you wrote a poem that describes *jus in bello* finely.'

James nodded, and Bethia let out the breath she was holding, while Will slipped from the room. He returned quickly with a nod to her.

'I have a gift for Your Grace which I hope you will do me the honour of accepting,' she said.

James rubbed his hands together, eager as any small child.

Bethia had travelled to Scotland with kists full of material. The fabrics of the East were much in demand, she understood from correspondence with John. And Bethia well knew her silks and camlet, velvets and twills after many years as a supplier to the sultan's harem. She had brought not only fabric for clothing but also for furnishings and wall hangings. The bold patterns favoured by the Turks were something she thought it likely would command a high price for their rarity and opulence. Yesterday she had sent an urgent message to Pittenweem for this delivery and John had not let her down. It had not been possible to bring the most exotic fabric of all from Turkey – the cloth made with gold and silver thread – for this was restricted for use by the sultan and his immediate family. Nevertheless, she hoped the king would be well pleased with his gift.

She signalled to Will, who led forward John's servant with a bundle in his arms which he and Will spread before the king.

'What is this?' James said, pointing to the yellow

motif which repeated across the hanging.

Bethia dipped her head. 'A tulip, Your Grace. It is a flower found wild upon the hills around Constantinople in spring. Suleiman the Lawgiver planted them in his gardens, where they grow in abundance.'

The king frowned and Bethia stared at the floor of dark-stained wood, fearful she had committed some solecism in referring to another monarch in his presence.

'Tell me about Suleiman,' he said, leaning forward.

And so she did, even making him smile when she described how that sultan had a place where he could listen in to whatever discussions and meetings his court were having, and then to look thoughtful when she told of how Suleiman also had a secret passageway out of the palace enabling him to go, in disguise, amid his subjects.

Then suddenly he stood up and stretched, saying, 'Enough of this sitting. Bartas, there is some good hunting to be had nearby. Let us away.'

He then strode out of the chamber with his entourage hurrying after him, by which Bethia understood their audience was at an end.

But the king did have something further to communicate to her, for a note arrived that evening, its seal stamped with his insignia. Cecy leant over Bethia's shoulder while she unfolded it and Will drew near.

'Is he making you a gift in return,' said Cecy eagerly.

'I don't think so, else it would have accompanied the letter,' said Bethia smiling.

'Maybe it's a grant of land or a post in his household,' Cecy said.

But Bethia was frowning as she read.

'What is it?' said Will taking a step closer.

Bethia tossed the letter on the board. 'Apparently I am in breach of the Act Against Luxury.'

Chapter Seventeen

Alesoun Pierson

Bethia and Cecy stopped by a pedlar selling ribbons in the busy market. Bethia rubbed the silk between her fingers and the pedlar frowned but did not prevent her from touching. Her hands were clean, she would leave no grease marks and, in any case, the ribbons were of questionable quality and not likely to withstand much wear. She sighed, thinking of the magnificence of the Grand Bazaar in Constantinople – and the letter from the king's secretary instructing her in the minutiae of the Act Against Luxury passed in the year of our Lord fifteen hundred and eighty-one.

Will had been beside himself when he read it. 'I told you, and John told you. We both told you and more than once. Only the wives or daughters of earls, dukes, lords of Parliament, knights or landed gentlemen may wear velvet, a variant of hues, buttons of silver or gold or,' he flicked his hand at Bethia's bodice, 'jewels sewn into their clothing. You are fortunate indeed that the king is granting you some dispensation, but I, as your minister and brother, insist you borrow one of Cecy's gowns while we are in St Andrews.'

And so today Bethia found herself wearing a sombre-hued and rough woollen gown covered by a plain shawl in the Mercatgait examining inferior ribbon.

'Come,' she said, linking arms with Cecy, 'let us to the castle.'

The castle looked very different from the one Bethia remembered. Of course, much of it had had to be rebuilt after the destruction caused by the bombardment which ended the siege. She had expected what was there before would have been restored, but Archbishop Hamilton had changed and extended the frontage so it was unrecognisable. The facade was more ornate than previously, with the Hamilton crest carved in the stone above the arch of the new entrance. Will had told of how the wealthy Archbishop Hamilton had spent lavishly on the repairs, refurbishment and ower grand frontage, but that all this demonstration of wealth and power had come to naught. Hamilton was hanged for his opposition to the core tenets of Church reform and, in particular, for his involvement in the murder of Mary, Queen of Scots' illegitimate brother, who was regent at the time.

'He wanted to take us back to the bad old days,' Will had said, 'and we could not allow it.'

The castle, for all its grand new frontage, looked derelict and unlived in.

'I thought the current archbishop resided here?'

'Aye, I believe so,' said Cecy. 'But Patrick Adamson is an odd creature. Papa says he's sickly and has some wise woman attending him.'

'And clearly the king does not lodge in the castle during his visit. He'll be in the comfortable rooms his mother once used.' Bethia felt sad then, thinking of the young king amid his dead mother's things.

'We should not linger here, Aunt,' said Cecy. 'It does not feel safe.'

Bethia shivered. But before they could move away, the door within the large gates opened and a woman was hustled out, her arms gripped tightly by the guards on either side of her.

Her head hung down and she groaned loudly as she

was dragged past them and other curious onlookers who had drifted over to see what was going on.

'Who is she?' Cecy asked of the fishwife standing near who was holding a bloodied blade in her hand, the small, shiny scales attaching to her capacious sackcloth apron glistening in the light, and her fingers wrapped in stained bandages. It was impossible to do that wretched job without suffering a myriad of tiny cuts to the fingers, as all the fishwives of Pittenweem could testify.

'Yon is Alesoun Pierson. They're ca'ing her a charmer, but I ken she's naething but a witch.' The woman spat as though to ward off evil spirits.

She then turned and stared at Bethia. 'Ye look like ain o' they cunning folk.'

Bethia drew back, stunned by the fishwife's effrontery.

'That is no way tae speak to yer betters,' said Will, appearing suddenly.

The woman slunk away behind her neighbours, who were following the witch as she was dragged to the tolbooth.

'Why would she think I can remove the effects of maleficium?' said Bethia as Will took her arm.

'Because there is a power about you,' said Cecy leaning around Will.

Bethia blinked. She did not speak till they were back in the safety of their chamber.

'What did you mean about power? I am no sorceress or charmer. I cannot counteract the effects of acts of witchcraft.'

'It is difficult to explain but there is a strength within you. Almost as though you could remove the devil from those troubled by him,' said Cecy.

'So you are *not* calling me a witch?'

'Of course not, Aunt Bethia.' Cecy came close and stroked Bethia's arm. 'But I do think you can help people.'

Bethia shook her head. 'I do not see how. And please do not speak of me in such a fashion again. I have enough troubles with what I wear and being the lady from Turkland, without adding to them.'

Cecy paled. 'I am sorry, Aunt. I did not think.'

Will, who had left them at their door to go and seek more information about Alesoun Pierson, returned.

'She has been providing comfort to Adamson, who had the sweating sickness which he could not rid himself of. Yet it is most peculiar that *he* should have sought her assistance, for it was he who first ordered an inquiry into her strange practices four years ago, and especially into her claim that God had permitted the fairy folk to teach her. An accusation of using dark arts was brought and she was likely to be burned for her sins, but the woman exerted a great power over Adamson himself – which to my mind is evidence of her association with the devil. I am less certain of these fairies of which she is said to often speak.'

'She did not look to be a dangerous creature,' said Cecy. 'Aunt Bethia has far more presence than her, as I have just been saying.'

'Please, Cecy, wheesht,' said Bethia.

Cecy put her hand over her mouth and flushed.

Will turned his startled gaze upon Bethia and then became quietly thoughtful.

'How did Alesoun escape death four years ago, and what has she done to draw the force of the law down upon her once more?' said Bethia, as much because she wanted to distract from talk of these mysterious powers she supposedly possessed as to learn the truth of the story of Alesoun Pierson.

'Adamson was sick at the time and she is said to have cured him completely. That is suspicious, you must admit. How would some ignorant woman of Byrehill have the knowledge to do so unless she was aided by fairies or the devil?'

'Mayhap she is simply very skilled with herbs,' said Cecy.

'Perhaps,' said Will, but he didn't look convinced. 'I must go, as Adamson has prepared a feast for the king. 'Tis likely that he will seize the opportunity to give a lesson, and Melville and I needs be there to refute the corruption he'll try and insert into the king's head.'

Will returned some hours later, face flushed and in such a state of excitement Bethia hardly recognised her normally dour brother. 'Melville spoke with great eloquence and courageously showed Adamson's doctrine to be naught but plain papistry. The king in turn gave some injunctions to the university for reverencing and obeying the bishop, but it was clear he was drawn to Melville's knowledge and impassioned speech.' Will gave a turn around the chamber. 'Then the king left to go riding, but Monsieur du Bartas remained and had speech with us.'

Bethia noted that Bartas had been elevated to Monsieur so was not surprised when Will said, 'Bartas has sound judgement. He said that, although Adamson was a learned man, Melville is far above him in spirit and courage.' Will rubbed his hands together, adding, 'I think we are in a fair way to gain the king's support for presbyteries.'

Bethia was happy for her brother, but of greater concern to her was the fate of Alesoun Pierson. 'I will go and see her. Can you get me into the tolbooth?' she said to Will, after he'd finished his tale.

He shook his head. 'That would be most unwise. You might even be accused of conspiring with her.'

Bethia swallowed.

'There is nothing we can do to help her,' said Will quietly. 'In her success as a supposed healer lies her guilt. And Adamson himself is again likely to be accused of

128

heresy and excommunicated – even the king cannot save him.'

'It is better you stay away, Aunt,' said Cecy.

'Do not go,' said Will. 'Please. For not only will it place you in a vulnerable position, it will be perilous for us all. Promise me, Bethia!'

After a moment Bethia bowed her head in acceptance of Will's judgement, but she felt shamed by her capitulation. Instead, she arranged for a daily meal to be delivered to Alesoun in the tolbooth.

But by the time they left a day later for Pittenweem, Alesoun Pierson had already been taken to Edinburgh, where she was to stand trial for witchcraft.

'The trial will be carried out most thoroughly,' Will said. 'No one is found guilty unless the evidence of witnesses is robust. We have sound processes for these trials. The king takes a great interest and would not permit anything to go ahead without due process of law. In this we can place absolute faith in him.'

But Bethia did not feel comforted.

Chapter Eighteen

Wise Woman

Bethia returned to John's house to find all in confusion. The cattle owned by John's neighbour had been seen to act most strangely, leaping and dancing around the rig as though possessed. The neighbour was convinced the beasts were bewitched and that Violet had set a charm upon them. Bethia could scarce believe she had just left accusations of witchcraft in St Andrews to find them on the doorstep in Pittenweem.

'This has naething tae dae wi' you, Violet, and is a' aboot our dispute o'er land,' John was shouting as Bethia walked into the chamber where the whole family was gathered.

Disregarding all, she went to Father and bent to kiss the top of his head, while he reached out to pat her hand. She drew back quickly, for he smelt oily. She would insist on washing his head later when the stramash had died down. She smiled quietly to herself – there would be another stramash at the mere suggestion of washing where only wiping with linen was thought necessary.

'What land dispute?' she said to John. She smiled to Ephraim as she went to sit by Violet who was hunched on the settle with no work in her hands. A most unusual circumstance for this busy and unassuming woman.

'He claims the corner o' the home field – *my* home

field – is his. We walked the boundaries when I bought the land and the previous owner was clear – that corner is mine.'

Bethia narrowed her eyes trying to visualise the piece of land John was talking about. 'The far corner?'

'Aye,' said John belligerently.

'But it's tiny. Is it really worth all this fuffle? Why not just give it to him?'

'Dinna be daft, Bethia. Gie an inch and the man will tak an ell.'

The evening was marred by John's bellicose face and Violet's worried frown. John was all for having it out with the neighbour now and rose several times to go and speak with him. Bethia, certain it would quickly descend into shouting and fearful it might end with punches thrown, earnestly counselled awaiting Will's return, and calling on his assistance in his capacity as minister to the parish.

Will had escorted Bethia and Cecy back to Pittenweem. They were determined to stay no longer in St Andrews – and in any case Cecy needed to return to her familial duties. Will then promptly turned around and went back to St Andrews. It seemed Andrew Melville still had need of him. Bethia thought he would be better to stay away from Melville and his attempts to instruct the king but Will said he must support Melville, for he agreed wholeheartedly with him. James's Melville's assistant was already lined up to cover Will's services this Sunday so Will considered he would be more useful in St Andrews than Pittenweem.

It took a long time for Bethia to fall asleep that night, a restless uncomfortable tossing and turning not helped by the small feet sticking into her back. Initially she'd been accorded a chamber, and a bed, of her own but the house, although large, was crowded, for Father commanded his own room, leaving only four others of indifferent size for John and his many children to pack tight into. Eventually Bethia spoke with Violet and offered to take some of the girls with her, a generosity she regretted every night when the six-year-old, who slept between her aunt and her nine-year-old sister, managed to swivel herself around so she was lying crosswise, her feet sticking into Bethia's back. Bethia suggested one of the other sisters could come into the bed instead but Aggie did not at all agree it would be a good thing. She begged so pitifully to stay 'cosy in the big bed' that Bethia could not gainsay her. Instead, she brushed and plaited Aggie's hair, as she had regularly done for her own granddaughters at home in Constantinople, while whispering stories in Aggie's ear of the magnificence of the Topkapi Palace where the sultan kept lions.

John agreed to await Will's return before confronting his neighbour, but a message came that he was required urgently in Edinburgh. A lucrative shipment of wood from the Baltic had arrived and the master was complaining the shipment of Scottish leather, hide and rabbit skins which was to go back in return was of poor quality.

'You can aywis ask James Melville for his assistance if Will doesna soon return,' said John as he left early the next morning. 'I must to Edinburgh, but Symon will be my eyes and ears and take care of you all in my absence.' He looked to his eldest son, who nodded assurance at him with a most solemn expression upon his youthful face. John hesitated for a moment then added, 'And stay away from yon lassie.'

Bethia followed them out the chamber, which was already hot and stuffy even though Father, who was being tended by Violet, had yet to rise and demand the fire be fed despite the summer sunshine. She was happy that John had decided to take Ephraim with him to Leith, for a letter had recently arrived from Samuel in Constantinople urging that his son seek every opportunity to create trading connections while in

Scotland. John, ever mindful of expanding his own trading empire, was eager to support his nephew. And since Will was in St Andrews, he could not object to the loss of his Hebrew teacher.

'You seem remarkably sanguine today?' said Bethia. 'But do you not think you should stay? I am fearful your neighbour will take things further.'

'Aye weel, it's no the first fight we've had wi' Macdougal and I doubt t'will be the last. I've tried tae buy his land but he refuses to sell.' John paused and gazed into the distance. 'And I dinna entirely blame him. He needs what land he has to grow food to feed his family. Now I must awa before yon bugger in Leith does the dirty on me again. He ay seizes his chance, when I'm no there, to slip some extra intae his ane pocket that should be going into mine.'

'I don't know why you work with him then,' said Bethia.

John sniffed. 'Oh, he's a clever fellow, and it's aywis better to keep yer enemies close.'

'Grissel would no doubt keep a watch on him, if you asked her.'

John's face brightened. 'Aye, that is a very good thought.'

He went off whistling, leaving Bethia worrying what she might have set in motion. But she soon forgot Grissel in her concern for Violet, who was white-faced and more pinched-looking than normal.

'What lass is Symon to stay away from?' she asked, but Violet was too preoccupied to answer, busy as she was staring out the window. The shutters had been flung wide despite Father, who was now ensconced in his chair, complaining loudly about the draft.

'Look,' said Violet standing before the open window.

Bethia followed the line of Violet's pointing finger.

'What are they doing?'

'It's branches from a rowan tree. They must nae touch

the ground else it will not work.'

'What will not work?'

Violet turned, eyes wide, and Bethia could see Violet's hand shaking where she clutched her shawl to her breast. 'The rowan is tae ward agin witchcraft. See they are nailing it above the byre door.'

'Huh!' said Bethia, 'a waste of good nails.'

'And look, yon wicked man is picking the twigs off and gieing them tae that trauchled wife o' his. She'll nae doubt sew them intae the seams o' their clothes.'

Bethia crossed herself and then caught Violet's horrified expression.

Macdougal must have seen them watching for he came close to the dyke which divided their properties, dropped his breeks and bared his arse. Symon, who'd come up behind them, hooted. 'A smelly wee bum for a smelly wee man.'

Violet slumped on the settle, arms wrapped around herself. 'Janet, his wife, is a good woman, but as for Macdougal, I dinna ken whit's come ower him. He's no been richt since all his sons died one after the ither from the measles. Now they only have the three lassies, and a man needs a son.' She gazed up at Bethia. 'But Janet's a braw cook and makes fine pies.'

Bethia shook her head and went to sit beside Father, feeling helpless. But she could not disregard what was happening when, having persuaded Father to take the air, she opened the front door with the auld man leaning heavily on her arm to find a mound of faeces piled neatly upon their doorstep.

'Christ's bones,' roared Father. 'It's that son o' Satan, Macdougal, wha's done this. Let me git at him.' He shook off Bethia's restraining arm and attempted to step over the offensive lumps but lost his balance.

'Look oot, grandfather. You near planted your face in that,' said Symon grabbing him around the waist from behind.

Bethia left Symon to deal with Father's spluttering fury and slipped out the kitchen door, down the garden path and through the gate. She lifted her skirts, for the grassy track was muddy from the recent rain, and set off for Macdougal's house. She found his wife pegging up her linens, which looked to Bethia as though they were in need of considerably more scrubbing.

'Mistress Janet,' said Bethia, touching the woman gently on the arm.

'Whit dae ye want?' said Janet, leaping back in fear and dropping the shirt she was hanging up into the muck.

'We are neighbours, and neighbours should assist one another, not get into fights,' said Bethia, drawing Janet to sit beside her on the low stone wall. 'But how can we women sort this?'

'I didna want this feuding, ye ken. I'm sorry,' said Janet. 'Especially no wi' a fine lady like yersel', but ma man willna listen. He's got the bit atween his teeth and he won't let go.'

'Did you know he left a pile of shite on our doorstep and my Father near slipped in it?'

Janet gasped. 'I did not.' She stood up. 'And I won't have it.'

'Wait,' said Bethia. 'Let *us* find a way to settle this together, for I suspect if he learns I'm here then you and I will not get a chance to speak again.'

Janet nodded slowly and sat down. 'But he'll no listen. He's an angry man,' she said softly.

Bethia took Janet's hand in hers and squeezed it gently. Janet squeezed back and they sat in silence gazing out at the sea. A light breeze brushed across the waves and the susurration as they rolled over the sand to touch the shore soothed the soul.

The breeze shifted and Bethia was suddenly assailed by the smell of the nearby privy. She had hoped if she sat here an idea would come to her. She thought of

Machiavelli's book *The Prince*, which she had read several times. If Machiavelli was here, he would come up with a cunning plan, she was certain. But she could think of nothing but appealing to Macdougal's better nature, if he had one.

She noticed the lacing of Janet's sleeve had come undone and reached over to fasten it at the shoulder. The skin beneath was visible – a large purpling bruise revealed. Janet flinched at Bethia's gentle touch and tugged her sleeve over it.

'I slipped,' she said, 'and knocked against the door jamb.' But she gazed at the ground as she spoke, then stood up. 'Please go afore he sees you.'

Bethia also rose. 'I will speak with my brother. He is the minister, after all, and I know he will not tolerate this behaviour from one of his parishioners.'

'It's no like that. The harvests hae been poor and the bairns died last winter.' Janet brushed a tear away. 'He cannie do the fishing since he hurt his hand and he's feart for us, 'tis all.'

'I still do not think that reason enough to do you harm.' Bethia lifted her skirts and leapt lightly over the muddy puddle, went around the corner of the house and walked straight into Macdougal. She could see he was surprised to find her there and made sure she got the first word in.

'Master Macdougal,' she said, dipping a small curtsey.

Wrong-footed, he bowed clumsily in return.

'I was just speaking with your wife, seeking her receipt for cheese pie. I understand she is known the length of the East Neuk for her pies.'

'Aye, she's no a bad cook.' He preened, fluffing out proud as any cockerel. 'And we hae oor ane oven. Nae need to pay the baxter for the use o' his.'

'I have heard that she is an excellent housekeeper.'

'Aye, and housekeeper,' he mumbled.

'She is shrewd too, for she would not give me the receipt, which she says is a secret passed down from mother to daughter within her family.'

He stared at Bethia and she wondered if she'd gone too far.

But then he nodded slowly. 'A secret, aye that wid be richt.'

'And so I have asked if she will bake me two of her excellent pies and I will pay her for them,' said Bethia crossing her fingers behind her back and hoping God would forgive her this small distortion of the truth. She also hoped Janet would be quick enough not to betray her … and herself.

But it was soon evident that Janet was nobody's fool, for she appeared the next day with a tray containing the two pies, while Macdougal lingered in the background.

'All is well,' said Bethia when a shrinking Violet called her to the doorstep. 'Stay,' she muttered to Violet, who was about to slip away.

Bethia smiled at Janet. 'And that would be the three pennies we agreed.'

'Weel it took me longer than I thocht, so I am thinking a penny more wid be richt,' said Janet stoutly.

Bethia swallowed while Macdougal nodded agreement eagerly in the background.

'Ye ken I'll be selling them in the market. Macdougal thinks it's a braw idea.'

'That *is* a good idea,' said Bethia, producing the coins from her pocket and holding them aloft, 'and I will give you an extra penny for the supplies to get started. Are you not proud of your clever wife?' she called to Macdougal.

He looked startled but nodded. 'And here is my good sister,' Bethia patted Violet's arm, 'awaiting an apology for the accusation of maleficium.'

She held onto the coins while Janet's outstretched hand wavered.

He shifted from foot to foot but finally dipped his head, mumbling he was sorry.

'And it will not happen again?' Bethia prompted.

He hesitated then gave a curt nod.

Bethia dropped the coins into Janet's hand, laid the pies on a plate in the store cupboard and sent wee Aggie to return the tray.

'What did ye do wi' the shite?' said John when he and Ephraim returned a few days later and were regaled with the story.

'Dug it into the ground where the second crop of beans are to be planted,' said Symon.

'Good,' said John. 'I wouldna want it wasted, whatever the source.'

Bethia raised her eyebrows while Father humphed in his corner.

'So the grand lady o' Turkland wi' her mysterious powers prevailed.'

'I do not think that at all amusing, John,' said Bethia.

'Aye weel, Macdougal has had a hard year o' it and Christ Jesus teaches us forgiveness. I can turn the ither cheek when there's reason tae do so. But you, Symon,' John glared at his son, 'are tae stay away from the eldest Macdougal daughter.'

Symon flushed as all eyes turned to him.

'Pah,' said Father. His face lightened. 'But I have to say they pies are no bad, no bad at all. I'll hae anither slice, Violet.'

Chapter Nineteen

Symon and Kristene

John was beside himself with fury: eyes bulging; fists clenched; face red as a beet; body rigid. Meanwhile, Father was leaning back in his tall chair, which occupied an inordinate amount of space in the crowded chamber, gnarled hands resting on his small pot belly, benign expression, clearly enjoying the drama unfolding before him. Violet nudged the child sitting on the settle next to her to stand up and give Bethia a seat while John spluttered out his rage at Symon standing hangdog before him.

'What has Symon done?' Bethia whispered to Violet, who was wringing her hands in a most distressing fashion. Violet shook her head and her eyes filled with tears. Bethia took one of Violet's hands in hers and stroked the calloused skin. She was conscious of how soft, white and unworked her own hands were by comparison and then she thought of her life as *kira* to the sultan's harem. It might not have been a life of drudgery but it had been like living on a knife edge – one move which displeased and she might die a cruel death. Many times she had passed through the palace gates and seen the executioner's servant kneeling to clean a bloodied axe, the red water pooling on the pale stone before swirling down into the drain. She released Violet's hand

and felt for the small crucifix tucked deep in her pocket. Her lips moved as she sent up a prayer to the Virgin to watch over her family in faraway Galata.

John finished his tongue-lashing by pointing out that Symon might be near on twenty years of age and about to become a father but wasn't too old for a thrashing.

Bethia gasped and John flicked his hand. 'Aye, the bluidy fool's been sticking his pizzle where it shouldna hae been.'

'The bairns, John!' said Violet in shocked tones.

Father winked at Bethia and she realised it was not so much the overall scene he was enjoying, but John's discomfiture.

'I must awa and tell your Uncle Will. You've brought disgrace upon our family, and him the minister.' John left the room, slamming the door behind him so hard the frame shook.

Violet went to Symon and, wrapping her arms around him, a small, slight mother holding her tall son, pressed her face against his chest. Symon, who'd recovered his composure with remarkable speed, grinned over the top of his head at his aunt.

'You do not appear overly troubled,' said Bethia wryly.

'Ach, Kristene's a bonny lass. I would hae married her onyway. This will just hurry it along and now her parents and pa must gie their permission.'

'You mean Kristene, who is your neighbour's daughter?'

'Aye,' said Symon.

'The neighbour who accused your mother of being a witch?' said Bethia, beginning to feel a similar outrage to John.

'She had naething tae dae with that,' said Symon.

'I do not think that at all wise,' said Bethia.

'Wheesht,' said Violet, and Bethia was so surprised to be hushed by the usually meek Violet that she said no more.

Symon did not appear quite so light of heart when he and Kristene had to sit on the repentance stools at the kirk the following Sunday, but at least they had not been reduced to wearing only a shirt and shift as usually happened.

'There is some benefit in having a brother who is also the minister,' John was heard to mutter when told the errant couple could remain fully clothed.

They sat low before the congregation, cheeks flushed but heads held high. However, as the service went on they both began to droop, until by the second hour they were sufficiently hunched over to satisfy the most diligent members of the congregation of their shame.

'Thanks be to God that is over,' said Bethia to Violet, as they filed out of the church.

Violet shook her head, and John, overhearing, corrected his sister. 'They are back again this evening and every Tuesday too, for the rest of this month. Be grateful Symon didna sin wi' a married woman,' he added when Bethia looked at him aghast. 'They must take the penitent stool for six months followed by a further three weeks wearing sackcloth and, if there is a child, pay a fine of twenty shillings or else be jailed – and the bairn cannot be baptised till the parents repent.'

'Life was simpler with the confessional,' said Bethia wearily.

'Hush,' said John, while Violet hunched, so her neck all but disappeared, protecting herself from the corruption of Bethia's words.

'Why did Symon not wait till he was married before …' Bethia's voice faded away.

They were by now safely inside the house, where Father was dozing by the fireside, excused church in case he caught a chill in the cold wind that was blasting in off the sea.

'How is your neighbour taking it? They have brought

141

shame on his house as well!'

'Hah!' said John. 'Macdougal's rubbing his hands now, thinking I'll hae to tak on him as weel as his daughter.' John sniffed. 'He'll soon ken how wrong he is.'

The wedding was to take place as soon as the penance was done and the young couple had demonstrated sufficient knowledge of the catechism which they must be able to recite diligently, distinctly and plainly. Bethia undertook to hear them, asking the questions while sitting with John Craig's small book resting in her lap.

What are we by nature?
The children of God's wrath.

Were we thus created of God?
No, for he made us to his own image.

How came we to this misery?
Through the fall of Adam from God.

What things came to us by that fall?
Original sin, and natural corruption.

What power have we to turn to God?
None at all, for we are all dead in sin.

What is the punishment of our sin?
Death eternal, both in body and soul.

'The author attended university at St Andrews,' said Will, nodding his approval when he arrived one day to find Symon, Kristene and Bethia studying diligently.

He directed the young couple to memorise the next section and lowered himself into Father's empty chair.

'Craig was a monk in an Augustinian monastery in

Italy where he was set to study and refute the forbidden books of Calvin and Luther. Instead, he found his true calling as a reformer, but when he was discovered, the Inquisition took him. He escaped before he could be burned at the stake, eventually returning to Scotland. I cannot think of a man for whom I have more respect. He was an excellent leader of the Church Assembly and is chaplain to the king – but he is old now and does not go about much, else I might have taken you to hear him preach in Edinburgh. He's been working on this catechism for some time and it will soon go to the Assembly for final approval.'

'Should you be using it then?'

'Oh aye, there's no doubt it will be adopted, and the doctrine is as solid as the rock upon which Saint Peter built his church.'

Will then called Symon and Kristene back, took the pamphlet and insisted Bethia be tested too, which she did not much care for.

Who may deliver us from this bondage?
God only who bringeth life out of death.

How know we that he will do it?
By the promise and sending of his Son Christ Jesus in our flesh.

What kind of person is Christ?
Perfect God and perfect man, without sin.

Bethia, sitting up tall on the settle, was feeling pleased she had so far kept up, but then Will jumped to those she did not know so well.

To what end are we thus redeemed,
and brought in hope of that endless joy to come?
To move us effectually to deny all ungodliness,

143

worldly lusts,
and unrighteousness, and so live godly, soberly,
and righteously
in this present world, looking for the coming of
Christ,
for our full redemption …

She stumbled halfway through and Symon stepped in, finishing the response.

'Hah!' she said, snatching the pamphlet from Will. 'Do you even know the responses without the book in front of you? *What shall be the final end of all these graces?'* she read out.

Will stared at her and burst out laughing.

'God shall be glorified for ever in mercy, and we shall enjoy that endless life with Christ our Head, to whom with the Father, and the Holy Spirit, be all honour and glory for ever. Amen,' said Symon, and winked at his uncle.

And Bethia understood she had been toyed with and Will knew the answer very well.

'If you are able to speak as ably before the presbytery then the wedding banns can be called. But you, Bethia, need more study before you can be granted a ticket to attend Communion,' said Will.

Father appeared then from his ablutions and Kristene slid out of the room, after a nod and squeeze of the hand from Symon. Will noticed but Bethia was pleased he did not remonstrate. Symon, for all his youthful age, was a clear-thinking fellow who had no doubt about the path he wanted to tread and was single-mindedly following it. Bethia smiled, remembering John's sudden appearance in Constantinople all those years ago because he *had a mind to go.*

And Bethia was happy for Symon that he was no longer in disgrace. John, after his first explosion of fury, had accepted the marriage should take place as soon as Will would allow it and before *Kristene's belly grows ony bigger.* It was Violet who was left with the challenge of finding space for the happy couple within her burgeoning household. But Violet, as Bethia was coming to understand, thrived on taking care of others, and was never happier than when her family were crowded around her. Chattering, laughing, arguing, making up, playing, and fighting was all as one to Violet as long as she could be the mother in their midst.

Chapter Twenty

Flight

Will seemed more and more satisfied as the lessons in Hebrew continued.

'I think Ephraim is accepted now. Before, I feared it was not sufficient that I was his blood relative should any questions of his antecedents be raised, but now with James Melville praising Ephraim's knowledge of the texts, albeit within the Old Testament, he should be safe.'

'You are a good man,' said Bethia.

'I try to be,' said Will humbly, then frowned. 'But Ephraim must show due diligence in his studies of the New Testament. I will insist he spends more time with me every day until he can answer the catechism with speed and confidence. Fewer days out on the boats and more with the Word of Christ Jesus is required.'

And, in the blink of an eye Will was back to being filled with his own righteousness and Bethia profoundly annoyed by it.

Yet, Bethia later reflected, neither of them should have been complacent where Ephraim was concerned. He was a seventeen-year-old lad with a wheen of ideas and an able accomplice in his cousin Symon.

'Dinna fash yerself, Bethia,' said John when she wondered what Ephraim and Symon were so busy about. 'Symon is a sensible lad – despite his recent transgression

– and, as the elder, will keep your laddie on a straight path.'

Bethia chided herself. At least Ephraim was with Symon and not finding an excuse to linger in Will's house conversing with Edane, which he seemed increasingly inclined to do. But, as it transpired, both lads had needed an eye kept upon them – and a tight rein.

It was Cecy's good mother who came screaming into Will's house one morning when Bethia, Violet and Cecy were having a companionable coze. It was not often that Violet especially had the opportunity to sit down for a blether, so Bethia could not help but glare when the door was flung wide and Nannis burst in.

'Oh, they laddies,' she shrieked. 'Where is the meenister?'

'He's gone to Grangemuir, Mistress Beattie is near her end,' said Cecy calmly. She took hold of Nannis to lead her to the settle but Nannis tugged her arm away.

'No, no, ye dinna understand. We hae to stop them.'

'Sit down!' said Cecy.

Bethia stared at Cecy, didn't know her niece had it in her to be so fierce.

Nannis sat down abruptly.

Cecy held her hand up as Nannis opened her mouth to speak. 'Which laddies?'

'Symon, Ephraim … and our Donald.' Nannis's voice rose as she spoke and *Donald* emerged as a wail. She clutched her hands to her heart. 'Oh, ye hae tae stop them.'

'What are they doing?'

'I dinna ken but Syffy says they're awa tae the cliff wi the small sail frae ane o' Andersoun's boats.'

Bethia stood up and all three women stared at her. 'Show me,' she said in a choked voice.

Nannis led the women along the track, fast as a wee woman with short legs could go, but Bethia, for once heedless of falling, went faster. They passed the site of the new tolbooth, noisy with masons chipping at the stone and the calls of men hauling buckets of plaster and rubble up the scaffold. It was Tuesday, and Will would preach in the old church adjoining it later this afternoon, when work must stop for several hours else no one would hear *The Word*. A few of the men lifted their heads to stare at the hurrying women, eyes bright in dust-caked faces, but the master was on the prowl and soon called their attention back to their work.

The path skirted the walls of the old priory where Will had begun a school in what had formerly been the prior's lodgings.

'What *is* going on? What do you fear?' gasped Cecy as she drew abreast of Bethia. But Bethia was concentrating on where to place her feet as the path twisted down a short steep incline. The track levelled out again and Nannis took off at as near a run as a plump woman could achieve. Cecy, younger and fleeter than both Bethia and Violet, lifted her skirts and ran after her, while Bethia tried not to slip. Whatever Ephraim was up to, falling and causing herself an injury would not help matters.

The sea spread out in front of them now as Nannis's scurrying feet led them unerringly along the clifftop. The tide was well in with only small patches of stony beach visible below, the shoals of dark, jagged rocks hidden beneath the deep blue. The path dipped then rose steeply, and Bethia, panting up the incline, could feel the sweat pooling at the back of her neck where her hair had come loose.

On the landward side, behind protective dykes, barley rippled in the breeze, turning gold against the purpling flowering hemp in the next rig and beyond the last of the peas, pods poking from dying white flowers. Behind the fields a line of washing flapped next to the cluster of farm buildings built low against the harsh winter winds. The track dipped and curved, and it was as she reached the next summit Bethia saw the white spread of sail take to the air, like a huge handkerchief tied with rope at all four corners. Dangling in its centre was Ephraim. She stopped hand to mouth so that Violet behind knocked into her, nearly sending them both over the edge. By the time Bethia had regained her balance Ephraim's brief upward motion had ended and he was dropping like a stone to the sea below. Violet shrieked to add to Nannis's screams, for Symon and Donald were holding the end of a rope tied around Ephraim's waist and both were in grave danger of being pulled over the cliff. Donald let go, and Symon, at the last moment, did too, and fell sprawling at the edge.

The sail floated, spread across the water like a giant dead seagull, with a bump in the centre where Ephraim's head was pushing up beneath it. Ephraim could swim, for Samuel, knowing the lure of the waters of the Golden Horn when he was a lad, had made certain his sons learned. What Bethia didn't know as she knelt to work out a way down the cliff, was if he could breathe with the weight of the sail pressing down upon him.

Symon was already scrambling down with Donald following close behind, having evaded Nannis's grabbing hand, when Ephraim emerged.

'It nearly worked,' he shouted breathlessly as he bobbed in the sea. 'Did you see I flew. I truly flew.'

Symon was in the water now too, gathering up the sail with Donald's help. 'We need a stronger wind. The breeze was too light,' he said.

'And the sailcloth too heavy,' said Donald.

'Aye, you're right,' said Symon.

Bethia by now had found her way onto the stony shoreline mostly by dint of sliding down on her bottom, to the great detriment of her skirts.

'We must use something lighter the next time,' said Ephraim as he went to put his feet under him.

Bethia opened her mouth to say there would be no next time, ever, but before she could speak, Ephraim, with a groan, sank back into the water. Symon left the sail to Donald and went to his aid.

'I think I banged my foot against the rocks when I landed,' said Ephraim.

'I'm not surprised,' said Bethia, made caustic with relief.

Symon helped him out of the water to a seat on a boulder. Bethia knelt and examined the foot while Nannis shrieked from above that Donald must come home with her – at once.

'You have cut it quite deep,' said Bethia. 'Why did you not keep your boots on?'

'They're heavy and would've weighed me down.'

'Man is not meant to fly,' said Bethia severely. 'As you have amply demonstrated.' She stood up arms akimbo glaring at the two young men. 'You should both have known better – and should not be leading Donald astray. There will be no more of this.'

They hung their heads but she could see them both trying not to grin at one another.

Bethia had expected John to side with the lads. After all, it was just the kind of mischief he had excelled at when he was young, but he surprised her.

'God's blood, Symon,' he said, 'ye are soon to become a father. What are ye aboot trying to fly? You are the older and should hae mair sense. I will be keeping you so busy from now on there will be no time for play. Donald will go off to the university in St Andrews and that is Will's business. But Ephraim will rope some other young fools in, for the lads, and lassies, of this village dance after him like he is a prince come among them. What are we tae dae wi' him?'

'Tounis College,' said Will when applied to. 'The principal there has already heard speak of Ephraim's skills with Oriental languages, and Andrew Melville supports the idea. Ephraim will go first as a student, and if he shows himself as able and willing, then he will be given some classes to teach.'

And so it was decided, Ephraim would go to Edinburgh. And Bethia, while sad to be parted from him, reflected that it was best he go for several reasons … not least the amount of time Edane had spent *nursing* him while he rested his injured foot.

Part Three

Edinburgh

November 1587 to March 1588

Chapter Twenty-One

A Gift

'I have a gift I wish to give you,' Gilbert said one day when Bethia was visiting Balcarrow and they were sitting at their ease in the solar. 'And I hope you will accept it in honour of our long friendship.'

Bethia told herself that there could be no harm in such a gift and sat forward in her seat eagerly, but before she could find out more, Elspeth's head appeared around the door.

'Forgive me, Master Logie, but I would appreciate your final approval on the composition.'

Gilbert removed his hands from his pocket and they both rose and followed Elspeth up the spiral of stairs into the small chamber, with north light as she had requested. Holdfast came to greet his master and then gave Bethia's hand a gentle nudge with his wet nose, which she felt strangely made welcome by.

'Holdfast is my companion here,' said Elspeth smiling. And Bethia was pleased to see her friend so quietly content, especially as it was she who'd suggested to Gilbert he commission a painting by Elspeth. She was less sanguine when she saw the elements of the composition that Elspeth was working on.

'Oh my good Elspeth!' she said, reaching out to pick up the skull.

'Don't touch it,' said Elspeth. Then speaking more gently added, 'It is positioned so the light falls on the curve of the skull to give it that burnished look.'

'But why …'

'A skull? The composition is a reminder of the brevity of life.'

Bethia nodded, although she was by no means certain she would want such an image constantly before her – but then it was not her wall on which it would be hanging. She caught sight of the glint of something tucked behind the skull's yellowed teeth and, being careful not to touch, bent to examine what was within. Straightening up, she deliberately did not look at Elspeth but could not help the wry smile. Elspeth had placed a crucifix within the skull. It would likely show as only reflected light but still they would all know it was there – and what it meant.

'Perhaps the candle might be lit?' said Gilbert thoughtfully.

'No, I think not. Or, at the very least, it must be guttering so it is nearly extinguished, else it does not fit with the overall meaning,' said Elspeth.

'Ah, I see. We shall leave you to it,' he said, ushering Bethia out the room.

In the solar once again, he said, 'Elspeth asks my opinion then disagrees with whatever I suggest. She can be a most obdurate woman.' He shook his head. 'But let us finish our interrupted conversation.' He tugged a small bag from his pocket and sat down.

'What is it?' Bethia asked, as she too took a seat.

He smiled, but she could see by the way he would not meet her eyes he was nervous.

''Tis only a poesy ring in recognition of our long friendship,' he said, dangling the bag from his fingertips.

Poesy rings usually had a poem or symbol of love inscribed upon them, so were more than the simple sign of friendship Gilbert implied. Yet, made curious, she took

155

the soft velvet pouch and quickly undid the knot. She tipped the ring onto the palm of her hand. A gold band with an interlocking pattern of … was it leaves … or hearts. She put on her new eyeglasses, which Gilbert had recently had brought from Cupar, and held the ring up, the gold winking in the candlelight, fearful what the inscription might say and how she would react.

'*Let liking last*,' she read aloud. And felt a curious sense of disappointment. She had expected something more intimate, perhaps '*You never knew a heart more true*', for it was how she thought of him; faithful and true … *like a dog*, a little voice said in her head, and she was discomfited.

She became aware Gilbert was shifting on the settle as though he was sitting on thistle spines and slid the ring upon her forefinger. It was too large for the fourth finger of her left hand, which was said to be where the vein of love was sited, but that was as well. She held her hand out, twisting and turning it in the light.

'It's a beautiful ring, Gilbert. I thank you.' She leaned over and kissed his cheek where the scar down the side of his face puckered the skin and the beard was sparse.

He touched his hand lightly to the spot and she could see him reddening in the candlelight.

'It is a symbol of our long friendship,' Gilbert repeated.

'Yes,' she said firmly. 'We have liked one another since first we met and you helped me escape from the terrible burning of poor Wishart.'

He nodded, and again she felt strangely cast down that he was not offering her more. And yet she didn't want anything more than friendship from him, did she?

'I have a favour to ask,' she said, knowing she was being as naughty as a small child to place Gilbert in what he would likely consider a position of obligation.

Gilbert's eyes never left her face and she realised he was waiting for her to go on.

'Ephraim has been in Edinburgh for some months now and I very much want to see him.'

She paused, hoping he would jump in and she need not spell her request out, but Gilbert did not oblige.

'I would be grateful beyond words if you would escort me there.'

Gilbert tilted his head to one side watching her quizzically, almost like an owl on the branch before it dives.

'John says he is too busy to go to Edinburgh at the moment,' she said in a rush. Actually, what John had said was, 'It's autumn, and naught but a bluidy fool would cross the Forth except at most urgent necessity at this time of year.'

'And John has no objection if I escort you there,' said Gilbert slowly.

Bethia straightened her back. 'John does not order my comings and goings. I am a widow and may make my own choices.'

A twinkle came into Gilbert's eye as she spoke. He stood up and bowed. 'In that event, my lady, I should be honoured to be your escort.'

'Thank you, Gilbert,' Bethia said looking up at him. 'You are the best of friends.'

'I try to be,' he mumbled, and sitting down again began to discuss the arrangements.

And John, when she told him later, suddenly seemed to have changed his mind, saying that it was as well she leave Pittenweem for a wee while.

Bethia blinked, wondering if the family had grown tired of her. It was, after all, more than six months since she'd arrived, but John denied it.

'No, no – why would ye think such a thing? 'Tis only the blethers still going around in the village aboot you being a wise woman after ye sorted out Macdougal. I dinna like it. If ye're away for a month or so then all will be forgot by the time you return.'

'Oh!' said Bethia, 'I see.' And she did.

Father was made unhappy when he learned she would be leaving him, albeit for a short time, for Bethia did not mention John's suggestion of at least a month. It took the combined efforts of Bethia and Violet to assure him she would be back before he knew it.

'Aye, weel bring my Grissel wi' ye,' he said. 'I dinna ken whit she's daeing in Edinburgh in the first place?'

Bethia and John glanced at one another but neither chose to respond.

Inevitably it was a cold and uncomfortable journey, but Gilbert had arranged for an awning to be rigged, and the sea was restless rather than rough. The men had to take to the oars else they would have made no progress for the breeze was slight, although the wind got up after dawn and a sail was raised to speed their passage. Despite the layers of woollen clothing she was wrapped in, Bethia was so stiff with cold she had to be assisted off the boat and it took some time huddled by the fire of a nearby house before she felt able to make the final push up the hill to Edinburgh.

Nevertheless, with remarkable ease, she found herself in John's land embracing her beloved grandson, who seemed happy enough despite his complaints about the amount of studying he had to do. All was comfortable till she glanced over to see Grissel lingering in the background. After a moment's hesitation Bethia gave a nod – uncertain how she should greet a bastard sister who had until recently been the closest of servant companions – and Grissel responded with the slightest of curtseys. It was all so awkward.

Chapter Twenty-Two

Bitter Cold

Bethia, curled up in bed, could hear the fire crackling in the grate and see the light dancing behind the curtains which Grissel had drawn around the bedstead. Although the bed was tight-strung and well provided with mattresses she could not get comfortable. But then she had experienced nothing but discomfort of varying degrees since she'd left her well-appointed home in Galata and should be accustomed to it by now.

The door opened and closed, the bed curtains wafting in the draft. Grissel slid the chamberpot beneath the bed and then settled down on the pallet, which cunningly was lowered from the wall at night and tucked away during daylight hours, and Ephraim slept in the small antechamber.

The room which housed the bed was also where John conducted all his business while in Edinburgh. The many other rooms making up John's land rose seven levels high, alongside equally tall neighbouring lands, and were all let to families. Nice, respectable families of course, but still it was peculiar to know that each time you passed someone on the stairs within your own home that they had as much right to be there as you.

John had sniffed when she'd said as much when she first arrived from Constantinople. 'You have become spoilt, Bethia. It's nae wonder you've been named the grand lady o' the Turks. There is a great shortage of accommodation in the city and I would be a fool not to profit from it. And there are tenements to be found everywhere, even in Pittenweem – else where would poor folks live?'

Bethia tossed and turned in the soft bed in which she could not get comfortable, while Grissel snored on the pallet by the embers of the fire. Truth to tell, she had been as eager to see Grissel as Ephraim. Fortunately, Grissel was quickly restored to herself, blethering gaily about the neighbours and her life in Edinburgh. But still there was an awkwardness between them. Perplexed by how to make things better, Bethia eventually fell into a fitful sleep where Mainard came to her, abjuring her to take care over and over till she grew impatient.

She awoke when the dim light of day filtered into the room through the opaque glass and, feeling a sudden longing for the sun, she clambered out of bed and up onto the window seat, pushing open the wooden shutters below the glass. A fine drizzle was falling cloaking everything in grey. She shivered as the raw damp enveloped her, coughing when the foetid air from below caught in her throat. She had lived amid crowded squalor before, but the Turks could teach the Scots a lot about how to keep a city, and themselves, clean.

And echoing Bethia's thoughts, Grissel rose up on one elbow and groaned. 'Whit an awfie smell to wake up tae.' She fell back and scratched her head and once started couldn't stop. 'And whit I wouldna give for ane o' those bathhouses like we had in Constantinople.' She sat upright. 'Could we no set one up. People here are verrie dirty!'

Bethia giggled. 'Time was you didn't think so highly of using the *hamam* yourself.'

'Aye weel, I grew used to haeing a body that smelt sweet, and ye do feel a whole lot better after a visit to the bathhoose.'

Bethia sniffed. 'It'll never take on here. People believe immersing yourself in warm water is dangerous, for it opens the pores – and they're fearful they'll get the pox. 'Tis said it's caught from such places.'

'Hah! If that was the case then they'd be an awfie lot o' pox-ridden Turks, and I niver saw that.'

'And,' said Bethia, seriously considering it, 'finding a supply of running water would be near impossible. Look at the difficulty we have getting a clean bucket of water from the wells, and the Nor' Loch is filthy.'

She rose and dressed, and it was a great relief to have Grissel wield the hairbrush once more. 'No one can care for my hair as well as you, Grissel,' she said, and caught sight of Grissel's smile of delight to be so praised.

'When will Ephraim return?' Bethia asked, for he had left at six bells for his first class. It was no wonder he had asked if he could live in college with such early hours to keep. She would tell him he might before she left for Pittenweem.

'Ach, they make that laddie study ower hard. I'm feart his heid will explode wi' all the learning that's being stuffed intae it. We'll no see him much before evening.'

'And what do you do with yourself all day?'

'Weel,' said Grissel slowly. 'I cook a meal for Ephraim and there's aywis the cleaning.'

'It must be restful after all the years caring for our big family.'

'Aye, it is,' said Grissel wistfully.

Bethia had been there only a few days when Gilbert, who'd lodged with an acquaintance further down the High Street, came saying there'd been a dispute amongst his tenants and he must return to Fife before they set fire to one another's houses or some such foolery. 'I will come back for you soon, for I assume you're not yet ready to leave,' he said, nodding to the needlework design the two women were engaged in creating.

Bethia nodded. She had not mentioned John's

instruction that she should bide in Edinburgh for at least a month.

The weather grew colder, and one morning Bethia was awoken by an intermittent thumping which she could not place. She parted the drapes around the bed and climbed down reluctantly. Shivering, she saw the fire was near out and, crouching low, blew and blew trying to coax the grey embers into flame. The ashes floated around her face and she coughed while Grissel slept on.

Creeping back to her warm bed she noticed the lace of frost slithering and crackling across the window panes, which explained the peculiar noises she'd been hearing. She pulled the covers over her head leaving only a peephole to breathe through and curled her knees up to her chest aware of the cold place next to her. There would always be an empty space where Mainard once lay.

The next morning the streets were white with hoarfrost and the sky a deep blue with a myriad trails of the black smoke from thousands of fires patterning it. The cold at least had the benefit of dampening the stink of the streets and the soil cart. Grissel came rushing into the kitchen, tightly wrapped in shawls, mittens, bonnet and the tip of her nose turning from blue to red saying there was a beggar huddled in the corner at the side of the steps who looked to be frozen stiff.

'The man is as lifeless as a stone,' Ephraim said, stamping his feet and tucking his fingers under his oxters, for he'd run out without a cloak to see if he could render assistance.

'Poor fellow.' Bethia looked thoughtful and turned to John, who'd arrived the previous day and sat, hands wrapped around a hot bowl of porridge.

'In Constantinople we have soup kitchens for the poor. 'Tis part of the Moslem faith that they be cared for – and the sultan takes a lead.'

'Well good for him,' said John.

Bethia opened her mouth to say that she did not consider this a matter for sarcasm and then closed it again. 'I was wondering if we might do something ourselves.'

'Yes, Nonna,' said Ephraim. 'We should.'

'Well, you'll no be used to the cold after the heat o' Constantinople,' said John.

Bethia laughed. 'It gets bitter cold in winter there and the Golden Horn sometimes freezes over.'

'In any case we hae a levy to raise funds for the poor so there's nae need for you to dispel largesse.'

Bethia blinked. 'Is that how I seem, John?'

John, shovelling porridge in his mouth, didn't deign to reply.

'But clearly not everyone benefits else we'd not have a frozen corpse lying in our doorway. I suspect Calvin's creed of the deserving and undeserving poor is in force here too?'

John was silent, while Ephraim went to the kitchen, calling out for food.

'There *is* a distinction made, isn't there?' said Bethia, unwilling to let it go.

'I am unaware of such distinctions,' said John stiffly.

'That doesn't mean they aren't made and that any who fail an inquisition into their circumstances won't be left in great need.'

'So, what would you have me do?' he said, exasperated.

Bethia walked up and down the chamber, skirting around the bed, table, stools and chairs, past the kists pushed up against the wall and the chamberpot which was sitting mid floor, still unemptied. 'We shall send Grissel out and she will find those in desperate need.' She paused, thinking how it might work, and more importantly what objections Grissel might make. She went to the door and called for Grissel, who was busy

163

packing a basket for Ephraim to take. But far from showering them with a multitude of objections, Grissel looked thoughtful, almost as though a burden had slid from her back.

'I hae given out food already,' she said.

John's face flushed, but Bethia held up her hand for him to be silent while Grissel spoke.

'Long ago in Antwerp, when you had gone wi' Will,' she looked to Bethia, 'and Master Mainard was imprisoned and they took the hoose, I had naewhere to go and lived on the streets.'

'Until Ortelius helped you,' Bethia said slowly.

Grissel nodded, her head bobbing up and down like an apple being dooked. She looked at John and spread her hands wide. 'I had tae help the mother and child I found. Then there was an old woman bent near double and twa wee lads in naught but their shirts, and a young lass nae mair than thirteen years old and ripe for the plucking if she was left wandering the streets.'

'How have you done all this?' said Bethia, for John appeared struck dumb.

'Weel,' said Grissel slowly, keeping her eyes fixed on Bethia, 'I telt them tae stay very quiet …'

'They're in Ma Wilson who died's room, aren't they?' said John.

'No all o' them,' said Grissel stoutly.

Bethia burst out laughing, as much at John's expression of outrage as Grissel's temerity.

'The twa wee laddies disappeared – they were a wild pair, even worse than you.' She nodded to John. 'And the auld woman was wandered and her daughter came and found her.'

'So you have a woman and bairn living in that room?'

'Aye, and the young lass. But I was haeing a think,' she said, turning to Bethia, 'I could dae with anither pair o' hands in the kitchen, especially wi' you visiting …'

'What! So ye can be falling ower one another?' said John.

But Bethia could see his heart wasn't in it, and Grissel, ever quick to spot a weakness, said, 'So can I tell the lass we hae work?'

John raised his eyes to heaven. 'If ye must!'

Thirteen-year-old Megy was installed in the kitchen by that afternoon and the woman and baby joined one of the other tenants, a very respectable widow, in the chamber she rented from John.

'And our widow *is* satisfied with the arrangement,' he said when Bethia raised her eyebrows. 'She says she was finding all the stairs difficult and the young mother can fetch and carry for her, cook her meals and generally tend to her.'

'And the baby?'

'Och, that's the best part. She's delighted by the bairn since she has no kin of her own.'

Bethia was dubious. Small children, as she well knew, could be boisterous. She went to visit and was relieved to see John's tenant holding a sleeping bairn upon her lap while its mother quietly mopped the floor in the background. Everyone looked content and Bethia felt great fondness again for Grissel and her big heart.

Chapter Twenty-Three

Megy

'Megy needs a contract,' said Grissel. 'The auld besom next door says Megy will be had up for destitution if she doesn't hae one.'

John frowned. 'Then gie her one. She's your servant, no mine.'

'Servants dinna hae servants,' said Grissel.

'Ye ken your naebody's servant now,' said John impatiently.

Bethia, observing this exchange, watched a slow smile creep across Grissel's face.

'Can I truly hae a servant?' she said in tones of wonderment. Then, as quickly became practical, 'What fee should I pay?'

'What do you think she's worth.'

'Weel,' said Grissel slowly, 'she is a steady worker, although a wee bittie slow.'

'Then you must teach her to be faster,' said Bethia.

Grissel's brow furrowed. 'Fourteen shillings in every six months, dae ye agree? Or mebbe it's too much.'

'It's up to you,' said John, winking at Bethia. 'However, if you hae doubts aboot her as a worker I would make the contract only till Whitsunday and you can renew it after that if you're happy wi' her service.'

Megy, when told of her good fortune, accepted her fee

of fourteen shillings – which she wanted Grissel to confirm added up to twenty-eight shillings a year – but then asked for her bounty.

'She's a canny one,' said John when Grissel relayed Megy's demand. 'What did you say?'

'I telt her nae to be sae cheeky.'

'And then gave her a bolt of cloth,' said Bethia.

John roared with laughter.

'Her clothes were falling apart,' said Grissel. If I am to hae a servant, she maun be a respectable one! And,' she said thoughtfully, 'I'll teach her how to do sums or else she'll get cheated in the market.' She rubbed her head then looked to Bethia. 'Would you show me how to do the writing again?'

Bethia nodded. She had tried to teach Grissel her letters a long time ago but Grissel could never see the purpose and did not attend. Calculations had been a different matter and Grissel could do the workings of any transaction in her head with remarkable speed.

'Thank you.' Grissel dipped a curtsy.

John laughed. 'What's wi' the curtseying?'

'If I am tae be mistress to Megy then I maun show her correct ways,' said Grissel, and minced out of the chamber, closing the door on the sound of laughter behind her.

Gilbert returned ready to escort Bethia back to Pittenweem, saying her father was eager to see her.

'There was nae need for Logie tae come, I can see ma sister safely home,' Bethia overheard John muttering to Grissel.

'Dinna grumble, Father will be happy.'

Bethia felt a lump in her throat. It was most peculiar to hear Grissel call their shared parent *Father*.

But the weather worsened, one storm following close after another. Father would have to wait. And then Yule was upon them. The new religion did not mark the seasons in the same way. Candlemas, Whitsunday, Lammas, Martinmas, All Hallows day and Yule were all considered to be inextricably linked with the practice of the old religion and thus any celebration now forbidden. Indeed, John told her she must not wish others 'a happy Yule', for the Kirk sent clatterers out to catch transgressors. Bethia said it was all very dreary, and were people meant to do nothing but read their Bible, attend church and work, but John kept his head bent over the column of figures he was adding up.

Bethia felt ashamed then. I am no better than a scold, she thought. But when John seemed no brighter the next day she inquired as to his well-being.

'For you seem most wearied.'

He gazed at the piles of notes he was surrounded by, each containing details of transactions he had made, as though he didn't see them. 'I miss Violet,' he said, then followed it up quite fiercely, saying, 'I hope Symon is keeping a watch over the cod fishing. 'Tis a most profitable business in winter, since all can be done frae a line cast at the shore. Ye ken, ma best fisherman is a wee laddie no more than nine years old.'

'Surely he should be in the school Will set up?'

'Aye, weel, he has a widowed mother and three wee brothers. She told me he's saving the family, proud enough tae burst she was, and now he's teaching the next brother down how to fish alongside him.'

'Have you never thought to move to Edinburgh? The merchants here seem to have it all sown up.'

'Aye, I have, but Violet doesn't like it here, and then there's Father. It's easier to bide in Pittenweem.'

John sat gazing at his papers and, after a moment, bent his head to them once more. There was a knock on the door, which Grissel opened. Gilbert appeared, with a book tucked under one arm.

'What are you reading?' Bethia asked after they'd

exchanged greetings.

'A book by an Englishman called John Foxe, about martyrs to the Protestant faith.' He looked at Bethia. 'It tells the tale of George Wishart and …'

'We were there at his end,' said Bethia softly.

She listened carefully as Will read Foxe's account of Wishart's life and death. 'It is much as I remember being told at the time. I never met the man until I saw him on the pyre, but Will heard him preach. Do you think it's true that he deliberately provoked Cardinal Beaton, particularly by his hedge sermons in Ayrshire, and that he *chose* a martyr's death?'

'Aye, weel, if he did, I would think he regretted it before the end,' said John, stroking his beard.

'Cardinal Beaton made sure it was quick by the amount of gunpowder he ordered hung around Beaton's neck – and I *know* this to be true,' said Gilbert.

'Aye, well, Beaton still had the man put to the flame, so he wasnie that compassionate,' said John belligerently.

'Foxe writes of other Scottish martyrs,' said Gilbert peaceably. 'And there are woodcuts here which capture the horror most vividly.' He slid the book across to Bethia. 'Here's one of the burning of the martyr John Lambert at Smithfield.'

But Bethia waved the book away. 'I do not want to look.'

'We maun celebrate Yule – we can dae it verrie quietly,' said Grissel in her usual abrupt fashion as she laid a tankard of ale on the board by Gilbert and Bethia was grateful for the change in subject.

John sat up, looking brighter. 'I dinna think discretion and Yule are good bedfellows, but Will isna here to chide us so let's see what we can do. If I was in Pittenweem there would be pigeons to be got from my doocot and rabbits from the warren.'

'Your own doocot! How mighty you are become and why did I not know of this? Where is it?'

'I've only recently had it built,' said John, looking slight shame-faced, and Bethia felt bad to have called him out in front of Gilbert, with his tower house, walled garden, extensive lands and large barn above which the doves were kept.

Bethia followed Grissel into the kitchen where Megy, was tending the pot at the fire. She could smell the beef and onions likely in the base of the cauldron and knew there would be bags of beans, a few eggs and a dismembered chicken, separated by inserts of wood, all cooking together.

'What can we get that is special for Yule do you think?'

'We'll go tae the market tomorrow,' said Grissel, nodding at Megy who'd fallen silent before the great lady. 'If we offer enough coin then we'll get what we seek.'

A search among what small stores were held in the kitchen yielded preserved quince but little else in the way of delicacies. A visit to the apothecary produced comfit, which was normally used for relieving a cramp of the stomach, but Grissel said the sugar-coated seed could be used in sweetmeats. Next day the kitchen was rich with the aroma of boiling mutton to make blood puddings and dough boiled in a syrup of sugars for biscuits, which Grissel twisted into knots before leaving to bake on the hearth. The bread came back half burnt from the baxter's oven but there was so much food no one overly cared. Ephraim was able to join in the secret festivities and Bethia was glad he was released for a few days from his studies.

The aroma of cooking smells drew John's tenants in the tall house to his kitchen door, which led out the back stair. He agreed they should each be given a blood pudding and a gingerbread sweetmeat, saying, 'It'll no doubt be a welcome variation to oysters, porridge and kail.' Then added, as though excusing himself, ''Tis not permitted for them to eat what we do in any case. Our king recently reinforced the laws on food,' he explained to a curious Bethia.

'Which are?'

'Well, as a man of means, I am permitted four dishes upon the table. The king, of course, may have as many as he cares for. Although …' he brightened, '… with Logie here we can have more since his family sits among the lords o' Parliament.'

Grissel surpassed herself with Ephraim's assistance. Using marchpane purchased at considerable expense from a confectioner, they created a subtlety of great magnificence by sculpturing the paste into a tower house, which John praised saying it was not unlike the one in Pittenweem.

'Ach, it's far grander than yon wee ane in Pittenweem,' muttered Grissel.

There was ale to drink and Bethia and Gilbert had wine brought from France – and which she but not Grissel was lawfully permitted to imbibe – but Bethia missed the cool sherbet drink of Constantinople. In thinking of it she felt sadness drop over her like a heavy shroud, crossing her hands over her stomach to hold in the ache of longing for her family.

They managed no more than three days of Yule celebration. An elder of the kirk lived in John's house and, although he'd been quick enough to take the proffered pudding and biscuit, he trotted down to see the minister and report them for their excess – and for making a celebration in the first place when none was permitted.

'Aye, and a poor kind of Yule it was too,' said Grissel, 'with no dancing, no Lord of Misrule and no bean cake.'

'We could have had a bean cake,' said Bethia. 'I forgot.'

'Hah! What use is a bean in a cake if its finder cannie be king for the day?'

'Let's do it,' said Bethia, 'and thumb our noses at John's miserable sot of a tenant.'

But next day Grissel had a swollen red cheek and a fiery pain in the jaw and all was forgot in persuading her to have the tooth drawn.

Chapter Twenty-Four

Grissel's Alehouse

'Grissel has had an idea,' Bethia said, interrupting John as he wrote some notes in his commonplace book. She looked down at the fine handwriting, always surprised that John, for an impatient man, took such care over what he committed to paper.

'What now?' he said, dropping the quill on the board and folding his arms.

Bethia, aware Grissel was likely listening outside the door, chose her words with care. 'The chamber you have unoccupied is at street level.'

John stared at her. 'Stating the obvious, my dear sister. And I plan tae fill it before Grissel brings in ony mair waifs and strays.'

'You have one shop …'

He raised his hand to stop her. 'If you're going tae suggest we open another shop, I'd already considered it, but I need someone who willna compete wi' the haberdashery and fine linens and I dinna want anyone selling foodstuffs. We hae enough problems wi' rats from the market without gieing them something else tae feed upon.'

'Grissel suggests an alehouse,' said Bethia.

It was Bethia's turn to hold up her hand as John opened his mouth in rebuttal, but before either could speak Grissel burst in.

'Let me tell it,' she said in a great breathy rush. 'It is a guid place for an alehouse tucked up the close and sae near the top o' the High Street.'

'And how dae ye propose to fund it – as well as pay me the rent?'

'Weel … I was thinking, if you were our money lender …'

'What!'

'Hear her out,' said Bethia laying a gentle hand on John's arm and fascinated to know more herself.

'I'll buy ale wi' the money you lend me and repay you with interest.'

'And dinna forget the rent.'

'Aye, of course.'

John stood rubbing his chin and gazing at the window. 'But I don't need aybody in the middle. I could dae it all myself.'

Bethia snorted. 'You, a burgher of Edinburgh, are going to spend your nights – and possibly days – serving in a tavern?'

'Dinna be daft. The lassies can do that and I'll just pay them a fair wage.'

Grissel flushed and her whole body drooped.

'John!' said Bethia.

He grinned. ''Tis fine. If Grissel does well I can turn a fair profit as her patron. In any case, afore we can do anything, I maun get the permissions to open an alehouse. There should be no difficulty but I will take it to the next meeting of the toun council. And after that we'll discuss terms.'

Grissel, being Grissel, took action before the permissions came. She had not acted as assistant to Bethia for all the years Bethia supplied goods to the harem without developing an astute eye for business. Quietly, she cleaned and lime-washed the dark hole that was to be the alehouse, and demanded Ephraim's assistance when there was somewhere she couldn't reach.

'The chimney needs cleaning,' she said to Bethia. 'A bird's nest has fallen in and is blocking it.' But instead of paying the sweep she sent the two wee laddies, who had returned and were again receiving regular supplies from the kitchen, to climb up and clear it.

She scoured all the dishes and drinking vessels that she purchased with a handful of straw and a sprinkle of potash, rinsing them several times in boiling water, and Bethia thought this would be the cleanest drinking place in Edinburgh, if not the whole of Scotland – but then Grissel had been trained thus by her mother Agnes, from a young age.

By the time John came home waving the paper on which it was inscribed that one John Seton Esq. had the permission of the Burgh Council of Edinburgh to open an alehouse, Grissel had her wee bothy near ready to go.

'We will sell wine as well as ale and beer,' she said.

'You are seeking wealthy customers then?' said John.

'Aye,' said Grissel, as though that should have been obvious. 'I want a nice sort of person and not a lot of drunkards. I'm no running a tippling hoose, and since you are a burgher we may sell wine.'

'Drunkards are good for business and can be any sort of person,' said John, but Grissel was not convinced.

She was a comfortably-off woman having never married, had worked in service all her life and, as well as saving her wages, had made considerable sums supplying goods to the servants in the harem who, like their mistresses, were not permitted to leave its narrow confines.

She purchased the stools and low tables, and had a counter built. She also spent near five pounds on ale, being sure to buy from a woman because everyone knew they were the better brewers, but left the purchase of wine to John.

'They rich merchants will nay sell to the likes o' me,' she said, 'and if they did are likely to overcharge.'

Bethia could see John was quietly impressed by Grissel's enterprise. 'I think she'll turn me a nice profit,' he said. 'And because we are near the top o' the High Street we can charge mair. Less smell and more salubrious up this end,' he added in explanation, although Bethia needed none.

Megy too was beside herself with excitement. On a windy January day the doors were opened and John and Gilbert were their first customers.

'Now can we return to Fife?' said Gilbert when he went upstairs to report to Bethia that all was as it should be within Grissel's new domain.

She smiled, touching him lightly on the arm, saying, 'I thank you for your patience. We will leave for Leith as soon as the winds are in our favour.' She did not add that John thought she had now been away from Pittenweem for long enough for any talk of wise women and fairies to have died down.

But on the morrow the winds where whipping around corners, down closes and shaking the tall wooden staircases by which people climbed the many stories to enter their tenement homes. So instead of departing, they went to the kirk, passing through the stinking narrow passageway between the rows of Luckenbooths to reach its doorway.

Bethia sat with John on one side and Ephraim on the other, while Grissel sat behind with Megy, and Gilbert with the family with which he was lodging. She twisted in her seat trying again to work out why St Giles always looked smaller than she remembered from her youth.

'Yes, it is smaller,' said John in answer to her whispered question. 'The south corner has been subdivided into a meeting place and tolbooth for the burghers. The old tolbooth was near to collapse and no one seemed to care enough to make repairs, even when

Queen Mary commanded it during her brief reign.'

The minister climbed the pulpit to give his sermon while John whispered that the prisoners who'd previously been held in the tolbooth were now kept in an attic above the church nave. Bethia thought this most peculiar and wondered if they could hear the minister from up there.

The sermon was long, as inevitably the minister had much to say. Bethia glanced at Ephraim and saw he was near to dozing off, and John, on her other side, looked like to follow. She gave each a dig in the ribs. Her legs twitched and her knees hurt. She leant forward to rub them until John elbowed her. She bent her head and clasped her hands as the minister said a long prayer. The back of her exposed neck felt damp and, reaching a hand around to rub it, she felt another droplet fall. She lifted her head and gazed up at the roof above, blinking as water hit her in the eye. John nudged her. She ignored him, sliding along the seat and pushing against Ephraim on her other side to make space, and he near fell off the end of the pew. There was a pause while the minister stared at them, and half the congregation opened their eyes to see who was disturbing a solemn moment when all attention should be on communion with God.

John was furious when they left the church and strode ahead up the sloping street on cobbles slippery from rain. Bethia held the pomander close to her nose to block out at least some of the noxious smells which pervaded the whole city and carried sickness to every corner. She clutched her cloak, for it was growing colder by the moment, and hurried after him.

He turned and glared at her. 'Must ye ay mak sich a spectacle of yourself so that all will know the grand lady come from Turkland is among them? In showing yourself up, people are likely to wonder about your faith regardless of who your brothers are. I dinna want some business contact to be choosing to gang elsewhere

177

because there is ony doubt about which faith we adhere to.'

He strode on, but John's tempers had always been of short duration, and he could usually be easily wheedled out of them. By the time they'd climbed the worn stone stairs to his rooms all seemed to be forgiven.

'Where is Ephraim?' John asked when they were divested of cloaks and bonnets.

'He saw a friend, I think.' She had assumed Ephraim was following but was not about to again stoke John's irritability by saying so.

'He makes friends with ease that lad,'

'Like his Uncle John.'

Bethia could see the vexation drain out of John like removing the bung from a cask of ale. 'Why is the roof of our once glorious St Giles leaking?' she asked as they sat down to eat.

'It is remarkable how long you were away and how many perilous events you are unaware of.' John leaned back in his chair and wiped his greasy beard with the towel draped over his shoulder for that purpose, while Bethia wiped her hands on her own towel. He belched and Bethia flinched. 'You have become ower fastidious, sister. Does the sultan no relieve the pressure of wind in his thraw?'

'The palace is a place of silence where communication is frequently by hand signals. Such a sound would be considered an insult to the sultan, uncouth in the extreme, and likely lead to the maker's instant removal, if not early demise.'

'Aye, well I'll remember that should I ever happen to find myself in the august company of a sultan.'

'But what of St Giles? What are these many perilous events I have been fortunate to miss – although I may say we had plenty of our own. The harem is full of intrigue and one of the most perilous places I've ever found myself to be.'

'But it did make you a wealthy woman.'

She inclined her head. 'That, I cannot deny. The *kira*, as supplier of goods to the harem, is in a most fortunate position on the one hand.' She stretched her hand out palm upwards. 'But on the other,' she extended her left-hand palm downwards, 'we are vulnerable. The sultan's favourites want information, and if you do not bring it then they will discard you for another.'

'How did you retain your position for so long?'

'I can tell you but only under pain of death should you reveal it to anyone.'

'Hah!' said John pushing his chair away and standing up. Bethia flinched as it screeched over the floorboards.

'But how did you stay in favour?'

'By having a son who was a skilled medic who doctored many of the most important people in the palace.'

'Jacob, the Moslem?'

Bethia nodded, although she did not care for this way of describing her second son.

'And by having a daughter-in-law with the sweetest nature who the women of the harem could not but love.'

'Ah, I can see you had it sewed up tight as a blood pudding.'

Bethia waggled her finger. 'And most important of all, a servant who talked with every other servant she met and was known to all within the Grand Bazaar.'

John let out a burst of laughter. 'Grissel! I should hae kent she'd be down the middle of awthing.'

'She was, and is, invaluable and I would not interrupt your interrogation nor your pleasure in it but what of St Giles's roof? Why are there holes in it? It's bad enough all the windows are without their once beautiful coloured glass, making it a cold, draughty place, but why must we sit with water dripping on our heads whenever it rains – which is a constant here?'

'Ah weel, you must hold William Kirkcaldy of Grange

179

to account for that.'

Bethia went quiet for a moment. 'I well remember him. He was the calm and considered one during the siege in St Andrews. Will said Kirkcaldy didn't want Cardinal Beaton killed in that savage manner but to be given a lawful trial. Indeed, Kirkcaldy was the one who insisted Will got into the deep pit to hide with me,' she shuddered, 'when I was too terrified to climb down myself. But what does he have to do with St Giles's roof?'

''Tis where he made his last stand against the king's men. Of course, King James was naught but a bairn, but Kirkcaldy, in a remarkable about-turn, had pledged his support to Mary, Queen of Scots.'

'Had he reverted to Catholicism?'

John pursed his lips. 'I know not. I think he was a wee bit o' a romantic perhaps.'

'But was Mary not a prisoner of the queen of England by then?'

'Aye, but you know these nobles, forever at one another's throats. So Kirkcaldy found himself again besieged and made a last stand in St Giles. They knocked holes in the roof to fire on the hordes below who were aided by troops sent by England – for Elizabeth did not want Mary to again be queen of Scotland. In the end they starved them out.'

'Not so many rats to eat in St Giles as there were in the castle,' said Bethia.

'You ate rats in St Andrews Castle?'

'We did. Quite the delicacy, especially when you have nothing else. But what happened to Kirkcaldy once they forced him out?'

'They hung him,' said John.

Bethia was silent, for there was nothing else to say. She put her hand to her neck but of course there was no crucifix there.

A few days later, and finally on their way back to Fife, Bethia asked Gilbert about Kirkcaldy of Grange.

'You fought against him at St Andrews and yet he turns coat and becomes Mary's supporter.'

'I have nothing but respect for William Kirkcaldy of Grange. He was true to his heart always. A most honourable man.'

'As are you,' Bethia said shyly.

He looked her full in the face. 'I try to be,' he said.

With which she could not but concur.

Chapter Twenty-Five

Companionship

Bethia felt in a strange limbo, that uncertain waiting chamber that was not recognised by a Calvinist Scotland where the faithful went from death either to a preordained heaven, or hell. It was over a year since she'd returned to her ane country and slowly she'd grown accustomed to how her life had changed. There were even aspects of her twice-weekly attendance at the kirk she found uplifting – although she might not feel so if Will were not their minister. His sermons provoked, challenged and made a connection with God she had not experienced before. It was no wonder people were still flowing in from far and wide to listen to him. The folk of Pittenweem frequently complained their church was overfull of strangers and yet there was also an element of pride that their minister should be so extolled.

Father was happy as long as Bethia was by his side and content if she left him, but only to go to Balcarrow. He spoke of Grissel frequently to anyone who would listen, proud of the success John said she was making of her new business.

Bethia visited Balcarrow regularly to see Elspeth. There she could have her confession heard by the priest and attend Mass on occasion. Father Richard was a gentle soul in constant fear of discovery. Bethia was comforted by his presence and by the connection she was again able to make with God and the Virgin through him. She was also aware of the risks Gilbert took by concealing the priest and that the priest took by his very existence. Elspeth said that only a few on the estate knew of Father Richard. Those were the people who cleaved to the old faith and they would not disclose his presence to anyone. But it took only one disaffected tenant or one loose tongue.

'Where does Gilbert keep him hid?' Bethia asked.

But Elspeth did not know, nor did she want to know. 'Most likely there will be a priest's hole carved out between floors,' she said when Bethia persisted in wondering.

'Well I am glad he is here,' said Bethia, 'and will pray each day that he continues to bring us comfort – and avoids discovery.'

'The king will not trouble about it as long as Master Logie remains discreet,' said Elspeth.

Invariably Bethia would meet Gilbert out walking with his dogs during her visits and speak with him – although, since the gift of the friendship ring, she no longer sought him out. Holdfast came to greet her each time and even went so far as to lean gently against her legs, careful not to overbalance her. The terrier, however, still gave short, unfriendly barks and eyed her with suspicion much like Gilbert's daughter. Bethia had given up any attempt to make friends with Isobel. It was a hopeless case, but the elder daughter Helen, who all had said was a harridan, Bethia found to be welcoming when they'd finally met. Far more welcoming than her sister.

One day Isobel made the journey to Pittenweem unattended by Gilbert. Bethia, fetched from Will's home where she and Cecy had been engaged in a most enjoyable blether, for once without Nannis in attendance, came reluctantly.

Isobel rose when Bethia hurried into the chamber, for

a small dart of fear had worried at her. Perhaps Gilbert was unwell or Father Richard had been discovered.

Isobel dipped the smallest of curtsies.

The chamber was empty for once since Father was taking a nap and Violet, surrounded by small children and busy about the kitchens, evinced a reluctance to join them which Bethia did not at all blame her for.

'Is all well at Balcarrow?' said Bethia breathlessly.

'Aye,' said Isobel, reseating herself and regarding Bethia as though she was some curious object.

'Although there is one thing amiss, and it is why I have come to speak with you,' said Isobel stiffly.

Bethia sat upright.

'My father is the best man I know.'

'Even better than Alexander of Anstruther?' said Bethia, and then covered her mouth with her hand. She had not meant to speak her thoughts aloud.

Isobel leant forward as though Bethia hadn't spoken. 'I do *not* know what your intentions are towards my father but I would ask you not cause him any further hurt.' She raised her hand when Bethia was about to speak. 'I once asked him why he waited so long to marry. He said there had been a lass he cared very much for who had married someone else and it took him a long time to recover. It was you was it not?' She sat upright staring at Bethia.

Bethia swallowed. She could dissemble – how should *she* know of the women Gilbert of Logie had loved? After some uncomfortable moments while Isobel waited, clearly determined she would have an answer, Bethia spoke.

'Your father has always shown concern for my well-being.'

'Humph!' muttered Isobel.

'It is true that there was a time when he sought to marry me, but that was forty years ago.' Bethia paused, remembering when Gilbert had come to Antwerp and, concerned for her vulnerability as the wife of a Converso, had proposed she return to Scotland with him. 'We are the best of friends but that is all.'

Isobel looked sceptical.

'See,' said Bethia, realising she had proof. She tugged the ring off her forefinger and stood up to pass it to Isobel. 'This is the ring he recently gave me.'

Isobel took it. 'This is a poesy ring,' she said, 'the gift of which is about more than simple friendship.'

'Read the inscription.'

Isobel held the ring up to the light twisting it in her hand. Her face coloured as she read. 'I thought you would cause him pain once more,' she said, passing the ring back to Bethia. 'But it seems all he seeks from you *is* friendship.'

'Yes,' said Bethia simply, and was surprised by how sad she felt in acknowledging the nature of Gilbert's connection to her. 'Whatever I may desire, your father has made his intention clear. We are to be no more than friends.'

Isobel stared at her while Bethia tried to swallow the painful lump in her throat.

'Alexander wants to marry me and Father has encouraged it,' Isobel said suddenly.

Bethia blinked, surprised to be the recipient of Isobel's confidence. 'He will be a fine husband,' she said.

Isobel nodded slowly and rose to leave. They said their farewells on the doorstep and Isobel went to where the groom stood ready to assist her onto the horse.

'You have not sought my advice, Isobel, but I would say this to you – good men are not easily come by,' Bethia called to her.

There was a ghost of a smile from Isobel, now astride her horse. 'Please call me Izzy,' she said, as she clicked her heels to set the animal in motion.

And so it was that when Cecy brought the news that Alexander of Anstruther had at last prevailed and was to take Isobel Logie as his wife, Bethia was not surprised. She was invited to the feast to celebrate their nuptials but Father was sick and she did not go.

'You willna leave me lass,' he said, weakly.

'I am here, Father.'

'No,' he gripped her hand with surprising strength for one who could barely lift his head from the bolster to drink. 'You will stay in Scotland till I am gone.'

'But Father …'

'Swear it,' he said gruffly then his hand fell away.

She stared at him while Violet fussed with a potion which she insisted Father drink.

He sipped it reluctantly, clearly struggling not to vomit.

'What did you give him?' whispered Bethia.

'A mix o' powdered almonds, the brain o' a chicken and the top o' the milk wi' a sprinkling of sugar,' mumbled Violet. ''Tis a braw broth for a sick auld man.'

'He is not so very sick, is he?' she asked Violet as they slipped from the chamber.

'I hae seen him much sicker and still make a full recovery,' said Violet, raising her eyes heavenwards.

Father attempted to extract a promise from Bethia again the next day.

'I can see you are better, Father, so do not try those tactics on me.'

'Hah!' he said. 'I will die and then you'll be sorry, if you have gone awa and left me.'

'I will not be sorry, for Grissel can very well substitute for me,' she said tartly.

'Oh, ma heid,' groaned Father. 'Fetch Violet, for she at least is my good daughter who will not leave me for Constantinople, or Edinburgh.'

'You are clearly much recovered,' said Bethia. 'I will fetch Violet and hope you do realise how fortunate you are to have her.'

But as February held them in its freezing grip and Bethia was unable to make the journey to Balcarrow, and with Ephraim, and Grissel, in Edinburgh, she found herself surprisingly lonely. She had Cecy and Violet, of course, but both were busy women around whom their households rotated like the sun around the earth – or the other way if what that fellow Copernicus claimed was to be believed.

She thought on the letter which had reached her from Samuel, before the winter storms set in. He wrote they were well, trade was good, and of how they missed her and Ephraim.

> *But do not think to return, Mama. It is not safe with the Spanish and their vast Armada patrolling the seas. 'Tis better if you stay in Scotland and one day I will make the journey to visit and meet my many Scottish relatives. And do not fear Ephraim will leave. He knows his duty and I believe him to be content in that far country of the north, despite the wind and rain which he claims to be unceasing.*

Bethia had held the letter to her breast when first she read it, and had perused it many times since. Once she had got past the pain, which was like a knife to the heart, she knew her son to be wise – and that he was giving his permission for her to stay. And yet she didn't know if she could stay here – but she did not belong in Constantinople either. It was in this moment of vacillation and weakness that Father caught her and finally extracted a promise that she would not leave while he still had breath.

As soon as there was a brief cessation in the strong northerly wind she went to Balcarrow. It was a rare calm and still day, unusually warm for the season, and she found Gilbert in the new enlarged herb garden, discussing the layout with the gardener. He looked pleased to see her and invited her to sit down on the bench which he'd recently had installed.

'We are sheltered here,' he said, 'and it is a pleasure to be outdoors after the weather we've recently endured.'

Bethia did not dally but told Gilbert straight away of what Samuel had written.

'I do not understand,' Gilbert said. 'Is he advising that you do not return, ever?'

Bethia sighed. 'There is a difficulty, for I do not belong anywhere. In Galata I am a Catholic among Jews. They are not unkind but always I am on the periphery. And the Levantines, which is what the Turks named us Latin Catholics, do not have the same protection as other religious groups.'

Gilbert looked confused.

'The Turks allow certain faiths, like the Orthodox Christians and Jews, to follow their beliefs in a way we could not begin to imagine in Scotland, or indeed the rest of Europe.' Bethia sighed. 'We could learn from them.'

Gilbert's eyes grew large but then he slowly nodded his head. 'It would be remarkable were we Catholics permitted to practise freely in Scotland but I cannot ever see that happening. I suppose always there is the fear we may try to reinstate Catholicism as the religion of Scotland.'

'Yes,' said Bethia batting away a fly which was dancing most insistently, and unseasonably, around her head. 'In Turkland, the various religions tolerated are all small groups in comparison to the Mussulmen.'

'But I do not understand. If you are permitted to worship as you please, what is this protection you are lacking?'

'It was the legal recognition that we're without. There's a chief rabbi for the Jews who consults with the sultan's officials when needful, but there was no such equivalent for Latin Catholics. It may be because

Catholics are a small and disparate group from many countries and don't share a common language, but it meant we didn't have the administrative and political structures that the other faiths did. Our only connection was our religion. There is a place of worship I attended, where mostly French diplomats and merchants went – and France has a treaty with the sultan allowing *them* certain privileges.'

'And did that not afford you protection too?'

'It did, while Scotland was Catholic and the Auld Alliance with France held sway, but now our countries have turned their backs on one another.'

'And were you in danger?'

'I was an anomaly,' she said slowly.

'What do you mean?'

'I did not fit anywhere, and I know it was awkward for my sons – well two of them – to be staunch members of the Sephardi community with a mother who is a Catholic.'

'And what of your third son?'

'Oh, he converted to Islam fifteen years ago.' She laughed and was aware how forced it sounded – had forgot she had never told Gilbert of Jacob's choice.

Gilbert looked truly horrified. 'And your husband permitted it?'

'He was made unhappy, but how could he stand in Jacob's way, when he himself had converted? And it is not unknown for Jews to do so. It makes for an easier life to belong in that way, although that was not why Jacob did it. He felt a true calling.'

'But … but …' Gilbert spluttered, 'what of your son's eternal soul?'

'Jacob is a kind and loyal man. And that, I pray, will assure his place in heaven.'

Gilbert sat in silence staring at his hands while the terrier settled across his feet and Holdfast gazed up at him thoughtfully.

189

'What will you do?' he said, his voice thick in the heavy silence which lay between them.

'I do not know,' she said slowly. And then with forced gaiety, 'Perhaps I should marry?'

He looked at her gravely. 'Why?'

She drew her head back. 'Protection?'

'You have your brothers and Ephraim for that.'

Bethia contained a sigh. 'For companionship.'

'My dogs are my companions,' Gilbert said. 'Perhaps you should get a dog.'

After a moment Bethia rose, dipped her head without meeting his eye and made her way out of the gardens, staggered as she passed through the gate and caught onto it to right herself. She found the carter at his leisure in the kitchens, directed that she was ready to return home and left without even a farewell to Elspeth.

Chapter Twenty-Six

Accused

This was the time of day that Will worked on his sermons, a rare moment of quiet in a busy, noisy household as the grandchildren were all at their lessons. He was deep in the Scriptures when John burst in.

'A message came from Grissel and we hae to go to Edinburgh.'

Will stared up at him. 'What are you blethering about?'

'There's nae time to lose. They've taken young Ephraim.'

'Who has taken him?'

'He's in the tolbooth accused of secret Judaising.'

Will dropped his Bible, Matthew verse one and the generation of Jesus Christ, the son of David, the son of Abraham forgotten. He leapt to his feet and tripped over a stool.

John steadied him. 'Mind how ye go, yer nay as young as ye were.'

Will ignored him, calling for Cecy.

They spoke together in rapid French. Will could see John had caught the gist, which was he was leaving for Edinburgh now, and would she pack him a small bag while he gathered the papers he wanted. Cecy left the room, her usual tranquillity undisturbed, and returned quickly with a satchel and a walking stick.

'I don't need that,' said Will taking the bag and waving the stick away, but she silently held it out to him until, with a whuff of exasperation, he took it.

'We'll go from Burntisland?' asked Will.

'Aye, all the big boats are out at the fishing. If we take Andersoun's wee crear it'll tak us about four hours tae sail tae Burntisland. We can rest overnight and catch the early morning ferry at high tide.'

'What about Bethia? She will most certainly want to come.'

''Tis better if she does not,' said John firmly. 'She's only a reminder o' the strange and exotic country of the Turks from which Ephraim hails, whereas we maun present ourselves as the esteemed preacher of the true religion wi' his brother the merchant.'

'Aye, you're right, but knowing our sister she will take some persuading.'

But Bethia surprised them both by concurring with their assessment, albeit reluctantly, and they were soon making for Burntisland, leaving their anxious sister and equally worried father behind.

That night, as the brothers sat together over a jug of surprisingly good ale, Will had more conversation with John than he'd had these past twenty-odd years.

'Your no sich a dour bugger as ye used to be,' said John after they had laughed together over Father's stories – for if Father had once been boastful of his sons' achievements, he'd a new subject in his daughter and especially of her meeting with the sultan. A tale, which grew by the telling, of how Bethia had spoken to Suleiman and he had been most curious to learn of the Christian faith, so much so he was near to converting.

'Hah, you're the dour one these days,' said Will. 'It's hard to see the wild young devil you used to be in the sober, rich merchant you've become.'

John leaned back on his stool and clasped his hands

behind his head, displaying the patches of sweat beneath his oxters. 'Calvin himself says wealth should be used to generate wealth.'

'I think *that* is an oversimplification.'

'Well he certainly had no issue with lending money and charging interest, which is a' contrary to the papist obsession wi' usury.'

'You are not wrong,' said Will and caught the small smile of satisfaction that flickered across John's face. 'But that was about helping destitute refugees who'd come to Geneva to restart the businesses they had to leave behind when they were forced to flee.'

'*And if ye lend to them of whom ye hope to receive, what thanks shall ye have? For even sinners lend to sinners to receive the like,*' said John.

He nudged Will, whose mouth had fallen open. 'See, I ken mair than you think.'

'I think you are being selective in your quotation. Calvin also said *let us take heed that wealth may not lie heavy upon us and become an obstruction in the way to the Kingdom of Heaven.* He thought it essential that we show charity to those who find themselves in poverty through no fault of their own and that we should give succour to them.'

John dropped his arms and leant forward. 'Since our beloved sister, or perhaps I should say sisters, returned, I am never done *giving succour*. I find it remarkable the Turks hae any wealth left, for according to Grissel they Moslems are constantly giving, and especially during yon big festival they have.'

Will grinned. 'Aye, I heard of the offering up of a chamber to the destitute in Edinburgh.'

'Let us hope it will gain me entry tae the Kingdom of Heaven, for I've practised mair generosity since Bethia and Grissel returned than I have in my whole life before.'

The smile faded from Will's face, for he did not consider this a matter for levity. 'Then it is good they have shown you the path.'

'Was Calvin truly sae generous himself? He no doubt had a fine home and a good income?' said John.

'You are quite wrong. Calvin's house was small, his furniture borrowed from the city council, and he refused any increase in what was a small stipend for such heavy responsibilities.'

'I stand corrected,' said John quietly, and Will greatly appreciated his brother's willingness to admit he was wrong.

'But I am then surprised by the size o' manse that James Melville is building – it's bigger than ma hoose!' John said indignantly.

Will inclined his head and considered what John had said. Perhaps Melville was being ower grand.

There was silence, not with the heaviness of anger but a quiet reflection.

'Diligence, discipline and frugality,' said John. 'They are the way tae a life weel spent.'

'And charity.'

'And charity. We'll never be allowed to forget that with Bethia and Grissel ay snapping at our heels.'

They moved on to talk of John's newest business aspirations and how eager Symon was to take up the reins. 'He's a determined lad,' said John, speaking with an exasperated tone which did not quite mask the hint of pride. 'And although I was angry wi' him for forcing a marriage to yon Kristene, I think t'will be the making o' him. She's a sound lass.'

Will spoke of his favourite grandson, Donald, and his hopes that Donald would follow him into the ministry. 'For he is a most studious and God-fearing lad.'

'Better to put him to the study of law,' said John. 'It would be maist useful to have a lawyer in the family.'

Will shook his head. 'Scotland needs ministers more than lawyers,' he said abruptly.

'I swear the lawyers are making mair money than we merchants, and increasingly they're inveigling themselves into positions o' power which used to be held by the clerics in the bad old papist days. They're everywhere in Edinburgh. I wanted Symon to study law, but he's no a bookish lad – much like myself.'

Will grinned.

Then they grew solemn, thinking of what could be done to aid Ephraim. Will said that once they'd visited Ephraim, they must speak with the college principal in Edinburgh, under whose tutelage Ephraim was.

'Robert Rollock is an able fellow who has taken on a vital task in training more ministers. There are many parishes who have to share a minister, and use the services of a reader when a minister is not available, which are in desperate need of sound leadership.'

They left the walled town of Burntisland early the next morning. Soon they were passing Inchcolm Island, where much of its deserted abbey still stood thanks to its inaccessibility to those pillagers of stone, tranquil against the dazzle of the rising sun. Looking back, Will watched as the hills of the Fife hinterland grew smaller and sent up a prayer of thanks that he lived in such a beautiful, and mostly tranquil, place.

They were in Edinburgh by afternoon and quickly discovered Ephraim was being held in a cell high up in St Giles Church. Will was not comfortable with the House of God being put to such a use, nor with the instruments of punishments outside it constraining the narrow High Street even further. Today there was a man in the pillory, iron collar around his neck, while a few bairns threw stones at him in a desultory manner.

'Get oot o' it,' John shouted, and they ran away. 'At least the hangings aren't held here,' he said to Will as they passed through the doorway.

'That is something to be thankful for,' Will muttered.

They were led up the steep turnpike by the jailer, who

tugged on his forelock when he saw the minister. Given how little hair the fellow had, Will did not consider it altogether a wise move.

They found Ephraim pale and shivering. 'I do *not* understand why I am being incarcerated,' he said, biting on his lower lip and clenching his fists in a vain attempt to stop the shaking.

John took one look at the cell, which contained nothing but a bucket and a pile of verminous-looking straw, and commanded the jailer to take him to the fellow in charge at once. He jumped to attention, and locking Will in the cell with Ephraim, set off back down the spiral stairs following hard on John's heels.

'Where has Uncle John gone?' said Ephraim plaintively.

'To insist you are moved to a cell which at least contains a bed,' said Will, breathing through his mouth, for the smell within this confined space had him close to vomiting. 'But what did you do? You must have done something to bring suspicion down upon you.' Will went to lean against the rough stone wall and then as quickly stood up, for it was damp and slimy.

Ephraim spread his hands wide. 'I swear, Uncle, I do not know.'

'What did you say to people about your background?'

'Nothing more than what I had agreed with Nonna.'

'And what was that?'

'That I am her grandson accompanying her to Scotland, who will attend university while I am here. It is what Uncle John advised, and given both he and you are well-known pillars of the Church, we thought it would be sufficient.'

Will grunted. 'I'm not sure I would describe my brother as a pillar of the Kirk, more as someone who does the minimum necessary to keep the presbytery at bay. But tell me,' Will lowered his voice, 'you are circumcised, I assume?'

'Of course.'

'There is no *of course* about it.'

'Jesus Christ was circumcised.'

Will's eyes widened at the abruptness of Ephraim's speech but he let it pass. 'Has anyone had sight of you?'

Ephraim blinked, and even on his dark skin, the flush was visible. He shook his head. 'I do not think so. My ablutions are a private matter.'

Will nodded. 'And women?'

Ephraim's mouth dropped open. 'Uncle, I can assure you I have led a blameless life since, and before, I arrived in Scotland …' he hesitated, '… apart from my attempt to fly.'

Will could not help but smile at the response.

Another jailer appeared at the cell door, the long strands of hair which had been smoothed over his head dangling limply to one side revealing his shiny bald pate. 'I am sorry, Meenister, but you must leave now.'

Will stooped and passed back through the doorway. He stood at the other side and reached out to clasp Ephraim's hand. 'I will go now and see your college principal. He is a sound young man and I am certain will be able to assist,' he said with a confidence he didn't feel – for why had Rollock done nothing so far?

'Thank you,' said Ephraim, the quiver in his voice audible.

'My nephew is to be moved,' he said sternly to the guard.

'Aye, your worship, he is.'

'We'll have you released soon, son. Stay strong.' Will went down the stairs swift as his stiff old legs would go, while his heart smote him to leave the poor lad in this place.

Chapter Twenty-Seven

Robert Rollock

John was waiting outside St Giles. 'I hae arranged a better cell and regular food,' he said. 'We should hae sent him to St Andrews University after all, but Grissel was watching oe'r him, and not much usually gets passed her. And he has friends among the students including Kintour's son. Ye ken, Kintour,' he said when Will looked blank. 'I do much business wi' him.'

'Then I will to see Robert Rollock, if you can glean what you can from this Kintour.'

John nodded, turned on his heel and left.

Will had heard Robert Rollock preach at St Giles. Although he was not an ordained minister, he was a young man of piety, sound doctrine and a breadth of knowledge which had had him appointed as teacher to the newly formed Tounis College. Edinburgh had lagged far behind in forming a university. The university at St Andrews had been in place for over a hundred and fifty years and both Glasgow and Aberdeen for near one hundred years before Edinburgh followed suit. Will had been puzzled why it was so long delayed and why the town council, concerned it would fail, had left Rollock as its sole teacher for the first three years. It was a lot to guide ninety young lads through a four-year curriculum to gain a master of arts, unsupported. But finally the good burghers had confidence that Edinburgh's town college would survive and had appointed Rollock as its first principal, permitting him in turn to appoint regents to lighten his heavy teaching burden.

Will walked down the noisome close to the college, skirting a group of small children engaged in rambunctious play and was near knocked into the gutter by two strapping lads careening wildly down the steep slope one chasing after the other.

'Take care, ye pillicocks,' he roared, startling a woman who was leaning out her window several stories up to hang washing on the line stretched across the close so much so that the garment she was pegging out slipped from her fingers and landed at his feet.

'Och no, ma petticoat,' she shrieked.

Will stood guard till the woman came rushing out of the doorway, for the bairns had stopped their play and were eyeing the linen with interest. It would be a happy mother who so acquired such a garment for free.

'Thankee, my lord,' she said, putting her hands to her flushed cheeks to cool them.

He thought to correct her, to say that he was no lord, only a servant to the true Lord. Instead, he inclined his head and carried on, taking care not to slip on the slimy cobbles and wishing he'd brought the walking stick Cecy had pressed upon him.

The college was still in its temporary accommodation in the duke's lodge by the high Flodden Wall and close to the theatre in the Cowgate, which the king was fond of attending – much to the disapproval of the Kirk. However, the city fathers were clearly now confident this new university would survive since a site had recently been acquired at St Mary's in the Fields and building work begun.

Robert Rollock was teaching, Will was told, but would soon return if the minister would care to wait in Rollock's chamber. He was offered some ale but declined it, pleased to see Rollock had a respectful servant, but then Will had heard the stipend was forty pounds per annum – a sum which would allow for a comfortable living.

Rollock appeared soon after and seemed genuinely pleased to find Will in his small offices.

'Reverend Seton, is it not?' he said, before Will could introduce himself.

Will bowed and Rollock did so in return.

'Sit down, sit down,' Rollock said, gesturing to the tall chair behind his desk.

Will was gratified to be the recipient of such courtesy, which was not always the case. He found the disrespect with which the young often treated their elders surprising, something that would never have been tolerated when he was a lad. Not that Rollock was a lad, he must be nigh on thirty years old. Will studied him. He was a small man with dark close-cropped hair and a long but neatly trimmed beard. The sides of his face were clean-shaven and his cheeks rosy as a young girl's. But, as Rollock moved so the light pushing through the mottled window glass shone on him, the rosiness was revealed to be an angry rash. Rollock smoothed his cheeks and Will was embarrassed to be caught staring.

'Does it pain you?' he said softly.

'Only if I forget to put on the lotion which the apothecary makes up for me.'

There was silence then and Will gazed at the floor as he thought how to continue a conversation begun on an intrusive note.

'I recently enjoyed a sermon you gave at St Giles,' he said.

A slow smile spread across Rollock's rosy face. 'And I yours.'

'You have been to the kirk at Pittenweem?' Will was surprised Rollock had not made himself known if that were so.

'No, this was a number of years ago at Holy Trinity in St Andrews.'

'Oh aye, you must hae been naught but a laddie.'

'I think I may have been made regent by then, but in any case, during my time at St Andrews you were much talked of.'

There was a kind of awe in Rollock's voice which had Will shifting uncomfortably in the oak chair – not so much because he didn't like it, more because he did. Wise words from Proverbs went through his head and he adjured himself to be mindful of them: *When pride cometh, then cometh shame: but with the lowly is wisdom.*

'We have begun the teaching of divinity,' said Rollock. ''Tis a pity you do not live here for I could have drawn on your experience. Classes from you would be valuable to our earnest young men.'

Will was grateful the conversation had taken this turn, for he had been wondering how to introduce Ephraim into it.

'My nephew is among your students.'

'Oh!' said Rollock leaning forward on his stool. 'I was unaware of that. It is good he came here instead of to St Andrews as might have been expected. He's not called Seton, else I'm sure I would have noticed him in the lists.'

'He is my sister's grandson. His name is de Lange, Ephraim de Lange.' Will clasped his hands tightly together watching Rollock's reaction to Ephraim's name.

Rollock clapped his hands together. 'I know him. His Hebrew is excellent, better than his Latin by far. James Melville recommended him but I did not understand he was your nephew. His skills in Oriental languages could be of great use to us.' He clapped his hands on his knees this time. 'Very great use indeed. I was considering offering him a position as a tutor, for we are in desperate need of a teacher of Hebrew.'

'I am gratified to hear this,' said Will. 'But there is a difficulty which I hope you can help me resolve – one which I thought you might have foreknowledge of.'

Rollock shook his head. 'I am not aware of any difficulties regarding your nephew. If it was some of the other lads then perhaps, but my information is he is a studious enough fellow – and well liked.

'Ephraim is being held in the tolbooth. He is accused of proselytising,' said Will bluntly.

'What! Just because the lad knows his Hebrew well?' Rollock leapt to his feet. 'I will go there at once.'

Will held up his hand. 'Unfortunately, the case is not straightforward. Let me explain.'

Rollock sat down slowly, eyes fixed on Will.

Will fell silent, wishing he'd prepared more carefully, for he was not certain what to reveal and what it was better to keep concealed about Ephraim's family history. He studied his hands and picked out the dirt from beneath his fingernails.

'My sister's husband was a Converso from Antwerp,' he said slowly, still picking at his fingernails. Then was sorry he had begun there, for it implied Bethia was a papist, which was not at all helpful to Ephraim's situation. He lifted his head. 'De Lange is dead now and my sister has returned to her home in Scotland. Of course, she could not make such a journey unattended, nor would her sons have permitted it. Ephraim came with her to take the opportunity for study here in Scotland.'

Rollock's forehead wrinkled mightily and Will knew he was not explaining at all well. He was a fool and should've rehearsed this discussion with John before charging down to the college.

'So Ephraim is the grandson of a Converso, which makes him a … Catholic?' said Rollock slowly.

Will hesitated, but he had gone thus far and must trust to the innate goodness he sensed Rollock had. 'Well no. He was brought up as a Jew.'

'Ah,' said Rollock gently scratching the side of his

head. 'That would explain the depth of his knowledge of Hebrew – and the Old Testament. But what is the boy now – a Jew or a Christian?'

'He has taken instruction as a Christian.'

'And that is where his true faith lies?'

Again Will hesitated, but Ephraim had declared his intention to follow the Protestant faith and seemed serious about his devotions. 'I believe it to be so,' he said firmly. 'And I could not support his petition that he has been wrongfully imprisoned otherwise.'

'How long has he been held for?'

'Several days I believe.'

Rollock's eyes grew large. 'What I do not understand is why I am only hearing of this now, and from you? I find it difficult to believe that at least some of his friends were not aware of his incarceration. And even more difficult to understand why his regent did not inform me of it.'

Will opened his mouth to say that the more pressing matter was to secure Ephraim's release, but Rollock was before him and, leaping to his feet, said, 'Our first stop is the procurator. And I have full confidence he will authorise the lad's release. I cannot imagine how he might gainsay you, as a hero of the Reformation, supported by me, the principal of the Tounis College.'

He grinned at Will, who could not help but smile back.

The door opened and a young man's head appeared around it, eyes darting from Rollock to Will.

'Ah, Browne, I am going out on urgent business. There should be nothing of import for you to deal with while I'm away.'

'I have a class at the next bell,' said Browne, stepping into the room, where he stood rubbing the palm of his hand over his knuckle. 'Should I postpone it and make myself available to you?'

'No need.' Rollock went to go through the door which Browne held open. Halfway out he halted. 'Have you heard anything of young Ephraim de Lange?'

Watching, Will noticed how Browne's eyes slid away at the question.

'Nothing, Principal,' he said breathlessly. 'Only that he has failed to attend class for several days.'

'And did you ascertain why he had not attended?'

'Why no, Principal. If I was to chase up on all the lads who miss a day then I'd never be done.'

'I see,' said Rollock. 'I thought we kept better discipline than that. We'll discuss it further on my return.'

Browne blinked and bent his head, one hand still smoothing the knuckles of the other.

Rollock led the way out into the street, Will following. Neither spoke as they climbed the hill to the tolbooth, Will because he was made breathless and Rollock because he seemed deep in thought.

The procurator fiscal had the heartiness of a man of girth but was skinny as a spindle shaft.

'Ah Principal Rollock, 'tis good to see you. I have been meaning to invite you for a discussion about the teaching of law at our college but here you are before I could get to you. Good, good.' He shouted for his clerk to bring some of the claret. 'From France, you know – shipped by your brother,' he said nodding to Will. 'Ah, you are surprised. 'Tis my business to know what takes place within my city walls, so far as I am able.'

'You employ watchers!' said Will, and then could have clapped his hand over his mouth. It was the curse of old age, this unintentional speaking of one's thoughts aloud.

'Oh, no, no. Hardly,' said the fellow, laughing in what to Will seemed an overly hearty manner. 'Only concerned citizens.' He narrowed his eyes. 'But I assume you are here about the Jew, who I understand by some strange connection is related to you.'

Will opened his mouth but Rollock was quicker.

'I too am here about this matter, which closely concerns me, for not only is Ephraim de Lange a most studious and devout pupil, he is also to become my assistant in the teaching of Oriental languages. I cannot think why he has been so defamed and most earnestly beg you to release him.'

The procurator held his hands wide. 'This I cannot do, for we have a date for his hearing already set. And we have a credible witness who has evidence of de Lange's apostasy.'

'Please tell us who this witness is,' said Will, speaking softly so the anger would not show. 'I am certain he must be mistaken. I myself have examined the lad and will swear he is no relapser.'

The procurator sighed, long and loud. ''Tis unfortunate I did not have this testimony sooner for it might have been sufficient but, as I have said, the date is set for only a few days hence and we maun go ahead.'

Chapter Twenty-Eight

A Hanging

Bethia arrived in Edinburgh the next day, accompanied by Gilbert of Logie.

'I could not sit idly by. And Gilbert,' she looked gratefully towards him and he had the grace to flush when Will stared at him, 'offered to accompany me.'

And what good will this do, was what Will wanted to say, but somehow, adopting the gravity required of a minister of the Kirk, he restrained himself. But really, what good would it do to have a woman widely spoken of as *the Turkish lady* and who he was fairly certain was a secretly practising papist, and her paramour who he strongly suspected also cleaved to the Pope of Rome, here?

He realised Bethia and Logie were awaiting information and gave a slight shake of the head. 'Ephraim is held prisoner still. I have met with Robert Rollock and he will speak on Ephraim's behalf. It appears he thinks highly of the lad.'

'You sound surprised,' said Bethia sharply.

'It seems Ephraim has unexpected depths,' Will said, raising his eyebrows.

'And why should he not? Building a flying machine requires a degree of ingenuity and a deal of tenacity,' said Bethia.

Will could see a smile creeping across Logie's face,

which vanished when Will glared at them both.

'Tell us what is happening?' said Logie.

Will felt a surge of annoyance. Who was Logie to pitch up here unasked and start behaving in this lordly manner? He stared at the man, wanting to say *this is a family concern.* But honestly what was the matter with him?

Logie, perhaps realising he had come on too strong, spoke again. 'Your sister is most anxious.'

'Aye, I'm well aware of that,' said Will dryly. He softened his tone. 'As indeed am I. But we are hopeful all will soon be resolved. John has spoken with Lord Kintour, whose son attends the Tounis College with Ephraim. It seems Ephraim is as well liked here as he is in Pittenweem. His friends were concerned when the lad disappeared and raised it with their regent but he did not pass the information on to Principal Rollock, who was unaware of Ephraim's incarceration till I met with him.'

Bethia took her cloak off and sat down with a thud on the chair in John's cluttered chamber and Logie moved to stand behind her. 'But why was he taken?'

Will could not help but notice how Logie stuck to Bethia fast as a burr tangled in her clothing. Even now he was gazing upon her as though she might vanish if he glanced elsewhere. 'Lord Kintour's son was apparently baffled when he learned Ephraim was arrested. It is only thanks to Grissel and the contacts she inevitably made amongst all the watchmen, porters, street sellers and anyone else up for a blether and a joke that Ephraim's whereabouts were discovered so quickly after he went missing.' And, as he spoke, Grissel came bustling into the chamber, cloak and bonnet still on.

'Ah, there you are,' said Bethia. 'Now we shall get to the heart of the story.'

'Ach, paur laddie. I hae just been to tak him his midday meal,' said Grissel, divesting herself of her outdoor garments and tossing them on John's bed in a most casual manner. 'He's putting a brave a face on it a' but I ken he's feart as a wee beastie inside.' She turned her head and stared at Will. 'And whit are ye daeing tae get him released? It'll no happen standing around here jawing.'

Will clenched his fists to stop himself roaring at her.

'We are all anxious, but must stay calm,' said Logie in a tone of voice that, surprisingly, was calming.

Bethia meantime had risen from her seat and taken Grissel's hands. They both stared at him. It was bad enough to have one sister, and here were two of them now, and united against him.

Will swallowed. 'A date has been set for …' he hesitated, didn't want to call it a trial, even though it most probably was, '… Ephraim's case to be heard. A few days and he should be among us again. Logie, I am sorry, but there's nae room here. We are bursting at the seams as you can see.'

'My good friend Morrison will put me up. He and his family occupy a comfortable house in a close behind St Giles. Bethia has also been invited to bide with them while we are here.'

Will looked curiously at his sister but she had turned to Logie behind her, saying, 'Perhaps we should go there now. They have been so kind I would not wish to offend by tarrying when the dinner hour is upon us.'

In answer, Logie picked up her cloak and carefully wrapped it around her. Will could see Grissel watching, eyes narrowed in speculation. As soon as Bethia and Logie had said their farewells and departed, she turned to Will, saying, 'I'm thinking she does mean tae hae him after a'.'

With which Will could do naught but concur.

It was an uncomfortable few days. Sunday was church, which went some way to relieving Will's mind. He held his Bible in his hands and still, twenty-eight years after the Reformation, it was a matter of wonder and joy to him that he could turn its pages and read the Word of God now accessible to all … well, those that could read.

But even when he was listening to the preacher's sound doctrine and feeling the connection with God, the fear for his nephew sat heavy upon him. At least he need not worry ower much about his own flock, for he'd sent a message to James Melville to cover for him. He knew this was an imposition, for Melville had Kilrenny kirk as well as Abercrombie and Anster's, but Will had on occasion done the same for him – and Melville had an assistant, which Will did not. He must make certain he was back in his parish by next Sunday though.

On Monday he passed through the Grassmarket on the way to see an elderly parishioner who had recently removed to Edinburgh to live with her son and his family. The old woman, who he didn't much care to remind himself was his sister's age, had become frail and confused. Will had contacted the son saying his mother needed care. He was pleased to find her ensconced in a tall chair, with a bolster at her back and one on either side to prevent her from sliding down the seat. Two small children were crouched at her feet, before a glowing fire, playing a game that involved flicking pebbles threaded on strings at one another and a great deal of giggling. Her cheeks were rosy and she appeared well fed and more alert than when he'd last seen her. He sat with her till the noon bell rang and, refusing the proffered invitation to join the family for their midday repast, set off back through the Grassmarket. He was eager to learn what further information John might have garnered, for his brother collected stories like John's wife collected buttons – as Will had good reason to know. He'd recently spent a rather tedious half hour when Violet emptied out a pouch on the board and described where each button – most of which were made of horn, although amid the small pile glinted a tarnished silver one – had been found.

He came to a halt suddenly, his way blocked by a large crowd. God's bones, a hanging. A familiar enough sight but not one that Will ever willingly bore witness to. The crowd were in jovial mood – although why those born under the planet Jupiter should be considered especially prone to merriment escaped him. It was not much passed noon but already leather bottles were in evidence. Men, and some women, were staggering and flinging their arms around one another in maudlin affection and as a means of keeping themselves upright.

Will pushed his way through, but before he could make good his escape, two miscreants were brought out, paraded before the crowd and their crimes declared – one for breaking into a house and stealing a silver tankard and the other for the making of false writs. The crowd grew rowdier as the ropes were placed around their necks and the sacks over their heads, although not before one of the men had blubbed, begging to be freed. They were pushed off the stools on which they stood and dangled twisting for longer than Will cared to watch. Yet, troubled that no minister was there to speak with them and bring some comfort before their demise, he lingered, whispering some words he felt appropriate from one of his favourite psalms.

> 'O Lord, thou hast searched me, and known me …
> Whither shall I go from thy spirit? or whither shall I flee from thy presence?
> If I ascend up into heaven, thou art there: if I make my bed in hell, behold, thou art there …
> I will praise thee; for I am fearfully and wonderfully made: marvellous are thy works; and that my soul knoweth right well …'

The kicks had grown weaker and finally the men hung limp. The executioner went to cut them down.

There was a rumbling behind and Will turned to see a large cartwheel being rolled over the cobbles which was then heaved up onto the platform by four sweating, panting men. Will shoved his way forward, determined to speak God's word with the lad shuffling in chains behind them before he met his end – however well deserved. The purpose of the wheel now became evident, for the prisoner was bound spreadeagled and face down upon it before Will could clamber up himself.

'Wait,' he shouted. 'I would have words with him first.'

The executioner overseeing the binding growled, 'Get awa wi' ye, unless you want tae join him.' But then, taking a proper look at Will, he stopped.

'Sorry, yer honour, I didna see who ye were. Gie, the meenister a haund up,' he shouted to one of his subordinates, and Will took the fellow's proffered hand and was himself hauled onto the platform.

The prisoner was young, barely more than sixteen summers, and underfed. Will crouched down so he could see his face and the lad stared at Will with desperate eyes flicking back and forward. He bucked against the rope most cruelly cutting into the thin flesh covering his jutting bones, but to no avail. Will stood and rested his hand on the boy's shoulder.

Silence fell among the crowd and Will was aware of being watched intently, which was awkward, for he was at a loss for what was appropriate in such a situation. *'Our Father which art in heaven, hallowed be thy name …'* he intoned, for you could never go wrong with the Lord's Prayer.

As he finished, the lad groaned, mumbling through the clout stuffed in his mouth and twisting in terror. Will glanced behind him to see the executioner walking with slow steps towards the laddie, the long sharp blade of the coulter hanging from his hand so it skimmed across the wood of the platform, scraping a line as it went. Quite

211

why the cutting blade of a ploughshare should be the implement of punishment in this case was beyond Will.

He bent again and squeezed the boy's shoulder. 'It will be over quick,' he whispered. 'I will see to it.'

Will stepped back. 'God will look kindly upon you if you act with merciful speed,' he said to the executioner.

The man nodded, announced it was a just punishment for the murder of a street seller from whom the lad had been attempting to steal, and set about his task with alacrity. Five blows and all four limbs and the lad's spine were broke. A final blow to the head and the boy was dead.

'We dinna usually dispatch them sae quickly,' he muttered to Will and, indeed, some among the crowd were jeering, for they had expected a more drawn-out entertainment.

The body was cut down and taken away, along with the others, to be flung into a pit in unsanctified ground. The crowd dispersed and Will walked slowly up the narrow curving close to the High Street and into St Giles, where he prayed most fervently for Christ Jesus to watch over the young lad's soul.

Chapter Twenty-Nine

The Book

Will barely closed his eyes all night. When he did briefly drift off, the scene played out in his head over and over, the snap as those stick-like limbs were broke reverberating in his ears. Such a fate would not be dealt to Ephraim if he was found guilty. He might be banished or perhaps hung. At least the Protestant Kirk did not burn heretics in Scotland, unlike its predecessor. The last burning had been two years before the Reformation, and that a frail elderly priest who had turned to the true religion – a shameful episode.

Eventually he rose and pushed aside the bed curtains, leaving John sprawled on his back snoring, and went in search of the brandy bottle. He found it on a high shelf in the corner of the chamber and took a swig. It was not a drink he was partial to and he may as well not have bothered, for all it did was incur a violent fit of coughing. He tried to contain it so as not to disturb his sleeping brother but the cessation of the snores were enough to indicate his lack of success.

Will could see movement lit by the dying glow of the fire as John propped himself up on one elbow.

'Whit are daein', man?'

The coughing began again, and Will bent double, his shirt billowing wide around his knees. John got out of bed and slapped him on the back, harder than Will considered he deserved, but still he coughed. John put his arm around Will to hold him up but Will could not get his breath.

'Grissel,' John roared, but she was already risen from her truckle bed next to the kitchen. Between them they held Will up until he could breathe.

Grissel retreated to her slumbers while John took a piss in the pot, the sound of his stream hitting the porcelain loud in the room. 'God's bones, man, I'll be glad when you are awa tae Fife and I can get peace tae sleep,' he said as he climbed back into bed.

'As will be I. 'Tis long time since I was travelling and forced to share a bed, and then more usually with a stranger.'

'And I more usually share a bed with someone very familiar, who is considerably softer and sweeter smelling.'

'I hope that's Violet you're referring to.'

John sniffed. At which point Will thought it wise to probe no more, for he had no desire to be party to any further details of John's past transgressions than he already knew. He clambered into bed himself and tugged the covers from John's grip.

'Sometimes I forget yer a meenister and need tae watch ma tongue, else, before I know it, I'll be sitting on the penitent's stool in front of the whole kirk,' said John once the tussle with the blankets was over and they were lying quietly. 'I preferred it when we could tell our transgressions quietly in the confessional and carry oot our penance privately.'

'That *is* the point,' said Will, 'for a public accounting means the transgressor is less likely to reoffend, and his neighbours, made fully aware of his sins, will be watching.'

'Weel, I dinna ken what the point of that is. Since it's already foretold whether we will enter the Kingdom of

Heaven or are damned to hell from the moment of birth then why should I strive to live a life where all the joy is sucked oot o' it?'

Will sat up. 'You misunderstand the doctrine of predestination.'

'Aye, aye,' said John hurriedly. 'But now is no the time to instruct me, better in daylight when I'm fully cognisant.' He rolled over and began to snore with suspicious speed.

Will lay on his back, arms behind his head. He could see, in his mind's eye, the document he had helped devise on questions and answers concerning predestination while he was at Calvin's side in Geneva.

'If God's ordinance and determination must of necessity take effect, then what need any man to care, for he that liveth well must needs be damned if it be so ordained. And he that liveth ill needs be saved if it be so appointed.' Will had not realised he'd spoken the words aloud until John groaned, muttering, 'See, I telt ye.'

'For to have either good will or good work is a testimony of the Spirit of God … being graced in Christ they grow in holiness … a thankful remembrance of God.' Will paused, searching for words that felt just out of reach. *'God will give according to his purpose and promise that which we require.'* He smiled, satisfied he'd remembered these wise words. His thoughts drifted to Ephraim. Where did this lad raised as a Jew but with Christian antecedents, albeit papist, belong? Was he already damned according to this creed? No, Will did not think Calvin would've said so, and Ephraim had shown great willingness to embrace the true faith. He drifted off into a peaceful sleep where Calvin came to him and touched Will lightly on the forehead.

He awoke with a start to a finger poking his eyelid. Grissel was bent over him, face close to his. She let out a shriek when he opened his eyes.

'What are ye about, Grissel, trying to scare me into the next life?'

215

She straightened up and crossed her hands over her heart. 'Ye werena moving. I thocht ye were deid.'

'Christ's bones, woman, get away with ye.' He flung the covers back, which had Grissel covering her own eyes, for his shirt had ridden up and more of him was exposed than any woman had had sight of in forty years. He reached for his breeches, dropped last night in a heap on the rough wooden floor.

'There's a message come from that principal fellow.' Grissel waved the paper in her hand.

'Give it here.' Will read the few lines quickly, aware Grissel was watching him intently. 'Fetch me a clean shirt.'

She picked up the shirt, freshly washed, pressed and carefully folded, that was lying on the large kist tucked away in the corner.

She had his black robes ready for him to don next, then he sat down on John's high-back oak chair and hauled his boots on, which he could see Megy had cleaned as instructed.

'I will keep yer porridge warm,' Grissel said.

'Thank you, for looking after me so well.'

She grinned at him. 'What else is a wee sister to do.'

'How long have you known?'

'I think I aywis knew, in ma heart.'

He thought to say more, but now was not the time. 'Where is John? Does he ken about this letter from Rollock?'

She shook her head. 'He's gone doon tae Leith.'

Rollock's cheeks seemed even redder today, glowing in the dully lit chamber above the white of his neckcloth and black robes. He stood up when Will entered. He did not acknowledge nor even seem aware of the bow Will gave, nor did he return it.

'What has happened?' said Will. He took a deep

breath and consciously dropped his shoulders from where they were hunched up by his ears. Whatever was going on there was no point in becoming as agitated as Rollock.

'That snake, that … that … serpent … that Judas. He has borne false witness against de Lange.

'Who?'

'My assistant Browne. I can only think he was jealous of your nephew's knowledge of both Hebrew and the Old Testament … for I have never encountered any student who can so ably quote large tracts from memory before …'

'What has Browne done?' said Will cutting across Rollock, who he had not found previously to be garrulous.

'It is he who has accused de Lange of apostatising.'

'How did you discover this?'

'Browne came to me weeping and telling of how he had mentioned to a clerk who works for the court that de Lange's antecedents were most dubious and he had seen a strange book within his possession with mysterious hieroglyphs engraved upon its cover.'

Will flinched as though a sharp knife had been scored across his flesh. Bethia and he had near been undone in Geneva because of Ephraim's aunt and that wretched book of the Jews she had hid. He clenched his fists to control himself and said as calmly as was possible while he could feel his heart thudding within his chest, 'Have you had sight of this mysterious tome?'

'I have not, even after a search of de Lange's chamber was undertaken.'

'Nothing to indicate an accusation of Judaising is well founded amid Ephraim's possessions?'

Rollock smiled grimly, 'There was an Old Testament in Hebrew, and I can only think it is that which made Browne suspicious and brought about his accusations.'

'Can the fellow not recognise Hebrew when he sees it?'

'It seems not.'

'What do you use him for?'

'His Latin is good and he has taken on some of my general classes allowing me to focus on teaching divinity, which I consider a priority.'

'But what has me curious is why Browne did not come quietly and tell you of his suspicions instead of placing de Lange, and indeed your college, in such a precarious position?'

Rollock rubbed his cheeks, a habit which he would do well to break since it made them even redder. 'Aye, I put that very question to him and his response did not convince. He claims he did not want to trouble me and thought it best for the welfare of my college that it be dealt with swiftly by the law courts. Then I would in no way be implicated in de Lange's very serious crime.'

'How very thoughtful of him. Why has he decided it now expedient to make you aware of his involvement? And why the girning as he told you?'

A faint smile ghosted across Rollock's face at the use of a word which would normally be applied to a whining child. 'I think he came to me because he had *not* understood he would be required to give evidence in court against de Lange and, discovering this to be the case, came grovelling in the hope that he would retain his position.' He glared at Will, and Will thought he would not care to be in Browne's boots. Rollock might appear to be the very epitome of kind reason, but threaten his college at your peril.

'I will dismiss him. There is no place for disloyalty here.'

'Who did the search of the chamber? Can we call on them to bear witness there was nothing untoward?' Will shifted from one foot to the other. His hip was paining him today.

'I have given much thought to an appropriate defence and have come to the conclusion it is better to go to court with the sword of God unsheathed.'

Will blinked; he had no idea what Rollock was blethering about.

Rollock gestured at Will to sit down and, drawing his own chair close, bent to explain.

Will rose on the morning the case was to be heard feeling he had barely slept since he arrived in Edinburgh and with a parched throat and eyes dry and gritty. John, who seemed without worries, or at least worries which overly troubled him, had snored his way through the night yet again and sat shovelling great spoonfuls of porridge down his gullet as though he hadn't eaten for days – nor consumed a whole roasted pigeon by himself the night before. Will heard the door to the street way below bang shut and the sound of heavy footsteps as more than one person came slowly up the turnpike. Grissel went to open their front door to find Bethia with the faithful Logie behind. Bethia rested one hand on the door jamb, leaning forward to catch her breath.

John looked up and spoke what Will was thinking. 'What are ye daeing here?'

'We are only come to wait,' said Bethia, moving into the chamber and lowering herself onto a stool.

'Oh aye, that's fine then. As lang as you're no coming tae the court.' John rolled a slice of bread up and opened his mouth wide to stuff it in.

'Your manners have not improved these past fifty years.'

John grinned at her, the rotating lump of masticated bread white against the pink of his mouth.

'Aye, ye were a cheeky wee laddie then and ye've niver grown oot o' it,' said Grissel, arms akimbo.

John rolled his eyes. 'It's bad enough to have one big sister … but two. It's mair than ony fellow should hae to put up wi'.'

Grissel grinned with pleasure, but Will could see Bethia's lips grow pinched at this open acknowledgement of Grissel's relationship to them. Well, she must become accustomed to it.

Grissel brought him his cloak while Megy placed John's across his shoulders. Bethia sat twisting her handkerchief in her hands while Logie gazed anxiously upon her. She had once confided to Will that sometimes Logie's presence felt as though she was being wrapped in a thick, over-warm blanket. He wondered if she still considered it so.

With a nod to them both, Will set off down the twisting stairs, placing each foot with care on the worn and uneven steps.

Chapter Thirty

The Trial

Rollock was outside the tolbooth. Will could see him pacing, four steps then turn, four steps then turn, as he and John strode down the High Street. They reached Rollock and Will studied him for signs of doubt as to their agreed course of action. If they were to sway the justices then Rollock must present as authoritative not agitated. His cheeks were less red than usual but no doubt the slight chill in the early morning air was cooling to their fiery heat. He held himself stiffly, almost as though if he bent he might break, but otherwise appeared composed.

He greeted them. 'Let us to it,' he said and led the way into the chambers.

Ephraim was brought down, his face pale and glassy-eyed as a recently dead corpse.

The charges were read out – that one Ephraim de Lange secretly followed the blasphemous rites and practices of Jewry while falsely attending the true Kirk.

There was a collective intake of breath from the watchers, for this was a rare and unusual case and the lad was also the grandson of the grand lady come from among the heathen Turk. There was always satisfaction in seeing the mighty come about their just deserts before God.

Browne was called and came initially diffidently,

shoulders slumped. When he saw all the eager faces watching him, it was as though he grew in stature, until by the time he completed the short walk to the witness box there was a cocky swagger to his movements. Then he caught sight of Ephraim, who had come alive enough to glare at him. Browne faltered but, after a moment, sniffed, tossed his head and looked to his audience for approbation.

He told the story of finding Ephraim, head bent over a book overfull of strange symbols engaging in devil worship. When he was asked where the book was kept, he did not know.

'I searched his room most thoroughly but he must have some devious place of hiding as all apostates do.'

The watchers whispered to one another nodding their agreement.

'And did you have any other cause to suspect him?' intervened the judge, resting comfortably against the high back of his oak seat.

Will shifted on the narrow bench.

'He once said that Mary was the Mother of God, which we all know to be incorrect.'

The prosecutor nodded sagely, raising his eyebrows as he looked to the procurator. 'I have no further questions,' he said.

Will and John had persuaded Bethia that Rollock had best act as the defence for Ephraim, 'For he is a widely esteemed as a most godly and learned man.' Bethia had been ready to pay for the best lawyers in Edinburgh but had reluctantly acquiesced, saying they understood more of Scotland than she did, and she found much of what went on here in this post-Reformation land perplexing.

Rollock stood up and shook out the folds of his black robes before fixing his eyes on Browne.

'I am curious. If Ephraim de Lange is a secret Jew, as you claim, how would he have knowledge of Mary?'

Browne looked nonplussed. 'He … he …' Rollock

waited, head tilted to one side in a display of exaggerated patience. '… he has picked up words like a child but without any understanding of what he speaks.'

Rollock turned to Ephraim. 'Who is Mary?'

'The Virgin and Mother of Christ Jesus.'

'And would you ever have referred to her as the Mother of God?'

'No.'

Ephraim's answer was unequivocal and emphatic, Will was pleased to hear.

'Hah!' muttered Browne. 'He would say that.'

Rollock, who had moved closer to Browne as he questioned him, walked back to the lectern from where prosecutor and then defence in turn posed their questions. He picked up a tome, and despite its heavy weight, brandished it in one hand, waving it at Browne. 'And is this the book which you saw de Lange reading from?'

There was an audible gasp from the crowd, who leaned forward as one to get proper sight of the devil's work.

'It looks to be.'

'Here, let me bring it close so there can be no doubt.' Rollock held the book in front of Browne's face.

'It is, for there is Satan's handiwork.' Browne jabbed his finger at the engravings upon the cover as Rollock pulled the book away.

Rollock held it aloft once more, waving it before the straining crowd. 'Far from being the blaspheming of the Devil, this is a work most holy. It is the Old Testament writ in the ancient Hebrew language. The language of Moses, and Jesus.'

Will swallowed. Jesus's first language would have been Aramaic. Yet he would also have spoken Hebrew, so Rollock was correct.

'It is the Word of God,' said Rollock softly so that the crowd strained to hear. There was silence while Rollock laid the book reverentially on the lectern.

It was Rollock's turn to jab his finger now. 'Browne, you are an ignorant fellow. These unfounded accusations are nothing more than a display of envy.' He turned to the transfixed watchers who were nudging and whispering to one another. 'And what does the apostle James have to say of envy?'

They looked to their neighbours and then to the floor, clearly fearful this man who seemed like to a minister, but was not, would point at them demanding if they knew their creed.

'*For where envying and strife is, there is confusion and every evil work*,' said a thin, reedy voice.

'Good lad,' said Rollock, and all turned to look at the boy standing amid them, who smiling hung his head while his mother next to him sat so puffed up with pride she was near bursting.

'James three, verse sixteen,' added the laddie, and the mother began to fan herself wildly.

Rollock, turning his back on the watchers, folded his arms and slowly shook his head at Browne. 'I put it to you that not only are you *not* competent to tutor at our Tounis College, you displayed malice towards a scholar. These are not the values and behaviours we should be demonstrating to young men who are in a godly place of learning.'

The crowd muttered their agreement.

The procurator released Ephraim into Rollock's care, with an injunction to follow life as a God-fearing Christian. Much to Will's surprise, and consternation, Rollock raised his hand indicating he wanted to say more. The procurator too appeared surprised but nodded his permission.

'Jews are the ancient people of God. They are of the seed of Abraham of whom the flesh of Christ came. Jews should not be considered or treated as other infidels. It was to them the Scriptures were consigned and from them were we handed down the gospel and the law. The Jewish Church, in their best estate, had the love and affections of a sister to the, then pagan, future true Church. And though now in their rejected state they are enemies to the gospel, yet they are beloved for their fathers' sake.'

There was silence. The procurator sat very still and Will suspected that he had no idea how to respond.

'It is my intention to appoint a regent to teach Hebrew to our scholars, for it is an ancient language most pertinent to their learning,' said Rollock.

'That is a matter for the college,' said the procurator, clearly relieved that he could make an ending to Rollock's diatribe.

'What was that all aboot?' muttered John as they pushed their way out amid the throng while Ephraim hurried home ahead of them to apprise Bethia of the happy outcome.

Will, pondering Rollock's words, did not immediately reply and was nudged quite fiercely in the ribs.

'His words were most apposite,' said Will softly. 'It is as Calvin himself would have said. Jews are the custodians of the Scriptures, biblical prophecies and the law – they are a people in covenant with God. It was right that Rollock should remind us of that.'

'Does that mean Ephraim could choose to follow Jewish practices openly?'

'No, of course not!' said Will sharply.

The family gathered around the table in John's chamber with Grissel taking the stool proffered to her, briefly.

'Will ye sit down,' Will said after Grissel jumped up to fetch first the bannocks which Megy had forgot, next to top up the ale, then for no reason Will could surmise beyond making sure all was being done as she wished in the kitchen.

Grissel cuffed him lightly across the head and kept

doing what she was doing.

'Are you staying on in Edinburgh?' Will asked Bethia, who was peeling a roasted egg.

She glanced at Logie.

'I am entirely at your service ...' his voice trailed off.

She smiled at Logie, a smile of such loving sweetness it took Will's breath away.

'But you would like to get home to Fife,' she said.

'Aye, but it's of no moment if you would prefer to stay with your brothers longer. We have already removed to another neighbour's,' he said to the table at large, 'as I did not want to presume on my friend any further.'

She patted him gently on the arm. 'No, I must go home to Father. He'll be in a right fankle worrying about this one.' She nodded to Ephraim, who was struggling to keep his eyes open. He had changed his coat and immersed his head in a bowl of water so the wet strands clung to his forehead and the sides of his face, but still the stench of prison adhered to him.

'If the winds are fair, we'll leave tomorrow. With the rumours running about the Spanish then the sooner we are safe in Fife the better. Can you be ready, Ephraim?' said Logie.

Will, opening his mouth to speak, saw Ephraim blink and widen his eyes. He waited to hear what the lad was about to say before giving his unsought opinion.

'I think it best I stay here for the time being. I would not want to disappoint Principal Rollock.'

John clapped Ephraim on the shoulder. 'Good lad.'

'Aye,' said Will, before Bethia could remonstrate – which she was clearly about to do. 'Most unwise to disappear now, and especially when Rollock has put his head in the noose for you.'

'I will not go without Ephraim,' said Bethia. 'Look what happened when I left him here.'

'Nonna,' said Ephraim, gazing at her earnestly, 'you would not have it said I was a coward who ran away.'

'No, I would have it said you are a clever fellow who had the wisdom to leave while he could.'

Will could see Logie squeezing Bethia's hand under cover of the board. She turned to him, a pleading look upon her face.

'Will spoke fair and true words. We can stay longer, despite the bed bugs,' said Logie.

Everyone around the board stared at them and Bethia flushed, pink as a young lass.

'In our separate beds,' she said loudly.

John roared with laughter and nudged Logie, while Ephraim said, 'Nonna!' in shocked tones.

'Aye, 'tis true,' shouted Grissel from the open kitchen door. 'Though when there is nay fear o' bairns I canna think why you're paying for twa rooms.'

'I will go home to Father,' said a flushed Bethia reluctantly, 'but *only* if Ephraim removes from his room in the college and lives here *and* if John stays for a while in case of trouble.'

'Aye, that's fine,' said John, and Will noticed how his eyes drifted towards Megy, bending over to place some of those strange dried figs come from Africa on the table, bosom on display. He sighed, hoping it was only his eyes that John was applying to the lassie, for she was a bonnie one.

'Aye, Megy and I will watch oe'r you, lad,' said Grissel emphatically, but she too was staring at John as she spoke.

Will gave a slight nod. All would be well if Grissel was in charge.

Before he left for Fife himself, Will made certain he had a private conversation with Ephraim. He could see the lad was still shaken by his experience and, although Ephraim had spoken bravely about how he must stay in Edinburgh, Will wanted to further reassure him.

'You need have no fears now, my lad,' he said. 'Rollock has declared before all his belief and conviction in the benefits you will bring to his college. I have no doubt he is an honest man who will in turn show you both loyalty and care.'

Ephraim nodded and Will could see he already looked less pale and wan.

Chapter Thirty-One

My Heart is Thine

Bethia had been surprised to find Grissel so content, even happy, living in Edinburgh, but then Grissel's business was thriving. Even John was heard to say, with a satisfied clap of the hands, that the alehouse had been a sound investment and was making him a good return.

'And she's become a wad wyfe, too, as weel as a tavern keeper,' he had said.

'What is a wad wyfe?' Bethia had asked, thinking it did not sound at all respectable.

'She's lending money tae ithers and charging interest. Och, she's a clever woman oor Grissel,' John said proudly.

'I am glad she is content,' said Bethia faintly, thinking that Grissel was in a fair way to end up the richest among the Seton siblings. She could not help but smile at the prospect of John's indignation should Grissel outdo him.

But for Bethia, it was a blessed relief to leave this smoke-wreathed city which was overfull of people, dirt and rats. And strangely, it was not John's home in Pittenweem with its views which connected to the ever-changing sea and sky with such perfection, nor her spacious house on the steep sloping streets of Galata which she longed for, but Balcarrow, with its long view of the hills and the sea in the far distance, the quiet measured rhythm of its days and the clean air.

Gilbert took her back to Fife. She could see Will and John glancing at one another, but after all, he had brought her here. And he treated her with such gentle courtesy, nothing ever too much trouble. Bethia had been in such distress about the news of Ephraim's imprisonment that she had turned to him without a second thought, despite their last awkward, indeed painful, parting. As ever, Gilbert had not been found wanting.

'I am always there for you in time of need, Bethia,' he had said, and so it had again proved to be.

On the return journey they stayed overnight in the royal burgh of South Queensferry, named for the saintly Queen Margaret, who had established a free ferry to take pilgrims across the Forth to the abbey in Dunfermline. Bethia sighed, thinking of the pious acts this long-dead and canonised queen was said to have enacted, including feeding the poor and, on occasion, washing their feet just as Jesus had once done for his disciples. There could be no more saints in Scotland now. Sometimes she was truly baffled by this new Kirk. What could be the harm in celebrating goodness in this way?

Gilbert had arranged lodgings in a tower house close by the harbour. 'There should be no bed bugs here,' he said as they sat down to a private supper, for their host had already retired for the night.

'It looks to be well kept,' said Bethia glancing around.

'We will take a boat early tomorrow to Wester Kinghorn, or I should say Burntisland, for so the town was recently renamed when it was made a royal burgh.'

'Why is it called that?' said Bethia, shifting on her seat.

'It's said to have something to do with the burning of fishermen's homes on an islet which was incorporated into the newly built harbour.'

'Oh,' said Bethia distractedly, reaching into her pocket.

'The sea does not look quite so rough closer to the river mouth. We can but hope it remains that way and we have a reasonable crossing. It was a longer journey by land from Edinburgh but I think we were wise to choose that over crossing from Leith.'

'The goldsmiths in Edinburgh are as fine as those to be found in the Great Bazaar in Constantinople,' said Bethia.

Gilbert looked at her oddly.

'There is a particularly excellent craftsman called George Heriot who has a Luckenbooth by St Giles. Do you know of him?'

'No, I have not had that pleasure,' said Gilbert slowly.

'John does,' said Bethia. 'Master Heriot was recently made a burgher of the city and is a leading light in the guild of goldsmiths.'

Gilbert had his head tilted to one side by now and she could see he was wondering if she had joined the ranks of the insane. It was all going wrong. She could not think how to let him know her feelings, and felt as tongue-tied as a sixteen-year-old lassie.

She wrapped her hand tight around the small package in her pocket, tugged it out and thrust it at him before her courage deserted her.

Gilbert stared at the soft leather pouch in her hand. 'What is this?'

'A gift,' said Bethia impatiently. 'Just open it.'

Gilbert worked to untie the knot while Bethia leant forward watching. She waited barely a few moments before snatching the pouch from his hands and untying it with deft fingers. She was aware Gilbert was frowning as he watched her.

'Hold out your hand,' she said as she loosened the strings.

Gilbert held out his hand.

She could stop now and he would never know, could claim she was playing a trick on him.

'Bethia?' he said softly.

She tipped the pouch up and the ring dropped onto his palm.

He gazed at it, a thick band with a bevelled edge, and tilted his hand so the gold shone bright in the candlelight.

'Heriot said it is made from eighteen carat gold. He said you do not want a ring made from twenty-four carat, which is pure gold, because it will wear away. And I want this ring to last.'

She could see him swallowing and the flush rising up his face – this face that was so very dear to her. But why was he saying nothing, only looking at her in such a peculiar way?

'But perhaps you do not want a ring?' She went to take it from him.

His hand closed over the ring before she could seize it.

'I wonder,' he said holding it up to the light. 'Does it have an inscription, for a poesy ring should, you know?'

Now it was her turn to swallow. Up till now she could have said it was a simple gesture of friendship such as the ring he had given her – but once he read the words engraved within this band of gold there was no going back. Only forward … or apart.

'I cannot make it out,' he said fumbling in his pocket for his eyeglasses. 'Ah, that is better.'

Why was it taking him so long to read four words.

He took the eyeglasses off and laid them on the board. 'Is this true?' he said, his voice thick with emotion.

Unable to form the words in reply, she nodded.

He reached out and she placed her hands in his. 'And my heart has always been thine,' he said.

Gilbert and Bethia were married fourteen days later.

'What's the hurry?' said John, eyes twinkling.

'I have waited for forty years and I will not wait a day

longer,' said Gilbert, capturing Bethia's hand.

He would have married sooner but Bethia had asked that they hold off till both Ephraim and Grissel could join them.

Grissel came in a great flurry and brought Megy too. 'We hae closed the alehouse for a week,' she said, made breathless by her own audacity.

'Aye weel, makes nae difference tae me,' said John. 'You will hae to pay the rent, closed or no.'

'John!' said Bethia.

'Whit?' he said spreading his hands wide. 'Grissel is a woman of business and kens weel she has tae take the rough wi' the smooth.'

On her wedding day, Bethia was dressed by Grissel. She wanted no other and was disappointed when Grissel asked if Megy could join them.

'She is ma dochter,' said Grissel. 'I havena birthed her, I ken, but she is as dear tae me as though I had.'

'Like my sons were to you,' said Bethia.

'Aye and no,' said Grissel. 'Megy is all mine, your laddies I had aywis tae share.'

Megy fetched and carried and managed to pin Bethia's headdress on so firmly that it took the combined efforts of Izzy and Gilbert to remove it later, for Anstruther had requested that the newly pregnant Izzy might remain overnight at Balcarrow and indeed would have preferred she did not risk the jolting of the cart at all – for it was out of the question she come on horseback.

Bethia and Gilbert were married by Will in the solar at Balcarrow, surrounded by their family.

'I will not test your catechism,' said Will, 'for I trust you know it.'

'*What are we by nature?*' Donald called out.

'*The children of God's wrath*,' responded his siblings.

'*Were we thus created of God?*' Donald came back.

'*No, for he made us to his own image*,' shouted the lads and lassies in return.

233

'*How came we to this misery?*'

'*Through the fall of Adam from God,*' shrieked the grandchildren, made hysterical by their audacity, while the terrier ran in ever-decreasing circles yapping with excitement.

'Enough!' said Will in his loudest and most ministerial voice, although Bethia could see he was trying not to laugh.

Will waited for the children, and dog, to grow calm before he continued. Bethia stood with her hands in Gilbert's and they smiled at one another, for there was no urgency. They had made their commitment and would not again be parted in this life.

They said their vows, both with absolute certainty, and then there was the hand fasting. It was Grissel who tied the ribbons around their wrists, binding them together while Will spoke a blessing.

'I have another poesy ring for you,' said Gilbert quietly as they sat together at the wedding feast surrounded by their noisy families.

'I do not need one,' she said.

'I wanted to give you my true sentiments, as you did on my ring,' he said with a smile. 'Something to match "*my heart is thine*". I want you to understand how deeply I feel, have always felt.'

'Oh Gilbert,' she said, touching his hand. 'I know.'

He slipped the ring upon her fourth finger, where it rested against the vein of love.

'You must tell me what it says else I'll have to fetch my eyeglasses to read it.'

He smiled. '*Love of thee is life to me.*'

'Then we are united in thought and feeling,' she said, smiling in return.

The family lingered, but eventually, by late afternoon, everyone had left, except Izzy, and Father Richard came creeping from his hiding place to give the blessing.

And then Bethia knew she was truly Gilbert's wife.

Part Four

Armada

March 1588 to August 1589

Chapter Thirty-Two

Doomsayers

It was the twenty-fifth of March in the year of our Lord fifteen hundred and eighty-eight, and the first day of the New Year in Scotland.

'I do not know where I am,' said Bethia plaintively to John. He and a beaming Symon had ridden up to Balcarrow to bring tidings of the birth of Symon's son. And after the congratulations were over and Bethia was assured that Kristene's time of trial did not last for more than a day and a night and was bravely borne, and how puffed up Father was by the birth of this great grandchild, she could not help reverting to the date, which was causing her both frustration and some anxiety.

'How can we lose ten days, where have they gone? Between the Julian and Gregorian calendar I do not know where I am,' she repeated.

'But we have not changed anything in Scotland,' said Gilbert soothingly.

She caught her lip between her teeth. Gilbert was the perfect husband except when he spoke to her in that tone, the same one he used to calm his dogs and horse. She swallowed her annoyance. They'd had their first, and she hoped only, argument the previous day. Izzy, on a visit to her former home, had let slip that John had asked Gilbert if he would marry Bethia.

'John was fearful for you because of the stories in the village that you are a wise woman,' Gilbert had said later when Bethia confronted him. 'He thought it was only one step from there to naming you a witch and that you would be safe here with me.'

'And so *that* is why you wed me.'

'Bethia!' he had said in exasperation.

'No wonder you once said your dogs were sufficient companions.' Her eyes narrowed. 'So you *were* going to ask me. If I had only waited you would have proposed …'

His eyes brimmed with mirth. 'But I much preferred that you did.'

'And you married me because John asked you to,' she said tearfully.

'You are being very foolish,' he had said softly. 'I *would* have wed to protect you, but you cannot know what your love has meant to me. You understand full well that I spoke thus because I judged it less painful to live alone than with a wife who did not care for me in the way I cared for her. I had one loveless marriage, Bethia, I could not have borne another.'

She was silent for a moment and then went to him, taking his hands in hers and kissing the palm of each in turn. 'And I did not truly know that I loved you until I thought you no longer cared for me in that way.' She looked up at him. 'It was my time of pain, although much shorter lived than yours.'

He had wrapped his arms around her then and all dissent was forgot.

'Ach, dinna fash yersel, aboot the calendar,' said John to Bethia, and she started. 'You sound like ane o' these soothsayers wringing their hands and saying we're all doomed because of some alignment of the planets or crashing of meteors.'

'But why does everything have to align anyway? In Constantinople they have the great celebration of the month of Ramadan and the dates are never the same but shift according to the year, and all is easy. It's said the Pope changed to the Gregorian calendar because Easter was ten days out but Jesus Christ was crucified on April the fourteenth. I ask you, what is so difficult about using that date consistently?'

'How dae ye ken the date of the crucifixion?'

Bethia had to think for a moment. How did she know? 'Oh, because it's in the Jewish calendar.'

'What!' said John and Gilbert in unison, while a watching Symon stifled a laugh at their reaction.

Bethia flicked her fingers at them. 'And I don't understand why we can't be the same as the rest of Europe and have New Year on the first of January.'

'I dinna understand why ye're getting in a fankle aboot losing ten days one moment and the next complaining because New Year isn't in January.'

'Well, t'would be fitting,' said Logie tugging on his ear. 'Janus is the god of beginnings and openings.'

'But he's two-faced,' said Symon, much to Bethia's surprise. Symon must've had a more liberal arts education than might be expected in Scotland – but then John had always enjoyed the singular, a trait which had clearly rubbed off on some of his offspring.

'That is because he faces both the future and the past,' said Gilbert.

'See,' said Bethia, feeling justified. 'January is more appropriate than ushering in New Year on the chariot of Mars, god of war.'

John laughed. 'Aye, 'tis as weel Will is no among us. He'd no be happy wi' all this pagan talk.' He grew thoughtful. 'These shifts in the calendar *are* a bother for those of us daeing business on the continent, though. When we agree delivery times they hae to be given using baith the Julian and Gregorian calendars, which makes it easier for dishonest fellows to hoax ye, and for a richt mess in the account books.' He stretched his legs out and took a sip from his glass of claret. 'And what of all this hand-wringing ower the year fifteen hundred and eighty-eight? We've had ither years that were said to be the end o' the world and naething came o' it. And now there's consternation because some fellow called Regiomontanus made a prediction a hundred years ago.'

Gilbert glanced at Bethia and she thought of their recent conversation when Gilbert had voiced his disquiet about Protestant Bibles being available in English, and thus now accessible to all who could read. 'It makes people more fearful,' he said. 'They are delving into Daniel and Revelation and seeking out passages which prophesy the end of the world is nigh upon us. This is why priests are necessary, for they sensibly interpret the wisdom of the good book which is beyond the understanding of people who live short and brutal lives. Let them have some mystery and beauty, and some days of celebration in their time on earth, else their lives are barely worth living.'

With which she could not but concur.

Symon continued the discussion on doomsaying. ''Tis more than what Regiomontanus wrote, Da. The almanacs count the years since God made the world. They calculate 'tis now five thousand five hundred and fifty years, which is a number of great significance.'

John leant back, a smile of pleasure on his face that his son should so display knowledge. 'Aye, very true,' he said.

'And it is said the world will end in the sixth millennium, which is now upon us.'

Bethia stood up and went to pour some of the Rhenish wine which John had brought as a gift. 'I cannot live as though the end of the world is nigh. All I can do is say my prayers, study my Bible, love my family and give succour to the poor.'

'Spoken like the good woman you are,' said Gilbert, as he held out his glass for her to fill. Their fingers brushed and she smiled at him.

'But still I do not understand, where are the lost days to go? Even if we do *not* join all of Catholic Europe in cleaving to the Gregorian calendar and simply shift New Year to the first of January, we will lose the last three months of the year. If it had happened this year where would January, February and March have gone? We would have a nine-month year.'

'Aye, but it'll mebbe no much matter,' said John, leaning back in his chair, arms behind his head straining the lacings around his armpit. 'This time next year we could a' be pairt o' Spain and following the Gregorian calendar.'

'But, Da,' said Symon, ''tis England who are the enemies of Spain.'

'Word has it Elizabeth gifted James five thousand pounds to help defend our kingdom against the Spanish,' said Gilbert. 'And there's still talk of Mary, Queen of Scots last will and testament, that she is said to have penned before her death, cutting James out of the succession and making Philip next in line to the throne of both England and Scotland.'

'Our king will dae naething to offend Elizabeth. He'd be a fool if he did, wi' his eye on the succession, although I'm no sure it'll dae Scotland muckle good to hae him king o' England as weel,' said John. He sat up with a suddenness that startled Bethia. 'If the Spanish were to tak England then the Pope of Rome would likely drive them on to take Protestant Scotland.'

'We would all be forced to be papists again,' said Symon, his face wrinkling in disgust.

John glanced at Bethia and she was surprised to see he looked almost apologetic.

'The Spanish are a cruel people,' said Bethia, thrusting her head forward, daring anyone to disagree. 'Their dealings with Mainard's family and others like them were vicious.'

241

Symon stared at her. 'What happened, Aunt?'

'They were banished from Spain and many were tortured and burned.'

'Then we dinna want the Spanish living next door to us.'

'We hae no quarrel with Spain and it will be maist unfortunate if the trade routes are cut,' said John. 'But the king will withoot doubt sacrifice his people to fight England's corner, for all his hopes of succession will vanish in a puff of smoke should Philip take Elizabeth's crown.' John rubbed at the back of his neck. 'Either that or he'll treat with Philip so that he becomes king of England as Philip's cipher.'

Gilbert placed his glass upon the side table and stood up. 'There is something here you may find interesting,' he said.

He moved over to the shelves which contained his books. Bethia had noticed the collection had increased significantly since she took up residence and was aware it was yet another way in which he tried to bring her pleasure.

'I have recently acquired pamphlets on the exploits of Sir Francis Drake in Spanish territories.' He slid two booklets from the shelf and held them aloft.

Symon went to join him and Gilbert passed him one.

'*The true and perfecte news of the worthy and valiaunt exploites performed and done by that valiant knight Syr Frauncis Drake,*' he read aloud. 'May I borrow this, Uncle? I will take excellent care of it.'

Gilbert placed his hand on Symon's shoulder. 'Take the other one too.' He passed both to Symon, who sat down, hunched over as though to protect his treasure.

'*How should we know the worthy deeds of our Elders, if those learned Poets and Historiographers had not set them down in writing, as Joseph did for the state of the Jews, Homer and Euripides for the Grecians and Quintus Curtius for the life of Alexander the Great,*' Symon read aloud. '*At what time*

242

heretofore was there ever any English man that did the like till now and herein I record his wondrous exploits.'

'Weel the author has grand aspirations as to his ane fame to set himself up alongside Homer, Euripides and the Old Testament,' said John.

Symon, head bent over his pamphlets, took no further part in the conversation and they drifted on to a discussion about the strong winds which had blown March in, John and Gilbert agreeing they were worse than usual.

'We would not have come today, had they not slackened and the rain held off. So wet I dinna ken when I'll get my barley sown.'

Bethia did not want to discuss the weather, for it was all a part of the general sense that the end of the world was like to come – yet another sign, along with the prophecies, almanac predictions and astrologer readings.

'Read us something from your pamphlet,' she called to Symon, abruptly cutting across the men's blethers.

Symon needed no encouragement. 'The writer is telling of how ill-treated the local people of Santa Domingo and Cartagena were by their Spanish captors and how Drake relieved that misery and by his sword set them free.'

'Surely not single-handedly?' said Gilbert.

'No,' said Symon abruptly. Then flushed, realising how impatient he must sound, and that to his elder.

'… all at once ran valiantlie,
Their shot discharged, with
weapons then,
They lay one load on either side:
Though five to one, yet durst not bide. …'

'God's blood, is the thing in verse?' John said.

'Aye, and it's very exciting. Drake was outnumbered five to one and yet the Spanish gunners laid down their weapons and fled. And then Drake and his men sat down and enjoyed the feast of roasted meats which the Spaniards had left behind.'

'Sounds like my kind of fight,' said Gilbert, winking at John. 'And by such writings are legends made. Who knows, Drake may become as lauded as that Greek explorer fellow Ulysses.'

'Aye,' said John standing up. 'And perhaps we could hae someone make verse about Will's exploits too, including being thrown out of the castle window in Rouen by his enemies and surviving unharmed only because he landed in a dung heap.' John laughed long and loud at his own wit, while Gilbert smiled as much from politeness, and Symon, who'd clearly heard this story more than once, buried his head in the booklet.

'You should write about your life, my love,' said Gilbert. 'You too have had some remarkable adventures.'

Bethia wrinkled her nose. 'I doubt anyone would be interested to read the exploits of a woman.'

'Why no?' said John stoutly. 'Ye've had at least as many as Will.'

Bethia rose and touched John lightly on the head. My wee brother, she thought, ever my supporter.

Chapter Thirty-Three

Edane

Will was working on his sermon for Tuesday and, although he well knew pride was a sin, he could not help but feel pleasure at the way the words flowed from his pen. He finished with a flourish, laid down his quill, scattered sand over the paper and shook it off in the receptacle he kept nearby for this purpose. He read the last few lines, then thought to add some words from Ecclesiastes. He picked up his pen, dipped it in the ink and prepared to write as the door was opened with such force it banged off the wall leaving a dent in the plaster.

'Meenister, you hae tae come at once,' shrieked Nannis.

Will stared up at her then glanced down at the paper where two large blots of ink had dropped onto his sermon. He placed the pen carefully in its holder while Nannis danced from foot to foot impatiently.

He pressed both hands flat on the desk and rose so he towered over her, but he should've known Nannis wouldn't be daunted.

'Come, Meenister, come quick else ye'll no catch them. I saw them, I did. They was walking alang the beach thegither. I didna think it was proper even though they are related, ye ken.' She gave a wild laugh. 'Whit am I saying, course ye'll ken.'

245

'Slow down, Nannis. What are ye blethering about?'

'Just come, *Meenister* and I will show ye.'

She beckoned and Will sighed but followed her.

'Ye'll need tae be quick else they'll have parted company and ye'll no catch them. It's doon at the shore. I wis collecting seaweed for ma garden, ye ken I hae permission. Lord Anstruther gie'd it tae me,' she said defensively.

'He gave it to everyone as long as they stuck to the beach on the far side only,' said Will wearily. He went to add, *and by the sound of things that's not the beach you were collecting on* but held his tongue. 'Who is it you have seen doing what?'

But Nannis was off down the hill at a great rate, indeed so fast on a path slippery from last night's rain Will was fearful she'd end up flat on her face. She led him along the edge of the cliff, which tumbled down to the jagged shore. The damp rocks looked sinister, and the sun, emerging from behind a bank of clouds, dazzled so that he had to narrow his eyes to see his way. He tripped on a stone hidden in the long grass and, stumbling to regain his balance with arms flailing, near fell on top of Nannis bustling along before him. The breeze off the sea was blowing her skirt so it wrapped around her legs and she tugged constantly to free herself, but without slackening pace.

She stopped with such suddenness that Will had to leap to one side.

'Look!' She pointed to the rocks below.

At first Will could see nothing. He followed the line of Nannis's stabbing finger, but only a seagull perched on a rock, sharp-beaked and smooth-feathered, caught his eye. Then a movement, and he curled his hands so tight his nails dug into his palms. The young woman below with her back to them and facing out to sea was Edane. And sitting on the rock next to her, so close a blade of grass could barely have slid between them, was Ephraim.

246

Will opened his mouth to shout and hesitated. Would he be creating an uproar where there was nothing but cousinly friendship? All he need do was send Ephraim back to Edinburgh early, or wait a few more days since the new term was about to begin.

'Aye, watch them now,' said Nannis, who he had forgot for a moment was with him. She echoed his thoughts, saying, 'I ken it looks to be innocent, but wait a wee whilie and ye will see.'

And just in that moment Edane glanced over her shoulder and up to where they stood. She leapt to her feet. A startled Ephraim followed and the flush that suffused both faces said it all.

'Och no, not ma bonny granddaughter and the Turk,' cried Nannis, again echoing Will's thoughts. She gazed up at him. 'Ye ken, I hoped it wisna so but ane look at those guilty faces tells the hale story.'

Will did not reply, only gestured most emphatically to Edane that she should come. She climbed over the rocks with alacrity, leaving Ephraim standing alone. The lad's whole body slumped, and for one brief moment Will pitied him. Then Ephraim straightened and followed her.

'We were going to tell you,' said Edane, standing in front of her parents, for Will had gone to the harbour and, finding Andersoun repairing one of his boats, insisted he return home. Then Cecy had been brought in from the garden, where she'd been sowing peas. Both stood, Cecy with earth clinging to her hands and muddy apron and Andersoun with a dusting of sawdust sticking to his sweaty face.

'We want to marry,' said Ephraim stoutly. He looked to Andersoun. 'I was coming to ask you this evening. That is what we were meeting to agree.'

Andersoun sat down upon the settle and stared at his daughter. 'I had hoped you might make an alliance with

247

Peddie's son.'

'Sorry, Da,' said Edane, looking genuinely apologetic. 'But ...' she gazed at Ephraim, '... once I came to know Ephraim and learned he cared for me too, I knew there could be no other.'

'Aye,' said Andersoun glancing at his wife, 'I can understand that.'

'No,' shrieked Nannis. She turned to Will, hands clasped together as though in prayer. 'Meenister, ye cannie let the lass marry him. He's no from these pairts and doesna belong here. He will tak her awa to Turkland.'

Will swallowed but remained silent.

''Tis a fair point,' said Andersoun. He looked to Ephraim. 'I must think on this, son.'

'Pleeease, Papa,' said Edane, eyes filling with tears.

Will could see how difficult it was for Andersoun to gainsay his daughter. Edane had them all wrapped around her little finger.

'It's they wicked Spanish coming and all they evil omens. It's got awbody upside doon,' wailed Nannis. 'My Edane is a good girl and else would niver hae got caught up wi' him.' She pointed a finger at a startled Ephraim.

And well may Ephraim be taken aback at such venom. Will had never seen Nannis do anything other than fawn over him, as occurred with most of the women he came in contact with. Aye well, it would do him no harm to understand what a shaky pedestal upon which he stood.

Will became aware the kitchen was filling up, as Andersoun and Cecy's children, no doubt attracted by the noise, slipped into the room to watch and listen. 'I think,' he said hoarsely, and coughed to clear his throat, ''twould be better to continue this discussion in private with only those directly involved. Andersoun, you may use my workroom.'

Andersoun nodded slowly. 'Ephraim, wait in the garden and I will call you.' He opened the door, beckoned to his wife, then said, 'You too, Edane.'

Nannis went to follow her son, but Andersoun stopped her with a 'Not now, Ma,' and shut the door firmly behind him.

Nannis stood wringing her hands and Will felt pity for her. He rose to guide her to the settle but she shook his hand off her arm. 'I ken't how it wid be when Andersoun married intae your family,' she spat, and pushed passed him. His surprise was so great he did not follow her. All these years when she'd seemed so puffed up that her son had married the minister's daughter and yet she would speak to him thus! The front door slammed; she must have gone. Well, now he might have some peace from her constant visits, demands and interference in his daily life and synod business.

There was a sea of faces staring at him, seeking reassurance. This was a noisy and busy household, couldn't be anything else with so many bairns, but what was occurring this day had unsettled them all.

'Let us to the shore and collect seaweed for the small field. Your mama will be mighty pleased with us if we so do.'

Their chatter rose to a clamour as the lads and lass flowed out of the chamber behind him. When they returned some time later, wind-blown and salt-encrusted, pushing the handcart piled high with weed and bringing the smell of the sea with them, it was to find Edane at work in the garden alongside her mother, Andersoun gone back to his boat repair and no sign of Ephraim.

'Well?' said Will to Cecy, once the circle of watching children had been sent about their business.

'Andersoun says Edane is too young and must wait two years at least, for Ephraim too is no more than a lad. If their sentiments have not changed then he will not

249

oppose the match but Ephraim must think very carefully if he wants to stay in Scotland, for Andersoun will not countenance it otherwise. And he must have the means to support a wife, which he will do as regent to the college principal.'

Will tilted his head thoughtfully.

'Does that meet with your approval, Papa?' said Cecy, forehead wrinkling.

'I believe it is a wise course,' said Will, who was aware of Edane listening, a smile creeping across her face.

She came to him then, this most beloved of grandchildren, and leant her head against his arm. 'Thank you, Grandpa,' she said.

'But,' he said, 'I must be absolutely convinced that he is a true follower of the Protestant faith.'

'He has told me that is so,' said Edane.

'Then there will be no difficulty. Although his own father must also be applied to for permission, which may not be forthcoming.'

But no one in all of this had considered Bethia. A few days later, having been apprised of the prospective nuptials, she descended on the household like a furious storm whipping in off the German Ocean.

Will considered it most unfair that he took the brunt of the blast, given that it was Andersoun and not he who had made the decision as to whether Ephraim and Edane might wed.

'This cannot be,' she shouted at Will, who was deep in his Bible wrestling with a passage in Luke which had him confused as to its meaning.

'What cannot be?' he said slowly, although he already guessed.

'Cousins cannot marry. The Church does not permit it.'

'The *Catholic* Church may forbid it but in the reformed

Kirk there is no such restriction. Why, in Genesis Leah marries her cousin Jacob. And I doubt there will be any objection to cousins marrying amongst your family in Constantinople, since Genesis is from the Old Testament.'

'Don't you give me instruction on where Genesis is to be found,' spluttered Bethia. 'I am not one of your ignorant parishioners.'

'In any case,' said Will calmly, 'they are not first but second cousins, and 'tis only first cousins the old laws forbad from joining together.'

'Bah!' said Bethia, and Will had to swallow a smile. He remembered when they were children how she would remain unnaturally calm in the face of his anger and how often it provoked him to greater anger. It was curious to experience this power from the other side.

She dropped onto the stool opposite and covered her face with her hands. Immediately he was contrite and came to stand by her side resting his hand on her shoulder.

'Oh Will,' she said. 'What am I to tell my son? That he will never see Ephraim again? And Mirella, she will be heartbroken. How can I have let this happen?'

'Bethia, you made the same choice when you married Logie. I do not think you can demand any different of Ephraim.'

She wept then, and he stroked her back, for there was nothing else he could do to bring her comfort.

Chapter Thirty-Four

Disquietude

It was an unusually stormy summer with a resulting poor harvest and an inevitable rise in food prices, and that, combined with the increasing rumours of various sightings of the Spanish Armada off Scotland, caused grave anxiety amid Will's flock. Given the disquietude, Will considered it most unfortunate that there continued to be an outpouring of predictions about the significance of the year. Sitting at a board strewn with papers one morning in early August, he leaved through a discourse written by an Englishman. This Richard Harvey was claiming they should all expect *either a finall dissolution or a wonderfull horrible alteration of the worlde* in this year of our Lord fifteen hundred and eighty-eight Harvey wrote in tortured tones, Will could almost hear his voice and a certain relish in his doomsaying, that the disorder would swell until it culminated in a thunderous crescendo, after which irrevocable changes would be embedded – or 'poof', Will flicked his fingers – the world would be consumed by a fiery cataclysm. But then, judging by what the astrologers were discovering, that was not so improbable. Comets did shoot across the sky, and what was to prevent those blazing implements of Satan from crashing into the world? And the movement of stars could and did cause an imbalance in the body's humours

– and all this was yet another way in which God punished sinners.

Will sat staring at his desk unseeing for a long time. Eventually he stood up, went out into the rain-soaked garden and gazed up at the ominous dark clouds forming and reforming above like they were pushing one another out of the way. These astronomers and astrologers were like a den of dragons blasting out burning air imputing all failings of nature, accidents of misfortune, oversights and errors to the skies and revelling in their prophecies of perdition. And in the end, certainly the last time this doomsaying occurred in fifteen hundred and eighty-three, all their lamentations had proved to be a gross error and the same was likely to be the case this year – in spite of the Spaniards.

Nevertheless, his heart did quail when he thought on the most recent prophecy, which claimed that it was in this year the impact of the perilous conjunction of the planets five years ago was to be realised. Yet if the world was to be blessed by the second coming of Christ, as some prophesied, then that could only be a matter of *joy* – after the cataclysm.

No, he must let go of the doomsaying of these fools and attend to allaying the fears of his flock, exhorting them to come to God with a faithful heart and trust to his care and that of his Son Christ Jesus. And with his purpose clear, Will went back inside to write a scorching sermon on searching within our hearts to seek purity and root out all sin.

The town worthies now directed that the young men were to spend at least two hours each day, except Sunday, at practice at the butts. Having skilled archers was important but, as Will repeated many times, the power of prayer was greater.

The burghers of Anstruther and Pittenweem met, along with their respective ministers, to discuss a shared defence of their villages. For, given there was barely a mile and a half between them, if one was attacked then the other was equally at risk. There had never been any further trouble from English pirates but some fool of a writer had recently described the East Neuk as 'the coast of gold' because of the wealth generated through its fishing, coal mining and salt panning, which was as good as saying there was rich pickings to be had for any freebooters who cared to come and seize it.

Pamphlets about Spanish cruelty were circulating widely and Will thought that life was much simpler before the printing press when rumour and gossip could not be so easily procured. There was something about holding a printed document in your hand, whether it contain truth or lies, or a mix of both, which gave credence in a way the spread of the spoken word alone did not.

Yet not all such booklets could be dismissed. *The Spanish Colonie, or Briefe chronicle of the acts and gestes of the Spaniardes in the West Indies* penned by a friar by the name of Las Casas made for grim reading. Bethia, on a visit to Father and greatly preoccupied by Las Casas's pleas, read aloud the prologue, which was dedicated to Philip of Spain's son, while Will and Logie listened in shocked silence.

'He begs that that the prince ... *be moved most earnestly to desire his Majestie, not to grant or permit to those tyrants such conquests against this Indian, peaceable, lowly & mild nation which offendeth none ...*' read Bethia. '*And calls them wicked, tyrannous, and by all laws either natural, humane or divine, utterly condemned and accursed.*'

'A brave priest to write with such passionate honesty,' Will said. 'But the power and wealth Spain is garnering by the actions of these conquistadors will make for a happy king.'

'Aye, weel said,' muttered Father. 'It is true that kings are avaricious.'

'Las Casas says they make no attempt to convert,'

Bethia said, 'but slaughter all, condemning them to hellfire and eternal damnation. And yet they claim their colonisation is about bringing the faith to the indigenous people. He writes it has always been the manner of doing wherever they have entered, to demonstrate a cruel butchery so that those spared tremble in constant fear.'

'Their lies have been stripped away,' said Will. He looked at Bethia and Logie in turn. 'And so any attempt by Catholic Spain to take England should be resisted by us most fiercely.'

There was silence, broken by Logie saying in a voice which had recently become strangely hoarse, 'You will receive no argument on that from us.'

To which Bethia nodded slowly.

'But I do not think what Spain has done is any worse than any other invader – look at the English rampaging around Scotland when they were trying to force the marriage of our queen to their king,' said Logie.

'I think the scale of the subjugation of peoples of a whole continent displays a level of viciousness not seen before,' Will had said slowly. And then Father had a coughing fit which had them all anxiously crowding around him, till Violet appeared with a spoonful of some concoction the apothecary had made. Father flapped his hands feebly, waving it away, but was eventually persuaded to swallow.

'Filthy stuff,' Father grunted when he could speak again, glaring at Violet, most undeservedly, Will thought. Eventually, he was restored to his more querulous good humour when she gave him a soothing drink of warmed wine with herbs. The conversation then shifted onto more mundane and less barbaric matters, to the relief of all, Will suspected.

Will left soon after to find his good son arrived home, bringing with him yet another pamphlet that he'd picked up in Leith.

'I think you will want to read this,' Andersoun said,

dropping it on the desk. 'It concerns matters close to us.'

Will reluctantly picked it up, read the title *The Baptizing of a Turk*, and paled.

Andersoun nodded and stomped off, calling for Cecy to bring a basin of hot water to wash the fish scales off his large, work-hardened hands. Will opened the pamphlet and began to read with a sense of dread. By the time he'd finished he was annoyed with Andersoun for making such a to do, but Andersoun was barely literate and likely made anxious by the title. The eponymous Turk had been naught but a Spanish captive whom Sir Francis Drake, during one of his many forays along the coast of Spain, had in turn captured. Indeed, it had a happy ending, for the Turk had willingly converted to Protestantism when he reached the shores of England, despite having previously resisted all attempts to turn him into a papist. Will sat flapping the pamphlet against the back of his hand and wishing that Bethia might so willingly be turned. What was it that made her cling so determinedly to false idols and spurn the good plain worship of the true Kirk? He dropped the booklet and, resting his elbows on the board, put his face in his hands in despair. She was a most obdurate woman.

Sir William Stewart, who had recently been granted the Barony of Pittenweem by the king, was suddenly much in evidence. Will supposed he must show he deserved the acquisition of lands that had previously formed rich pickings for whoever was prior ot the monastery. But really he was a fussing old woman, even worse than Nannis, for she at least did some good. Stewart sent his men shouting around the streets that the Spanish were like to come soon so that the village was in such ferment of fear that women were practising hiding their bairns beneath the bed, and those which had some sense, in the woods that rose on the slopes behind their homes.

An order was pinned to the mercat cross requiring a state of readiness and calling a *wappenschawing*, where all would gather, with what weapons they had, so that they might be counted. And the folk dug deep to find something to use against the cruel Spaniards and their whips. On the twentieth of August Will was there for the weapon count, which included ancient spears, swords gone rusty as well as the more obvious bows, staffs, ploughshares and even some long clubs normally utilised for the playing of golf. He remembered tales of the attack on nearby St Monans years ago by the English, and how it was told the people, including the women, rose up to defend their town and expel the invader, and his heart burst with pride for the doughtiness of his people. For all that Scotland was a lowly country, the Scots would fight to the end to defend their land. In this moment of unnatural pride he forgot Flodden and the flower of Scotland which fell there, he forgot Solway Moss which led to the death of another king, he forgot the Battle of Pinkie and the many recent small defeats at the hands of England and remembered only Scotland triumphing at Bannockburn two hundred and fifty years ago. And he was sure there must be other times too but could not bring them to mind in that moment.

He wandered amid his parishioners, the young, the old, the comfortably-off, the poor and the infirm, for everyone was there in a great muddle. Sir William Stewart bellowed to his men to get them into some sort o' order and *pick oot they fellows fit tae fight*. His men moved into the crowd, pushing and shouting, but to little avail. Finally, Will could bear it no longer and roared for silence. At the sound of their minister's voice all other voices did fall silent. Will could see Stewart glaring at him from his position on horseback. He gestured to Stewart that he should take over and eventually Stewart had the motley collection of village defenders lined up.

In church the next day, Will led the congregation in

prayer, asking God to watch over them and especially to protect them from the Spanish – for judging by the state of readiness he had thus far observed, they would not manage it without God's aid.

Chapter Thirty-Five

Visitors

The wet and stormy August continued. Day after day the boats could not put to sea and the wind and rain whipped through the narrow closes as fierce as any Spaniard. Sir William Stewart regularly called muster at the mercat cross and set the men to practising their archery at the butts, but it wasn't easy to fire an arrow straight with the gusting wind likely to blow it off target. Stories were rife that the Spanish had landed to the south in Dunbar, to the north in the Tay Estuary, Aberdeen and Cromarty and even St Andrews – which set the good folk of Pittenweem to a level of fervent devotion with their prayers which Will wished they might show more frequently.

One day in late September Will strode the mile and a half along the path to Anstruther to meet with James Melville. The sea, for a change after all the recent tempests, was sparkling blue and as innocent as a naughty bairn hiding he's been dipping his finger in the jam – which was precisely what Will had caught two small grandchildren doing just before he left the house. He'd waggled his own finger at them and they'd grinned back guiltily in return.

'I shall have to tell your mother,' he said. The bairns hunched fearful and Will dipped his own forefinger in the among the fresh-picked bramble jam, licked it and winked at them.

Shrieks of laughter followed him as he fled out the back door.

'I saw that, Papa,' called Cecy, as he made good his escape.

'Have you heard?' said Melville coming to greet Will with every evidence of pleasure. 'King Philip's most "fortunate fleet" has been defeated. At last it is over.'

'Yes, the news came this morning,' said Will. 'Although I believe it's not quite the triumph the English are lauding it to be. Strong winds are said to have played as much a part as Sir Francis Drake and his skilful seamanship in vanquishing the *invincible* Armada.'

'Aye,' said Melville. 'But who would ever have thocht it would be over so quickly. When I think on the last Assembly in Edinburgh and how terrible was the fear, piercing was the preaching, earnest and fervent the prayers amid the abounding sighs and sobs. And at that very time of lamentation, the Lord of the Armies who rides on the wings of the wind was conveying those monstrous ships around our coasts and dashing them to pieces on the headlands and islands of the country they had come to destroy.'

Will thought that Melville, who was at times inclined towards hyperbole – which was in part what made him such a powerful and popular preacher – was verging on the whimsical here, but it turned out to be not so far from the truth. As the wet and windy summer blew into an equally stormy autumn, the broadsheets went wild with the tales of the scattered Armada harried up and down the east coast of England and Scotland, chased by a relentless Sir Francis Drake and his flotilla. By late autumn, the English ships had returned to the safety of their harbours, confident that, of the one hundred and thirty ships which had set out from Lisbon in July, none remained off English waters. And then the stories came that many of the Armada ships unsunk by either Drake or storms, had been blown far north and were to be found off the coasts of Orkney, Shetland and even as far as Norway on one side, and Ireland on the other, desperately seeking any harbour and the supplies that would provide. And every attempt they made to reach Spain was frustrated, for God had mounted a campaign against them where they fought both storms and headwinds whatever they tried.

Then, early one morning in November, Will was awoken by a loud banging on the front door. He had recently taken to sleeping on a pallet in his workroom thereby relieving the pressure in the house by giving up the chamber which had formerly been his alone. The banging came again and Will leapt to answer the door, still in his shirt, before the whole house was awoken.

'Meenister, you're needed,' said the fellow standing on the doorstep.

Will didn't stop to ask why, assuming it was either death or transgression that he was being called to with such urgency.

'Wait here,' he said, pointing to the shelter beneath the outside stairs, and closed the door on the chill air creeping into the house.

He hauled on his breeches, black robes and black skull cap, tucked his Bible into his satchel and joined the fellow in a few minutes. He got a better look at him now despite the gloom, for the sun was still an hour off rising, and realised it was one of Melville's bailies.

'You are to tak ma horse. Gang tae the harbour where ye'll find the meenister. He said tae say he kindly requests yer presence.'

Will stared at him, but the fellow untied the reins from where the horse was most inappropriately tethered to the mercat cross and handed them to him.

'What *is* going on?' Will said as he prepared to mount.

'The meenister telt me tae say only that he needs ye,

261

else I'd blether on, and ye must go quick.'

Will thrust his foot in the stirrup, swung his leg over and clicked his tongue to get the horse moving.

'Ach, I forgot,' shouted the bailie after him. 'You'll find him at Anster East harbour.'

Will didn't stop to find out more. He set the horse to a gallop as soon as he left the village, despite the risk of a stumble on the rutted path in the grey light of dawn. As he drew nearer he could see a ship drifting in the bay. There were few boats around at this time of year and the fishing boats mostly safely moored in the harbour were only putting out on rare days when the weather looked to be favourable. He pulled on the reins bringing his horse to a halt and narrowed his eyes. It looked to be a lugger, which had likely encountered fierce weather for its sails were tattered. He peered at the ship, finding it difficult to make much out with the rays of the sun rising behind it. His eyes watered and he wiped them. Finally he could see the many small figures clustered on the deck, far more than he would've thought safe for a ship of that size.

The horse's hooves clattered over the cobbles but Will barely slackened his pace until he reached the harbour. He leapt off the horse leaving the reins trailing and, stiff-kneed, hurried to where a small group, including James Melville, was gathered gazing out to sea. There was a rowing boat putting out from the ship and Will could feel the tension as they watched its progress. It drew closer and he could see by the dress of its occupants that these were not men from around here.

'Spaniards?' he hissed to Melville.

'Aye,' said Melville, eyes fixed on the boat, which was drawing close to the wooden pier and the ladder with which to mount it. 'That is why I particularly wanted you here for I remembered you speak Spanish.'

'It is a long time since I last did.'

'Do your best.'

'Their officers will likely speak Latin.'

'Aye, and they may have an interpreter among them too. Given they were to invade England, one would be very necessary. I wanted you to listen for what might be said amongst them.'

Will nodded, Melville was an astute fellow.

They moved to the edge and stared down at the group in the boat. The captain, judging by the richness of his dress, sat in the stern hands clasped together as though in prayer. The sailors rowing appeared barely to have the strength to pull the oars, their bare arms thin and pale, shoulder bones jutting from ragged shirts. The only other occupant of the boat was a small man sitting hunched in the prow.

'They are unarmed,' muttered Will.

'Aye, I noticed,' said Melville.

The captain spoke and the man in the stern leaned forward and translated his words.

'Our commander asks if he may come ashore.'

'He may,' said Melville.

Will became aware of the murmur of voices behind him as folk emerged from nearby houses to discover what was about and why their minister and the one from the neighbouring parish were at the harbour so early. There were calls when they spied the ship and even more when the captain slowly hauled himself up the ladder and appeared before all in his shabby magnificence.

Will and Melville took a step back to give the man space. Will placed himself slightly behind Melville. He might be the senior by many years, but it was Melville's parish.

The captain stood before them, near as tall as Will, with thick grey hair and the weather-beaten face of a man who has spent much of his life at sea. They stared at him and he bowed, then dropped to one knee and bowed, even lower, so his lips came near to touching Melville's foot.

There were gasps from the watching crowd.

Although the Spaniard was of a stout frame, there was something hollow and shrunken-looking about him – and his men looked close to death. After a moment Melville spoke, and Will thought it of significance that the captain had waited for Melville to speak first, which was not something a commander of men was likely accustomed to doing.

The sun rose, spreading vibrant yellow light across the scene, which dimmed each time a cloud passed before it, as if sending a divine message. Although what that message could be was uncertain – the light felt heavenly while the darkness seemed of the underworld.

'My bailie tells me you have come not to give mercy, but to seek it.' Melville spoke loudly so that all could hear, his voice harsh in the stillness. The captain awaited a translation and Will wondered that Melville had not spoken to the man in Latin, but perhaps he did not want the listeners to misconstrue. Latin was forever a reminder of the Catholic Church.

'I am Jan Gómez de Medina of the ship *El Gran Grifon* and commander of the ships providing supplies to the Spanish fleet.' He spoke with quiet humility so Will considered it unfortunate that his translator did not follow his lead but adopted a tone of booming bombast.

Will glanced behind him at the crowd which was swelling with each moment that passed. He could see folk running along the clifftop path to reach them, so it was clear the word had already spread to neighbouring villages. The appearance of a stricken ship would always draw folk in any case. Where a living is made from the sea, all will come to aid a rescue hoping the same will be done for them, should they find themselves in such a position off a strange coast.

Medina continued as though the interpreter hadn't spoken. 'His glorious grace King Philip brought together a mighty fleet and army to avenge the intolerable wrongs

264

and grievous injustices inflicted upon the peoples of the Spanish Empire by the treacherous nation of England. But for our sins, God has turned against us, driving us past the coast of England and subjecting us to storms sent by divine providence over the past several months. Many of our ships have sunk in merciless seas or been dashed against inhospitable shores. Those few of us whom God has chosen to survive have endured bitter cold and suffered great hunger. We come here to kiss the hand of the king of the Scots ...' Medina paused here and bowed low once more '... and beg of you to render us assistance.'

Will watched Melville and sent up a prayer that he would show a true spirit of kindness, as Jesus Christ would have done.

Melville began to speak. 'Our friendship cannot be great, seeing your king and you are friends to the greatest enemy of Christ – the Pope of Rome. Our king and we defy that son of Satan and his cause against our neighbours and special friends of England.' Melville paused to let the translator catch up. 'And yet we, as Christians of a better religion, are moved by compassion. A compassion that is not manifest to our merchants residing among you with peaceable intent pursuing their lawful affairs who have been violently taken and cast in prison, their goods and gear confiscated and their bodies committed to the cruel flaming fire in the cause of religion. But among us you will find *nothing* but Christian pity and mercy, leaving God to work in your hearts concerning religion as it so pleases Him – for we *will* give you assistance.'

Medina bowed and gave his grateful thanks, saying he had met Scotsmen before in Cadiz, some of whom may have come from this very town, and had always shown them courtesy. Melville glanced at Will, who stepped forward and addressed Medina.

'As my fellow minister has said, we will do what we can to aid you. The Good Samaritan did not turn away and nor shall we. How many men do you have on board?' He spoke in Latin for he did not want the watching crowd to become fearful of the numbers of Spaniards likely flowing off this ship, which might be great enough to overpower the folk of Anstruther.

Medina replied, also in Latin, his voice hoarse as though he was already exhausted from speaking. 'We number two hundred and sixty.'

Will took a sharp intake of breath and saw Melville, out of the corner of his eye, start.

'Many died when my ship foundered far to the north off your island of Fair Isle. The *El Gran Grifon* was crowded, for we had rescued sailors and soldiers from other ships which sunk in the fearsome storms as we were blown north.'

'We cannot have all your men come ashore yet. We must speak with the local lairds,' Will said. This time he spoke in English so all might hear.

Medina nodded his understanding when the translator had finished speaking. He turned to climb back down the ladder.

'Wait,' said Will.

Medina stared at him, and Will, realising he'd spoken in Spanish, cursed himself.

'You know our language, sire,' said Medina.

'A little,' said Will reluctantly. 'In any case, I think you may stay ashore while we confer.'

He turned to Melville and spoke in Scots so the translator would not understand. 'We'll tak him tae Dreel Castle and Lord Anstruther can see whit kind o' man he is. God is wi' us here, but nae sense in gieing the devil an entry.'

'Aye,' said Melville, 'that is a guid way o' daeing.'

'I would bring my second in commands, if I may,' said Medina, when their invitation was explained to him.

Melville nodded and Medina called down to the boat.

Will felt sorry for the poor starving oarsmen having to

row out and back again. He stood on the quay watching while Melville spoke with Medina, or more correctly spoke at Medina, instructing him some more in the tenets of the true faith. Will was pleased to see the rowers were changed before the boat returned carrying three men in fine clothes which had seen better days. They were introduced as Capitan Patricio, Capitan Legorretto and Seigneur Serrano, who had all previously commanded supply ships which had sunk.

The group set out across the sand and over the stepping stones at the burn to Dreel Castle, followed by a great procession of watchers. Lord Anstruther, already apprised of their coming, came to welcome his guests, smiling and bowing. All four men responded with even deeper bows.

They were quickly called to the board, and Anstruther provided a surprisingly lavish spread given how little forewarning of their arrival he'd had.

Will found himself placed next to Captain Patricio and soon abandoned any attempt to disguise he could speak Spanish. All that time on the French galley shackled to a Spanish prisoner had borne fruit, for there was nothing else to do in their rest period and learning Spanish had at least provided some distraction.

'Our commander is an honourable man,' said Patricio. 'He is known to all as *El Buen.*'

Will inclined his head, pleased to learn his assessment of Medina was borne out.

'We have suffered beyond what I could ever have believed.' Patricio swallowed. 'It is very terrible when God turns his back upon the faithful.'

Will grunted. They were straying into territory where he did not want to go. 'I am surprised your men are quite so hungry given you had the funds for a ship to bring you here.'

'Hah!' said Patricio. 'The island where we were stranded called the Fair Isle – not a name I would have

267

bestowed upon it, for it is a miserable place stuck amid a vast cold sea – had not enough food to feed its own people. We offered gold but it was of no value to them. They shared what they could, but we were over three hundred men then, amid seventeen households.' He brushed his hand over his eyes. 'We left fifty of our men buried in that bleak land.'

They were starving and yet they had not seized what they wanted by force. Will impulsively reached out and squeezed the man's shoulder, feeling the bones sharp beneath his hand. He gazed at the other three senior officers. They did not look as cadaverous as their men, but then it would be no different to the galleys. The officers would take what food they wanted, leaving scraps for the rest, if they were fortunate.

'How did you manage to get away?'

Patricio shook his head. 'It was not easy. But eventually the factor came to gather rents, although the sums he could collect from such poor people were paltry. He was happy enough to take our commander, myself and a few others in his small boat back with him to the lands of Orkney, for a fee. There we became the guests of the …' He hesitated.

'The laird?' said Will.

'Yes. A good man by the name of Malcolm Sinclair.'

Will nodded thinking it likely that Andersoun would know Sinclair from when he fished around the Orkney Isles during the summer months.

'Sinclair was our host for many weeks until we were able to arrange boats to get our men from the Fair Isle to Orkney.'

Will inclined his head with respect that these officers had shown care for their men. It would've been all too easy to turn their backs and make good their escape leaving the sailors stranded, and starving.

'It is a very dark land,' said Patricio with a hint of weariness in his voice.

'In winter, yes. I sailed around that coast in the summer months,' said Will, deciding not to mention that he did more rowing than sailing, 'and at that time of year the sun barely sets before it rises once more.'

'We lost more men while we were on Orkney, as much from cold as starvation, but nothing comparable to the numbers on Fair Isle. Laird Sinclair arranged passage for us and …' he spread his hands wide, '… we find ourselves here.'

Will narrowed his eyes, wondering if they'd been seeking the lands of the Catholic nobles in Scotland, who were sympathetic to Spain's cause. Huntly to the north – no that was too far inland – Slains perhaps, or more likely Tantallon further south perched on a cliff above the sea, and home to the Red Douglas, a most determined papist. Perhaps it was naive to be offering the Spaniards assistance? He would pray they had not made an error of judgement …

Chapter Thirty-Six

A Kindly Folk

By the next day, when Lord Anstruther and Stewart from Pittenweem had gathered their men and made sure they were armed and wary, the Orcadian vessel was towed into harbour and its crew permitted to disembark. The men stumbled off the ship, some supporting their comrades although they could barely stand themselves. Faces drawn and with raw, bleeding gums, these skeletal figures staggered onto the quay. Will's heart was wrung; they were mostly young and beardless yet already as worn down as old men. The local folk watched with faces which displayed both horror and pity.

Suddenly a woman came pushing through the crowd and directed two sailors who had a third strung between them into her house. Others rushed into their homes, reappearing with bowls of kail and pottage, which they passed around. The sailors dropped to the ground where they were, bodies curving around the bowls which they drank from, picking out the pieces of fish and kail to chew slowly and savour every mouthful.

Will selected some sailors and soldiers he thought could undertake the walk to Pittenweem without collapse and led them there, with many stops upon the way. So a walk which would normally take at most half an hour took near two hours. Once there he arranged for the men to be billeted in the sheds and barns of his parishioners and none of the said parishioners objected. He was proud of his people; this was true Scottish kindliness.

He was feeling considerably less puffed up the next morning when Bethia again descended from her eyrie in the hills like a small Spanish Fury.

'What is this I am hearing?' she said loudly the moment she had been let in the house.

Will looked behind her, but she was, unusually, without her faithful shadow. Although, no doubt, she had travelled with a phalanx of outriders, for Logie would not allow it any other way.

'How could you permit it? Do you know how cruel Spaniards are with their torture, whips and Inquisition? Do you know how many Conversos they slaughtered – not caring if they converted with a true heart or no, assuming they were always apostates, crypto-Jews, Marranos – and only those with sufficient funds like Mainard's family could escape. And they have been running ever since. Till the moment of her death in Salonika, a thousand miles from Spain, Mainard's mother looked back with longing upon the country of her birth. A place she loved and yet could never return to.'

Will was stunned by the vehemence of her attack and for a moment could not think how to respond. 'But, but, but …' he stuttered, '… they are Catholics. I would have expected you, of all people, to be happy they were rendered assistance.'

'Pah!' said Bethia, making a movement as though to spit over her shoulder, which Will found most peculiarly foreign. 'Have you seen the latest pamphlet which is circulating? 'Tis a poem about Philip of Spain and begins most accurately:

'O waspish King,
Where is now thy sting,'

271

'They are a cruel and prideful people who would never have shown such mercy to us. Imagine if they had landed here with their forces intact, as was their intention in England, and how they would have abused us.'

Will could not help but say dryly in response, 'Somehow I think you and Gilbert would have been safe. But come ...' He gestured, leading the way to the kitchen. Opening the door, he pointed to the hearth, where three young men sat hunched by the fire, each knob of their spines visible beneath their thin shirts. They drew back as Will advanced.

'Would you have had me refuse assistance to starving lads?' He was about to say more but could see Bethia's face soften.

'Very well.' She nodded curtly. 'But the officers are the ones to watch. I hear they are living in comfort at Dreel Castle. Indeed, Gilbert has been invited to a banquet there to meet them.'

Her face flushed with anger once more as she spoke, the word *banquet* spat out with contempt. It seemed the happy couple might have disagreed.

Bethia had relented further towards the Spaniards when Will went to Balcarrow a few days later, displaying her more normal compassion at the tale he brought, after she expressed surprise at his rare visit. Will was not comfortable in Logie's home, forever fearful he would come across a crucifix or rosary or some other sign of that wicked creed and which he could not disregard. He knew the bonds of family loyalty should *not* be stronger than loyalty to God – and yet his sister had helped him many times as he wandered lost in Europe. Without de Lange's pecuniary assistance he would likely have ended up as miserable as the poor Armada wretches flooding the streets of the villages all around.

'James Melville was recently in St Andrews,' Will began.

She looked surprised he should tell her of Melville's whereabouts.

'Where he gathered information about the fate of more of the Armada ships. There is a broadsheet circulating entitled *Certeine advertisements out of Ireland concerning the losses happened to the Spanish Armie upon the west coasts of Ireland* that lists the names of all the principals of the Armada and their fate.'

She pursed her lips and he wondered at himself. Why was he trying to persuade her that all Spaniards were not evil? Nevertheless, he continued. 'I was present when Melville showed the broadsheet to their leader, Gómez de Medina. Melville read the first line … *this was the Lord's doing and it is marvellous in our eyes.* A statement most true.'

He could see Bethia wanted to interrupt but somehow contained herself.

'He read the names aloud of the captains who had died. *No,* said Medina, *oh no,* and vehemently shook his head. Then the tears began to fall, spilling down his face, and he made no attempt to hide them. He wept and wept as Melville read on.' Will fell silent, swallowing the lump in his throat.

'You could not have but felt pity for the man if you had been present, Bethia. *So many*, he said, over and over. And, Bethia, the ships were wrecked off Ireland as well as off the north of Scotland. Over sixty-five ships sunk or foundered and folk not ay as welcoming as we have been. Indeed, there are stories come from Ireland of men staggering onto beaches only to be slaughtered, then their bodies stripped as their attackers searched for jewels, silver or gold they might have on them, and any who survived later hung. Medina thanked us again and again for our generosity of spirit, calling us true Christians regardless of our faith.'

273

'I am sure the final comment must have gone down well with James Melville.'

Will gave a bark of laughter. 'I could see him pause but for once he didn't seize the opportunity to instruct Medina in how wrong thinking he is.'

'I am surprised you did not step in then,' said Bethia.

'Sometimes 'tis better to know when to speak and when to haud yer tongue,' said Will. 'And 'tis you and Logie's faith I have greater concerns about.'

She put her hand on his arm then. 'You are a good brother,' she said softly. 'And you must not fear for us. I go to the kirk, as you know, and I take Communion – with a true heart.'

'And yet …' said Will.

'The ceremony will always be lacking for me. I cannot help it, Will, any more than you could help but take the path you did.'

After a moment he nodded and they went on to speak of wider family matters, which was always safer ground. Nevertheless, he rode away feeling lighter in the knowledge that Bethia, secret recusant though she was, did not attend the kirk with a cynical heart.

Of course, it was inevitable that Ephraim should appear. He had been given leave to come by Robert Rollock because of his knowledge of Spanish – a form of which language he spoke at home in Constantinople. Will wished Rollock had not been so beneficent. He would have much preferred not to have Ephraim, with his easy charm, consorting with the soldiers and sailors of the Armada, who came from many nations under Hapsburg dominion and not only Spain. Yet he also understood that Ephraim would seize any opportunity to be with Edane during what was likely to be a long courtship for Andersoun wanted to make certain that Ephraim did not change his mind about staying in Scotland and try to spirit Edane away to Turkland, which he could do without the permission of her father once they were married.

And between one bell and the next, Ephraim had made friends and brokered peace between the local lads and the visitors.

'How did you manage that, and so quickly?' said Cecy when Ephraim strolled in and sat down on the settle next to Edane, quietly taking her hand in his.

Will stared at Ephraim and the hand was released.

'The Spaniards have a story to tell and our lads are of the sea so understand the perils they suffered very well.' He turned to Edane, half blocking Will's view, no doubt so he could obtain possession of the hand once more.

'That they have survived thus far is truly a miracle. God must have some care for them.'

'I doubt that,' said Will sternly.

'Tell us what they told you,' said Cecy quietly to Ephraim. 'I am sure we are most curious to hear.'

Ephraim pursed his lips thoughtfully and Will could see he was considering where to begin.

'Many of the Armada ships were galleasses.' He looked to his audience, including the children. 'The galleasses are …' he spread his hands wide, '… huge, which makes them formidable but also difficult to manoeuvre and, despite the great size of the Spanish ships, the smaller English ships could dart around them inflicting great damage as they did.'

'Did the Spaniards we have in Pittenweem sail on a galleass then?' said Edane.

Ephraim smiled at her and squeezed her hand. Will decided to let it pass.

'No. It seems Gómez de Medina was in charge of a squadron of urcas. They are smaller and more lightly armed since their purpose was to carry the stores and pack animals for the wider fleet. Medina's squadron were all ships owned by merchants from Northern Europe which were seized while they were trading in the ports of Andalusia last year.'

Will grimaced. John would not be at all happy when he learned that. Between pirates and kings, it was remarkable there were any vessels remaining in the hands of their original owners.

'His men say Medina has also been a soldier, so is knowledgeable and experienced about warfare both on land and sea. Even so, they found themselves confronted by the ship of Sir Francis Drake, no less. They had already engaged with other ships, despite being positioned well out on the left flank, and had no ammunition left. Drake fired at close range and then came about, crossing behind their stern and firing as he did. *El Gran Grifon* was raked by gunfire and round-shot, much of it below the waterline. Fortunately, another ship then crossed Drake's bows and the *Revenge* moved to attack it.'

Ephraim paused for breath but his eager audience urged him to tell more. Will had heard some of this before from Medina's captains but it was interesting to learn more from the perspective of his men.

'So there they were with a ship riddled with shot so its seams were leaking and the deck a morass of broken spars, fallen rigging and splintered wood. Medina ordered that they must reduce the weight they were carrying. This involved casting all the livestock overboard, including the horses and mules.'

There was a gasp from his listeners and Edane covered her mouth with her hand.

'There was no longer any requirement for them,' Ephraim explained to Edane. 'The Armada had failed and the invasion force would not now land on England's shores.' He clasped his hands together as though in prayer.

'It is to their credit that, despite the terrible trials they've faced since, the crews still talk with pity of the seas filled with horses swimming desperately to reach the ships which were leaving them behind.'

Ephraim sighed, but after a moment went on.

'Not all of the men come here are from Medina's ship. *El Gran Grifon* rescued drowning men from several wrecks which sunk or foundered, even though the commanders were told not to endanger their ships by so doing. But Gómez de Medina is truly a good man and disregarded those orders. Many times they thought they would die, for the strength of the wind was beyond anything they'd ever experienced and the waves so high they reached near to the sky.'

Will nodded. 'This tallies with what Medina himself told me. He said they patched the worst of the damage from Drake's attack with ox hide and what planks of wood they had, but it was never sufficient. Always the sea and wind would again rise to destroy their repairs.'

'And one night,' Ephraim continued, 'when they were so beset amid the torrent of storm, they saw lights flickering and pulsing across the black sky: red, green, blue and purple. They told me that *God in his infinite mercy sent us a gleam of light to pierce the darkness.*'

Will sniffed his disdain at such an interpretation thinking it was more like the fairies, driven by Satan.

'Yet still the storm grew. Daylight found them off a small rocky island – which was Fair Isle – knowing they *must* make landfall before the ship sank. They were forced to drive it up on the shore, but above the bay rose steep cliffs. The only way they could escape was to climb the mast till they reached a ledge high above and then clamber on up the cliff face, at any moment risking death by a fall either onto the deck or into the sea. And that is how all bar five – who did fall to their deaths – made good their escape.' Ephraim paused for breath and scratched his head. 'They hauled up the sea chests too, which are filled with Spanish gold, but they did not manage to rescue what few provisions they had left before the ship sank. I think they did not understand how

277

meagre the lives of the folk of Fair Isle would be and thought they could purchase what they needed.' He shook his head. 'Many died of hunger – and yet they did not steal from the islanders.'

There was silence in the chamber. A quiet pitying of the fate of this terrible Armada.

'Let us pray for their souls,' Will said, and bowed his head.

Chapter Thirty-Seven

The Crew

Despite their origins, those who met them could not but be charmed by the Spanish commanders, and *El Buen* in particular. There was a genial kindliness about him, a sense that the man fitted his epithet and was innately good. Even Will was heard to say 'he was nay bad, for a Spaniard,' and John, inevitably, was using the opportunity to forge future trade links with Spain and its new dominions.

Bethia, come to visit Father one day, found her brothers and Andersoun outside John's house blethering about their Armada guests – although they no doubt would deny they ever engaged in anything but serious conversation.

'It's no sae easy to get rid o' all they Armada fellows,' said Andersoun. 'The ship they arrived in is unseaworthy.'

'They scraped it ower the skerries at Fife Ness,' said John.

Andersoun nodded his agreement. 'Aye, it wis fortunate they made it this far.'

'Why did they not put in at Crail then?' she asked.

Andersoun shrugged. 'It was dark and daybreak found them off Anster.'

She left the men and went inside to discover John's

daughters in a huddle giggling over the Spanish sailors. It would seem that, even in their cadaverous state, some were found to be bonny, and now, several weeks in with plenty of kail and porridge inside them, were further recovering their looks.

Violet glanced at Bethia and came to whisper in her ear. 'Tell them,' she said.

'Tell them what?' said Bethia.

'That it does not do to take up wi' a foreigner.'

Bethia stared at her. 'I loved Mainard, and if I had to live my life over, I would not choose differently.

'Oh! I thocht now wi' Gilbert …' Violet's voice trailed away as Bethia looked askance at her.

After a moment she reached out and touched Violet's arm. 'I am indeed fortunate, however, to have had not one, but two, loving husbands.'

Violet's anxious frown eased, but only momentarily, for her daughters were leaning in whispering together once more. 'The sooner these Spaniards are awa' back to Spain the better,' she muttered. 'But for now I maun go see to their feeding. Come lassies!'

Her daughters rose with alacrity and followed Violet to the kitchen.

Violet was not the only mother made anxious, and, in any case, the villages around Anstruther Easter and Wester could not long sustain feeding an extra two hundred and sixty mouths, and this with the rest of winter to get through. By Yule, Medina and his commanders had left for Edinburgh, where they were entertained in great comfort by the Earl of Bothwell and a number of the other Catholic lords.

'The commander, for all his men called him *El Buen*, no longer seems to consider they are his responsibility,' Melville had said to Will.

'Melville sounded maist weary,' Will said when

repeating the story to Bethia and Father. 'We all saw the heavy iron kists removed from the ship. Melville says they are full of Spanish gold yet Medina did not see reason to use it to pay for the transportation of his men to Edinburgh, but skipped away before anyone quite realised the villages would be left wi' them all.'

Father snorted as he listened, one hand cupped around his ear while Will's voice boomed around the chamber. 'Aye weel. Melville will be wanting ony siller the parish has tae pay for the finishing o' this grand new manse,' he said, voice full of mirth. 'I hear tell that commander gie'd Melville one o' they chests o' Spanish gold tae help wi' the build.'

'That is nonsense, Father. Melville is a good and honest man. 'Tis a most wicked rumour to spread.'

'Hah!' said Father. 'That's whit awbody is saying.'

Bethia wondered how Father knew what anybody was saying given that it was winter and too cold for him to venture out – and he was growing deafer by the day.

'And why are you no getting a grand new manse built for you by public subscription and Spanish gold, like Melville?' Father said, clearly not about to be shut down by his son. 'Perhaps the folk o' Pittenweem dinna value you as much as the Anster folk do their meenister.' He folded his arms and slowly nodded his head.

Bethia watched Will's face grow from red to purple and reflected how easy it was to rile him still. Age didn't seem to have brought him serenity, at least in matters close to his heart. She reached out a foot and gave him a gentle kick and, when he stared at her, a shake of the head.

'Why would Will need a manse built? He has finer accommodation than Melville available in the priory … if he cared to use it,' she said.

'Aye, they monks looked after themselves very weel,' said Father. 'But papism must be seeping from the very walls of that auld priory itself, so I'm no surprised you didna move intae the place, son.'

'Numbers in the school are growing so it's good there's space to expand into,' said Will. 'And William Stewart was quick enough to take the great house there. But,' he said slowly, 'I could move into the prior's old accommodation.'

'And your house *is* very crowded,' said Bethia.

'Aye, it is that,' said Will.

He spoke with a certain weariness, and Bethia gazing at him felt a sudden rush of fear. Her brother looked old. But then they were old, even John was now creeping into his fifties.

She rose and went down to the kitchen. She'd come with a sack of oats which Violet was already overseeing making into a large pot of porridge, while outside a line of refugees from all corners of Spain's European empire stood shivering in the wind whipping off the sea and around the corner of the house.

'I dinna ken how much longer we can keep them fed and still hae enough left for ourselves,' said Violet as her daughters bustled around her ready to take the bowls out to *they puir Spaniards*.

Bethia thought of passing through Anstruther recently and how it did indeed seem that the Armada refugees outnumbered those who lived there. And not all were welcoming towards their foreign visitors. Will, speaking at the church on Sunday and most roundly condemning any fighting between the young men of the village and their guests, reminded all yet again of the tale of the Good Samaritan.

'I would not have it said that the people of the East Neuk of Fife did any less for those in great need,' he said from the pulpit.

'Aye, weel, they need to stay awa frae oor lassies,' muttered a lad behind Bethia.

'And,' said Will, 'anyone else caught fighting will be brought before the synod, incur a fine, be adorned in sackcloth for a week and spend a month of Sundays on the repentance stool.'

There was an intake of breath from behind and the speaker desisted. But it was a relief to all, except the lassies, when a few weeks after their commanders had left, the fishermen, in desperation, began to ferry men from the broken Armada across the Forth to Leith, from where they walked up the hill to Edinburgh – before the goodwill of the community entirely dissipated.

Will was particularly glad that Ephraim was among those who returned to that city. He did not entirely trust his granddaughter, so besotted did she seem, not to persuade Ephraim they should follow the path of Symon and Kristene and hurry the marriage along. And Kristene was already heavy with her second child. Oh, no, he did not want that for his beautiful granddaughter and her still so young.

Chapter Thirty-Eight

St Fillan's Cave

In March of fifteen hundred and eighty-nine, Will decided he would move to the old priory.

'Are you quite certain this is what you want?' said Cecy when he made his announcement as they ate dinner. 'Pass your grandfather the goose,' she said severely to one of her brood who'd been about to seize a plump drumstick.

'I have thought, and prayed on it, and I think it's time. It will be easier for parishioners to seek me out and to have a place of quiet reflection and private discourse,' he said, raising his voice over the dispute begun at the other end of the table about which brother had the better collection of bird's eggs.

'Wheesht!' said Andersoun. ''Tis time ye baith were oot in the boats wi' me. I niver had the indulgence of nesting when I was a laddie but had tae work tae feed us.' He glanced at his mother who'd joined them at the board and she nodded vehemently.

'You, Morris, will be out wi' me tomorrow, and Charlie, you'll tak yerself doon tae the rope walk and learn how to twist fibre into cable.'

He sat back in his chair, arms folded, and surveyed his sons with an expression of satisfaction.

The boys looked to their mother and Will saw they

expected her to intervene, no doubt claiming they were too young for such arduous duties, but she said nothing. He had hoped at least one of them would follow Donald to the university in St Andrews, but they were not at all studious lads.

'Maman?' appealed Charlie hopefully, and Will had to suppress a smile at the connivance of the laddie hoping that using the French would soften his half-French mother.

'You will obey your father, as you should,' she said.

Will could see, by the exchange of glances betwixt Andersoun and Cecy, that all had been agreed beforehand. He smothered a smile himself, but the next moment he was coughing and spluttering, and it wasn't anything to do with lads and nesting.

Nannis, leaning across the table, had spoken. 'I will keep hoose for ye, Meenister, when ye move tae the priory. We cannie hae ony o' they flibbertigibbet lassies working in yer kitchen without proper oversicht.'

Andersoun rose from his seat and came to slap Will upon the back, which at least stopped the coughing fit Will was suddenly assailed by.

Will saw Andersoun was made anxious by his mother's offer, but it wasn't until Andersoun bent to whisper in his ear, 'Let her doon gently,' that Will understood why.

There was silence in the room. For once even Nannis had said her piece and gone quiet. All eyes were on Will, while Cecy was readying herself to speak and rescue him.

'I think …' he said slowly, '… I think that might be helpful.'

He could see his family glancing at one another, uncertain as to whether they'd understood correctly.

Nannis leaned forward. 'Does that mean ye want me tae keep hoose for ye, Meenister.'

'I believe it does … but,' he said severely, 'only if that is all you do. I cannot have you interfering in parish business, and if you do not abide by this stricture then I will seek another housekeeper. Are we in agreement?'

There was silence in the chamber, all eyes on Nannis.

'Aye, Meenister,' she said, 'but I must hae control o' the kitchen.'

'Of course, that is understood.'

Cecy grinned and Andersoun squeezed Will's shoulder and went back to his seat, while an argument was begun between the lads and lassies as to who would get Will's workroom as a bedchamber. The only person who was silent was Nannis.

'We will discuss terms later,' Will said.

She wiped her eyes with the back of her hand. 'Aye, and I will gie a thocht to the best servants. I micht hae Annie Martin, for she's a hard worker.'

'And that ye will no!' said Andersoun in tones of ringing outrage. 'She's ma fastest filleter o' haddock.'

Nannis was not dilatory. The next morning, Will, on his way to bring solace to a widower – although he knew there was small comfort to be found for a man whose wife had died in childbirth leaving him with seven children, one of whose legs were so twisted he could not walk but must be carried everywhere – met her bustling breathlessly along the street. Behind her, Morris and Charlie huffed and puffed as they pushed a cart piled with household goods. And behind them trailed a young lass, her arms so full with linens she could not see where she was placing her feet and was every moment at risk of falling. At least the bundle would cushion her, nevertheless Will went to her aid.

'No, no, Meenister. Tibby can carry it fine,' said Nannis loudly while the lass hung her head.

Will took the bundle anyway and a woman scrubbing her doorstep knocked on her neighbour's door so that all could come and watch their minister carrying linens down the street.

'See,' said Nannis to Tibby. 'I telt ye the meenister is a kindly man. He only shouts loud in the kirk tae make certain God can hear him.'

'I telt the servant which rooms we would hae,' said Nannis as they ducked through the low doorway and into the narrow hallway of the accommodation the prior had once taken his ease in.

She led him up the stairs after instructing the lads and Tibby to wait till she had conferred with the minister about where everything should go. Will could hear the screech of furniture being hauled over the floor as they climbed, and Nannis, small and ample-bellied, quickened her pace.

'Tak care,' she shouted to the two men who were dragging desks over the wooden floor. She pointed. 'Look at the bluidy mess ye are making o' the polish. Sorry, Meenister,' she said, 'but it is a bluidy mess.'

'What's going on?'

'Och, we are moving the school tae the back o' the priory. Much better there and near the gates so the bairns dinna disturb ye. And from here we can see awbody that is passing up and doon between the harbour and the new tolbooth.'

Will opened his mouth to object and Nannis came to stand before him.

'Now, Meenister, you jist worry aboot the godliness of the folk o' Pittenweem and making sure we a' hae a place in heaven and I'll tak care o' yer comfort in this life.'

Will shook his head at her but could not contain the grin. He handed over the bundle of linens and set off back down the turnpike.

'Go on up,' he said to Tibby who was lingering by the door, 'and you lads can start unloading. There'll be a penny in it for all of you.' He waved Tibby away, for she was trying to kiss his hand. 'No need for that, lass,' he said, and hurried off to see his parishioner.

It was remarkable how quickly all was settled. Nannis, now that she had him under her dominion, was far less troublesome than previously. She was housekeeper to the minister and, although she would never be entirely cured of prying into everyone's business, her primary interest was ensuring Will was well fed and comfortable, and she had little time for much else. The regular payments Will made her for her work, he soon discovered, were, in part, used to help others – and in particular those who had been reluctant to send daughters, who were needed to mend nets or fillet fish or care for their siblings, to school. Nannis had made it her mission that all young girls, as well as boys, should be able to read their Bibles. And Will, from having found her alternately an object of pity and then an irritant for much of the sixteen years that Cecy had been wed to Andersoun, now felt respect for her – which frankly made a pleasant change from barely tolerating her.

'You are happy here?' said Cecy, when she came to see him on her daily visit.

'I am,' said Will. 'If it were not for the problem of what to do with our stranded Spanish sailors then all would be well in my life.'

'What do you mean?' said Cecy frowning. 'They have all been removed to Edinburgh and are no longer our concern.'

'Not quite all,' said Will wearily.

He had discovered them by accident when he was investigating the chamber he now used for study and writing his sermons. He'd expected it would also be where he met his parishioners, but Nannis considered that no one but herself, the minister and Tibby, when she cleaned the chamber, should be permitted entry.

Tibby was dusting the ridges of the carved wooden panelling which lined the room (those abbots really did like their comforts) while Will read his Bible. Usually, he would prefer the quiet contemplation of being alone, but the lass moved around the periphery in silence and he quickly forgot she was there. He studied one of the finest verses in the Holy Book, Isaiah 2 verse 4, reading it aloud softly to himself.

> *… And he shall judge among the nations, and shall rebuke many people: and they shall beat their swords into ploughshares, and their spears into pruning hooks: nation shall not lift up sword against nation, neither shall they learn war any more …*

There was a sudden thump which had him near dropping the good book.

'What was that?' he said to Tibby.

'Naething, Meenister,' the girl whispered.

'Blethers. There is something there.' He got up and leant his ear against the panelling. He *could* hear voices. He ran his hands over the smooth wood, then knocked on it. There was silence now, a heavy silence, as though someone was listening intently on the other side.

A thump came from behind him and he jumped. Tibby stood gazing at where his Bible lay open on the floor. He narrowed his eyes and stared at her, had never known her to be clumsy before.

'Who is behind the panelling, Tibby?'

She shook her head.

He stared at it. When he squinted he could see a break in the wood. It was like the Doges Palace in Venice that Bethia had told him of, with its labyrinth of secret doorways and passages. He felt around it with his fingertips and then snatched them away at the nip as a splinter of wood pierced the skin. Sucking on his bleeding finger, he studied the doorway. He could fetch a hammer and break through, but this was beautiful, old polished panels.

'Tibby,' he said severely, 'open this door.'

She hung her head, a wee slip of a lass. 'I dinna ken

how tae,' she whispered.

'But you *do* know who is hiding behind the panelling.'

She kept her eyes on the floor, but, after a moment, slowly nodded.

'So how did they get there?'

'They werena in the hoose, Meenister, I promise,' she said.

'How, Tibby?'

She glanced at the door and shuffled her feet.

Will waited.

'The cave,' she whispered.

'The one on the way to the harbour?'

'Aye, Saint Fillan's Cave,' she said, then covered her hand with her mouth. 'Sorry, Meenister.'

Will remembered there was a spring within the cave, once a place of pilgrimage where papists had come, believing tales of the cures that drinking its water would effect. Eight hundred years ago an Irish monk had supposedly lived as a hermit there and the insane used to be shut in the cave overnight, their desperate relatives hoping the spirit of Saint Fillan would effect a cure.

'Come,' he said, striding out of the room and down the spiral of stairs with Tibby slowly following.

They edged down the path, the mellow sandstone rock face behind which the priory was built rising to their left. The cave was somewhere deep within, and fishermen used it now as a store in the dark days of winter, and very occasionally, if the tide rose far enough, it was flooded. But Will had never had any cause, nor desire, to go inside himself.

He halted, bracing his feet to prevent himself from slipping on the steep slope, while he waited for the reluctant Tibby to catch up with him.

'Show me,' he said.

She hunched as though expecting a blow. Will waited. Suddenly she was off, scrawny arms and legs scuttling like a spider over the rocks. He followed, aware of how old, stiff and hesitant he was next to her sureness of foot.

The narrow entrance she brought him to dropped steeply into darkness. 'Is there a torch?' he asked. She shook her head. There was no fire to light one with anyway. Tibby stepped inside and Will came uneasily after her. She seemed eager now to show him, and the further inside he went the more hesitant Will became. He should have waited and fetched Andersoun, a party of men … and torches.

He descended shallow steps cut in the rock, sliding his hand along the cave side both to keep his balance and orientate himself. Andersoun had once told him that the name Pittenweem came from the old Pictish language meaning *place of the cave*. Will hadn't been much interested beyond surprise that his poorly educated son-in-law, who could barely read, should know of the Picts.

He stumbled and near fell. Then Tibby's small hand was upon his arm. He'd no sense she was so close.

'Not far now, Meenister.'

Will thought of those of unsound mind left alone in this darkness all night. Perhaps it was hoped the fear would effect a cure, and perhaps that Jesus might bring comfort and light to the afflicted in a dark place. He tutted, knowing that was naught but the false stories of papism from his childhood.

The cave wall was curving as he descended. Then he had a glimpse of light below: a light to guide a man through the darkness. He shook his head at himself. What was going on? This was naught but being in the dark, with some tales of a holy man who may have lived here clogging up his head. The wall fell away and he sensed he was within the bowl of the cave. He stumbled forward towards the light.

There were two of them sitting before a very small fire. Will wondered where they got the wood and hoped they weren't burning any of the fishermen's stores. They were only lads, one perhaps around Tibby's age, the other a boy of around ten years old. It was hard to tell their ages, so scrawny were they.

'Why are you here?' said Will in Spanish. 'Why did you not go with the rest?'

'They want tae stay in Pittenweem wi' us,' said Tibby.

Will turned to stare at the lass, who had drawn close to the older lad. 'They want tae become proper Christians. They want tae come tae the kirk and worship as we dae. Will ye teach them, Meenister, please.' She pressed her palms together imploring him.

'But how did they get here and why could I hear them from within my chamber?' Will said, as much to give himself time to think.

'There is a stair,' said Tibby. She led him into the far corner, and tucked behind an outcrop he could see the curve of stone steps in the flickering light, leading upwards. The abbot's secret stairs – more papist trickery.

'Tibby, how did you expect to get away with this? I assume you've been feeding them from my kitchen?'

She hung her head.

'But why not bring them to me.'

'I was feart you wouldna listen, Meenister. T'was better tae wait till a' the Spaniards went back to their hames and then ye couldna send them awa.'

Will felt shamed. Was he really so unapproachable? He sighed. 'It is not so simple, Tibby.'

'Why?' she said.

He was surprised by how bold she had become. He'd had more conversation with her these past minutes than in the few weeks since Nannis brought her to work at the priory.

He went back to the two Spaniards sitting hunched by the paltry fire which gave off little heat in this cold, dank place. They were watching his every movement with desperate eyes.

'Do you come to the Protestant faith with true hearts?' he asked them in Spanish.

The older lad stood up and pulled the younger with him. 'We do,' he said, with sufficient solemnity that Will thought his answer sincere.

He glanced down at Tibby, who was still standing with hands clasped as though in prayer.

'We shall keep them quiet here for the moment. You may feed them and bring firewood, and,' he looked around but they seemed to have nothing but the thin and ragged garments on their backs, 'some blankets.'

'Oh thankee. I kent ye were a guid man, Meenister.'

Will held up his hand. 'I must speak with my synod,' he said.

A small moan came from Tibby and she went back to wringing her hands.

'Do not fear, lass, for I am hopeful of a good outcome.'

Chapter Thirty-Nine

The Armada in Edinburgh

Bethia had not met the Spanish captains when they'd been staying at Dreel Castle although Gilbert had gone several times to dine with them, saying they were fine men.

'Did you speak through the translator?' she'd asked.

'Some of the time but it was too slow. We reverted to Latin, certainly with Gómez de Medina, for he's a well-educated man. Did you know he's the most senior ranking Armada officer in Scotland?'

Bethia did not but, after hearing this, was not at all surprised when she learned that the Spanish commanders had been invited to Edinburgh as guests of the Catholic nobles. And soon after, a message came inviting Gilbert to join them.

'I do not think that is wise,' said Bethia. 'The lords no doubt see Medina as a means of securing Catholic assistance for their cause.

'I am not comfortable to refuse, and, in any case, the king is surprisingly tolerant of the vagaries of his Catholic lords – and currently preoccupied with his marriage plans.'

'Then I will come too and I can see Ephraim,' Bethia said. 'In any case, I am now curious to meet these men before they depart our shores, which surely must be soon.'

He frowned. 'The crossing will likely be rough and certainly cold even in spring, however calm a day.'

'Gilbert,' she said, arms folded, 'I have travelled to Constantinople and back. I think I can survive yet another trip across the Forth, however old I am now become.'

He took her in his arms, whispering that she was a feisty wench.

She giggled, then pushed him away claiming he was messing up her hair.

'Ah, the hair,' he said. 'We cannot have that disturbed.'

And so she went to Edinburgh, where, more important than any Spanish captains, she saw Ephraim.

'You have prevailed in spite of the almost universal opposition,' she said, sitting down the day after her arrival to have a comfortable blether with him.

'I love her, Nonna. She is kind, and fierce,' he grinned, 'and I am the most fortunate of men, for Edane loves me in return. How could we not prevail?'

'But if you stay in Scotland you must adhere to the Kirk, else you will be in constant fear, forever looking over your shoulder in case you are revealed.'

'And is that any different to how you live?'

Bethia gave a start.

'I know you cleave to the Pope of Rome still, and Grandpa Gilbert too.'

She savoured the *Grandpa Gilbert*. It meant a great deal to her that Gilbert should be treated as belonging within the family. After a moment she said, 'It is different for us. We are old, and when we die it will die with us. As long as we make no attempt to engage others and do our observances in secret then we are unlikely to be punished. And Grandpa Gilbert is not without influence.'

Bethia thought of the story that was told of Mary, Queen of Scots at her execution, and the moments before she stepped forward to lay her head upon the block, when the Dean of Peterborough drew close.

'Your Grace,' he said softly, 'will you not take this last chance to forswear the false faith and join the Protestant Church.'

She had politely refused.

'We will pray for Your Grace,' he said.

To which Mary replied, 'I thank you, but to join you in prayer I will not do. You and I are *not* of one religion and I will spend my blood in defence of the true faith.' And Bethia swallowed back the fear which rose into her throat as she thought on that poor queen and the terrible choices that were forced upon her.

'Nonna,' said Ephraim, bringing her back to herself. 'You are not so very old. You have the stamina of great grandfather and will live at least another twenty years.'

'Thirty, if I take after him.'

'See!'

'But what of you, my beloved grandson. Can you give your faith and loyalty to this reformed Church in all its austere joylessness?'

'Nonna, within our family there are Jews, Catholics, Protestants and Moslems. All are paths which lead to God. There are aspects of the Protestant faith I do not overly care for but that was also the case when I was a Jew. I will live a God-fearing life with family at its centre whatever route I must travel, just as my father did and his before him.'

Bethia gazed at him, so young, strangely wise, and full of hope that all would turn out well. And yet she was made fearful by his wavering path. No one should pick and choose which faith to follow, for only the true one would lead to God. She sighed, saying, 'When I was younger than you, I witnessed the burning of a Protestant preacher. There is nothing to say such evil times are gone. We may again see a similar fate for any who do not practise the Protestant faith with a good heart.'

'But I *will* follow it with a good heart, and it is not so

difficult, for apart from my unfortunate incarceration, which was due to envy and nothing else, I have been welcomed here. I feel as though I do belong.'

'Oh, my boy. Are you certain?'

He nodded. 'I have made my choice, and in any case, when we embarked on the long journey to Scotland, I promised Papa I would not leave you.'

Bethia's eyes filled with tears. 'But I would *not* hold you to such a promise, for I do not think I shall ever return.'

'And I too have reason for staying.'

'You could take Edane back with you.'

He shook his head. 'I would not do it. I can be happy here and we will have a good life. I could not take her from all that she knows. It would crush her.'

'I think you underestimate Edane. She is not some wilting flower.'

'I well know that, else she would not have defied her family. But Uncle Will only agreed we could marry if I stay here. It suits me, and I will not break my promise to him or Edane's father, who have been so good to me.'

'So you too are become a Converso, except this time it is by choice. God does move in mysterious ways.'

'His wonders to perform,' said Ephraim.

And Bethia could see he truly believed what he said, which brought her comfort that all might be well.

Gilbert joined them then and they went on to talk of the Spaniards, for Edinburgh was full of Armada sailors, soldiers and some priests too. They were to be found slouched and shivering in every close and corner, beneath archways, in any empty doorway, all in great misery. Hollowed out with hunger and with little enough clothing to cover their nakedness, never mind to keep them warm – for what they had, had mostly been torn from their backs by locals seeking the famed Spanish jewels and gold when, half-drowned, they staggered from their wrecks onto Scottish and Irish beaches.

297

Edinburgh's beggars were angry at the incomers seeking alms without either licence or the medal to show they held one, but the Armada sailors and soldiers so outnumbered them they could do little. Word was that the kirk session at Perth had commanded its town gatekeepers not to grant entry to any Spaniards. But what were these poor fellows to do stranded so far from home?

Grissel was in her element as she and Megy ran yet another soup kitchen, in the Turkish way, and John could not object at her prodigality, for it was her own earnings from the ale house and her business as a wad wyfe that she was *squandering* – as he roundly told her. But even John, who was again in Edinburgh, could not but pity them.

'How will you manage when word gets out?' said Bethia. 'There must be nigh on six hundred of them crowding the streets.'

Gilbert blew out air. 'More like double that number I would say. And I learned today there's the remnants of an Irish regiment that was fighting for Philip among them too. And all come to Edinburgh seeking passage home, even those who were wrecked on the west coast of Ireland.'

'Aye,' said John, 'and their masters lording it in comfort with nary a care for all their men.'

'Megy has it a' worked oot. They will get tickets,' said Grissel folding her arms and puffing out her chest, which, Bethia reflected, was not inconsiderable. She did not remember Grissel being so large bosomed previously. She was a woman of comfortable size, since she'd always had enough to eat, but could in no way be described as fat-bellied. Now there was something almost *motherly* about her demeanour.

Megy came later that day with her bundle of tickets and a story of a fight at a tavern in Leith.

'Ane o' they Spanish officers stabbed a man,' she called excitedly the moment she entered the chamber.

'That is *not* good,' said Bethia, and Gilbert nodded his agreement.

'It was an Englishman and he's deid as a butchered bull,' said Megy.

'What! Surely an Englishman would not be foolish enough to be caught carousing down by the docks,' said Bethia.

John looked thoughtful. 'I think it maun be true. The king gave safe passes to the crews of *Vangard* and *Tiger,* two English galleons which arrived not three days past off Leith. Elizabeth will be curious about the Spanish in Edinburgh and nae doubt her men are here to gather what information they can while the king is hosting the English commanders at Holyrood. Ach, oor Jamie is no going tae be happy aboot the English and Spanish getting intae a brawl.'

'Yon laddie played the trumpet,' said Megy.

Grissel, Gilbert, John, Bethia, and even Ephraim, stared at her.

'The ane whit got stabbed – he was a trumpeter.'

'Oh aye,' said John, 'then no so easily replaced.'

By the next afternoon, John had been to Leith and gathered what information he could about the English commanders and their purposes. He and his fellow merchants were made uncomfortable by the proximity of these ships of war, which not so long ago had viewed them as prey, to their much smaller and less well armed vessels, and all were on edge to uncover the English intentions. He arrived back as Bethia and Gilbert were preparing to leave for the banquet and spread a piece of cloth across the board.

'Rather drab and dreary,' said Bethia. 'I do not at all care for that dull shade of brown.'

'This is a colour called *Dead Spaniard*,' said John, 'and is in great demand in London, so the English told me.

Everyone wants to be seen clothed in *Dead Spaniard*.'

'No!' said Bethia.

'Aye, and it's fetching a high price. I wonder if it would take in Scotland,' he said thoughtfully. 'And there's a new ballad of *the Strange and Most Cruel Whips*, which is been sung everywhere. London, it seems, has been seized by a' things Spanish – jist not the Spaniards themselves.' He gave a short bark of laughter at his own wit.

'You *have* been collecting a lot of gossip today,' said Bethia.

''Tis always wise to have an ear to the ground. Word is that the queen of England is demanding yon Gómez de Medina be given up to her. It appears he sailed extensively in the waters o' the southern Atlantic sea and will hae information her mariners would find maist useful.'

'Pah! you mean her pirates,' said Bethia.

Both men stared at her.

'I do not care for Elizabeth. She had our queen beheaded. What kind of a woman does that, and to her own cousin?'

She could see John smirking at her outburst and glared at him.

'We must away,' she said stiffly to her husband and swept out of the door.

Chapter Forty

Gómez de Medina

Gilbert had cautioned Bethia more than once he could not be certain she too would receive an invitation to join Bothwell and the other Catholic lords at Craigmillar Castle.

'And Bothwell is a dangerous man of quick temper inclined to wield both knife and sword at the least provocation. Although not much older than the king, he has already killed several men.'

Despite Gilbert's warning, Bethia was almost as curious to set eyes upon Bothwell as Gómez de Medina. This Bothwell's uncle had been Mary, Queen of Scots' third husband and, when her throne was seized, had fled to Denmark – a most unfortunate choice. What would it be like to know your uncle had spent the last ten years of his life in a pit prison where no light penetrated, chained to a post so low to the ground he could not stand and a descent into madness his only means of survival?

In the event her presence was requested – there were some benefits in being *the grand lady from Turkland*.

They travelled to the castle in great state, for Gilbert, as well as bringing three of his own retainers, had hired the two stout guards who John generally employed. Gilbert had been quite stern though when he realised Bethia's servant was not among their party and she would be unattended. She could've brought the girl who performed duties for her in Balcarrow but the lass had looked so fearful at the prospect of setting foot on a boat Bethia had decided it was best to leave her behind.

'Better not to bring her,' she said when Gilbert had remonstrated. 'I would likely have spent the crossing mopping the vomit off.'

'My wise wife,' he said, then grew serious once more. 'But still I do not like it that there is no one to care for you.'

Bethia would've liked Grissel to accompany her to the castle but Grissel had not offered and Bethia was not comfortable making the request. She said nothing of this to Gilbert, instead catching his arm and pressing her face against it. 'What are you speaking of – no woman could be better cared for than I.'

'And no man more fortunate than I,' he said with a break in his voice.

She was wishing she'd not been so sanguine as she dressed that afternoon in the spacious chamber they'd been allocated within the castle. When she and Gilbert had married the previous year she'd happily reverted to wearing her most ostentatious clothes, for she was no longer constrained by the Act against Luxury. Again, she was dressing in beaded and bejewelled clothes whose beauty she enjoyed, despite their weight. And silk was so much more soothing against the skin than rough linen. But it was heavy work getting herself arraigned in them without a competent servant to assist.

'You have led an interesting life, madam,' Gómez de Medina said when she found herself seated next to him in the gracious surroundings of the great hall with a feast laid before them, for the Scots Catholics were feting the Armada commanders as though King Philip himself was among them.

Bethia blinked in surprise.

'You are the Turkish lady of whom I have heard tell?'

She nodded, for she doubted there was another in Scotland.

'And I find it is correct you understand Spanish. You must tell me how this came to be.'

She swallowed. She had wanted to come here and now it felt perilous. She should've feigned ignorance when first he spoke in his formal Castilian. He would realise it was Ladino that she spoke as soon as she opened her mouth. Both the mix of Spanish and Hebrew words used, as well as her accent, would give her away. He was watching her now with those kindly eyes behind which lurked an astute mind. He had likely risen to his shipboard rank as much through ability as through patronage.

'I enjoy the study of languages and speak several,' she dissembled, replying in Latin.

She saw he understood that she was made uncomfortable by his probing. He moved on to asking her about her experience of living in Constantinople, saying, 'They are a warlike people, the Turks, although we bested them at Lepanto. It was the most successful unification of Christian nations ever, a great and true Holy League.'

She wanted to put him in his place, to tell him that Lepanto was as nothing to the Mussulmen, but restrained herself. In any case, she'd become weary of the topic.

'Of course, England and Scotland could never have joined us,' Medina said.

'No, our countries do not boundary the Mediterranean Sea,' said Bethia, deliberately misunderstanding.

He leaned in closer. 'King Philip was grieved, and angered, by the death of your Queen Mary at the hands of the English bastard queen – as no doubt were you. Kings and queens, appointed by God, are not beheaded – 'twas an act of barbarity. It is in part what drove Philip to bring together the greatest Armada the world has ever

303

seen.' He shook his head sadly. 'But God was not with us.'

Bethia was made uncomfortable by the mention of Mary and the assumption that she would want a Catholic again upon the Scottish throne.

'I respect our king,' she said stiffly. 'Despite his youth, he balances the demands of different interests skilfully while keeping Elizabeth onside. You cannot know what it was like to live here when her father, King Henry, was on the throne with his constant incursions into our country. We have had peace with more frequency recently, which is most unusual.'

'So you do not desire change?' Medina said.

Bethia became aware of Gilbert, from across the board, watching their exchange curiously. She would tell him all later, and of how they must live quietly in Fife. There were dangerous games being played here by the Catholic lords which they must distance themselves from.

Next to Gilbert sat Mark Ker, Commendator of Newbattle, for whose family she had nothing but contempt. Ker's father had been the abbot of Newbattle Abbey and, at the Reformation, had conveniently, and rapidly, turned Protestant so he became the wealthy owner of all the lands which had formerly belonged to that abbey. Ker had inherited a few years ago and yet here he was, a Protestant of convenience, sitting amid Catholics, indeed leaning back in his seat and laughing at something Bothwell had said.

She realised that Medina was awaiting a response. She would give him an honest one. 'I would not wish for Scotland the bloody turmoil the people of France have suffered these past thirty years, even if it did mean we returned to the one true Church founded by Jesus,' she said softly.

For all that she cleaved quietly to the faith of her birth and felt always the Virgin's presence watching over her, any attempt to turn Scotland back to the Pope of Rome would lead to bloody internal war. The country had managed by mainly peaceable means to become Protestant and that was in no small measure to both Queen Mary and her mother Mary of Guise as regent before her, having an understandable reluctance to kill and burn those of a different faith. Both women had behaved as true Christians to show such tolerance – and in the face of John Knox's rude aggression towards them.

She spoke quietly, almost to herself, and knew it was her truth. 'I do not think it is what our Lord would want.'

Medina sat in silence for a moment then rose and held out his hand. Confused, she placed her hand in his, and he bowed and kissed it.

Bethia, aware of Gilbert half rising opposite and the eyes of all the table upon them, could not help but blush like a lass.

Medina, again seated, waved his hand at the watchers, saying, 'There has been no sultan to match Suleiman the magnificent.'

Bethia, appreciative of him changing the subject, exerted herself to respond while thinking this man was indeed deserving of his epithet *El Buen*, and that *El Sabio* – the wise – could equally be accorded him.

'It was actually Suleiman the *Lawgiver*, for that is how he was styled by his people. I met him, you know.' Then she had to cover her mouth with her hand to stop the laugh, thinking of how Will still told of having once spoken to Queen Mary of Scots when she was a small child being taken to France, although he tended not to mention he was imprisoned as a galley slave at the time.

Medina inclined his head waiting for her to elaborate.

'Although it is perhaps an exaggeration to say I met him. I was in his presence but we were not permitted to gaze upon him, but instead must keep our eyes fixed upon the floor. Then he summoned me, for he had a question, and I was held tight by the arms and brought

305

before him. I cannot begin to describe the lines of janissaries in their tall plumes, the richness of the colours and the splendour of the Topkapi Palace. It was not only Suleiman who was magnificent but everything that surrounded him.'

'And what did he ask of you?'

Bethia felt the bubble of laughter rise. 'He wanted to know why, if everyone in the land of the Scots has red hair, I did not.'

Medina roared with laughter and again all eyes were upon them.

'Just a small amusement,' said Media waving his hand.

After a moment, conversation resumed, although Bethia could see Gilbert staring at them still.

'You said your first husband was in trade,' said Medina.

Bethia did not think she had said any such thing but nodded.

'You will have dealt with the Mendes family then?'

Bethia went rigid. He knows we are Conversos, she thought. The fear was there, but really what did it matter what some Spaniard shipwrecked off Scotland knew of her children's and grandchildren's antecedents, for they were safe in Constantinople – apart from Ephraim.

Medina continued as though he could not see the fear in her face.

'Although the Mendes family have now fallen into obscurity since the death of Dona Gracia.' He paused. 'We were fools to let them go. They would've been a magnificent asset to Spain to rival any magnificence Suleiman might display.' He lowered his voice further, speaking so quietly she had to lean in to hear.

'My grandfather was burnt at the stake for heresy.'

Bethia blinked, not certain if she had heard him correctly.

Medina nodded. 'Yes, I am descended from Conversos.'

'But how …?'

He smiled sadly. 'How did I become one of Philip's commanders when he insisted that all be untainted by Jewish blood? The king urgently required appointments to be made and his hard-pressed advisers ran out of time in which to inquire of the Inquisitor of Seville regarding my antecedents. And so, for my sins, I found myself a squadron commander.'

Bethia felt her shoulders drop and a sense of calm pervade her. He was no danger, indeed had shared the Converso peril. She had not intended to tell him that the queen of England wanted him delivered up, but now she leant forward whispering in his ear that he must find a way to return to Spain with all possible haste.

He nodded his understanding, murmuring that she had confirmed what he'd already heard, and they moved on to other matters.

When Gilbert came to escort her to their chamber, he had many questions once they were safely within, including commenting more than once what a handsome man the Spaniard was. She went up to him and placed her hand softly against the scar which puckered the side of his face, stroking it gently.

'Handsome is as handsome does,' she said. 'And no one, not even Mainard, has loved me as you have. And I thank you for it.'

She kissed him then. And Medina was quickly forgot.

But in the darkest hour of the night she awoke and wept. She had known from the moment she made her vows to Gilbert that she would never return to Constantinople, but sometimes it hurt. Of course, some of her grandchildren might risk the long journey to see her, but never again would she sit in a room surrounded by the now extensive family that had resulted from the union of Mainard the Converso and Bethia the Scotswoman. And she wept for Ephraim, who she feared did not understand what he had given up by coming with her, praying that he would not live to regret the choice he too had made.

She tried to contain her sobs but Gilbert rolled over and gathered her in his arms and, in being held, gradually they subsided. Gilbert was soon again snoring, and she lay, calmly now, reminding herself of one of Father's favourite sayings – *as you have made your bed so shall you lie.*

Chapter Forty-One

In Our End Is Our Beginning

Bethia and Gilbert rose early the next day and went down the hill to Leith where he had arranged a boat for their private use. The wind blew only enough to caress the waves, making the crossing tolerable, and Bethia sat quietly gazing out. To their left, in the near distance, sat the hummock of Cramond Island, only a mile off the shore and easily accessed at low tide. The tide was on its way out and she could see bent women collecting cockles from the exposed beach which was pooled with water and dotted with stones. She remembered Will's stories of running aground here when he was still enslaved by the French, along with the redoubtable John Knox, who had hated woman rulers almost as much as he hated Catholics.

Across the still water they were rowed accompanied briefly by a shoal of leaping porpoises. A couple of fishing boats taking advantage of the unusually clement weather drew near, come to trap the porpoises for their oil. The animals disappeared with the same suddenness with which they'd arrived. Bethia, although mindful of the loss of much-needed income for the fishermen and their families, could not but feel glad these joyous creatures had escaped death.

Over to her right the coast of East Lothian fell away,

the distinctive hump of Berwick Law, near where Elspeth had lived when she was in the convent, bold against the sky. They passed Inchkeith Island, where the now deserted fort built by the French against English marauders, when Mary of Guise was regent, stood solid against the light of the setting sun. The island had once been used as a place of quarantine for those with syphilis, and Bethia thought she would not care to step ashore there, for who knows how that disease might linger.

Before them, the curve of the Fife coastline extended away into the distance where the Firth of Forth widened into the sea. Darkness fell and Bethia retreated below the awning of sailcloth draped over the boom, settling close by the small cook-fire. Gilbert tended her, wrapping her in blankets so the only part of her that was uncovered was her face. She dozed through the hours of darkness and in the welcome yellow streaks of dawn glimpsed the long town of Kirkcaldy, whose mile-long street ran parallel with the shore.

Sunrise found the sea still flat calm, and they passed the castle of Ravenscraig on its rocky promontory, and soon after, the tower of Wemyss Castle. By late morning they were anchored off Earlsferry, where they disembarked and enjoyed a repast supplied by an enterprising fishwife. Later that day Bethia was back in her tower house with its parterre in the English style and the green tips of bulbs brought from the hills behind Constantinople poking through.

Word came that Gómez de Medina had been returned to Spain in a ship chartered by the Earl of Bothwell and that Bothwell had sent a message to *let the Spanish king know how many well-wishers he hath in this country.*

She was glad to learn Medina had escaped, but, hearing of Bothwell's message, Bethia made Gilbert promise that they would bide quietly at Balcarrow for the rest of their days. There would be no further conversing with these Catholic nobles playing a perilous game.

'You do not have to persuade me, my love. And all I need in this life is to be with you, for, as Pliny says, *without hearts there is no home*.'

Medina's officers were furious that he had left them behind.

'They dinna think he's sae *good* now,' said John leaning back in the settle, arms behind his head, while Father nodded sleepily in his chair, during one of Bethia's regular visits.

'He had to go quickly,' said Bethia, 'before Elizabeth caught him.'

John shrugged. 'The story is that the Duke of Parma has now sent ransom money, so we may finally be rid o' all these Spaniards constantly seeking alms.'

And indeed Parma had sent funds, and Queen Elizabeth surprisingly promised safe passage through English waters for the four ships he had also sent to take the remaining men of the Armada to Spain. But all did not go to plan, since the Dutch, lurking at Dunkirk, were not bound by any agreement the queen of England had made, and – perhaps angry that Medina had evaded capture – she didn't request it of them. They attacked the small flotilla and boarded one of the ships, where they tossed everyone overboard – Scots and Spanish alike. And, for a time, it was not safe to be a Dutchman in Scotland.

In August, a year after the Armada had been so roundly beaten and scattered and four days after King James had married his fourteen-year-old Danish princess, Father died. It was not unexpected, for he'd taken to his bed saying he'd waited for Bethia and Grissel to return but now he was tired and ready to join his maker. Despite his weariness, Father didn't lose his humour, whispering to Bethia a few days before he died that when he met Saint Peter at the Gates of Heaven he would tell him of how he had been both a good Catholic and a good Protestant.

'And surely one or ither o' those faiths will be sufficient for Saint Peter tae allow me entry,' he rasped.

It was the last coherent words he spoke. Bethia, Will, John – and Grissel summoned hurriedly from Edinburgh – kept vigil for two days and nights. On the third morn, as the sun rose over a wind-whipped sea, the space between each laboured breath grew longer. They leaned forward thinking each one was his last till finally the long silence came. Father had left them.

Bethia stood up, one hand curled tightly around the crucifix clutched in her palm, and bent to kiss his forehead. Grissel flung the window wide allowing Father's spirit to fly. John covered his face with his hands and wept. Will stood gazing down at Father, then, with the gentlest of touch, pressed each eyelid closed and laid the pennies upon them.

Violet came to wash and lay him out with the help of Grissel. 'I want tae dae it,' she said when Bethia would have taken her place. And Bethia was relieved, for she did not know how.

Gilbert arrived from Balcarrow, despite the earliness of the hour. He stood quietly gazing down on the corpse then bent to kiss Father's forehead. When he straightened up he gazed in turn with an equal quiet thoughtfulness at Bethia.

'You have kept your promise and stayed till he breathed his last,' he said, his gruff voice oddly tremulous.

She went to him and took his hands in hers. 'But you know I will never leave you,' she said, wondering he should even think it. 'I made a vow and 'tis with you I will bide.'

An expression of such relief spread over his face that she near wept again.

'You will stay until *I* breathe my last,' he said lightly.

She inclined her head. 'But let us hope that *you* may be the survivor.'

'We will make a pact to go together,' he said, enfolding her in his arms.

Word spread as quickly as the Dreel burn flowing in spate, and first the villagers and then folk from near and far came. The queue to file past the corpse soon stretched from the house and along the shore, while a neap tide came flooding in to soak the feet of those slow to jump out of its way. Everyone wanted to touch this man who had lived for more than nine decades and hope some of his longevity might transfer to them.

It was a long procession of men who followed the wooden coffin – none of this wrapping of the corpse in only a cloth for the wealthy Setons – up the steep close to the graveyard. Father was buried in the priory grounds amid the graves of Catholics and Protestants alike, which to Bethia seemed fitting.

Women did not go to the burial, and a few days later Bethia went alone to the graveyard. The earth heaped high over the grave was dark from the rain which had fallen overnight, turning it from a smooth mound to rivulets of mud. Bethia had barely slept, thinking of Father lying beneath the soaked earth, and rose at first light. She had brought her crucifix and her old cloak to kneel upon while she said a prayer for the dead. Even if Father had died a Protestant, it would bring her comfort. When she was done, she rose and wandered around the churchyard.

Gilbert and she should decide where they were to lie once they were dead. She would like to be buried in this old cemetery by the priory and close to the sea but Gilbert would want her beside him in the family plot by their home in Balcarrow. In the end she had chosen him over her beloved children, and she would sleep the long sleep next him. Her heart smote her when she thought of Mainard buried so far away on Mount Hebron. He would arise when the long-awaited Messiah of the Jews came, but she would not be there … and could never have been. She'd made her choice when he reverted, her faith as a Latin Catholic never wavering. Even Will, for all that he disdained papists, had recently, and unbidden, said that however wrong thinking she was, he could not but respect that she had held fast.

As Bethia wandered among the graves in the brightness of an August day, the last words spoken to her by Gómez de Medina crept into her consciousness.

'My lady, you have lived a remarkable life and should make a record of it.'

She thought of Andrew Wyntoun, whose chronicles of Scotland contained many exciting tales bound up in some execrable verse. Could she attempt such an undertaking? She did not know if she wanted to, but what she would do was write an account for her grandchildren so they would know of their forebears, and their children would too, for many generations. Then it would not be forgot that once a lass from Scotland met a lad from Antwerp – and that is how they came to be.

She met Will as she came through the priory gates, his two converts following close behind. It was a matter of some pride to Pittenweemers that the Spanish lads had hid, under the protection of Saint Fillan, because they wanted to stay in a small, but godly, village. Their instruction into the Protestant religion was robust, for everyone felt they had a hand in turning them into true Christians.

Prancing behind them came the servant girl, eyes alight, for she was to marry the bonny older lad as soon as Will judged him to be a Protestant of sound doctrine.

Nannis stood in the doorway, arms folded watching, and Bethia gave her a smile and a wave.

'They are tae bide in ma wee house,' Nannis called, pointing to the Spanish lad and Tibby. 'But only once they're merrit. I'll hae no fornicating beneath ma roof.'

'Hush,' said Will, but Bethia could see the twinkle in his eye.

'You are away, sister?'

'Yes, Gilbert will arrive soon.'

'Ach, he's already there, awaiting you.'

He bent to kiss her cheek and moved on into his house. Bethia put her hand to her face, could not remember Will ever giving such a mark of brotherly affection.

Lifting her skirts, she walked carefully down the steep uneven path slippery with mud from last night's rain, for, as ever, she had forgot her walking stick.

Gilbert was standing with the horses. 'There you are,' he said, smiling.

She smiled in return. 'Yes, here I am.'

'I have your things.'

'Let me say a quick goodbye.' She hurried inside to say her farewells and hug Grissel, who was returning to Edinburgh and her business.

Grissel tensed at such unexpected sisterly affection but, after a moment, hugged her in return, even tighter.

'Keep an eye on Ephraim,' Bethia said.

'Never fear aboot that. I will keep baith eyes upon him.'

Bethia gave Grissel's arm one last squeeze and slipped down the stairs to where Gilbert was patiently waiting.

Reaching home some hours later, she climbed the spiral of the tower stairs and went into the solar to see how the portrait was progressing.

'I am working on the background,' said Elspeth, 'but will need you both to sit again. I do not think I have well-captured the affection that flows between you. And we should include Holdfast lying at your feet as a symbol of love and fidelity.'

Bethia gazed at the painting. It was to hang next to the portrait that Elspeth's false swain Antonio had made of

Bethia and Mother during the time of the siege, and which Father had gifted her when she married. 'You have captured us beautifully – and are a far better painter than that wicked Italian.'

Elspeth narrowed her eyes and studied Antonio's painting. 'I think you may be right,' she said.

Bethia continued up the spiral stairs, hauling on the rope and trying not to pant too heavily at the exertion required. She ducked her head to enter the low doorway of the small chamber Gilbert had given her for her very own. Its window looked down upon the gardens below and then to the expanse of grassy hill, where sheep roamed, before it fell away to the wide blue sea beyond. She sat gazing out for a long time.

Then she picked up her pen and carefully sharpened the nib, opened the jar of iron gall ink which looked to be fresh, and laid a sheet of paper before her.

Placing her eyeglasses upon her nose, she dipped the pen in the ink and began to write ... *This be the Chronicles of the Family Seton* ... She paused, inclined her head, dipped the pen once more ... *& the Family de Lange, once known as Mendoza.*

***

Please rate this book

If you enjoyed this book please take a moment to share your thoughts in a review. Just a few words and/or a rating are perfect.

Reader reviews help sell more books and keep your favourite authors in business!

You'll find some stories available to newsletter subscribers only and free to download on my website, www.vehmasters.com, which gives more glimpses into the Seton family's life. I send out a monthly newsletter giving insights into research and my writing with the occasional free gift which I'd be honoured if you subscribed to, again via the website…

www.vehmasters.com

Acknowledgements

I'd like to say a big thank you to my friends and family for their ongoing support and encouragement. And readers and bloggers, thank you for your kind reviews, and especially for inquiring when this last in series would be out… and pre-ordering it too.

Richard Sheehan thanks for the confidence your impeccable editing inspires and Margaret Skea thanks too for your wise advice on the story arc and telling me not to begin the book in Edinburgh.

To my beta readers – Ruthann Bow, Sandra Greig,

Margaret Lovering, Emma Watson, Alison Whiteford and Mike Masters, who all made very helpful suggestions and a special thanks to Zoe Masters for her detailed feedback which greatly improved the book.

A big thank you to the harbour masters of Pittenweem and St Monans for their assistance in working out where the harbour and moorings likely were in the 1580s and to Duncan Chisholm for showing me around the church and explaining how it would have been at the time. Thanks to the folk of Pittenweem too, especially those who were pinned down answering my questions. Pittenweem is one of my favourite places in the world and its Arts Festival every August an excellent day out.

I'd like to very gratefully acknowledge the resources I'm able to access through the National Library of Scotland, including their wonderful maps. And a special thanks to the National Trust of Scotland staff at Gladstone's Land in Edinburgh (which is well worth a visit) who gave me the idea for Grissel to run an ale house. John's Land is based on Gladstone's Land and Balcarrow on Balvaird Castle, although I have moved its location nearer the East Neuk.

Hugest thanks of all, as ever, go to Mike for all his support and help once again … including creating the map of Pittenweem, designing the cover and other images, and formatting.

Historical Note

There's lots of source material about the immediate post-Reformation period in Scotland, and my challenge was to stop researching and start writing. Many of the events I am ascribing to my fictional characters in *The Pittenweemers* actually took place – the events of this era are so remarkable you really do not need to make them up!

For instance, Andrew Melville did roundly and publicly scold the king in St Andrews (amongst other times), English pirates did attack ships off Pittenweem and Anstruther, the abbot did attempt to fly from the walls of Stirling Castle and fell into a midden and, most remarkably of all, the citizens of Anstruther did wake up one morning to find over two hundred and fifty starving Armada sailors and soldiers off their coast seeking sanctuary. And we know about much of this because of the remarkable diaries kept by the local minister of the time, James Melville.

Commander Juan Gómez de Medina of the *El Gran Grifon* was indeed known as *El Buen* by his men. I am indebted to the wonderful book *Armada* by Colin Martin and Geoffrey Parker for detailed background information and especially the tale that Gómez's grandfather was a Converso who was burned at the stake by the Spanish Inquisition.

The list of books and articles I read is long, and since this is a work of historical fiction I am thankfully not required to include them all. However, I would like to mention *The Wisest Fool* by Steven Veerapen, a biography of James VI and I, which dispels much of the misinformation about him, *The Time Travellers Guide to Elizabethan England* by

Ian Mortimer, and *Court, Kirk and Community: Scotland 1470-1625* by Jenny Wormald.

Finally, the tower house in Pittenweem High Street was not built until around 1590, however I have made it earlier. I'm also aware that swallows do not hibernate! However, this is what was once believed to happen when they vanished during the Scottish winter.

Please do get in touch if you want to chat about my books. I love a good blether with readers.

You'll find me at www.vehmasters.com

Glossary

afeard	afraid
ahint	behind
althegether	altogether
ain, ane	own, as in my own child, one
auld	old
awfie	extremely
ay, aywis	always
bairn	a baby, a child
blethering, blethers	gossiping, talking nonsense, inconsequential chatter
canny	careful, shrewd, wise
cheeky	insolent, naughty
clatterer	someone who made announcements for the church by clattering, ie making a noise with a clapper or ringing a bell and who would also have reported on any transgressions they saw
clout	to hit; also a cloth
cooried up	cosied up
dinna	don't
dinna fash yerself	don't worry
dither	to be indecisive
doon	down
dour	pessimistic, humourless
dreich	dreary, dull, gloomy

fankle	tangle, upset
frae	from
fuffle	to fuss or throw into disarray
gang	go
gey	very
gie	give
girning	whining
git	get
guid	good
hae	have
heid	head
hirpling	limping, hobbling
ken	to know
kent	known
lang	long
ma	my
mair	more
maun	must
meenister	the minister
merrit	married
micht	might, also power, force
nae	no
naebody	nobody
naething	nothing
niver	never
ony	any
oor	our

oot	out
oversicht	oversight
ower	too, over; as in overmuch
paur	poor
richt	right
sae	so
sair	sore
shouldna	shouldn't
skelping	smacking
spurtle	a wooden spoon
telt	told
thrashing	a beating, a whipping
thrawn	stubborn
toun	town
trauchled	downtrodden
twa	two
verra	very
wasnie	wasn't
wheen	a lot
wheesht	be quiet
whit	what
wi'	with
wid	would
yer	your
yin	one
yon	that, over there

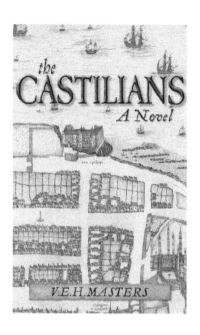

The Castilians is Book One of the Seton Chronicles

The Conversos is Book Two of the Seton Chronicles

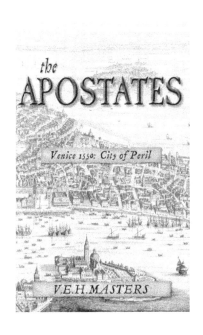

The Apostates is Book Three of the Seton Chronicles

The Familists is Book Four of the Seton Chronicles

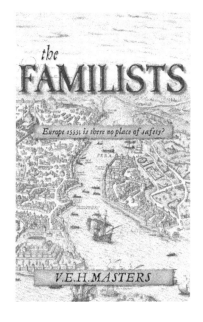

Milton Keynes UK
Ingram Content Group UK Ltd.
UKHW040911041224
3395UKWH00035B/226